The Pignapper

Erica Adams

Little Crow Publishing
32 Molyneux Park Road
Tunbridge Wells
Kent TN4 8DY

A CIP Catalogue Record for this book is available from the British Library.

Printed and bound in Great Britain

ISBN 0 9532239 1 4

This story follows on from *The Pig and I* in which, at the climactic end, Freda Field's cherished pig, Hermione, gave birth to nine piglets. Or, to be be factual, ten piglets. But one died which, strangely, was quite funny (though I, the author, admit I did weep all over the keyboard when the poor squashed-up little corpse was buried). Should I get him resuscitated, I wondered? (Oh, the power of being a writer.) And then I thought, no, my dinner's ready, so sod it.

This sequel tells of Freda's attempts to keep the porker family by opening up an Animal Park. And I don't want to give too much away, or you'll just read this bit and put the book down and go off and buy yet another copy of bloody Bridget Jones. Well, you just stay with flipping Freda Field, I say, because, even if you're thirty, single, over-weight and angst-ridden - well, *especially* if you're thirty, single, over-weight and angst-ridden - you'll need to see that older women, like Freda, still have a life (absolutely choc-o-bloc with magnificent cocks and dastardly dicks as it happens). And also, if you're hooked on the weed, like bestselling blockbuster Bridget, you should read this book - it'll be better than all the acupuncture, hypnotherapy and patches in making you give it up. And, if you don't, what kind of nut *are* you?!

For dearest Maurice
with all my love
and many thanks for your encouragement
and delicious meals
(even the pork ones)

One

'Charge people to look at your private parts!' mother's incredulous voice screeched down the phone.

'Not private parts, mother, private *park*. Charge people to see our private animal park - in our back garden. You know, like a children's zoo - but smaller.'

In the silence that followed while she digested this fact my mind raced. We'd had the idea when Hermione had first had the piglets, but abandoned it. But now, putting the idea into words again made it seem a real possibility. Our garden was big enough.

'Much more money in charging people to look at your private parts than charging them to see your back garden with one large sow and nine piddling piglets,' mother eventually responded, killing herself, then adding, 'Though, on second thoughts, maybe at your age showing off the porkers 'ud bring in more customers.'

'Very funny mother.'

'You could get them running naked across the grass and call it the Streaking Bacon Zoo,' she continued undeterred.

Her cackles were still bombarding my ear as I replaced the phone.

You wait, I thought. We *could* make it work. Bernard and I could run it and it could earn us enough to keep our little piggies so they wouldn't have to be sent to market.

I ran out into the freezing January air, across the crunchy grass, into the walled yard, up the ramp and through the swing door into the warm mobile home where Bernard attended our porcine family.

'You suggested it once, remember?' I blurted. 'When they were first born you said we could build a proper pig unit. But, I've been thinking, as well as that we could dam up the rivulets that run down from the spring and make a duck pond. We could advertise for people's unwanted pets. We could see if that woman from Rugged Farm would sell us her donkey. We could charge people to come and see it all, and then we could afford to keep the piglets.'

Bernard stopped, mid dung lifting. Our nine babes lifted their snuffling snouts from Hermione's milk bar. Even Hermione herself stopped grumbling and snorting. An uncanny silence settled. It was as if the atmosphere had been charged with magic pig comprehension dust.

As if the importance of Bernard's reply was realised by ten piggy brains. All eyes were fastened on Bernard.

'What about your dreams of making a name for yourself as a portrait painter? You'd have no time for art.'

I gazed at our porkers.

'You're just starting to get commissions,' he reminded me.

The trusting eyes of the porkers stared back.

'If it's between fame and fortune and our porky family ... I choose our porky family.'

'Great,' he said, scraping the dung off the tines, 'and I could train the piglets to do tricks to attract customers.'

Suddenly smiley Jesus, our first born, got to his tiny trotters and twirled round before crashing back down and latching onto a milk-swollen teat. The atmosphere broken, his brothers and sisters squealed and snorted their attention back to the nipple array and normal pig decibelity was restored.

That night, I shivered with excitement, unable to sleep.

'It wasn't a coincidence that Jesus twirled when you mentioned tricks,' I whispered to Bernard.

'Course it was,' he said sleepily.

'No. He was showing his aptitude and willingness.'

'So that he doesn't have to go to the abattoir I suppose?' Bernard said cynically, yawning.

'That, and to lead us to the promised land, not full of milk and honey, more like pig swill and dung, but heavenly anyway.'

'Yes ... heavenly,' he slurred.

And, as I lay in the darkness listening to his gentle piggy snores, I knew it would be. Forgetting for the moment that heaven was an unknown place without a bank or cash machine.

I rang our next-door neighbour - that woman from Rugged Farm - to tell her about our Animal Park idea and ask if she'd consider selling us her donkey.

'En't a bad idea,' she said, 'I'll come round.'

Ten minutes later she was banging on our kitchen door, having opened the side gate and come round the back.

'People usually come to the front door,' I said, miffed.

''Tis all right, the gate sprung back shut.' Her beady black eyes darted around. Then, 'Sit down,' she said, indicating our kitchen table, 'I got an idea.'

Annoyed at her effrontery, I nevertheless sat down and she took the chair opposite. Reluctantly, Bernard plonked himself down next to her.

'Coffee?' I asked, feeling obliged.

'No, no. Don't drink it, herbal infusions for me.'

'Oh, so sorry, we're plumb out of them,' I said, but she didn't seem to notice the sarky tone.

'My idea is for you to open up a gap in the hedge atween your garden and my field. I got long lush grass in there doing nothing, so you could keep more animals if you'd a mind to.'

Bernard's eyes sharpened and he scraped his chair round so he could look at her.

'The barn roof lets rain in when we got a real downpour,' she continued, 'and its walls need a bit of attention, but it en't too bad.'

With a sudden sharp clatter, that made her jump, Hermione entered the kitchen through the pig flap. My big fat girl cast an inquisitive eye at the small dark stranger sitting at the table before trotting off into the other room.

'She likes to get away from her babies and stretch out on the sofa,' I explained.

'I see,' she said, giving me a funny look before rushing on: 'The stable block's got four stalls, one for my Daisy, and three you could use. Mebbe you could get another donkey?' she said, face lighting.

'Maybe,' said Bernard doubtfully.

'Then Daisy got the company donkeys need - they're more sociable'n us humans. And, mebbe they'd mate and ...'

'Hang on,' said Bernard, laughing, 'we're not planning to rear donkeys as well as our pigs.'

Her dark hypnotic gaze hung on Bernard, then she shrugged.

'No matter. The stable block got a big room at one end where my straw and hay is kept. But you got to provide your own if you take Daisy on.'

'You mean, we *can* buy your donkey,' I exclaimed.

'No. You can *have* Daisy, you en't obliged to buy her, just so long as my son, if he ever comes home, can have access to her.'

I glanced at Bernard, but neither of us ventured to go into what *that* meant.

'We'd love to have your donkey,' Bernard said, 'but I'm not sure about taking on your field. The whole of our garden boundary is pig-proof with thick hedges in front of wire fencing going deep down in the ground and ...'

'Don't need to concern yourself 'bout that,' she cut in, pre-empting him. 'My land is securely hedged and fenced too.'

'Even the far side of the field where it runs alongside your farmhouse garden?' I asked distrustfully.

'Even there. En't no way through 'cept a gate in the hedge.'

I looked at Bernard, saw blooming interest.

'It en't no good for crowds o'visitors if there en't no parking space, but you could knock up a fence 'cross the field on level with the back o'the barn and turn top end into a car park.'

Bernard leaned towards her, eyes shining.

'And we could make two gaps in the upper hedge,' he said, 'so visitors could enter and exit from Nuthatch Lane.'

'Good idea en't it,' she said, beaming at me. 'Then, when they been and parked, they could walk straight into your Animal Park through the back doors of the barn.'

Wonderful rose tinted visions of laughing children dragging their parents through into the grounds floated into my mind. The sun shone continuously from a cloudless sky. Piglets performed tricks and danced jigs to ecstatic applause from the crowds. And I collected entry fees at the barn doors and served tea and biscuits in dainty china.

'How much rent would you charge, Mrs Oven,' Bernard asked.

And my internal film projection crashed. I'd forgotten about such a thing as payment.

'It'd be free for one year to get you started.'

'That's very generous,' I gasped.

'And another thing,' she added, in fact adding two: 'As I'm giving you Daisy that means you got to buy her feed and stuff, but I want to look after her, it'll save you trouble and she's all I got left in the world. And besides all of this, you got to call me Esmerelda.'

I stared at this slight swarthy woman and her dark mystical eyes stared back at me. She'd always been *that woman from Rugged Farm* to us. Mrs Oven to her face. Now she was Enterprising Esmerelda and I was finding it hard to adjust on both 'E' accounts.

Bernard and I chatted about it all evening and, even though we were still slightly dubious about her, we decided to accept the offer of the donkey and the field and its buildings.

'Visiting children would love Daisy, and the barn could be a tea room and gift shop,' I raved.

'And a snooker club,' Bernard shrieked, up there with me on cloud ten, then, catching my look, 'Getting carried away aren't I, a kiddies' rough and tumble area was what I should have said.'

The faint clatter of the pig flap and Hermione's high heeled trotters clacking across the quarry tiles came from the kitchen, then her inquisitive eyes atop her twitching snout peered round the sitting room door. Seeing we were there, she hurried in nodding a cursory greeting, before clambering up onto the sofa where she stretched out her porky legs and let out a long juddering sigh. Just to get those piglets off her milk bar for a few precious minutes was patently bliss.

I watched my girl, wondering how she'd feel if she understood our plans and realised that by this time next year her babies would be fully grown and still not flown the nest. Perhaps if she understood that the only place they could fly to was the slaughter house she'd put up with having them under her trotters for the rest of her life.

Unless, of course, the whole enterprise turned out to be a disaster and by this time next year all the piglets had been transformed to bacon and we'd spent all our savings so couldn't even afford to keep her.

'You look worried,' said Bernard. 'Let's go to bed. I'll put the pig out and lock the flap.'

I looked in the mirror as I undressed. *Say you're me,* I silently said to my reflection. *Say you're me now, at fifty-one, looking your best for years: newly slimmed; curly red hair brought back from the dead by Raymond; newly acquired modern wardrobe bought with newly acquired wealth (well comparative to a year ago); newly making a name for yourself painting portraits; newly freed from the rigours of work by leaving the village school. Say you're that person,* I thought-said to the freckle-faced, slightly chubby chinned woman, *would you risk it all for those pigs?*

'You're taking a long time,' called Bernard. 'Come on, get into bed.'

Quickly, would you? If you were her, would you risk all for those pigs?

Her twinkling green eyes latched onto mine and she nodded.

I knew you would, I smiled.

But, as I slid under the duvet, the knowledge that all our savings could get eaten away sullied my clear mind.

'Do you think it's worth all the risk?' I whispered.

And his hand abruptly stopped its gentle stroking.

'There's no risk, you know that. That's why our daughter and grandchildren are pigs.'

And, as the love-making took its natural course, I became convinced again. Not only was I blissfully joined to my long-legged handsome husband in love, but soon we'd be blissfully joined in running an Animal Park together.

'I think we can make it work,' I cried.

'We usually do,' he replied.

Two

Planning permission, for what must be the must luxurious pig unit in the land, was granted surprisingly quickly and pipes have already been laid under the lawn, one carrying electricity, the other, Bernard's brilliant invention, taking water from the constantly gushing spring behind the mobile home, by gravity to the foundations half-way down the garden. Surplus water being piped to our newly dammed-up pond.

It's so exciting. The brickie has started building the walls and every day I go out and try to picture each piglet happily living in its own apartment: Mary, Princess, Countess, Duchess, Lady and Hermione along one side, Jesus, Hamlet, Pudding and Pie along the other, and a large open yard in between.

One of the two extra apartments on the boys' side is to be used for storing bedding and a new wheelbarrow and pitchfork. The other will be a shower room for the pigs, a hosepipe attached to a tap, plus a proper electrically heated shower unit to use when it's chilly. And I've found the perfect shower curtain, patterned with pigs.

Bernard's ingenious plumbing system includes pipes to divert water directly into two zinc troughs in the yard with overspill outlets, ensuring a continuous flow of crystal clear spring water. It's brilliant and he's justifiably proud, dragging all and sundry in to look at the plans.

Today, I made out a cheque to the builder for work to date, then rang the bank to transfer money from our Higher Rate Deposit Account (which should be re-named Higher Rate than Peanuts Deposit Account, to be honest, judging by the interest.) But, as I handed it over, doubt settled like a sticky dark cobweb clogging my mind.

'Oh Bernie, is it worth it?' I whispered that night in bed.

'Well, it was last time,' he sniggered, going for it.

Into the sea of snapping snouts my bank manager throws five pound notes drawn from our account. With horror I watch the piglets shredding them into bits then devouring them. The bank manager looks over for confirmation that he should draw out more. I nod and another wad of notes is flung over and consumed by wildly gyrating mouths. When every note has vanished, demanding squeals rev up, louder and louder until I can hardly bear the din. I nod my consent again to the enquiring

Bank Manager and another bankroll is pigged down by the swine. I nod again but, this time, the Bank Manager shakes his head. Your account is empty he mouths, immediately vanishing.

'YOU'VE EATEN THE LOT' I scream, scrambling up onto the pig yard wall in my stiletto heeled shoes. I stare down into wild ungrateful piggy eyes. Then, knowing full well what I'm doing, I jump, bouncing from one to another, leaping with gusto on this living pork mat. Up and down I fly, higher and higher, tucking and twisting, laughing with glee, hearing ear-splitting squeals on each landing. Abandoned, I spring higher and higher, spinning, somersaulting forwards and back.

Suddenly, all squealing and screaming abruptly ceases and now each time I land there are popping sounds which gradually change to grim squelching. But still I continue to trampoline, trampoline, tramp-o-, trample, trample, until all the bounce has vanished and gravity forces me down. I stare down at the carnage, sob loudly as I scrape bloody flesh from my spiky heels.

Bernard shook me by the shoulders. 'Freda,' he whispered, 'you're calling out in your sleep. What's the matter, tell me?'

'I had a nightmare,' I cried.

'What happened?'

'All of the piglets died.'

'You're lucky,' he replied. 'I had a nightmare in which they were all alive, full size, and hogging down food as fast as I could shovel it in!'

Then he laughed long and heartily to let me know it was one of his "jokes".

'That's not funny,' I yelled. 'It's the problem.'

I rang my best friend, Cynthia.

'I won't be going to the art club each week,' I blurted.

'But why not,' she cried. 'It's our morning out together.'

'We've decided to keep all the piglets and run an Animal Park so there'll be too much to do.'

'You must be mad keeping the whole litter,' she muttered.

'It's that or sending them to the abattoir and how can you do that to your grandchildren?'

'Easy if they're pigs,' she mumbled in an undertone, deliberately just audible. 'I'll miss you,' she flared. 'I love our Tuesday mornings painting portraits together.'

'I'll miss them too - and you. But we're investing everything we have in this venture so ...'

'So if you had as big a pile of stinking money as you have of stinking shit, it'd make sense, but you haven't,' she cut in, surprisingly crude and harsh for Cynthia, so I knew she was really upset.

'You're not going through all that risk business again are you,' said Bernard, pulling up the duvet against the cold and cuddling me under it.

'No. The die is flung. There is *no* risk,' I said forcefully. 'We shall *make* it work.'

'But not tonight, eh?' said Bernard. 'Never have managed three on the trot.'

Yet, as I drifted to sleep, I still wondered. Would we, in six months time, be up to our eyes in filthy muck and clean out of money?

Three

The piglets have been in their newly built accommodation for two weeks and planning permission has been granted for the Animal Park. Yippee!

Yesterday, the new vet, Vernon Veal, came to check them over. The short wiry man with the tall forehead and sandy fly-away hair obviously loved our grandpiglets, especially Pudding. Kept picking him up and stroking him, lifting his one floppy ear and whispering 'Who's a little beauty then,' into it. I took to the strange little man immediately, in the same way that any mother would take to a man besotted with her child.

Back in the cottage, he said, 'I do so admire your enterprising spirit Mrs Field. Unless you have a crisis I shall visit once a month, and only make a charge if medicine is needed. Just until you get on your feet you understand.'

'Call me Freda,' I rushed, feeling all emotional and just holding back from throwing my arms around him and kissing him.

'Cheeri-ho ... um ... Freda,' he said, 'I'll be seeing you soon.'

Next day, the thirty-first of March, I hurried down to let my babies out for their last feed of the day. As I entered the yard I spotted Jesus, bright eyed and waggy tailed, skipping across to Mary who, with slow deliberation, turned her back on him. With a gleeful squeal that smacked of sly premeditation, he reared up and mounted her from behind.

Appalled, I lashed out at his fat pink rump, knocking him sideways onto the floor and he scrambled to his feet honking in loud unison with the cavorting Mary.

I knew then that soon I'd have to get his tackle amended or keep him away from the girls. This wasn't his first attempt and, in another few weeks, his equipment would be well primed and hazardously close to firing.

I glanced up the long grassy slope and saw Bernard emerging from the cottage. He waved down at me then banged on the food trough, bellowing his strange pig grub-up call: a peculiar warbling yodel, half Tarzan half Muezzin. An innovative vocal achievement of which he was unduly proud.

I unbolted the gate and the mob dashed through, pushing and shoving, grunting and snorting, streaming across the grass like an upward flowing river of pink blancmange. A warm glow engulfed me as I watched them go. God, I did love them.

Hermione, looking gigantic beside her babies, as usual quickly took the lead, closely followed by Jesus, then Mary - still fleet of trotters despite the shock attack on her virginity. Not far behind came Hamlet, then Pie, Lady, Duchess, Countess and Princess, all pelting along squealing in hungry excitement. I felt proud. This deliberate plan of making them run up the long slope twice a day to get to their feed kept them exercised and healthy.

Bernard let rip with his pig yodel again, this time pure Tarzan, and I half expected him to beat his chest and zoom out high across the garden dangling from a strand of wisteria. I watched the receding porker blobs jostling and weaving around each other as they put on a final spurt and the love in my heart was so intense it hurt me. That kaleidoscope of subtle pinks racing towards Bernard was our precious substitute for the sadly unborn grandsons and granddaughters held captive in our genes.

Suddenly I realised I hadn't seen Pudding, our flop-eared roly-poly boy, the greedy one, the unfittest one. I peered up trying to count the squiggly tails as the piglets clamoured round the trough.

'... five ... six ... seven ... eight fine little ones plus Hermione's big one. My heart fluttered. There should be nine little ones. But one couldn't go missing, they'd been rooting around the garden earlier, but there was no way out. I squinted up, trying to isolate each plump little body in a recount as they dashed around each other vying for best positions. But it wasn't possible.

'I think Pudding's missing,' I called up to Bernard. 'Can you see him there? Have I missed him?'

Anxiously I watched as he tried counting the swarming bodies.

'I think there's only eight,' he called back, 'and you're right - I can't see Pudding.'

Sleepy, rotund, slow-moving Pudding. Our most affectionate pig. With the kind of horrible dread in the core of my stomach, like the real mother of a real missing child must suffer, I stared around the yard where I'd just lammed Jesus off Mary. But it was patently devoid of pig. Just a few dollops of pig dung on the concrete.

Maybe Pudding had been tired and not heard Bernard's call or the ensuing commotion. But I knew that if that were so he must have been struck with an illness, sudden deafness ... or something ... I couldn't bring myself to form the word, even inside my head ... or something ... that sounded a bit like deaf, but was far far worse.

I rushed across to his apartment, looked in. No sign of him. I hurried along peering into the other boys' rooms, but there wasn't a snout or a tail or plump little body in any one of them.

I peered into the storage room but no pink body skulked amongst the bales of straw, packs of sawdust, bucket, wheelbarrow and pitchfork.

Gingerly, I drew back the plastic curtain that hung across the end cubicle where we showered them clean, always kept fully drawn to stave off mould. Screeches and vivid images of *Psycho* bombarded my head. But the shower room was empty. No stabbing, no blood, no murdered piglet.

I ran across the yard to the girls' side and looked into each of their rooms, but there was no Pudding.

I stood quite still in the yard, listening for sounds of movement, but the only sound was the thudding of my heart and the squeals of Hermione and the piglets hogging down their swill. No nearby grunts - no sounds of breathing.

'Pudding,' I called. 'Here Pudding, Pudding, Pudding.'

But he didn't appear.

I turned full circle. It was impossible. After their free time in the garden, they'd all been herded back for a rest. And there was no way he could have escaped from this new purpose-built brick building, and nowhere he could be hiding.

Suddenly my eyes were arrested by a large mound of dung with, what appeared to be, a footprint squashed in it, but smaller than Bernard's or mine. I went over, bent lower, seeing the blurred impression of what might have been a sole with horizontal ridges in it, and a deeper flat squarish heel.

I twisted my foot up to see the underside of my welly boot and saw it was deeply inscribed with circles and diamonds surrounded by thick and thin wedges. I knew Bernard's boot tread would be identical because we'd bought the same ones, except his were size ten, and mine were a seven. I was perplexed. No-one ever came in here but us. Could my precious Pudding have been abducted? Killed? Being transformed into sausages even as I stood here? Too tiny a body for the jumbo eight to a pound, but chipolatas or cocktail size just conceivable.

'He'll be all right. No-one could have taken him.' Bernard leant across the kitchen table and patted my hand.

'A little round Pudding who loves his food. He'd never miss a meal - and there was what looked like a footprint in the dung - he's been taken away by a loathsome kidnapper.'

I closed my eyes, feeling the ache in my heart leaching into my head.

'So a ransom note should soon appear,' quipped Bernard. 'And don't you mean a *pig*napper,' he added, always the sodding clown.

I pushed my plate of bread and cheese away, unable to continue.

'Come on,' cajoled Bernard, jumping up from the table, 'just because our fat lad hasn't eaten his tea there's no point in you not eating yours.'

He came back. 'Look, I've made this for you.'

Then he pushed a ham sandwich under my nose and wondered why I dissolved into tears.

'I thought it would make a nice change ...'

'But it's pig,' I sobbed, 'it's ham ... pig meat ... and at a time like this.'

'But it's not Pudding,' he replied.

As he spoke, Esmerelda came barging into our kitchen, unannounced and uninvited. She stared at my ham sandwich.

'Course it's not pudding,' she said.

Overcome by the terrible anxiety which over-rode my anger at her rude appearance, I sobbed, 'My Pudding's missing.'

'Well you could always knock up a jam sponge!' she said, turning to Bernard, adding, 'Is she often demanding like this?'

'No sign of him,' confirmed Bernard miserably, coming back in.

I plodded out into the cold twilit garden and searched again, knowing he wouldn't be there. Knowing our baby had gone.

Before bedtime, at about eleven, I tried again, taking a torch though it wasn't necessary because the whole garden was drenched in moonlight. But there was no trace of our dear boy, not whole or ripped into shreds.

'I love Pudding,' I cried into Bernard's back as we lay in bed.

I felt his arm move and his hand reach out and rest upon my tum, heard him sleepily snigger, 'I know that, I can tell.'

Why did he always have to crack jokes I fumed as I cried myself into fitful sleep, howling energetically upon each awakening, mourning the loss of my piglet whilst, at the same time, guiltily hoping the emotional turmoil, and physical flailing about, would burn off some fat.

I ran down towards the sound of hungry squealing, dreading that somehow another one of my precious toddlers would have disappeared in the night.

Easing myself through the metal bar gate of the yard, I blocked the charge of the hungry pig brigade. Jesus smiled up at me from the milling mass, his curly tail twirling. I bent down and stroked his head and another piglet's snout pushed up under my hand. I stared at its owner in disbelief. Pudding! It was the glorious face of my Pudding. No doubt about it. Our dear boy had returned. His tender eyes stared up at me as he rubbed his body against my leg and impetuously I lugged him up into my arms and kissed him.

Bernard's warble suddenly rent the cold air, setting up frenzied squealing all around me and such frantic writhing in my arms I had to rush him back down before he nose-dived. There, he joined his sisters and brothers in their desperate pre-breakfast dance. It was like witnessing lumpy pink soup being stirred by an invisible spoon. I ploughed through the bodies, opened the gate and watched them stream away towards Bernard.

'He's back,' I shouted to Bernard. 'Look, he's back!'

His startled eyes roved the oncoming stampede, then he grinned, jerking his thumb up as he saw him.

Alone, the shock of Pudding's reappearance hit me. It was impossible. The gate was covered with strong mesh so no little body could squeeze between the metal bars. The bolt was high and on the outside - inoperable by any animal, let alone a three and a half month old pig. If a fox had climbed in and grabbed him he'd certainly not be returned, certainly not without teeth marks and bloody wounds.

Thoughtfully, I began the daily task of tidying the piglet apartments and, as I replaced hoops, tubes, geometric coloured blocks, and so on, onto racks, I could only think it was an April Fool's joke. But who could have played such a heartless trick and where could he have taken him?

Back in the cottage we talked about the mystery disappearance and reappearance but came up with no solution. Bernard had just started to tell me about new ideas for piglet tricks when there was a knock at the door. To my surprise it was Cynthia's husband, Sidney, on the doorstep.

'Aye oop, Freda, did you know Hermione and her piglets is marching down Nuthatch Lane.'

The shock of his statement closed my brain down to its outrageous impossibility and I barged him sideways off the step as I blundered towards the front gate.

'April Fool,' he wheezed, trying to catch his breath from my brutal elbow attack.

'Stupid idiot, you nearly gave me a heart attack,' I cried, holding back from punching him on his bulbous nose as I helped him out of the hydrangea.

He followed me into the cottage and sank down on a chair at the kitchen table.

He crossed his legs and my eyes were suddenly riveted to his bouncing foot - I'd never noticed before how small his feet were. But if he'd taken Pudding as an April Fool's joke he'd have surely admitted it by now. No point in playing such a stupid trick if you didn't let on. Unless, of course, I'd scared him into silence.

'Just thought I'd drop by to tell you some champion news,' he said, breath now fully restored to normal. 'Me cousin Nesbit Batty has moved into The Bungalow.'

He beamed with delight at this imparting of what he obviously thought such a splendid piece of news.

If he's as crafty as you, Sidney Slocumb, I thought, there's not much call for celebration.

Before I could formulate a reply, the phone rang and, relieved, I went out to the hall to answer it.

'Hello Freda, how's your private parts?' mother asked.

I ignored what I knew would be a running joke for the rest of our lives. 'Guess what,' I gabbled, eager to tell her my news. 'Pudding disappeared yesterday and now he's come back.'

'I'm delighted,' she said in that mocking way of hers. 'But I've got more to think about than your piddling pig.'

'Oh yes, did you have a bad evening at the bridge club?' I replied, equally sarcastic.

'As it happens, yes ... but it's not that.'

'What then?'

'Your father's dying,' she replied.

Four

I drove to Tooting like a maniac, doing ninety on the motorway, taking chances, howling all the time. He might be cantankerous. He might be overbearing. He might be impossible. But he was my father.

'You'd better go up and see him without me,' mother said when I arrived. 'He's in a funny mood.'

With quiet reverence, I pushed open their bedroom door. Dreading what I should see, I peeped in. Father sat propped up on pillows, scowling. On the double bed beside him was a large cardboard notice. In large capitals, written in red marker pen and outlined in black, was the one word DEATH.

'Is this some kind of a joke!' I cried, rushing to him, grabbing his hand.

'Your mother clearly thinks I'm on my death bed, so I thought I'd label it,' he explained morosely.

'What's wrong with you? Why are you on your death bed? You must tell me. Mother wouldn't say.'

'I have an in-growing toe nail that's giving me gyp.'

'An in-growing toe nail!' I cried, enragement and relief flooding over me in equal douches. I should be at home now organising the Animal Park, not here with this sham.

'It's either that or the touch of lung cancer they say I've got,' he added.

'Oh father,' I whispered. And shockwaves of goosepimples shivered over me.

'My own fault. Shouldn't have smoked,' he said gruffly. 'People warn you but you never think the time will come, or you think you'll be old and have had your life so it won't matter. Well I am old, but it *does* matter - I don't want to die.'

In the silence that followed, I heard mother's slow footfalls on the stairs, heard her shuffling along the landing towards us. My mother not pounding up the stairs? My mother shuffling! It was almost as shocking as the news I'd just heard.

Her small figure appeared in the doorway and an emotion I can't describe stirred up inside me. The impish smile, the sparkling blue eyes, had vanished. Deep lines had appeared. She pushed a stray wisp of blonde hair from her face. She flung out her hand towards father.

'Meet Hector Salmon, the idiot,' she said. 'When he blacked my eye, just the once when we were young, I nicknamed him Sockeye Salmon. But his friends at the bank always called him Smoked Salmon, because of his chain smoking - a name he preferred because it made people think he was an expensive, tasty dish.' She ran her hand across her eyes. 'But it should have made them think of black gungy tar clogging up his tubes, of black shrivelled lungs, of ...' She trailed off, fighting for control.

In the silence that clung to the air, I struggled to think of suitable words. Mother's mouth moved in an ungainly dance, her chin quivered. Father sat rigid. But, suddenly, he picked up his DEATH sign and flung it across the room, skimming it like a frisbee.

'Your mother thinks I've had it, but I haven't. The doctors will cure me.'

Mother, regaining control, sniffled, 'I'm glad to hear you say it, very very glad.'

He shuffled his legs over the side of the bed about to stand, then thought better of it and dragged them back again, flopping his body back against the propped-up pillows. His eyes fixed onto her.

'I Hector Salmon *will* be cured,' he reaffirmed.

'Oh good,' she said, now fully controlled. 'Fish are cured by smoking and salting them. You're a Salmon who's had years of being smoked so, Freda, go down and get the salt cellar will you. We'll smother him in it.'

Then they both started laughing and I caught the look of love and fear that passed between them.

Five

The ad we put in the paper for people's unwanted pets has so far produced one adorable female kid, about six weeks old, as yet unnamed, one cockerel called Bert and one goldfish called Jaws.

The kid has attached itself to Hermione, following her around like a shadow and, strangely, Hermione who seems to be completely brassed off with her own offspring, butting them away with her snout, appears to love the little goat.

When the piglets have been shut back in the unit after their free roaming times, we unbolt the pig flap in the kitchen door for their housetrained mother to have free access, but she's stopped coming in to the cottage to be close to her new found friend who, thankfully, hasn't yet mastered the hinged flap. They even sleep together every night in the mobile home, Hermione eschewing her new luxury pad for her old familiar room and her new friend.

Bert, the cockerel, was like a fish out of water the first day here, but now he struts around the garden as if he owns the place and, at night, disappears under the shored-up mobile home. Unfortunately, he reappears at five, piercing the placid air with his raucous pre-dawn screeching. At the first harsh *Cockadoo*... I'm astir, and by the *doodledoo* I'm wide awake, never to get back to sleep again. I'd get rid of him if it was up to me but Bernard, who never wakes of course, loves him, raving all the time about the beauty of his rich iridescent feathers and erect red comb.

'Okay, it's *your* cock,' I sniped. 'You look after him, but don't expect me to help out.'

'Pity,' he murmured, nudging up to me.

And, after the ensuing marital merger, he held me close and whispered, 'You know what I think?'

'No,' I replied, sated with love and waiting for the endearments.

'I think Bert's too common a name for that magnificent rooster.'

'Cuss Bert!' I flared, viciously elbowing him from me.

'No *Cuth*bert.'

'No, Cussbert.'

'*Cuth*bert!' he ejaculated, for the second time.

Jaws has been released into the new duck pond which, currently, is a completely duck-free zone. When we do get a quacker though I shall rename the fish. He'll never know, and I'll feel better about it.

Today I'm going to see a rabbit that Sidney Slocumb's cousin, the new owner of The Bungalow, wants to give away. Nesbit Batty's his name - the man's, not the rabbit's.

I walked along Bramble Lane and, from a distance, saw a tall man, his back towards me, looking up at the branches of the oak tree in The Bungalow front garden. Strobes of sunlight darted fleeting patterns on his slick black hair as he stood, hands on thick jean-clad hips, black-vested torso arched backwards, muscular tanned shoulders fully displayed. Surely this couldn't be Nesbit Batty, cousin of stolid squat Sidney?

As I opened the garden gate the man turned and I saw from the front that he could indeed be a cousin of Sidney's for his bulbous nose was of the same strawberry class, but redder, even riper looking. And his droopy lids failed to hide grey eyes that were just as devious. He strode towards me, baring glaring white false choppers in a welcoming leer.

'Aye oop. Thee must be Freda Field who's after me rabbit,' he said. And his voice was like gravel attempting to be velvet. He took my hand, placing his other on top of it. 'Nesbit,' he said, 'Nesbit Batty - delighted to meet thee.' Strong alcoholic fumes invaded my nostrils as he kept a firm hold on my hand, staring searchingly at me. 'Has anyone ever told thee, I say has anyone ever told thee, what gorgeous green eyes thee possess?'

And I didn't know how to answer, so just shrugged and smiled inanely.

He squeezed my hand. '*And* what gorgeous red hair - 'tis magnificent, all them tumbling curls.'

And, strangely, for normally I like compliments, I felt like clouting him round the ear to dislodge his Grecian Two Thousand, or kneeing him in the balls.

'Come in and meet the rabbit,' he said, at last releasing my hand and leading the way to the front door.

I entered. A short slim woman with curly grey hair hovered timidly in a doorway off the hall wiping her hands on a floral overall.

'Meet the rabbit,' he guffawed, jovially amending it to, 'Nay, Nay. Meet the wife.'

The woman looked up at me, a smile playing nervously on her pale lips. 'Enid,' she said. 'The name's Enid Batty - take no notice of him.'

Her hazel eyes seemed to be trying to convey a warning message of some kind.

'Come on,' Nesbit said, taking my elbow, 'come and see me Dick. I say come and see me Dick.'

His wife shot me a rueful grin. 'It were his idea of a joke calling the rabbit that - it's an easy chat-up line.'

He drove me the short journey home, the large white buck rabbit in a roomy hutch on the back seat of his expensive-looking shiny estate car.

'Does thee want me rabbit for your own little kids?' he asked.

I prevented myself snapping that at fifty-one that wasn't likely and, instead, told him about our plans to run the Animal Park.

'That's enterprising, I say that's enterprising. Glad me Dick will be of help.' He gave me a wicked look, which I ignored.

'But we think we've taken on too much,' I rushed. 'The animals take up so much time and Bernard's trying to dig up part of the hedge to get through to the next door field. And the barn roof needs mending and lots of other things too.'

'Mebbe I can help,' he said.

And maybe I won't want you to, I thought.

''Tis champion we're neighbours,' he gushed as we pulled up in our drive.

I ducked the obvious response and hurriedly removed myself from his car.

Nesbit hauled the hutch out from the back then followed me round the sideway where I held the gate back as he went on through to the garden where Bernard was just trundling a barrow of old straw across the grass. He left it when he saw us and hurried over.

'It's kind of you to give us your rabbit,' Bernard said, taking the hutch from Nesbit, placing it down on the ground.

'Nay, not at all. Just so long as the rascal has a good home, that's all that matters, I say, that's all that matters,' Nesbit bellowed. 'Our lad is grown up and he stayed oop north, and Enid and I don't want the bother of him any more.'

Bernard crouched down and peered in. 'He's a good-looking chap,' he observed, opening the hutch door and inserting his hand, instantly yanking it out again screaming, 'He's bitten me.'

'Aye, he does that, him,' Nesbit confirmed. 'Next time, approach him wi' a carrot and he'll ignore thy finger - that's if thee's pronto.'

Before either of us had time to gather our wits and tell him his rotten rabbit was unsuitable for our requirements, Nesbit said, 'Freda tells me there's lots of jobs need doing here to get the Animal Park up and running. Worry no more. I say worry no more. I can help thee.'

Bernard, winding a hanky round his bleeding finger, looked fleetingly relieved, then said, 'Thanks for the offer, but we couldn't afford to pay you what you'd be worth.'

'Nay, nay. Not to worry about payment. I say not to worry about payment. Give me a chance to be neighbourly and give me something to do.'

'I'd have to pay you,' mumbled Bernard, unconvincingly.

'Nay, I am happily set up for rest of me life, me. I've sold off me Batty Building concern and taken early retirement down south here in same village as me cousin Sidney - ex mayor of this district,' he added, jutting his chest out.

'I know Sidney well,' I informed him, 'last year I painted his portrait - and his wife, Cynthia, is my best friend.'

'Ah well, that means we'll be bosom buddies too,' he beamed, his eyes dwelling on my breasts so that, embarrassed, I hunched my shoulders forward in an effort to diminish their size.

'And there's more ways than mere brass to pay for willing help, besides it'd get me out of Enid's way,' Nesbit hastened, as if he'd gone too far in the first part. 'So thee and me'd be helping each other. What needs doing first? I say what needs doing first?'

Putting down your revolting rabbit - bobbiting your Dick, I wanted to reply.

I lugged the hutch containing the finger-mauler to the junk room in the mobile home, while Bernard led Nesbit down the garden to look at the part of the tall laurel hedge that needed removing.

Six

One month since drink-sodden slimy, but very useful, Nesbit appeared on our scene. He has helped Bernard uproot a section of hedge creating a wide gap connecting our garden to Esmerelda's field. And, single-handed, has mended the barn roof and is now making good the walls.

Whenever I trundle a wheelbarrow of five pound notes in the guise of straw, hay, oats, vitamins or carrots over to the stables for Daisy, I skirt the bottom of the field, giving the barn wide berth to avoid his crude remarks. If Esmerelda's there I stay a while, even though it does make me feel ill watching her cast bounteous quantities of straw down, and feeding the donkey ad lib. As I keep saying to Bernie, Esmerelda still has all the pleasure of the donkey she's "given" to us, while Muggins pays for it. Spot the silly ass!

This morning it was bucketing down and I, in my role as chalet maid, squelched down to the lucky piglets to tidy up their playthings in their snug dry rooms. Two dangling patter-snout balls in Pie's room had become too entangled to undo. As I wielded my penknife, holding the soft balls in one hand and hacking at the thread with the other, I hoped that Vernon Veal's blade would be sharper when, tomorrow, he neuters my poor boys.

'I beg you Freda, do not concern yourself about payment directly,' Vernon Veal insisted, as we walked over the boggy lawn towards the pig unit. 'You can settle in a few months when your enterprise is up and running - and be assured I will just charge you the minimum.'

'That's very good of you,' I sighed.

'It's my pleasure. I revel in being with animals. There are so many fascinating things one could do with them if only one were authorised.'

'What kind of things?' I asked, intrigued.

'Experiments - to establish their true feelings.'

'How could you do that?' I asked, now not only intrigued but vaguely perturbed.

'Oh you know,' he replied, wafting his hands around in the air, 'wiring up their brains to voice synthesisers, getting them to talk about their emotions, that kind of thing.'

Suddenly, I wasn't so sure of him. Nervously, I opened the gate and let him through to where my innocent lads waited unaware of what was in store, for it wasn't their brains and voice boxes that were to be tampered with today, it was their manhoods.

Vernon threw down a waterproof pad and knelt on it as he opened his black box of implements. As I hurried out, anxious to leave, I looked back then stopped dead in my tracks, eyes riveted to the small ridged soles of Vernon's boots. About the same size as the imprint in the dung that may have been left by the pignapper! Was he the one? Had he borrowed poor Pudding to try his vile experiments on him? He had shown him extra attention the day before. As I watched, Vernon rummaged in the open black box and I could see the contents but knew I wouldn't recognise a voice synthesiser - unless it shouted out at me, and then only if it spoke in a Dalek voice. Slowly, he removed a scalpel from a sheath, harsh stabs of sunlight flashing from it. My poor, poor lads. Quickly I fled.

An hour later he knocked on the kitchen door. 'All done,' he said, 'with hardly a squeal between them.'

I felt faint and must have shown it.

'All for the best Freda. No more worries about hormone-packed Jesus getting his sisters in-pig.'

I pictured the laddish smile on Jesus's face as he'd tried to mount Mary. Poor little swine. No more urges. No more skittish fun with the girls. No more dangly bits.

Next morning as I ate my muesli, I pictured Vernon Veal eagerly devouring soft squidgy lightly sautéed devilled kidneys. Only they weren't devilled kidneys, they were devilled nuts. To my consternation, as I scraped the last spoonful of oat clusters from my bowl, I found I was wondering how they would taste but, luckily, a knock at the door halted that flow of loathsome thought and Cynthia came in saying she wanted to see how we were doing with our Animal Park. No doubt attempting to make amends for her negative comments about piles of stinking money and piles of stinking shit when I first told her. (Nasty un-Cynthia like words that had painfully stuck in my mind, like undigested food in colonic pouches.)

'Come and see,' I said, one final vision of Vernon selling my pigs' balls to the deli in Orlford invading my head before vanishing for good.

'It's so exciting,' I babbled as we walked down the garden, 'Bernard's taught the piglets loads of tricks. They can balance balls on their snouts then flick them up into a kind of netball net.' As I spoke I wondered if the boys' missing paraphernalia might make them top-heavy and unbalance them. 'They can play patta-snout with soft dangling balls. They can throw frisbees. They can place circular blocks into circular holes. And other shapes. All nine of them can do all those things, they're so clever. And Jesus can even skate board down a ramp.'

'Even more miraculous than walking on water,' Cynthia grinned, her teeth sliding out into full view.

I linked my arm into hers, elated we were back to being friends. Those cheery buck teeth had confirmed it.

We entered the pig yard and Princess, the pinkest of the litter, skipped out from her apartment, snorting a greeting. As she did so, I saw Countess, the long-snouted mean greedy one, sneak into the vacated room then hasten out with Princess's frisbee gripped in her teeth. She was like that. Stole anything she could, not because she wanted it but because she was a kleptomaniac. Sometimes I guiltily thought that if ever there were a time we couldn't afford to keep all of them, she'd be the one with the one-way ticket to the pork pie works.

Duchess, more ginger than pink, and Lady, a pale blush colour, joined us, squealing and capering, tails a-twirling. I knew the boys were lying low because they felt sore - in every sense of the word. Duchess, the brazen one, rolled over as usual hoping for one of us to tickle her tum.

'When are you going to let paying customers in?' Cynthia asked, bending down and obliging.

'We're having a trial run with my old class from the village school. If it goes well we'll open the doors to the public soon after - that's if anyone comes.'

Slowly, we walked along the boys' apartments looking in at them. Jesus, then Hamlet, then Pudding, then Pie glowered back up at us with undisguised hostility that was hard for me to bear.

We crossed the yard to the girls' side where we saw that Mary and Princess had joined Lady in her apartment where they all sat staring at one of the colourful matching games that Bernard had bought from the Early Learning Centre. Incredibly, they appeared to be trying to work out how to get a trapezium shape into its hole and, as we watched, Lady carefully nudged it with her snout 'til it was the right way round and it dropped straight through. Immediately they capered around together, squealing, and, when we clapped, each one spiralled round in a circle as Bernard had trained them, then knelt down taking their bows.

Euphoric optimism engulfed me. We were on our way for sure.

'They're truly amazing!' Cynthia exclaimed, and my heart felt as if it would explode with pride at our clever family.

'Come on. I'll show you our little kid,' I said, 'she's so sweet and she and Hermione love each other - spend every second together, one cropping the grass, the other rooting around in it. Or they're snuggled up together, asleep.'

We left the females to their fun and games and the males to their morose recuperations and squished our way up the garden towards the old yard housing the mobile home.

'I can't see them around the garden so I expect they're taking a siesta in there. They often do about this time,' I explained.

I led the way up the ramp and through the swing door. Immediately opposite, Hermione was stretched out asleep on the straw in her blue painted room. I looked around but there was no sign of the little goat. A snake of fear slithered around inside my guts. 'The kid's not here,' I whispered.

'Probably grazing somewhere out of sight,' Cynthia sensibly suggested.

Hermione opened her eyes. She smiled at me then looked down to where the kid should have been nestling against her. I saw the shock in her eyes. Saw her head jerk from side to side. Watched her haul herself up, heard her plaintiff honking call.

'No, no, she wouldn't have gone off, they always stick together,' I said, turning back down the ramp with Hermione close on my heels.

'She'll be all right,' Cynthia called. 'You told me yourself that there was no way an animal could get out of your garden *or* the field.'

I knew she was right. I was panicking for nothing. The kid had become bored, or hungry, and had wandered off and was having a feast on the grass out of sight at the far side of the barn or stables. I stopped, but Hermione galloped on by.

Cynthia joined me and we linked arms again. 'What do you think of Sidney's cousin then?' she suddenly asked, distracting my worried thoughts.

This was a loaded question and I wasn't sure how much I should say.

'I'm grateful for all the work he's putting in,' I began cautiously.

'But he drives you mad with innuendo and smutty chat up lines.'

It was a relief that she knew.

'He's a letch when he's had a drink or two, the same with all females - even with me. And I reckon we should teach him a lesson, don't you?' she stated.

'Yes,' I replied, emphatically. 'But only after he's done all the work here.'

And we both creased up with laughter as we ambled back to the cottage to make a cuppa and work out a plan.

But, even as we sat round the kitchen table, laughing at outrageous things we could do to him, I was longing for Cynthia to leave so that I could ring mother about father, then go out and search for the kid.

'He's tired,' said mother, 'but he always is after the chemo.'

'How about you?' I asked.

'I'm tired too, tired of this dull life, stuck indoors with him. The only time I ever get out is to peg up the washing. That's my treat. Pathetic isn't it. *And* I'm tired of his daft requests.'

'Like what?'

'Like asking me to ask you if you'll set up a salmon farm in your garden pond as his memorial. The Hector Salmon Salmon Farm. I mean, it's stupid having two words the same together.'

I wondered if he was serious or just winding her - and me - up. At any rate I felt easier. If my father was still in winding up mode he wasn't too poorly.

After we'd said goodbye, I hurried out to hunt for the kid, but she was nowhere. Not again, I thought. Not another animal missing. Fear hacked at my innards with a machete knife.

Just before bedtime, Bernie and I went out to look again. Translucent scarves of cloud drifted across the moon's full bright face, casting eerie shadows on the wet ground. Bernard went off to check around the stables and the barn whilst I mooched around the back garden.

Hermione, honking sadly, stayed with me, nosing into long grass and nettles, risking a painful snout. At midnight, we gave up the search and gave in to poor dejected Hermione by letting her sleep on the sofa indoors.

'I wish it had been your bloody cock that had vanished,' I cried to Bernard as we consoled each other in bed.

'That's *very* encouraging,' he grumbled, snatching his hand away from my favourite erogenous zone and making me wish I'd kept my trap shut.

Vernon Veal's long fangs emerge from his parted scarlet lips as he leers down at the bleating struggling kid lying on a table, its little hooves cruelly shackled together. In each hand he holds a two pronged metal implement which he suddenly lunges into each side of the little goat's head as if spiking a corn on the cob. 'Now we shall see,' he hisses ...

Cussbert's raucous reveille pierced the nightmare and, grateful to him for once, I leapt out of bed, glad to escape. Downstairs, I found that Hermione had vacated the sofa and the cottage. I dashed out, still in dressing gown and slippers, now dreading my precious girl would be missing too. I pounded up the ramp then stopped dead. There they both were, in the room opposite, cuddled up together as if nothing had happened. I clasped the kid's tiny head gently in my hands, easing it slowly right then left. Not one hole punctured her tiny skull, not one speck of blood stained her fine white hair. Her strange horizontal pupils gazed placidly at me showing no sign of distress.

Now *I* had a strong desire to wire her brain to a voice synthesiser so she could tell me where she had been!

Seven

Bernard is still besotted by the beauty of Cussbert. To hear him talk you'd think it was the most handsome rooster in the Kingdom, if not the world. He is now terrified a fox will get him one night *(If only!)* and has been busy making a run enclosed by special heavy gauge mesh guaranteed to be fox proof. The whole contraption - known as an *ark and run* in poultry housing circles he proudly informed me - is shaped like a giant Toblerone packet lying lengthwise on the ground, its lower side open to the grass, its two sloping walls filled in with the protective mesh for two thirds of the way and solid wood for the last third, that part being the ark, partitioned across by a triangular wall with an archway cut in it. Thus, unfortunately, rendering Cussbert completely safe from attack.

I had hoped that when Bernard shut Cussbert away in his DIY fox-proof night quarters positioned at the far end of the garden, the cock's screeching pronouncement of a new day would be fainter and hopefully later due to the darkness inside the ark, but if anything it's amplified and even earlier. When I suggested to Bernard that we reposition it in the field, Esmerelda unfortunately overheard.

'Oh no you en't doing that,' she said hotly. 'That'd be too near my house. I had a cockerel once and had to wring its neck 'cos I couldn't stand it.'

I wondered if she might be persuaded to do the honours on our one!

Then, as if to try to make up for being uncooperative, she actually engaged in conversation, asking if I believed in spirit deities. What, like gods of whisky and gin, I quipped, but she's got no sense of humour. Thought you might want to join our female circle, she muttered sullenly, then clammed up when I asked what they did.

It's strange that the two people I see most of these days are her and Nesbit, both of them peculiar. Nesbit has worked so hard on the barn that I really wished I liked him. Once or twice he's been quite pleasant, but then the hip flask comes out and Mr Nice Guy disappears and Mr Obnoxious Fucking Big Mouth takes over.

Thank goodness the animals are normal.

I was worn out when I went to bed, but next morning at five, the other Mr Obnoxious Fucking Big Mouth opened his beak and I wished

I had the same strength of hand and strength of personality as Esmerelda to do a bit of neck wringing myself.

'Bloody cockerel's woken me up again,' I ranted, heaving myself over.

'Why don't you sleep with cotton wool stuck in your ears,' Bernard sleepily suggested.

'Why don't you sleep with cotton wool stuck up your arse - *and* your fucking cock,' I yelled, driven to vulgar obscenities by lack of sodding sleep.

It was Thursday, the day Elizabeth Blessing had said I could speak to the year three class about their forthcoming visit to our Animal Farm.

They sat on the floor, cross-legged, gazing up at me. 'You'll be pleased to hear that, next week, you are all going to be guinea pigs,' I started.

Laughter and squeaking guinea pig impressions flared up then slowly simmered down.

'That means you are going to be the first visitors to experience my brand new Animal Park,' I explained.

Twenty-five pairs of eyes shone back at me and excited chatter swept through the classroom, all along the lines of: Hooray, no work/no school/ no maths/no spelling, etc. etc.

Then Harry, still only eight but looking bigger, shot up his hand. 'I *love* animals,' he said, and I was delighted that one child at least seemed pleased with the actual idea of the outing and not just the getting out of work. 'But mum won't let me keep any,' he continued, 'so can I borrow one of yours?'

'No,' I laughed, 'it's not like a library.'

'Just for a day, miss,' he wheedled.

'Harry, you know it's out of the question. No.'

'Just one of your piglets - you wouldn't miss one out of nine.'

I stared at him. How did he know there were nine! Had I ever mentioned how many? His pleading eyes stared back at me. Could this boy be the phantom animal borrower?

'Or, how about the little goat,' Harry persisted.

And now he was definitely the prime suspect until I suddenly realised that only last week I'd called in and asked the class for suggestions for the kid's name. So they all knew about her.

'Are you going to call it Billy the Kid?' little Penny asked.

'Yes, are you?' a dozen or so voices piped up.

Practically every child in the class had written that idea on their secret ballot paper because they'd just had a story about the notorious bandit read to them.

'Billy goats are males and our goat is a female and, besides, she won't always be a kid, so I've decided on Isobelle's suggestion of Kermit, because it's funny and because goats like to jump, just like frogs.'

'Can't wait to see Kermit the kid,' pronounced Harry.

And my thoughts were back on track. I tilted my head trying to surreptitiously read the size on his upturned shoe. Between the sole and the heel a faint number was etched. I think it was 38. I bent my head over more then saw that Harry was staring at me with a puzzled frown. Hastily, he uncrossed his legs and drew his knees up to his chin. But I'd seen enough. I wasn't yet up with EC sizes but I could tell just by looking that his foot was about the same size as the imprint in the dung. Now all I had to do was catch him borrowing.

That evening Isobelle, the successful kid namer, knocked on the cottage door and handed me a cardboard box with a hole-pierced lid. Her father hovered in the lane outside the gate.

'Dad says it's surplus to our requirements,' she said solemnly, 'so you can have it for your Animal Park. A *real* guinea pig.'

I peeped inside and bright button eyes peered back at me.

After she'd left, I rang the RSPCA.

'Is it safe to put a guinea pig in the same hutch as a rabbit who bites fingers?' I asked. 'Just until we can get another hutch.'

The man on the other end assured me they'd be all right together. 'Rabbits are okay with guinea pigs, yours probably associates fingers with food. Keep an eye on them at first though.'

Carefully, I opened the door of the large hutch and threw a carrot in for Dick. Gently, I placed the black, brown and white little guinea pig at the opposite end to the big rabbit. I closed the door and surveyed them through the mesh. Dick began greedily nibbling the carrot, his mean eyes never leaving his new room mate.

The guinea pig trembled and I worried about leaving him with the savage buck. But, suddenly, the big rabbit lolloped over to him and sniffed around the quivering bundle of fur. I clasped the cage door at the ready to rescue him. I held my breath. But, to my utter amazement, Dick dropped a chunk of carrot held in his mouth at the guinea pig's paws. The little creature stared up at Dick then down at the carrot. His took the welcome gift up in his tiny paws and nervously began to nibble.

Dick hopped back to the bulk of the carrot at the far end and began gnawing again, his eyes still on his new fluffy companion.

I was touched by the unexpected generous gesture from the finger mauler. I breathed out. They were going to be all right together. Nesbit's misunderstood Dick just needed a friend.

Early next morning, even before seeing to the piglets, I jogged across to the mobile home where the hutch was housed in the end room. As I passed Hermione and Kermit a coldness came over me: there was something about their quietness and scared-looking eyes that frightened me. Fear hung in the air like the Hitchcock shower curtain. Something dreadful had happened here last night. Could the pignapper have returned?

A frightened moan sounded as I entered the room. I stopped then realised it came from my own throat. I laughed out loud at my stupidity, hearing Hermione's answering honk from her bedroom behind. Hugging myself to stop shaking, I made my way towards the rabbit hutch, weaving my way round the old wheel barrow, flower pots and hosepipe to the wooden bench on which the hutch stood. I bent my head down, stared in.

Thank god, they were still there, the rabbit up one end and the guinea pig fast asleep on its side facing me, looking incredibly sweet. I threw the rabbit a carrot to distract him and reached in, inserting my hand under the guinea pig's body to lift him out but, as my fingers curled round the little bundle of fur, they entered a soft wet hole in his back and I screamed out, throwing him down, where he stayed, unmoving, eyes staring, quite dead.

'You bloody Dick, you've eaten him,' I sobbed, picking up a hammer with my sticky hand, opening the hutch to smash up the guinea-pig-mauling rabbit who, but such a short while ago, had only specialised in fingers, at least as far as I knew. But, it was a futile gesture and, slowly, I put the hammer back down, seeing its haft stained with dark blood, before I ran for it.

Later, Esmerelda took the hutch and the unbeaten-up rabbit away, saying she'd deal with it if I couldn't.

Next day, still depressed by the murder of the guinea pig, I mooched through the gap to go over and ask Esmerelda how she'd "dealt" with the assassin, but before I got there Nesbit ran out from the barn.

I backed away as the whisky scented breath assailed my nose.

'By heck Freda, thee's looking ravishing, I say thee's looking ravishing,' he said, baring his false gnashers at me.

I backed away some more, but the distance between us remained the same as he kept on advancing.

'I'm right sorry me rabbit gnawed a hole in yer guinea pig,' he said cheerily, edging closer.

'It was awful, I hate your rotten Dick. Esmerelda took him away, or else I'd have killed him with my own bare hands,' I cried, the big white buck in my tormented mind transmuting to the big red smuck in front of me.

'Enid's gone to her mother's,' he pronounced, the subject of the killer rabbit apparently over. He winked one drink-sodden eye. 'Think on Freda, why not come round and see me, it could be fun.'

'No way, Nesbit,' I snarled, turning on my heels and hurrying off.

'Spoil sport,' he bellowed after me.

With relief I reached the stables and looked back, checking he wasn't following. Daisy was watching from the open upper door which hung down precariously on rusty hinges. She threw back her large head issuing stuttering brays of excitement. I stroked her nose, gave her a carrot, then unbolted the lower door. With a little joyous kick up of her hind legs, she trotted out.

I stayed there studying the dilapidated old timber building. Daisy's stall was the furthest left. Then came three unused stables permanently bolted shut - plenty of room to house more animals some day. Maybe another donkey or a Shetland pony? A shiver of excitement ran through me as I thought of how we could grow.

I wandered past them to the door at the end, seeing the dryness of its lower edge scalloped into raggety holes. Esmerelda had told me this opened on to one large room, but I'd never been inside. Tentatively, I lifted the latch and entered the gloom.

A gentle cooing made me look up and there, poking over one of the rafters of the tall pitched corrugated iron roof, was the white head of a dove, its glinting eyes peering down at me. A sharp flacking made me look higher where two ghostly white birds flew from one short cross beam to another. As my eyes grew accustomed to the dim light, I spied other inquisitive eyes in eerie white faces peering down from high corners where they nested.

For a while I stood unmoving in the still room, cocooned in the gentle sounds of the doves and the sweet smell of hay. Eyes fully accustomed to the dimness, I began moving around, passing loose hay piled carelessly in a corner, seeing old mildewed reins hanging on a rusty nail and an ancient saddle on the floor beneath. A dented bucket lay on its side by a high pile of bales of straw. I now knew where to come if we ran out of money, I thought bitterly, thinking of the barrowloads of our own stock we'd trundled over for Daisy.

Propped against the wall was a besom, its twigs cobwebbed with disuse. I moved past it to the darkest corner where I discovered an old cupboard hanging crookedly on the wall. Wavering, for I didn't know if I should really pry, at last I dared open it. Inside, ten clean packets of white candles were neatly stacked in two piles on a shelf. Otherwise, it was empty.

The creak of the door opening behind me made me start and quickly close the cupboard. For a second I didn't turn, eyes darting, searching for a weapon, spotting the broom. If it were Nesbit prowling round after me I'd have no compunction in clouting him with it. Slowly, I turned. Esmerelda stood silhouetted in the open doorway. Had she seen me snooping? I wondered guiltily.

'Thank you for what you done letting Daisy out,' she said, advancing towards me. 'I got up late this morning.'

'A night out on the tiles,' I joked.

'No, a night out with my sisters.'

'I didn't know you had sisters.'

'They en't real sisters,' she muttered, 'just a circle of friends.'

'What circle?'

She shuffled her feet.

'The inner circle of the Great Piddlehurst and District ...' she stopped, as if saying too much. 'Bet you still upset 'bout that guinea pig,' she hurried on, 'even though you en't had him more'n two minutes.'

She must have seen me bridle at the uncalled for snide postscript.

'O'course, you en't a born and bred country woman,' she quickly explained. 'That'd be why you're so soft 'bout creatures.' Her dark eyes held mine. 'Why not come round to me for supper tomorrow, cheer yourself up - you and Bernard.'

I was touched by her unexpected display of sympathy and accepted straight away, grateful for her thoughtfulness.

I should have known it would end in tears. Mine of course.

Eight

A dozen or so candles flickered life into the dark recesses of the room and twinkled pinpoints of light off Nesbit Batty's false teeth as he gabbed on and on. Brassed off already with his unexpected presence I sat staring, my eyes lured to his teeth like snails to slug bait.

'That's the advantage of your missus being away, I say that's the advantage of your missus being away, strange dark women invite thee round to dinner,' said Nesbit, dropping his voice so that strange dark Esmerelda attending to food in the adjacent kitchen couldn't hear. 'And, of course, if thee doesn't mind my saying so Bernard, being in the company of buxom redheads such as your good lady wife. Aye, that's an advantage. If Enid were home I'd be stuck there looking at her.'

Oh god, he was still as nauseating as ever. When I'd walked in and seen he was there, it was all I could do not to march straight back home where sitting on the sofa with my plump pink pig would be a million times better than sitting at Esmerelda's table with this red faced smarmy git.

Bernard, still unaware of the true nature of this man, leant across the table and clinked glasses with him, wishing him the best of health, thanking him profusely for all the work he'd done and was doing.

'Nay, nay, 'tis my pleasure,' Nesbit generously responded. 'Always enjoyed me building work. So thee's helping me out in me retirement by providing free materials and dilapidated buildings.'

As he spoke I felt his foot brush against mine in the unseen depths beneath the table. He cast me a wicked smile as he manoeuvred it around.

As I jerked my foot away from his, an idea shot into my head.

'Why don't you sit next to me,' I purred, pushing one shoulder forward in a hopefully sexy way. 'It's not right that a husband and wife should sit side by side.'

His eyes lit up, vying for glinting supremacy with his gnashers. 'Champion idea Freda, I say champion idea Freda. That way your Bernard would be sitting rubbing shoulders with our hostess so 't would be satisfactory all round.'

Quickly he rose, throwing me a look which clearly said that it wasn't just shoulders he hoped to be rubbing with me.

With a soft sigh that could probably only be picked up by a long-standing wife as a sign of inordinate annoyance, Bernard stood and, with an even deeper sigh, grabbed hold of his wine glass and stomped round the other side.

'Champion idea, I say champion idea,' said the automatic repeater weapon as he sat eagerly down, shifting the chair closer to mine in the process.

He took a large gulp of wine and, as he did so, his knee slid against mine - like an unsuspecting fox brushing up to a gin trap, I thought wryly. Gradually, his upper leg pressed against mine. Casually I picked up my fork, slowly I lifted it, speedily I plunged it full force into the top of his fat leg, instantly pulling it out again in one deft movement.

Through the spluttering of red wine and choking, he screamed.

At that moment Esmerelda came back in carrying a heavy tureen which she placed on a mat in the centre of the table.

Muted noises of distress came from my right.

'Sorry Nesbit,' I said, turning and smiling sweetly. 'My hand must have slipped.'

'Aye it did that and it blewdy hurts,' he moaned, rocking back and forth, hands encircling his leg.

'Sorry,' I said again, this time vaguely meaning it, though I wasn't sorry that his mind was now on his own leg instead of mine.

'Me trousers're ruined,' he groaned.

And, guiltily, I saw on his smart beige trousers, two blobs of blood oozing into the material either side of the crease.

'I've been thinking,' said Bernard, addressing Esmerelda, unaware of the extent of Nesbit's agony. 'What kind of a farm did this used to be?'

Esmerelda sat abruptly down. 'That were heavy.'

'What, the soil?' said Bernard.

'No the pot,' Esmerelda laughed. 'The kind of farm this used to be when my grandfather ran it were a thriving, well-run one. He grew all sorts: wheat, tatties, the lot. It were him that got the stables built for the horses that pulled the plough. Then, his son, my father, took over and it were still thriving and well-run. He were the one who got the barn built. I had a pony when I were a girl and I rode it through the fields we owned then at t'other side of the house.'

'Why was it called Rugged Farm?' asked Bernard and I wished he'd shut up till she'd served up because I was famished and dying to get started on whatever was in the steaming tureen.

'That were my family name,' she said sounding astounded that he didn't know. 'I were Esmerelda Rugged before I married an Oven.'

Nesbit guffawed loudly, apparently recovered from my fork tines attack. 'Talking of ovens,' he said. 'I say talking of ovens. I'm starving, me. So how about us getting started on yer 'ot pot?'

'Hang on a minute,' Bernard aggravatingly said. 'This is interesting. What did you and your husband grow here?'

Flickering light played on her face casting eerie shadows of her aquiline nose on each pale cheek.

'He grew fat here,' she finally said. 'He didn't grow cereals. He didn't grow vegetables. He just grew fat.' Her eyes clouded. 'He sold off the fields we owned on t'other side, he let the farm go till there weren't anything much left that could be passed down to our son.'

She pushed her thick dark hair back revealing a dangling earring of what looked like a small bone.

'What happened to your husband?' asked Bernard gently.

'He died.'

'How did he die, I say how did he die?' bellowed Nesbit.

'My son killed him,' she replied.

In the silence that followed I stared down at the old oak table, seeing the uneven shallow dents worn into its surface seemingly changing their shapes in the prancing light and shadows of the candle flames.

'But, if he behaves hisself, he won't be in clink for ever,' she said at last.

'Thee should re-marry, I say thee should re-marry, a handsome lass like thee,' said Nesbit, as tactless as ever.

'I en't never going to marry,' she snapped. 'Men en't hygienic. Spend too much time adjusting their scrotums for my liking.'

'Nay, nay,' said Nesbit, shocked.

'Yes, yes,' she argued, rising and at last lifting the tureen lid. 'I got to be germ free and celibate.' Then, completely changing the subject, she added, 'And he's looking forward to getting out o'prison so he can see what we done with the top field - cars to be parked there 'stead of crops. I've writ and told him and he said he liked that. Always liked cars he did.'

We sat in silence as she sniffed noisily at the steam. Then she picked up a serving fork and spoon and dipped them into the pot, stirring them round. 'Gotta find a prime bit for Freda,' she said, at last raising a leg of pink sinewy-looking meat and serving it onto my plate.

'What is it?' I asked not recognising the joint, or the aroma.

'En't no need to worry, it en't my cat,' she said, brightening at the joke, indicating a stuffed black cat that I hadn't noticed before, propped up in a shadowy corner, all thoughts of her murdered husband and murderer son cast aside.

'Sheba. Used to lie purring in my lap every evening - couldn't just bury her so I got her stuffed.'

'Didn't do the same fer yer husband, I say didn't do the same fer yer husband,' Nesbit quipped.

Esmerelda looked up from her stirring to gaze at him, her expression giving nothing away.

I sniffed at the steaming meat on my plate again. 'I know it's not a cat. We don't eat cats. What *is* it?'

She stopped in her search for the next joint, candle light flickering on her face, weirdly lighting up one eye.

'You'll be mighty pleased to know it's rabbit stew.' Then turning to Nesbit, grinning, she added, 'One way to deal with your Dick.'

I stared in horror at the dead leg on my plate. 'You can't expect me to eat a part of Nesbit's Dick,' I cried. 'Not that vile creature who ate my guinea pig while it was still alive.'

'En't nothing wrong with that,' stated Esmerelda. 'Not like you got to eat the rabbit while it's still alive. I killed it afore it went in the pot. An eye for an eye and waste not want not is my motto.'

As she spoke she delved around again and, with a sudden 'Gotcha', hoiked out a whole thinly fleshed ribby torso. 'That gotta be for you,' she said to Nesbit. 'It were your rabbit first afore you got rid of him, so you gotta have his chest.'

My brain ceased reeling for a nanosecond to wonder why being an animal's previous owner warranted the eating of its chest, but then set off reeling again.

'Champion. Aye, champion. Thee can't beat rabbit stew,' Nesbit said, eagerly tucking a paper serviette into the top of his shirt.

The pungent smell of the assassin rabbit rose up in steaming swirls, infiltrating my body through my nostrils, blending my innards to pulp.

'I've got to go,' I cried, dashing out through the kitchen to the back door, making it to a gooseberry bush before throwing up.

'I should have known,' I lamented to Bernard when he arrived back home. 'It was the worst evening of my entire life - and now I'm starving because I didn't eat a thing.'

'Actually,' said Bernard, 'I stayed on to be polite to Esmerelda, but Dick tasted jolly good and I was delighted to get my teeth into him, instead of vice versa. My tasty revenge.'

'But it was only your finger he bit, and you weren't dead.'

'That's why I was the one who came off worst,' he explained patiently, 'when you're dead you feel nothing, when you're alive it flaming hurts.'

'I'm not surprised Esmerelda's son murdered her husband,' I muttered, 'he's inherited her killer genes. She kills rabbits and cockerels at the drop of a beret.'

'Cockerels! That's horrendous!' gasped Bernard, his irritating patient understanding of Esmerelda's killing ways at last prodded into outrage.

Feeling better, I ate three cheese sandwiches then went up to bed where I couldn't sleep because the engorgement of cheddar invigorated my brain, causing it to worry about everything, including my poor father and mother but, most pressingly, about the Year Three guinea pigs who were coming to visit tomorrow.

'Supposing the children don't like it,' I said to Bernie's curled up back. 'We'd have to close our Animal Park before we'd even opened.'

I waited to hear his voice roar that that was impossible, but all he did was snore, selfishly leaving me wide awake to worry on my own.

'We *would*,' I told his sleeping back. 'We'd have to shut down if the children hated it.'

Oh god!

Nine

The children, dressed in casual clothes and trainers instead of their royal blue uniforms, lined up in pairs in the playground and Elizabeth Blessing came out to wave us off, saying she would pray for us all.

'Why, will it be dangerous?' asked timid Prunella.

'Of course not,' I laughed.

'So why is Mrs Blessing going to pray for us all?'

Good question I thought. 'To ... um ... to make sure you enjoy yourselves,' I lamely replied.

As I walked beside them I heard her say to her partner, 'It's not going to be much good - they've had to ask god to make us enjoy it.'

As we made our way along Bramble Lane I listened to their speculations about the visit, gradually realising that unless I could magically acquire a python or chimpanzee the day was doomed to failure from the outset.

Just half an hour after we'd arrived and they'd seen it all! They sat on the square of second hand carpet on the barn floor eating what was meant to be their packed lunches, but what had turned out to be their packed pre-elevenses. All that remained was the Piglets' Performance about which Bernard had been very secretive, not letting me see their progress because he wanted it to be a surprise. Listening to the children's grumbles about non-existent animals, the muddy walks and the empty duck pond, I was filled with despair. It was as if I'd promised them the Earth and given them a worm cast. The whole enterprise was a failure. Whatever made me think we could run such an Animal Park, Children's Zoo, Pet Farm, whatever you liked to bloody well call it. We knew nothing about the business and had no money to pay for experts, or even buy more creatures. It was a farce.

'Kermit is lovely,' said, Harry, cutting into my dismal thoughts. 'I stroked her - I wish I could take her home.' He sounded wistful and, again, my eyes were drawn to his shoes.

'I've got fifty pee to spend and there's nothing to spend it on, no gift shop, can't even buy an icecream,' grumbled Toby, biting with frustrated vigour into a pork pie.

'My dad says all pigs are good for is eating, not looking at,' Penelope piped up, adding, 'anyone want to swap something for half of my ham sandwich.'

'How about a handful of pork scratchings,' offered Suzie, sitting next to her.

'And there's not even a play area or computer games,' sniffed Molly, glaring accusingly in my direction.

And I didn't admonish her for being cheeky, knowing I'd let them all down.

'Hermione is too fat,' piped up Penelope who was a rather overweight piglet herself.

'Especially her tits,' sniggered Toby, and all of them except Harry joined in the smutty laughter.

I didn't even bother to explain about sows and their milk. I felt too fed up. Besides they all knew.

As we all mooched across to the area where the show was to take place I wished the whole blooming day was over so that Bernie and I could sit down together and discuss how to wind up this daft enterprise. Even if Elizabeth Blessing had been the Archbishop of Canterbury, or someone with equal clout, prayers couldn't save this debacle.

We plonked ourselves down on some of the bench seats, made by Nesbit, surrounding the oval arena, in the centre of which stood a long ramp, a platform at the high end, a gentle curve at the other. I studied the children's faces. Each and every one of them looked as if they'd rather be back at school battling with maths or spellings than sitting here in our field. Shoulders were slumped. Mouths were sullen. Disappointment reigned.

Suddenly, the faint strains of music that I recognised as a Sousa march drifted to us from the direction of our back garden. I looked over to the gap in the hedge just as the tall figure of Bernard appeared. He carried a tape recorder in one hand, twiddling with it as he strode towards us, increasing the volume. On the crook of his arm hung a bulging plastic bag. Beside him, in neat single file, the piglets marched along, more or less in time to the music. A burst of applause and swell of excited comments surged out from the revitalised children whose clapping hands gradually took on the rhythm of the march. As the strange little army marched into the arena, the music ceased and an expectant hush fell.

'Halt one two three,' yelled Bernard, and, with a bit of bumping and snorting, the piglets stopped, standing to attention, still roughly in a line.

'Partners,' called Bernard, and immediately Jesus trotted over to Mary, Hamlet to Duchess, Pudding to Princess and Pie to Lady. They spread out in facing pairs, snouts touching. Countess, the odd one out, scampered over to Bernard and sat down by his feet looking up at him. Bernard clicked his fingers and, immediately, she lunged her long tapered snout at the tape recorder button, switching it on. The first slow soothing notes of Ravel's Bolero eased out and the four pairs of piglets began slowly turning, snouts still touching, hind legs cross stepping sideways, leisurely at first, but pace gradually quickening to the pulsating majestic beat. I was entranced. Amazed.

A follow-up maths lesson burgeoned inside my head, as if I were still a teacher. *If the length of each piglet ('x' cms) is the radius of a circle what is the length of the circumference? Get out your compasses and describe the circle being invisibly drawn in the air by the piglets' tails. What is the diameter of the circle - think of the two piglet radii joined at the centre in a straight line.*

I wanted to jump up punching the air as I watched the magical performance. As the Bolero grew more tumultuous, the piglets side-stepped faster, little front legs beating time on the spot in the centre, bottoms zooming around with gathering speed. The glorious music thumped out with an intensity picked up by the pigs: faster and faster they circled round, then, as the music came to its crashing climax and abruptly stopped, the piglets flung themselves down on the grass in a dramatic ending better even than Torville and Dean.

The children clapped and cheered as if they would never stop and I felt delirious with pride. Here were my grandpiglets strutting their stuff - and they were *wonderful*. Bernard was going round to each of my resting babes giving each one a slice of apple and words of praise. When the children's excitement had died down, he turned to them, beaming, saying there was more. Then he clapped his hands and the piglets stood. I could feel I was grinning from ear to ear like a melon with a slice out of it.

Bernard suddenly called out 'Circle' and made motions with his hands like a tick-tack man, signs that were as clear as mud to me but obviously as clear as our spring water for the porkers for, eagerly, they took their positions forming one large circle. Bernard double clicked his fingers and Countess, who'd been left out of the previous thrilling performance, now trotted out into the middle, eyes bright.

Countess might be a nasty piece of piglet as regards stealing, I thought, but she was excellent at translating Bernard's clicks.

A ripple of giggles fanned through the children and, mystified, I followed their gaze to see Hermione and Kermit galloping full pelt through the gap towards us. They'd obviously realised they were missing something. As they neared, they slowed down to a trot, pulling up at the edge of the arena then, after a cursory look around, coming and sitting by me. I wondered if Hermione would be as proud as I was of her children.

Bernard took individually named piglet dishes out of the plastic bag. He placed each small metal dish beside its owner, then did a bit more finger clicking which galvanised Countess into dashing around the circle snatching each one up in turn and taking it to the middle making a pile of them. I was the only one watching, besides Bernard and the pigs, who knew she did this naturally, being the kleptomaniac swine that she was. Each time Countess stole another one, the children cheered louder and Kermit gustily joined in with bleats, though I noticed Hermione sat silent and po-faced, not joining in with the encouragement being given to the black sheep of her litter.

After more titbits were given out, and more congratulatory words spoken, Bernard announced the show was ending with a grand finale. Then, from out of his bag, he removed a skateboard, placing it carefully on the platform of the ramp. As he lifted Jesus onto it, the others, with much excited squealing, began spinning round and round. Jesus, bright eyed and twirly tailed, stood sure-trottered on the board, head turned to face the front.

'Ready,' said Bernard.

Jesus adjusted his trotters slightly.

'Steady,' said Bernard.

Jesus tensed.

'Go!' said Bernard, giving the back of the skateboard a gentle push.

Jesus zoomed down the long ramp, snout pulsating, ears and tail flying, legs slightly bent, perfectly balanced, taking off at the upward curve, briefly flying, landing to uproarious cheers.

I joined in the applause, waving to Bernard who waved back, radiant, emotional, long black lashes blinking over moist blue eyes. And I knew that no other two grandparents could feel more pride than we did then. The piglets' incredible performance had confirmed that, even though we were in want of more animals and amenities, we were ready to open the doors.

Ten

Enid Batty rang up out of the blue and asked if she could come round and see me.

Half an hour later she sat at the kitchen table nervously picking at her nails.

'I know about Nesbit,' she said. 'Wherever us've lived, it's been the same, him flirting with anything in skirts. No offence Freda. But I want you to know he's a good man really, help anyone out him, it's just booze that sets him off.'

She continued to stare down, picking at her nails, and I studied her. She was how I'd been eighteen months ago: colourless, insipid, lacking confidence. I wondered if I could help her.

'Cynthia and I have talked about your flirty husband ...' I began.

Her head jerked up.

'... and we thought we might try and teach him a lesson - make him think twice about his unwelcome crude remarks. Hopefully make him see how obnoxious he is when he's been drinking. We haven't come up with anything yet, but when we do, do you want to come in on it?'

Her face flashed into sudden beauty with a brief brilliant smile.

'Aye, Freda, if it makes him give up drink, count me in. I'd do anything to get my sweet Nesbit back - the one I married before he got hooked.'

After she'd left, I related it all to Bernard. It was the first time I'd divulged the nasty habits of our willing worker and he was incensed.

'Count me in too,' he said hotly.

I rang Cynthia and told her of our two new recruits. 'We must try to think up a plan quickly.'

'Right,' she replied, 'I'll come round on Saturday and won't leave until we've worked one out. Be prepared for imminent Nesbit Action!'

Vernon Veal made his monthly visit this Wednesday, this time to give them their first injections against Erysipelas, which is vet talk for measles. I hovered outside, too cowardly to be present when the needle struck, yet at the ready to dash in to comfort if needed. But I didn't hear one squeal and at last Vernon emerged, his large nostrils stretched sideways by the broad width of his smile.

'Not a whimper from any of the little loves,' he said, flapping one hand in limp wrist fashion. 'But in six months they'll need another jab.'

As we made our way over to the mobile home, Cussbert ran up to us, clucking and squawking, and Vernon, an enigmatic expression on his face, scooped the cockerel up into his arms, gently turning him this way and that, eventually replacing him on the ground and pronouncing him a very fine specimen with no trace of fowl fever.

Fowl fever for that loud mouth had never entered my head, extra voluminous voice box fever that necessitated a larynxectomy or throat cutting, had often!

I led through the swing door to where my bulky girl was stretched out on the straw, her little shadow Kermit snuggled up to her. And after a cursory look at my pig he turned his attention to the little goat, stroking her snub nose and fondling her burgeoning horns in a funny way for a vet, more like a doctor enjoying a cute little female patient too much. But, far from responding positively, the kid bleated loudly, apparently in fear, and when he lifted her fragile leg to examine the hoof the bleating cries became pitiful, abruptly stopping, as if paralysed with terror, when he extracted a swiss army knife and began paring the hoof down.

As I patted poor Kermit's quivering back whilst he saw to the other three hooves, I made up my mind to get rid of this suspect man and employ another vet.

'Won't charge you for doing that,' he said, straightening up.

Making me change my mind quickly. After all, he might be weird but he was good at his work.

'It's another job that has to be done quite regularly,' he stated. 'And don't worry, they all create at first but eventually they get used to it, even enjoy it.'

Did I imagine the devious veil sliming his eyeballs. Was there evil darkness inside his head that he was trying to hide?

'I'm afraid I'll have to charge for the piglet injections,' he said. 'But you may leave it for a month or two, or more.'

I thanked him then, trying to sound nonchalant, asked, 'What kind of experiments did you say you'd like to do if you were allowed to?'

He glanced at me sharply, then, as if deciding to trust me, said, 'Pick up their thought waves - register the minute electrical impulses using ECG.'

'And then what?'

'Connect the wave patterns to a computer in tandem with a voice simulator.'

'How?' I asked, 'How could that be that done?'

'Oh, it's so *great* to meet someone who's interested,' he said, baring pointed off-white canines that wouldn't have been out of place on a werewolf.

'Always interested in animal experiments,' I mumbled.

'I've written the software but it's not yet perfected,' he continued enthusiastically, 'but the computer already responds to the brain wave patterns.'

'How do you mean?' I asked, not liking the sound of this at all.

'Well, say someone hurt the animal in question, the resultant spiky pattern would activate the electronic voice simulator to say something like, *Ow, that hurts!* or whatever words I decide upon.'

'And how would you hurt the animal?' I asked, trying to sound calm although, inside, all my nerves were quivering on red alert.

'It doesn't matter how, that's not the point. Pain was just an example. You could try the opposite - give the creature pleasure and the resultant brain wave pattern would activate the simulated voice to say something like, *That's nice*, maybe in a soft voice.'

Despite my fearful apprehension I was becoming genuinely interested in the innovative idea.

'How else could you use it?'

His steel grey eyes bore into mine.

'All this is just between you and me you understand - you mustn't tell a soul - not until the whole invention has been patented and the software perfected.'

'You have my word,' I reluctantly agreed, crossing my fingers.

'Good. Okay, then. Another application would be to feed the animal different kinds of food - if it likes it the brain-wave will be different from if it doesn't like it. The voice will be programmed to say, *That tastes nice*, or *I don't like that*.' He threw his arms out, waggled his hands high. 'Don't you see Freda, animals would be virtually talking, and their vocabulary could gradually be enlarged. Imagine two pigs mating, for instance. Instead of their usual grunting climax, the voice could be programmed to cry out *The earth moved for me baby, how about you*? You know, more like humans,' he added, without any trace of embarrassment.

I looked sideways at him. Saw the rapture on his face. Now I was dead worried. What did he do to my pets when he borrowed them for the night? Was he some kind of pervert? How I wished the animals could really talk and let me know.

When Vernon had left, I studied the calendar and saw that Pudding had vanished the day after his March the thirtieth visit, and Kermit had gone missing the day after his April the twenty-ninth visit. Today was May the twenty-eighth. From the pattern that was emerging, I guessed an animal was due to be taken tomorrow. I rushed out and imparted this revelation to Bernard.

'That does sound too much of a coincidence,' he agreed.

We decided that tomorrow night, May the twenty-ninth, we'd keep watch in turns from a deck chair at the window of the end room of the mobile home. From there virtually the whole back garden was visible.

Every animal had been checked and shut in its rightful place, and I began the first watch at nine. By ten o'clock the moon had risen, switching its welcome spotlight onto the scene. I peered out wanting, and yet dreading, to see Vernon vet skulking around. Slowly, the static scene mesmerised me and I closed my eyes.

Bernard came to relieve me at midnight.

'I've seen nothing and no-one,' I truthfully said.

'Don't wonder at it,' he said, shaking rain off his head. 'It's pitch dark and pouring.'

After two hours lying awake in bed worrying that I wouldn't get up at two, I tottered downstairs and outside across the soaking wet grass, glad it had stopped raining and that the moon was back into shining mode though spasmodically dulled by dimmer switches of wispy cloud.

'The only skulking thing I've seen has been a fox, so it was a good job I had the foresight to build Cussbert's ark and run,' Bernard said, the pronouncement obviously making *him* ecstatic - but not yours truly.

At four o'clock when Bernard returned he shook me awake then instructed me to go inside and get some sleep!

At six o'clock he joined me in bed where I'd just lain awake for the whole past hour since the cussed cock had crowed.

'A total waste of time, the vet must have decided to take a month off to avoid suspicion,' Bernie said weakly, before immediately zonking out. Leaving Muggins to do the full animal maintenance procedure by myself, thankfully discovering in the process that every animal was present and unmolested.

I was still dead beat the next day when Cynthia came round for the *Devising a Punishment Plan for Nesbit Batty* meeting.

By the end of the session we had dreamt up a scheme that was so absolutely OTT that, if we dared to pull it off, Nesbit would give up alcohol and chatting up women for life - unless of course it turned out he enjoyed it.

'We can borrow some of the gear from my friend at the stables,' said Cynthia, as she stood to go.

'And probably I can get some from Poppy Bambridge, she rides too,' I said, 'and I'll buy a couple of metres of the narrow red ribbon.'

I opened the front door for her to leave.

'Now we have to wait for Nesbit to make the first repulsive move,' Cynthia said, eyes sparkling.

As I closed the door after her, a frisson of excitement trembled through me. Would we really dare to do it? When Bernard and Enid heard what it was, would they still want to be included?

Next morning, after all the animals had been fed, watered and mucked out I wandered over to the barn and stealthily peeped in to make sure Nesbit was working in there. Then I raced back to the cottage and rang Enid.

She listened to the plan in silence, then said, 'By heck Freda, that's going a bit far is that.'

'Yes, but do you want your husband to be punished for his constant unwelcome flirting? Especially if it makes him realise what we all think of him and it persuades him to give up the drink?'

There was a long pause, then. 'Aye, Freda, I'll go along with it if thee thinks it'll have the desired effect. But I must say I'm astounded - Cynthia an ex-mayoress and thee a respectable pig owner.'

And, when I put the phone down I too was astounded. Astounded that between us, we'd thought up such a plan. Were we covert perverts about to enjoy the sick joke we were waiting to play I wondered as I dashed out to tell Bernard.

Eleven

Considering it was the late May Bank Holiday Monday, it had been a glorious day. Late afternoon and, so far, no rain, snow or sleet as was normal in England on workers' holidays. But days off for me were as non-existent as penguins in a desert - and just as unnecessary, because I *loved* my work.

Eagerly, I opened the yard gate, fending off quivering kissy snouts as I eased myself through, savouring their grunts and squeals of greeting.

I glanced up the long grassy slope and saw Bernard emerging from the cottage. He waved down at me then banged on the trough, bellowing his strange pig grub-up call: a peculiar warbling yodel, half Tarzan half Muezzin. An innovative vocal achievement of which he was unduly proud.

I unbolted the gate and the mob dashed through, pushing and shoving, grunting and snorting, streaming across the grass like an upward flowing river of pink blancmange. A warm glow engulfed me as I watched them go. God, I did love them.

Jesus quickly took the lead, closely followed by Mary. Not far behind came Pie, Lady, Duchess, Countess, Princess and Pudding, all pelting along squealing in hungry excitement. I felt proud. This deliberate plan of making them run up the long slope twice a day to get to their feed kept them exercised and healthy.

Suddenly I realised I hadn't seen Hamlet, our prince among piglets. I peered up trying to count the squiggly tails as the piglets clamoured round the trough.

... five ... six ... seven ... eight little ones. My heart fluttered. There should be nine. But one couldn't go missing, they'd all been shut in their secure quarters all night.

Was this deja vu or was I asleep and in some ghastly recurring nightmare? Only, this time, it was Hamlet, not Pudding.

I squinted up into the sunshine, trying to isolate each plump little body in a recount as they dashed around each other vying for best positions. But it wasn't possible.

'I think Hamlet's missing,' I called up to Bernard. 'Can you see him there? Have I missed him?'

Anxiously I watched as he tried counting the swarming bodies.

'I think there's only eight,' he called back, 'and I think you're right - I can't see Hamlet.'

Inside my head I heard the robot voice of Vernon's voice simulator shouting: I BEG YOU, DO NOT CHOP OFF ANOTHER TROTTER, IT HURTS!

Hamlet, take heart, I silently comforted, *these ordeals are not usually scheduled to last long.*

When the eight piglets were back safely inside the unit, Bernard and I plodded around searching, poking in, around and under hedges and outbuildings, knowing that if Hamlet's mysterious evaporation into flimsy air turned out the same as the other two vanishing tricks, he'd reappear soon. But supposing he didn't?

After dinner, Bernard said he'd go out and stay on watch for a few hours, hoping to catch the mystery animal thief returning his plunder.

Sadly, I left him to it and went inside to ring mother, as I do every day.

'How's father?' I asked.

'He's looking at me right now,' she replied, 'just as handsome as ever but tired.'

Oh god! Father had to be in a bad way for my mother to say something complimentary about him. I knew he'd had chemo today.

'When he's finished this course of treatment, why don't you both come and stay with us for a while?' I suggested.

'Yes. Yes please,' she replied.

My spirits rose. It would do them good. They needed TLC and I needed to be the one to give it. And, besides that, I needed to have them close to me.

'You can help us find out who the mystery animal borrower is,' I said. 'Hamlet's been taken - hopefully soon to be returned.'

'Can't wait,' said mother with no hint of her usual mockery.

After we'd said our goodbyes I wandered into the sitting room and sank into an easy chair to watch TV. Very soon my eyes closed and, when next they opened, I saw it was gone midnight.

I tottered out into the garden and into the mobile home where I found Bernard slumped in a deck chair, head lolling backwards, mouth agape, throat vibrating with gentle snores.

'Come on, time to get to bed,' I said gently. 'We'll see in the morning if our sweet prince has been returned.'

'But not by whom,' he protested, rubbing his eyes, then following me indoors and up the stairs as if sleep walking.

Next morning when Cussbert's five a.m. crowing bombarded my ears, instead of muttering the usual oaths, I silently slipped out of bed, threw on my track suit and ran out into the dim garden and down to the new yard.

Hamlet, my dear prince among piglets be back in place, I beseeched as I hurried to his apartment. And *Yoricks* he was there! Snuggled up in a nest of straw, eyes shut as if he'd never been absent.

I dashed in, scooped him up in my arms, brushing my face against his warm soft skin, breathing in his sweet porky tang. But all my sleepy ungrateful grandhog did was let off a barrage of bad tempered snorts accompanied by such vigorous wriggling that I couldn't hold him and had to hurry him back down. I stared at his podgy body as he settled himself in the straw. It was in pristine condition, completely unscathed. But, what about his inner soul, I wondered, how had that suffered?

O! that this too too solid flesh could speak I thought, rather proud of the literary connection.

Twelve

'By heck Freda, you look champion this morning,' Nesbit called over from the open window of the barn.

I'd made the mistake of going to visit Daisy taking the short route past the barn, not realising he was in there. He threw down his hammer and hurried out to me, standing overly close, within whisky fume range.

'Thee's got such grand red curly hair, I say such grand red curly hair,' he said, having the temerity to tap it upwards with the palm of his hand as he spoke.

I stepped back away from him.

'Is it like that all over?' he whispered slyly, sneaking within breath smelling range again.

I went to back away again, then remembered the plan and stayed put.

'Wouldn't you like to know?' I said, flashing a smile that I hoped was seductive.

His drink drenched eyes sharpened. Then doubt crossed his face in drifts like a breeze in a cornfield.

'What's the matter?' I asked, jutting out my hip sexily, patting at my hair, 'Were you having me on. Didn't you really want to know?'

Nesbit's incredulous eyes held my gaze, then wavered.

'Aye,' he said shortly, 'I would like to know - any inquisitive hot blooded male would. 'Tis obvious.'

'Come round this evening when Bernard's out,' I whispered, 'at eight o'clock precisely.'

'Aye, I will that,' he confirmed, running trembling fingers through coal black grey-rooted hair.

I cast one more, hopefully, coquettish smile, then turned on my heels and hurried away to inform the others.

Up in my bedroom, Cynthia, Enid and I were in hysterics as we changed into the gear borrowed from Poppy Bambridge and Cynthia's horse riding friend. Cynthia sat on the edge of the bed hauling on a pair of tight jodhpurs. Enid and I were already clad in ours and were angling our feet into tall shiny boots.

'Wait till we see your husband's face,' Cynthia screeched to Enid. And we all fell about, although I noticed Enid's face straighten before ours did.

By five to eight we were all ready and in place. At eight o'clock the doorbell heralded his arrival.

'Hello Nesbit' I crooned as I opened the door to him.

'Hello babe ...' He stopped, worry clouding his eyes which were now severely at odds with the bright smile still frozen on his face.

I thwacked my horsewhip too zealously against my thigh, trying to disguise the pain as I drawled, 'Come in Nesbit, I've been looking forward to this.'

He gave an involuntary step backwards before blundering forwards across the threshold into the hall. There he halted and with trembling hand hoiked out his hip flask from his back pocket, taking a quick swig.

'Dutch courage?' I asked, trying to raise an eyebrow.

'Certainly not,' he squeaked, screwing the lid back on then, as if to prove it, lunging at me, full glutinous lips puckered for a kiss.

But I side stepped saying, 'Not yet, Nezzie, the time isn't right.'

Out came the hip flask again and I waited, watching his colour heighten as the fire water kicked in. He looked me up and down, an expression hard to fathom on his face.

'Thee looks sexy in them breeches, I say thee looks sexy in them breeches,' he said in a false treacly voice that made me want to vomit.

I beckoned him forward, turned, feeling his heavy hand slap on my bum as I led him into the sitting room. But I didn't react, just winked at Cynthia who stood in the centre, high booted legs astride, horse crop in hand. He had stopped dead.

'What's me cousin's wife, doing here?' he wailed. 'And dressed up in riding gear same as thee!'

'We thought you'd like some fun and games,' Cynthia answered, flicking her whip in the air in a vain attempt to make it crack. 'And don't worry, we'll not let cousin Sidney know.'

'But ... but ... why?' he stuttered, his face now puce.

'Because you're always asking for it, Nezzy,' I said softly. 'Admit it, go on, anything in skirts. You chat 'em up - you've been asking for it.'

Cynthia stepped towards him, flicking her whip ineffectually again. 'So, Freda and I, two of the skirted species who've been on the receiving end of your lewd chat up lines, are about to give you what you ask for.'

Nesbit took another swig, then smirked inanely.

'But it were only good clean fun weren't it, I say it were only good clean fun.'

'Let's have some more fun then Nezzy baby,' I crooned, 'good, clean or otherwise. Show us what you're made of - for starters get your shirt off.'

Excitement and fear dappled his face.

'Nay lass,' he said patting his smart turquoise shirt, 'ta very much but I'd rather keep it on.'

'But what you'd rather do doesn't come into it,' Cynthia informed him. 'And, while we're about it, hand over your flask.'

As his hands shot protectively to his back trouser pocket, Cynthia pounced, deftly undoing the top button of his shirt. Instantly his hands flew up to stop her. Immediately, I went for his back pocket, bringing his hands back down. Cynthia undid the second button and the performance was repeated until all the buttons were undone and the shirt was yanked off by the pair of us.

'Nice tits!' she remarked staring at his powerful chest as I flung the shirt down on the sofa.

Girlie-like, he shot his arms up across his nipples and, taking the chance, I snatched the flask from his pocket, chucking it down on the shirt.

'And what muscles,' I giggled, forcing myself to touch his bare shoulder.

Nesbit stood ramrod straight, arms folded across his chest, apparently unable to move. His eyes flickered nervously from one to the other.

'Now the trousers Nezzy baby,' I whispered in his hairy lug hole.

And instant mobility returned as his hands swooped down to his jeans.

'Surely you weren't teasing us all along with the suggestive things you said you'd like to do to us,' I goaded.

'Aye, but it weren't *my* trousers that were to come down,' he protested, knuckles whitening as he gripped the waist band.

Cynthia sidled up to him, pressed her homely body against his, then suddenly lifted her arms and grabbed both his ears, brutally twisting them. He bellowed, hands flying upwards passing hers flying down to tug at his fly zip. In splendid co-ordination, I tugged at the jeans from behind forcing them part way down.

'That hurt,' howled Nesbit.

'Let that be a lesson then,' she replied sweetly, 'if you don't co-operate and get 'em off, it could prove even more painful.'

I saw, as he saw, the steely look of someone who meant what they said in her taunting dun eyes.

Little groans now came from Nesbit. 'Nay, thee can't do this,' he protested, but as Cynthia menaced him, flicking her whip, he obediently pulled the jeans right down and dutifully stepped out of them.

I stared in disgust at his grubby green and white striped boxer shorts, trying to reorganise my face to show the same kind of lascivious desire he showed when he looked at my breasts.

'Now Nesbit Batty, get down on all fours,' I commanded.

'Nay, nay,' he protested, as if already taking on his required role as a horse.

'Very good,' congratulated Cynthia. 'Soon you will get your oats.'

'Am I in some fantasy nightmare?' he wailed looking round wildly.

'No, this is for real Nezzy, and, play your cards right, it could be a fantasy dream.'

And so saying, she whacked him one with her crop.

'Nay, nay,' he groaned, in full horse-speke again.

'Yes, yes,' she snapped, whacking him again.

And I had the feeling she was over enjoying it.

Awkwardly, he knelt, arms stiff, backside jutting. He twisted his head to look up at me - fearful excitement flickering in the drunken orbs.

Cynthia, on his blind side, shook with silent mirth, hands clapped over her mouth.

'Relax cousin-in-law,' she spluttered, 'enjoy what's to come.'

'And we can all live out our fantasies together Nezzy baby,' I purred.

Cynthia flicked her riding crop at his rump.

'You are our stallion, Nesbit Batty,' she said, emitting an uncontrolled snigger as she lifted her jodhpured leg. 'And I intend to ride you first.'

Clumsily she mounted, sitting astride his back, little legs dangling.

Nesbit sagged and Cynthia, clearly having a ball, whacked his rump again, rapping, 'Straighten up you idle nag!'

And, amazingly, he obeyed.

I pulled a length of scarlet ribbon from my pocket and slowly waggled it in front of his face.

'Wh ... what's that for?' he stuttered.

'I don't know,' I said especially loudly. 'Shall we thread it through his mouth and use it as reins, or would it work better around his penis! What do you think wifey?'

And, with those cue words, Enid marched in, striding straight to her husband who, discharging pathetic little groans, attempted to stand but couldn't because Cynthia was astride his back and Enid and I held him down.

His horror-struck eyes rolled round to his wife.

'Why are thee here? Why are thee dressed up like one of them?'

'Because I *am* one of them,' she said softly, 'I'm a lass, though thee seem to have forgotten it. And I'm here to help teach thee a lesson.'

He struggled to get to his feet again but was no match for we three.

'What lesson?' he asked, almost crying.

'A lesson to teach thee not to get drunk and be disgusting to decent lasses.' She turned to me and, keeping beautifully to our rehearsed script, continued, 'As legal mare of this randy stallion, I should be the one to ride him.'

Quickly Cynthia dismounted and Enid took her place.

'Give up drink Nesbit sweetheart,' she pleaded leaning forward, 'return to the nice lad thee were when us was young - when the only female thee paid any attention to were me.'

Nesbit didn't move or speak, just stared ahead like a resentful donkey carrying too heavy a load.

Enid ruffled his hair, a look of intense sadness in her eyes.

'Thee's a silly fool, thee,' she said. 'I love thee when ...'

She didn't finish, for he forced himself up, clasping her legs to him, so she was piggy-back riding. He didn't speak. Just stood there, holding her.

'Thee's not said owt,' she whispered.

'Aye lass. Aye, I'll try and stop,' he muttered, letting her down gently.

'Jolly good,' called the voice of Bernard and all eyes turned to the partly opened window at the front end where Bernard stood looking in.

'Brilliant,' he pronounced. 'I got it all on video.' He waggled the video camera at us to confirm it.

'After all the building work I've done for thee,' Nesbit howled, grabbing up his trousers, jabbing one foot in after the other.

'We're most grateful for that,' Bernard replied, 'and if we ever make money we'll pay you for your labour, but, in the meantime, you take this home with you ...' He held out the tape. '... and whenever you feel inclined to chat up someone else's wife put it on and watch it to see what a complete berk you look when you're drunk - and to see how much your Enid loves you.'

Nesbit, hauling at his zip, strode over and snatched it from him, then returned to the sofa to grab up his shirt.

Enid, bright eyed with hope, looking amazingly fetching in the jodhpurs and soft green top, took his arm.

'Come on home thee silly bugger,' she said, 'I've never seen thee sober up so quick afore!'

And as we waved them off I wondered if Nesbit had really learnt his lesson - and, if so, for how long.

Thirteen

I still don't know what awoke me. It may have been the faint smell of smoke in the bedroom or it may have been a bad dream. But, still in the drowsy trance of sleep, I forced myself from our snug bed to look through the window. And, as if suddenly doused in icy water, I was shocked into instant awakening.

Tendrils of flame licked the night sky and flurries of orange tinted smoke belched up from the direction of the stables. I screamed the terrible news to Bernard, still peacefully asleep and, without waiting for a reply, ran for it.

Bare-footed, I lifted my long nightdress and hared across the bumpy grass towards the gap in the hedge, then rounded into the field seeing with horror the blazing building where Daisy was incarcerated - and, for all I knew, already incinerated.

The scorching heat hit me as I sped nearer and I stopped, gasping for breath, seeing the far end was already a roaring inferno and hungry infant flames were licking the raggety lower edge of Daisy's bolted door. Thick smoke poured out through the open top one and I knew I had to get in there, and quick.

Suddenly, a stuttering terrified braying set up and, galvanised, I moved forward. Nearer. Nearer. Towards the infernal heat. Coughing. Choking. Eyes smarting, streaming, straining to peer through the turbid smoke. But it was too much and I backed away, defeated, screaming out as a stinging pain darted into the top of my head. Wildly, I flicked at my hair, dislodging a glowing cinder. I stumbled away and another red hot needle pricked into the top of my foot, making me kick out madly, displacing a fiery ember onto the smouldering grass.

A sudden hideous splintering roar made me scream out again and run back further as the far end of the roof and burning rafters smashed down, shooting glowing cinders up into the velvet blackness of the sky. In awe, I watched them mix in a kaleidoscope of patterns with twinkling pinprick stars. Sudden dragon flames reared up, roaring fiercely in their hungry search for new wood. I cried out, then shook with fear, seeing a buckled corrugated iron sheet balancing upright, its corner stabbed deeply into the ground. I ran back further, fearing the next one could be stabbed deeply into me.

Hysterical braying rasped out again, choking, throaty, terrible to hear, and, knowing it would be too late soon, I forced myself forward once more. But again the unbearable heat and choking smoke beat me back.

Abruptly, Daisy's grating cries ceased. Had the sweet donkey died? I strained my ears to hear her through the crackle and roar of the fire. I stepped forward, stopped in agony, fingered my scorching face to check if its flesh was really melting. A sharp heart-rending whinnying scream suddenly cut through the din. She was still alive, but I had to do something soon.

My eyes scoured the appalling scene, and then I saw it. Through a fleeting gap in the smoke and flames, in the centre of the blazing front wall, the jutting cold water tap. If I could reach it, drench myself, I might stand a chance. Another beam crashed down at the far end, flinging up more hissing sparks and roaring flames. I wavered, but another terrible braying scream forced me forward into the abyss.

Coughing, choking, placing each bare foot carefully between patches of burning grass, I picked my way towards the silver glimmer of the tap. Forward. Forward. But the heat and smoke were intolerable and I stopped, closing my streaming eyes. But Daisy was dying. I re-opened them and the fearful rush of heat that smashed into my eyeballs forced me to shut them again. Blindly, I stumbled forward, then halted, thoughts a-jumble. Bernard, Hermione, the piglets and the rest, they all needed me and I was recklessly putting my life at risk for Esmerelda's donkey who could already be dead.

But Daisy's choking scream bit through the infernal air again and impelled by the pitiful sound I stepped forward, arms stretched, hands blindly feeling into searing hot space. Slowly, agonisingly, one foot after the other, I proceeded. It was too hot. Blistering hot. Too hot to bear. Like walking into the sun. Then suddenly my waving hands felt hot metal. Gasping, crying, I gripped and turned, hearing the water gush out, dipping my head under, unsure if my scalp really did sizzle as the water hit and the terrible heat was sucked out, or if I imagined it.

I opened my eyes, crouched lower, drenching the whole of my body, pulling my arms out of my long sleeves, wriggling the sodden nightdress up over my head, till at last I was blindly cocooned in cool wetness.

Still crouching to protect my ankles and lower legs exposed by the raising of the nightdress, I stumbled back towards Daisy's stall, flames eerily lighting up the inside of my thin wet cotton sheath with strobing flashes. At last I dared part the garment's front opening to look through. I was nearly there! But I'd had it. The heat was too much to go on.

Gasping for breath in the choking smoke, half blinded with tears, I stared at Daisy's locked coffin through the slit. It was so near. Over the smell of burning wood, I imagined the reek of fresh meat cooking.

Spurred on by the horror of Daisy being cremated alive, I inched forward, crying out in agony at every burning step until at last I reached the smouldering door. Clasping the hot metal bolt with my "oven glove" nightie, I wrenched it sideways. Immediately the door fell open and flames that flickered at the inside of the blackened door abruptly flared up, fuelled by air from outside.

Terrified of the flames and smoke, terrified of what I should find, I fought my way into the burning hell. And at last I saw her, cowering in the corner, eyes rolling, ears flat, mane shrivelled, patches of red skin visible through smouldering fur. But still alive.

I was within touching distance of her but I couldn't move. The water that had soaked me had now abandoned me and I was dying. A sudden explosive crash from the end propelled an inferno wave of heat that sent me reeling. Muddled now, I had the stupid notion it was the heat of the donkey's breath that had engulfed me. Poor thing. I shuffled forward until, at last, I could reach out and grab hold of a solid tuft in her shrivelled mane. I pulled. Pulled. Pulled, knowing if she would move my feet too would move. Move off the smouldering straw. Move off the agony. Must save her. Must save her feet. Must save my feet. Must. Must. I tugged and at last she let herself be led, through the flames, through smoke, through the heat, through the nightmare to the safety outside the door.

We stumbled out and I became vaguely aware of Bernard, vaguely aware of flashing lights, sirens, firemen. Vaguely aware of the distinctive smell of singed hair that I thought must be Daisy's, never for a minute suspecting it was mine.

Fourteen

Three days since the fire and this morning I'd seen myself in a mirror for the first time, and it was horrible. Little piggy eyes set in swollen livid flesh had stared back at me, but it was my hair that horrified me. Or lack of it.

Now Bernard sat on the edge of the hospital bed.

'They say you're lucky, all your burns are first or second degree so they should gradually fade,' he said.

'Gut my hair,' I cried through shrivelled lips, jabbing my finger at the frizzled mess that 'til four days ago had been my newly trimmed, newly permed, newly touched up titian crowning glory.

'Never mind your hair, what matters is you're safe,' he said, clasping my hand and immediately casting it away as I shrieked out.

'That's the gluddy grubble with ge-ing in a glazing inferno, you gluddy hurt,' I moaned, lips as taut as a ventriloquist's.

Just let him ask me to say gottle of geer just for the laugh, I thought. It'd be like him.

But he didn't chance his luck, instead he made sympathetic clucking noises like the rooster revving up to a full head of scream. When enough sympathy had evidently been demonstrated he ceased the irritating noise, saying:

'It was lucky the firemen could get their appliance into the field - if Nesbit hadn't already made the entry and exit holes in the hedge they'd have been stuck in Nuthatch Lane, and then the whole stable building would now be just a pile of charred rubble.'

I managed an 'mmmm,' even though at that very moment I couldn't give a toss. The fucking firemen hadn't got there in time to save Daisy had they. I'd done that on my tod.

'But it was a pity we'd already put up the dividing fence because they had to chop their way through it.'

'Mmmm.'

'Cost us a bomb and now three of the close-boarded panels are smashed up beyond repair.'

Couldn't he see that the only damage beyond repair that I was concerned about was the damage to my hair.

'Don't gother to stay,' I said, closing my eyes, weary of all his conversation.

But he ignored me.

'The police have been poking around and, strangely, Esmerelda tried to stop them, but of course she couldn't.'

I opened them.

'Did they disgugger how it gegan?' I asked, craftily lured into communication again.

'They didn't say exactly, just asked me if I could throw any light on why there was a circle of wax blobs on the floor of the end room where the fire evidently started and the damage was worst. I made a quip about throwing light on arson, to amuse them, but they had no sense of humour.'

I thought of a sardonic response, but couldn't be bothered to voice it.

An image of opening the cupboard and seeing packets of new candles crept into my mind. Could their burnt remains have been the wax blobs set out in a circle? Could Esmerelda have been responsible for the fire? And thus my hair! I ran my one unburnt finger through what such a pitifully short time ago had been a shock of thick shoulder length curly red hair and was now a haphazard moquette of long and short strands from which little dried up dark ginger bits showered down upon the starched white sheet on the bed. A tear dropped down on the frizzle, looking how I'd imagine a tiny portion of birds' nest soup to look.

Bernard smiled sympathetically and clucked again.

'You're bound to be upset,' he said. 'It's the shock.'

'It *was* a shock,' I cried, poignantly witty. 'A shock of hair.'

And I wished I hadn't bothered with the rashly exclaimed outburst because my tight parched lips now stung even more having just been ripped into shreds.

He went to pat my hand again then obviously thought better of it.

'They're discharging you when the blisters have healed, providing they don't get infected' he said. 'And then, when you feel up to it, I'll drive you to Raymond's and he can cut your hair into shape.'

'Gut short hair will make my face stand out,' I wailed, feeling, and sounding, pitiful.

'Your lovely lovely chubby face,' Bernard whispered, touching my cheek on a burnt bit, making me yelp.

And why did he have to say chubby. I *knew* I'd put on some weight.

He clucked again and the aggravation of that cussed sound made me throw the small amount of caution I had to the farting wind.

'You cluck just like gluddy Cussbert,' I snarled, lips splitting completely asunder. 'Gluddy clucking Cussbert. And it's getting right up my gluddy nose.'

Bernard's whole body recoiled from me as if he were physically wounded.

'My cock doesn't cluck,' he bawled indignantly. 'It crows.'

'Really now,' said a smirking nurse as she placed a jug of fresh water on my side table. 'That's a novelty.'

There was silence while Bernard coloured and while my brain tried to decide whether the physical pain of laughing was worth it. I compromised with a snigger that did me good. And then uneasy silence flopped down between us.

Eventually, I thought I'd better make an effort, because he had driven the twenty miles to Great Piddlehurst General to kindly visit.

'How are the giglets?'

'Fine.'

'Just fine?'

'Well I don't want to worry you now - not, you know, while you're in here recovering, because you're uptight and jangled enough, but I don't think our Animal Park is viable.'

'Not viagle?' I shrieked.

'I mean we've too many animals to feed and look after with no income whatsoever. And we haven't enough of them to charge people to look - it isn't truly an Animal Park, or Zoo, or Pet Farm. It's just our collection of family pets.'

'Gut what agout the giglet disglay?'

'The piglets are brilliant but they'll only perform once a day and paying customers will expect to see more than a half hour show, a kid, a donkey and a rooster.'

'Gut they'll end up as gacon,' I sobbed.

'And sausages,' Bernard said brightly. 'Don't forget sausages. And the Duchess could finish up as York Ham.' He beamed at me as he always did when he'd made a funny. 'Get it?' he laboured. 'Duchess of York.'

But his bad taste stab at a quip didn't vaguely amuse me.

'What agout Germit.'

'What about her?'

'Why not go the whole gluddy hog and joke agout kid gloves.'

'Nice one Freda,' he said. 'Didn't think of it!'

I tried to smile because he was getting up ready to leave, but it hurt and, besides, I didn't feel like it.

I watched him attempting to decide which bit of me to kiss as he said goodbye. Eventually he didn't chance the flesh and air kissed above my hair. My fucking frizzled hair. Somehow, nearly being devoured by fire, which I've just realised is also a foul four letter F word, has made me very angry. And I don't understand why, except that I was stuck in this hospital ward missing my pigs, missing talking to mother, and missing my busy lovely wonderful fulfilling life. And, on top of all that, was forced to eat National Health Service food or starve.

As Bernard disappeared, I gazed with longing at the grapes he'd brought, but knew they would make my lips sting. Why couldn't he have realised that I thought angrily, wishing he'd thought to bring marshmallows. Cut up in slivers of course.

But, look on the bright side, I mused. If my blisters didn't erupt, and my burns didn't re-offend, and I stayed on my best behaviour, I'd be up before the parole doctors who'd consider my conditional discharge before very long.

For the hundredth time I wondered if saving the donkey was worth all of this misery. And then for the first time I wondered if her hair was in better nick than mine. I pictured the scorched fur and mane all grown back to luxuriant growth and wicked envy and anger gnawed into my soul. Bloody donkey. If I'd left her to incinerate, Esmerelda would have enjoyed eating her and my hair would have remained perfect.

After the lights had been dimmed, I lay back on my pillow deep in thought. Bernard was right. No way would I pay good money to see one sow, nine piglets soon to be grown-up swine, one kid, one donkey and a rooster, even though the piglets were entertaining.

A depressing cloud of gloom settled on me, almost as dark as the black clouds of smoke that had so recently nearly killed me and mucked up my looks. It had been a stupid idea, trying to set up an Animal Park. I knew it. I'd thought so before. We should have got shot of all our grandpiglets at the outset and then I could have continued with my portrait painting career. But, as I drifted into sleep, I knew that our lovely animal family was worth more than any oil painting, even a Monet, but especially mine.

Three more days of agony, NH food and Bernie's well-meaning chat. He cannot understand why I don't want any other visitors, not even Cynthia, that I don't want anyone to see me with my patchy skin and shrivelled hair. And I don't want to talk. I'm glad he comes. I do love him. But I'm glad when he goes, then I can wallow in self-pity and openly mope with only the nurses and doctors to see me, and the poor old soul in the next bed who doesn't count because even if I openly pulled the rest of my hair out in frustrated rage, then painted my head purple with yellow dots, she wouldn't notice because she's not with it. Not that I would.

Exactly one week since my incarceration and a woman pushing a trolley loaded with books trundled past the end of my bed, then stopped.

'You look fed up,' she said.

A nurse bore down on us, smiling.

'She won't be fed up any more. I've just heard she can go home tomorrow.'

But the joy that should have welled up didn't.

'Try reading this, it'll make you laugh,' said the woman as the disappointed nurse left us. And she handed me a cheerful vibrant pink book entitled *The Pig and I*.

When Bernie came to visit later I was forced by politeness to put the book down.

'You look preoccupied,' he complained.

'Hadn't you getter get gack to the giglets?' I said, lips now healing, but scabby and sore.

'Nesbit and Esmerelda are seeing to them so I can stay,' he said, happily sitting at my bedside for another hour.

The next day when Bernard came to take me home I was grinning as widely as my scabbed lips would allow, which in truth was negligible so he probably wouldn't have known.

'That gook has left me with a feeling of well-geeing - I am gositive everything will ge okay,' I said, taking the clothes he'd brought in for me from him.

'You haven't seen how much the piglets are hogging down these days,' he cautioned, just about to take hold of my arm, but warned by my pre-emptive squeak not to.

A nurse helped me don my baggiest dress and soft slippers, then I hobbled out of the flaking white room, down the disinfectant-scented corridor, through the automatic doors and into wonderful glorious freedom outside in the car park.

As I eased myself into the car, I knew with certainty that somehow we would carry on and make our Animal Park a success.

'Wait till you see what the piglets get through,' said Bernard gloomily as we headed back home. 'We'll never be able to afford to keep them.'

Fifteen

Bernard drove me into Great Piddlehurst and dropped me off at Raymond's Salon for my appointment.

'Good god,' Raymond shrieked as I hobbled in, 'what've you done with my year's work?'

It was true, every six weeks for a year now, he'd skilfully cut, re-tinted and permed when necessary, transforming the lank faded hair it had sadly become into a work of art. Like an artist whose work has been vandalised, he fingered my fire-nibbled tresses emitting little moans of distress. But soon, the creativity in him responded and he was explaining how he would condition and re-shape it.

Two hours later I looked in the mirror and my spirits lifted. Spirals of short hair framed my blotchy face in a becoming halo, somehow detracting from the chubby chin and patchy red burns. It didn't look too bad.

But back home glumness took hold, despite Bernard's oft repeated words about how nice I looked. I *knew* I looked bloody nice. I could see that in the mirror. It didn't need him rabbiting on about it. Even as I thought these grumpy thoughts guilt sludged over me. But still they continued invading.

'Oh shut *up*,' I snarled nastily.

And, sadly, no more compliments came, and he went.

'So you didn't really like my hair,' I snarled even nastier when he returned.

Two days later as, with stiff swollen fingers, I tried to clasp the handle of a cup of tea, the phone rang.

'This is Mrs Menabilly from the Land's End Animal Pet Farm here,' a woman with a Cornish accent announced. 'Only we don't want the animal pets any longer, we've had enough of 'em, so I'm ringing to see if you want 'em for your Animal Park.'

'How did you hear of us?' I asked, puzzled.

'My old friend Alfred runs the PDQ Pig Farm where you had your sow mated and where you buys your feed - he told me. And he said you didn't have much more'n a few pigs an' odds bits an' pieces - so you might want to have 'em.'

Having established that the *'em* was a mixed bag of various creatures "to be had in a whole lot not piecemeal mind," I asked her what the mixed bag consisted of.

'Oh, you know me dear,' she said vaguely, 'there's a couple of goats, water fowl, poultry, chipmunks, a lamb, that be about it - maybe a couple more.'

'No wild creatures?' I ventured.

'No, no,' she confirmed. 'Nothing like wild creatures here, except me husband but he's staying.' Her hearty laugh vibrated my eardrum with the rattle of her bronchial tubes. Between wheezy snorts, she added, 'Not one crocodile nor lion nor tiger if that's what you mean.'

I told her I'd have to discuss it with Bernard.

'You've got till tomorrow then me dear,' she said. 'Only we're not getting any younger and we've had it up to here with 'em. You're our last port of call - phone call that is.' Another wheezy laugh oozed forth then quickly died. 'Say yes and we'll get 'em to you somehow, free of charge. Say no and the whole lot of 'em goes to the slaughter house. It's up to you.'

I took her number and, thoughtfully, replaced the phone.

I'd just risked my life and forfeited most of my hair and half of my epidermis saving the donkey, now the lives of a whole menagerie were suddenly dependent on me. It didn't seem fair. But slowly it dawned on me that this phone call out of the Cornish blue was meant. It was our salvation. Customers would come pouring in to see a mixed bag of creatures and then we could keep our precious own.

Bernard and I talked about it all evening even though we both knew the answer right from the start.

'If we don't take 'em in,' I said, 'we'll be in the same canoe as Mrs Menabilly.'

'What canoe?'

'The canoe up the creek without a paddle taking our animals to be slaughtered,' I said, amazed at his dimness.

'Not necessarily slaughtered,' he said, pedantically. 'They could be given away to some other mugs who will feed 'em.'

'Not mugs, other animal lovers like us.'

'That's right, mugs. Ring her tomorrow and tell her we'll take 'em.'

'I knew you'd take 'em me dear, Alfred from PDQ said you had a kind heart.'

Then I heard her muffled voice pass the news on and I wasn't sure if she said Freda Field was giving them succour or Freda Field *was* a sucker. Whatever it was, the die was tossed, the Land's End animals' lives were to be saved and Bernie and I were to be even more up to our eyes in animal feed and the resultant brown stuff.

The next evening a convoy of two vans, a shooting brake and a Range Rover pulling a horse box arrived outside and Bernie and I rushed out to meet our new family. A jolly-looking plump woman tumbled out of the shooting brake, releasing a waft of surprisingly sophisticated perfume.

'Mrs Menabilly,' she announced. 'And you must be Freda and Bernard Field.'

Her twinkling blue eyes scanned Bernard's face then settled on mine. 'Burns aren't they? You been somewhere hot me dear?'

'You could say that,' I replied, raising my bandaged hands as further proof.

Meanwhile a tall thin white-haired man clambered out of the Range Rover and a young man and women alighted from the two vans.

'Me husband and two kids,' Mrs Menabilly introduced. 'Come to help us get shot of 'em.'

Then with seemingly undue haste the Menabilly clan rushed back to their vehicles and began unloading, while Bernie and I stood nervously aside.

'Now we'll see what we've taken on,' Bernard muttered.

'My god!' I squealed, as Mr Menabilly appeared at the back of the horsebox dragging a haughty-looking llama down a ramp.

'Where are 'em going dearie?' Mrs Menabilly called as she lifted a small lamb from the back of her shooting brake.

'In the back garden,' Bernard said and I wanted him to say: No, they're going nowhere. We won't be able to cope. Take 'em back from where you've come from. But instead he added, 'Take 'em round the side of the cottage, mind the strong spring on the gate.'

On wobbly legs I followed them as they took two of our new family round.

'You can't leave that llama with us, it's too big,' I cried to Mr Menabilly.

'I can. You took the job lot,' he said hotly, leading the lofty creature to the centre of the lawn. 'He's a lovely bloke but just watch out, he spits sometimes, though not often,' he hastened.

He cast me a smile which I knew was intended to be reassuring but which just look smugly victorious to me, then hurried away for some more.

Quailing inside but trying to look nonchalant, I sauntered over to the "lovely bloke" till I was within touching distance or, in his case, spitting distance. His supercilious eyes stared at me through long lashes. His nostrils quivered and his mouth began a surreptitious sideways gyration which I suspected was his way of working up spittle.

As I stepped back I heard the snort of a pig behind me. But ours were all shut away in the pig unit for the duration of the new animal stock delivery, *including* Hermione, despite her protests. I glanced over to the pig unit, seeing Kermit waiting patiently outside, proof that Hermione was still ensconced in there.

I turned to see the Menabilly daughter shunting a horrible looking black swine into the garden, its belly so low slung it brushed the grass. Its face so concertina'd with deep ridges and rounded furrows you'd think if its skin could be pulled out flat there'd be enough to make two more pigs' faces at least.

'This am Pot Belly Bella our Vietnamese Pot Belly,' she called down. 'And she's the loveliest of the bunch.'

That ugly crinkled creature was the loveliest of 'em! Suddenly I felt sick.

Then the Menabilly son, clasping a cumbersome three-tier cage to his chest tottered into view. His head peered round the side of it and, seeing he had reached the garden, he dumped it down, straightened up and rubbed his back.

'Them are the chipmunks,' he called. 'There was ten at the start, but there could be more now.'

'Wh... what do you mean?' I stupidly stuttered, going over to the complex cage and staring through the mesh at some strange little stripy rats with squirrel tails.

'Don't 'ee know nothing in Hampshire,' he said, guffawing loudly. 'One of 'em is up the duff.'

As the full enormity of what we were taking on hit me, I stood rooted to the grass watching the Menabillys off-loading and Bernard rushing hither and thither in an apparent frenzy of fear and excitement as birds and animals took possession of our land.

A sudden sighing gust of warm air on the nape of my neck made me squeal and spin round. The llama stood close to me and it was all I could do not to take off and run. Seconds passed as we stood staring at each other, then, slowly and very gently, he lowered his head onto my shoulder and held it there. I froze. Was he about to sink his big choppers into my flesh? Trembling, I raised my hand and forced myself to pat the long ridge of his nose. With a deep contented sigh of halitosis, he stayed there, nuzzling my neck.

'Ah look at 'im, he's taken to you already me dear,' Mrs Menabilly called over, on her way up from releasing feathered fowl down by the duck pond. Then she yelled down to her husband, 'Lardarse has taken to her, it's okay!'

'Go on me dear,' she encouraged. 'Give Lardarse some grass, that's what he's after. He likes to be fed - takes it as a sign of caring.'

Feeling stupid, with all the grass around that the llama could nibble himself, I bent down to pick some. And suddenly the llama's nose was at the seat of my pants giving a sharp shove and I was sprawled out on the lawn with the Menabillys laughing their silly heads off.

'He always does that,' Mrs Menabilly, howled. 'Our Lardarse never misses a chance with a bender.'

I picked myself up, red faced, seething, relieved that before they'd come I'd bandaged my fast-healing hands, though I'd thought it was to protect them from alien animal germs, not practical jokers. I glared at the stupid Menabillys, and then at the llama.

'That hurt my burnt hands,' I complained.

'Oh sorry me dear,' she said flippantly. Then, the matter obviously over: 'In case your Hampshire grass tastes different and puts Lardarse off staying, we've brung a sackful of cuttings from Cornwall. Give it to him after we've gone me dear, make him feel at home.'

But I didn't want that disrespectful arrogant llama to feel at home.

'We will not need it,' I said stiffly. 'Take your sackful of cuttings from Cornwall back with you.' *And stick it up your jacksy* I wanted to add, but didn't.

Mr Menabilly, rubbing his hands and grinning as broadly as if he'd just won the national lottery, came over.

'I've piled all their specially made signs just inside your garage,' he said. 'All professionally done by a signwriter - gives each animal's name and make, and says something interesting about 'em. Save you a bit of time, money and, by the looks and sounds of you, confusion.'

Bernard appeared, saving me the effort of a civil reply.

'Jolly good,' he said, without enthusiasm, nervously eyeing the llama still lingering by my side.

Mrs Menabilly, closely followed by two large goats, sailed into the garden, podgy right arm waving.

'These am the last me dear,' she called, heading towards me. 'Goofy and Goolie's their names.' She and the goats reached us, causing Lardarse to back away. 'Very affectionate creatures - gotta bond with me,' she explained.

Then suddenly the whole Menabilly family seemed to rush at us, crowding around.

The openly jubilant son said, 'Everything's unloaded and we're off.'

'They're all in good condition me dears,' Mrs Menabilly announced, energetically shaking Bernard's hand then, mercifully, miming the vigorous action above my bandages.

Out of the corner of my eye, I saw the goats' heads violently nodding up and down in time with her, as if attached by short tethers to her wrists.

'Goodbye and good luck,' said her husband, gleefully rubbing his hands together again.

'Won't you have a cup of tea before you go?' I unwillingly asked. But I needn't have worried.

'No, no, we won't stop. Me and the family's going straight back home to celebrate,' he replied.

'Champagne not tea' said the daughter, giggling.

'With brandy in it,' added the son jiggling his fists in the air as if his team had just scored.

Which, in a manner of speaking, I suppose it had done.

We followed them to the gate at the sideway where Mrs Menabilly tussled with the goats who, once forced away from her presence, bounded away to the bottom of the garden bleating pitifully. They really seemed to love her.

Out in the lane, we watched them get into their animal-free vehicles, heard the engines rev up, waved to their laughing phyzogs and then they were gone.

'What have we done!' we groaned in unison, turning back to our zoo.

Sixteen

Four days since we took possession of the animals and all but the goats seem to have settled down well.

Big Belly Bella has been given the vacant superior apartment in the pig unit, seeing as Hermione has eschewed it for her old room. When the Vietnamese intruder had first shown her peculiar face and sagging body to the piglets they'd snuffled around her and I could tell by their mystified looks that they were perturbed by her blackness and squidged up face. But, once the snorting inspection was over, they readily included her in their fun and games and Big Belly Bella, also no doubt at first thrown by their smooth pinkness, joined in with gusto, rolling in the straw with the mob and dashing around as best she could, the overt happiness of her joyous squeals at odds with the frowning furrows on her face. If only humans were that accommodating, I mused, touched by the fuss-free bonding of pink and black, smooth and wrinkled. The fact that Countess stole a frisbee we'd assigned to Big Belly Bella didn't count as an act of hostile racism because she'd still nick anything from anybody, white, black, pink or navy blue. She wasn't a likeable pig.

Lairy the Lamb was adorable and no trouble, just cropped grass from dawn till dusk, only stopping to run over to bleat a cheery greeting and rub against my legs whenever I went out. Already I loved him.

And Lardarse the llama was just as amenable as the sweet little lamb, merely chewing cud and cogitating all day long and, so far, keeping his sputum to himself, a lesson to be learnt by some of today's uncouth footballers in my opinion.

The ducks and geese quack and honk in apparent bliss on the pond. But, as they have one clipped wing apiece, they couldn't fly off even if they wanted to. And it's impossible to tell from their inscrutable eyes and expressionless beaks whether they're missing their Cornish home or not.

I throw the chickens handfuls of corn each morning and they scratch about all day in seeming contentment. There are only a couple of normal sized, typical looking ones, and they've both laid eggs which we've already eaten. I wonder Cussbert hasn't had his beady eye on these two good-looking birds, but he keeps himself aloof. The others are a mixed bag of black, brown, white, speckled and plain ones. Some with fluffy top-knots, others with peculiar hats or fancy trousers. The one thing that all the poultry have in common is that they huddle together asleep every night under the mobile home.

Goofy and Goolie are the only problem. Goolie, well named by the Menabillys, by the size of them, perversely acts as if he has none, his beard quivering with worry when any living thing approaches - even Kermit, the loveable little creature of his own species. And Goofy, the nanny with protruding front teeth, rather like Cynthia's, always follows his cowardly flights, both fleeing across the grass in a series of soaring leaps as if they half expected to take off and fly away like jumbo jets. Or, in their case, goat gliders.

Their cowardice was extraordinary really because they were the only two animals armed with bayonets on top of their heads, although Kermit's little buds were quickly growing. The only good thing about them was they didn't cost anything to keep, just nibbled away at the poor quality grass Lardarse and Lairy didn't want, and tugged loose twigs and branches off hedges and trees.

'The trouble is they'll gradually demolish the boundaries,' Bernard observed as we walked across the garden together, 'so we'll just have to tether them to stakes away from bushes or trees.'

'But how do we catch them? We can't get anywhere near. And, always supposing we could, we couldn't keep them tethered outside all winter, they'd freeze to death.'

Bernard stopped walking and thoughtfully stroked his chin. I stood beside him impatiently waiting for his inspiration to arrive.

'Esmerelda's bound to have the stables covered on her insurance,' he eventually said. 'So, when it's rebuilt, we can put them in the stall next to Daisy - we've just got to find a way of catching them. Are you any good with a lasso?'

I let his quaint idea that Esmerelda had insured the stables go.

'If I found I was good at lassoing, I'd make the most of it and string them up from a tree,' I said, setting off briskly again.

'But why!'

'Isn't it obvious: to throttle them. Get rid of them.'

Bernard halted, looking shocked.

'Well I don't suppose I could really do it myself,' I admitted, 'but I could get Esmerelda to. She's good at snuffing out animals. She'd probably invite us round to eat them - and I might give it a go. They're too unfriendly and unlovable for my liking, not like the rest of the Menabilly flock.'

Above the general background of squeals, snorts, quacks, bleats and twitters, came the sound of a wood tearing and we looked back in time to see Goolie dragging a stout branch from the laurel flanking the gap.

'That does it,' I exploded. 'I wouldn't really ask Esmerelda to do them in, but I am going to ring the Menabillys and make them take them back. Those horrible goats loved Mrs Menabilly, they had a special bond with her. I bet she's missing them.'

'Wasting your time,' Bernard said, puffing to keep up with me as, spurred on by the great idea, I started jogging.

'They made it clear we took them all in one job lot,' Bernard panted, peeling off to the pig unit, leaving me to deal with the phone call alone.

Indoors, I sat at the hall table and nervously tapped out their number.

'The Menabilly Pet Zoo has closed down, but if you would like to leave a message please speak after the tone.'

'Hello,' I said tentatively. 'This is Freda Field.'

'Oh, hello me dear,' her soft voice cut in, then hardening, 'We'll not take any of 'em back.'

'No, no, of course not,' I said shrilly. 'We just want to know how to get near Goolie and Goofy. You *must* know - you got them into your van, *and* guided them into our garden.'

I was appalled at the aggressive hysteria honing my voice.

'Oh 'tis easy me dear. Didn't I tell you. 'Tis Chanel Number Five. I were wearing it.'

'What!'

'Chanel Number Five. They love it. Go anywhere, do anything to get a sniff.'

'You mean lure them with a bottle?'

Her phlegmy chuckles crackled into my ear. 'Don't be stupid me dear. Goats can't read. No you wear it on your wrist, or anywhere come to that, and then you lure them. They're addicted.'

'It really works?' I asked, wondering if it was some sort of Cornish jest.

'It does me dear. It really works but, be warned, don't wear Chanel Number Nineteen. It doesn't just attract them, it drives 'em lustful mad - specially that Goolie. I can tell you, I've had some of it. Pinned me down on the grass with his willy as erect as one o' them old tin mine chimneys and almost as big. My husband came and saved me, but he's never mentioned that goat's chimney 'cos I think he were jealous. Men are insecure like that, have you noticed me dear?'

I ducked an answer out of loyalty to Bernard.

'So that's the solution,' I said, still needing reassurance. 'Chanel Number Five.'

'Yes me dear but, as I says, keep off the Number Nineteen, unless you fancy a bit of rough and tumble with a goat, that is.'

I waited for her wheezing chortles to die down.

'I would have given you my Number Five,' she said, 'but it's the equivalent to Number Nineteen on me hubby so I need it. Specially now we're getting on. Anyway, good luck me dear, goodbye.'

And that was that. The conversation was abruptly over. But, I had the information I needed.

I sped down to the village, parked in the High Street outside the chemist. Dived in.

'Chanel Number Five,' I rapped.

'Sorry, you'll have to go into Great Piddlehurst for that,' the assistant said.

'How about Number Nineteen,' I asked, wondering if it might be possible to lure them then run for it.

'Sorry, nothing as exotic as Chanel sells in Wood Hill. We've got lavender water.'

Disappointed, I drove back home.

As soon as I entered the hall, the phone rang.

'Hello Freda. He doesn't need more chemo for six weeks at least,' mother's excited voice said, 'so we can come down and stay with you - I can help with the animals and dress your burns.'

'That's wonderful news,' I exclaimed, a sudden rush of joy hitting the back of my knees making me sit down. 'But my burns are healing beautifully left uncovered, though sometimes I protect my hands. But help with the animals would be great.' I lowered my voice in case Bernard was around. 'I think we've bitten off more than we can munch,' I confided. 'There's so much to do all the time and Bernard has placed adverts in various papers and pamphlets in hotels saying the Animal Park will be opening soon and I don't think we're up to it and I'm so worried.'

It all came pouring out and the funny part was I hadn't known it was there.

'We'll come down tomorrow,' mother said firmly, 'and I'll bring my welly boots. Anything else I'll need?'

'You don't have any Chanel Number Five do you?'

'Yes,' she said, sounding puzzled. 'An old duty-free bottle, still half full.'

'Bring it down - it's to attract the goats.'

There was a pause, then:

'Sounds kinky, but I suppose it's up to you.'

And, before I could get in a word of explanation, she rushed: 'What kind of things can I do to help?'

'Basically, we just shovel food in one end and shovel up muck that comes out from the other end,' I said, quite appalled when I realised that that was indeed what we did basically do.

'I won't deal with poo,' she stated. 'Never could stand the stuff.'

And I didn't realise then quite how much she meant it.

Seventeen

They arrived at midday. I had been dreading that father would have become bent and frail in the few weeks since I last saw him. But, as he hauled himself out of the car I could see he was still as upright and thickset as ever, just marginally paler maybe.

'You look *great*,' I said, hugging him to me.

'Great for somebody dying,' he snapped, adding, 'I see you've had your hair chopped off. But just look what they've done to mine.'

'He's always on about the treatment making him bald, but he was bald before that even started,' mother said as she nimbly alighted from the driver's side.

I squeezed her slight body tightly in my arms. 'It's so good to have you with us,' I gulped.

'I *wasn't* bald,' he bellowed as he crunched over the gravel to the front door. 'I was just a bit thin on top.'

'Let *go*,' mother said, pulling away from me. 'You're hurting and it isn't me who gunged up their lungs with tar and toxins and is now paying for it - go and squeeze the life out of your father.'

The deep-felt emotions of sympathy and the desire to protect my vulnerable mother squittered out from me.

'You know where your bedroom is,' I said stiffly. 'If you don't like the red roses in the vase by the bed, just chuck them out.'

'Is something up?' asked mother as we climbed the stairs.

It was three hours since they'd arrived. Bernard had taken all their luggage up and they'd had scrambled eggs on toast and were now sleeping. All the deep-felt emotions of sympathy and the desire to protect them had crept back inside me again. My parents *never* slept after lunch or after a journey. When I told Bernard what I was feeling he said to remember they were both in their seventies. But that's just what I had been remembering, that and the cancer.

I heard the stairs creak and jumped up as mother appeared. She looked terrific. Newly blonded hair swathed on top with the usual fetching wisps hanging down, bright pink trousers in a soft material, topped with a baggy tee shirt in black. As she came closer, an old familiar perfume wafted to me, booting up my memory cells with fleeting images of parties, dances, and first love.

'I could hardly wait to get down here to see all the animals,' she exclaimed.

And as we went outside, a little hurt part of me wished she'd said *I could hardly wait to get down here and see you.* But then she showed that she cared by asking what needed to be done and how she could help with it.

Lairy the lamb was cropping grass just outside the back door and mother rushed to him, cooing and ahing as she patted his curly wool fleece. Just then Lardarse hove into view from behind the mobile home and mother froze.

'You-you said you had a l-l-llama b-but ...'

As Lardarse galloped full pelt towards us mother screamed and shot behind me, her trembling hands clasping my waist.

By now I'd grown quite fond and confident of Lardarse and had even stopped carrying a tissue with me.

'He's okay, let go of my waist and don't worry,' I reassured her, stepping to one side and exposing her to the oncoming llama who stopped dead staring at her with troubled eyes, mouth beginning to sway from side to side in increasingly rapid swings.

Mother's whimperings grew higher pitched and more terror struck.

'He's okay,' I reiterated, lifting a confident hand to tickle his soft muzzle.

His taut lips stretched even tauter and his baleful eyes swivelled back and forth, finally settling on me.

'He's okay,' I re-reiterated, quickly ducking sideways as a thin stream of spit shot out aimed squarely at where I'd just been.

Mother's whimperings had transmuted to a continuous high-pitched squeal.

'He's okay,' I re-re-reiterated, trying to hide my shock. 'He's just got to get used to you.'

I blanked my mind to the fact that it wasn't her he'd just gobbed at, but me. Screwing up my courage, I pushed at his strong curved neck, forcing him away, then slapped his backside, hearing mother's soprano squeal lower to a bass hum as the llama trotted away, gradually fading to silence when he'd disappeared.

'Those Hillbillys knew what they were doing when they got rid of him,' mother muttered as she turned to go back indoors. 'You'll not get me outside on my own while he's on the run.'

'Don't go back already.' I held onto her arm. 'You'll be okay. He's gone into the field and if he comes back, I'll ... I'll send him away.'

As I spoke I realised we had to get a compound made for him, and not just for mother's sake. Visitors wouldn't appreciate being spat at by a temperamental humpless camel, especially if they'd paid five pounds for the pleasure. Not much compared with what football fans paid, but our customers would be closer to hand. Or, more appropriately, closer to flying spittle. Bernard, as usual trundling a wheel barrow, hurried towards us.

'It's all too much,' he moaned. 'There's so many animals to feed and clear up after, and now Esmerelda's told me she wasn't insured so Daisy's roaming loose with no prospect of a stable being built. And the idea of putting the goats in there is a non-runner. And adverts are out stating we're opening at the end of next week.'

The hysteria in his voice matched the syndrome in my nervous bowel.

'What about asking your friend Robert Bambridge what he'd do if he were you trying to run this,' mother suggested, spreading her arms wide. 'He's a good businessman - might have some ideas.'

But before either of us could respond the sound of pounding hooves and excited bleats made us turn. And there, charging towards us, were Goolie and Goofy.

'It's your perfume,' I gasped, suddenly realising what her familiar fragrance was. 'Chanel Number Five, they've just caught a whiff of yours. Quick, get indoors.'

Bernard abandoned the wheel barrow and grabbed mother's hand and we all ran towards the cottage, hotly pursued by the goats. As we slammed the kitchen door behind us, Goolie's lowered horns charged full force into the pig flap torpedoing his head into the kitchen where he juddered to a halt, jammed from full entry by the height of his back.

Goolie lifted his head, raising the flap on his blunt horns. His startled eyes roved the kitchen, locked onto mine. He bleated, backed out. The flap crashed down and there was silence.

'We can't stay long,' quavered mother, as I dashed over and bolted it shut.

The screeching cockerel woke me up at five o'clock and I lay awake till ten to seven when I managed to nod off. But at seven Bernard shook me awake.

'Time to get up,' he sang out happily.

'Time to get Cussbert's neck wrung,' I snarled.

Half asleep, I got dressed then went through the routine of the early morning, going down to the pig unit whilst Bernard mixed up their feed in the kitchen of the mobile home, then releasing the pink army for their charge up the slope to the troughs. Then tidying and casting fresh straw down in their apartments whilst they hogged their food down, all the time worrying about mother's threat to leave.

Feeling even more tired after my strenuous chalet maid services, I tottered back out to the garden where the piglets had finished their feed and were scattered around enjoying their free time as they always did after a meal. I glanced around as I plodded up the slope but could only see four of the nine.

My stomach lurched. Surely the pignapper hadn't struck in broad daylight whilst I was inside? Surely he couldn't rustle five piglets in one go? It was impossible, I reassured myself. They'd have trotted over to the field out of sight: they were getting more daring. Wearily, I pushed open the kitchen door, expecting the lovely sight, sound and smell of percolating coffee. But instead received the appalling sight, sound and smell of five squealing shitting piglets. And it was then I realised that in my drowsy state I'd unbolted the pig flap for Hermione while the piglets were still on the loose.

'Get out!' I screamed to Princess as she cavorted up to me. 'Get out. Get out,' I screeched at the rest of them, flinging the door open wide.

'What's happened?' said mother, entering. Then, 'Good god, what a mess, what a stench.'

'It's all got on top of me,' I cried.

'How?' she asked, puzzled eyes scrutinising my head as she stood on tiptoe.

'Not literally. It's all too much. I can't cope.'

'There, there,' she said, right out of character. And it made me remember when once I had grazed my knee falling off the kerb and instead of getting a ticking off for playing where I shouldn't she'd given me a sweet.

'There, there,' she said again, this time nasally as she was now pinching her nose. 'You get away from all this, go and ring your friend Robert Bambridge - see if he can help you with your other worries. Go on. Shoo. Get out to the hall phone. Leave this revolting mess. Shut the door behind you. Ring your friend.'

I'd never loved my mother as much as I loved her then. I knew that even talking of the brown stuff made her heave. I knew that when I was a baby she'd treated terry towelling nappies as disposables if they'd been too soiled - *because they always made me throw up*, she'd related ad nauseum. And here she was taking over the job of cleaning off my hands, quite literally.

I tapped out his number.

'Hello Robert. Yes, we're fine thank you, yes very well, except we've too many animals to cope with and the stable block burnt down and that was where the donkey lived and it's all gone up in smoke and now we have a llama who spits and needs a compound built but Nesbit and Enid have gone off visiting relations up north and we've also got chickens and geese and ducks milling around and the goats are nervous and have to be tethered but we can do that now thanks to Chanel Number Five.

'Yes, yes, I will slow down. Yes, we've got a load of new animals and we open up next week. Yes, I'm all right. Except my father has lung cancer and he's here with mother staying but my mother already wants to go home because the animals attack her but I want to spend precious time with him because ... you know ... who knows how long and there isn't any precious time to spend even if they stay because I'm just too busy.

'Yes, yes. The pigs are very happy and Bernard has taught them wonderful tricks but they're growing so fast and eating so much and producing so much, you know, end product, that it's getting out of control. But they're happy as the proverbial pigs in the muck, spending all their time eating and playing and being showered and sponged clean by their human slaves ... and, now I think of it Robert, I realise those porkers are far *far* happier than me.'

'You sound at your wits end,' said Robert, 'and I can help. Just need a little time to think about it. In the meantime, you put your feet up, make a cup of tea.'

I replaced the phone feeling calmer, opened the door and entered the kitchen. It was just as I'd left it, minus mother. Stinking pig shit splattered everywhere. Grimly, I got out the bucket and mob.

Half an hour later when it was all cleared up mother appeared.

'Bought this for you,' she said handing me a bottle of perfume. She kissed my cheek. 'Drove down to the village specially. They didn't have Chanel Number Five and I didn't want lavender water because although I really quite like it, it's naff, but thought this would make you smile and help with the pong.'

I read the fancy label. *Vasser der gros Fart* it said.

'Should over-ride the pig poo pong,' she said, with the attempt at a modest look that went with someone who has gone to inordinate trouble to help out.

'You went off and left me with it,' I cried.

'All the thanks you get,' she said huffily to father who'd just appeared. 'You put yourself out to be a good mother and it's thrown back in your ear.'

'About time,' he snapped.

'About time it's thrown back in my ear?' she hotly queried.

'No, about time you put yourself out to be a good mother,' he roared, all signs of lung cancer having vanished.

'Bloody pigs,' muttered mother. 'It's not like this in Tooting.'

'No, in Tooting it's dog's turds and they're worse,' he growled.

She wheeled round on me.

'I told you when we first came, I never deal with poo. Why on earth don't you tag Hermione with an electronic device so only she can get through the pig flap? Unless you intend to housetrain the other nine.'

My zany mother always managed to amaze me. It was such a wonderful idea.

'Nor blood, nor vomit,' mocked father rather belatedly. 'You don't deal with them either. You're blooming useless. Good job I ...'

I went out and left them to it. They were getting too much like my old mum and dad for my liking. The ones before the C scare. But at least there was no mention of them going.

As I said to Cynthia when she rang me, I couldn't believe the speed with which Robert Bambridge got cracking. He's sent one of his workers called Larry every morning and evening to feed and muck out the animals. Larry feeds Lairy has been mother's recurring joke which is starting to wear a bit thin.

Another of Robert's workers, still on his books but apparently currently under-employed, is Carl the carpenter who has already made a large post and rail compound, lined with field fencing, for Lardarse so he can't chase after mother or visitors, although he could still long-distance spit if he'd a mind to.

And now Carl is replacing burnt rafters in the stable block and when that's finished he's going to replace buckled or missing sheets of the corrugated iron roof, then set about making the individual stalls fit for animal habitation again, so the end one will be Daisy's, and the next can be for Lardarse when the weather gets cold, and next to him the goats. And that still leaves a spare one to use as a sick bay or for any new animal that comes along.

Another two workers have rehung the drooping double doors in the back of the barn where people will enter once they've parked their cars. And now they are constructing men's and women's toilets at one end of the barn. Apparently we're lucky the sewage pipes run from Esmerelda's farm house to our cottage taking the low route across the field instead of the high one along Nuthatch Lane.

Robert visits every day to make sure his workers aren't skiving. Whenever I get close to him when he's talking to Carl, they clam up as if they're up to something secret. But I haven't a clue what.

I haven't a clue also how we're going to repay Robert, but the relief of the work being done is as if someone has lifted an elephant off my chest. And the most important thing is I've been able to spend time with father and mother, playing the occasional game of bridge, and actually having time to talk with them.

And Bernard, beautifully perfumed with Chanel Number Five, has tethered the goats to special uprights incorporating twirly-whirlys that allow the goats to wander round without the rope snarling up.

At the end of my long dissertation, Cynthia replied that she'd better get off the line because Sidney had something urgent to fax.

'But what do you think about what I've told you?' I wailed hoarsely.

'I am very pleased Freda. Oh, all *right* Sidney, she's stopping now.'

'Goodbye,' I said, mortified to realise she was fobbing me off.

'Goodbye Freda. Oh, by the way I'm working on an idea that might help you.'

What *is* it? I wanted to say. But pride wouldn't let me. My best friend's fax machine didn't have to fall on my head to know I'd talked too much. Because I didn't even think she had one.

'I need to tell you something,' father said.

'Tell me what?' I asked, vaguely wondering what Bernard was teaching the piglets because, through the open French windows, I could hear faint strains of The Sugar Plum Fairy coming from the field.

'My parents, your grandparents who died when you were four.'

'Mmm, I have a hazy memory of them, though it might only be because I've seen photos.'

'Well, they're not my parents.'

'Who were they then?' I asked, astounded.

'The Salmons - kind people who looked after me ... I didn't find out 'til I needed my birth certificate and couldn't find one ... it was after they were dead.'

He swallowed hard and his pallid face flushed pink.

'Apparently they were paid to look after me.'

He eased his knobbly fingers up and over the dome of his head as if the sparse hairs he'd been used to tidying were still there.

'That's the hard part to bear. Only they carried on looking after me as a son when the money stopped coming when I was five. So that makes it easier. An old aunt - in the family I'd always thought of as mine - told me. She also said that for the first three years my real mother used to visit me whenever she could.'

I didn't know what to say. This had come like a stealth bomber out of the blue. I put my hand up to twiddle with a strand of hair, also forgetting that my long tendrils weren't there. Hastily, I moved my hand up higher to run fingers through my cropped curls.

'Have you any idea who your real parents were?' I asked at last.

Now the heavy lids leapt back from his eyes, exposing twinkling emeralds. 'The old aunt told me that my mother was young and beautiful, always expensively dressed - she described a rich velvet coat with sable collar and cuffs, satin shoes, a primrose cloche hat. I have a vague recollection of the soft rounded face with blue eyes and sweet smile that she described. She said she thought the lady was someone high up whose position would be ruined by public knowledge of a child born out of wedlock. She said once or twice my father came to visit, at the beginning, when I was a baby. She described his shock of red hair and green eyes, his handsome freckled face. His height. His quick temper. How once they met up to see me together, taking turns to hold me, both crying. She told me that she thought the lady came from Windsor, she'd heard the name whispered. Since the old aunt died I've been trying to trace them, but it's only the last few months that I've been getting somewhere through the Internet.'

He made the strange little buzzing noise in his throat that he did when he was angry or excited. There was no doubt which one it was this time.

'Who do you think they are?' I asked.

'Father might have been a Scottish farmer who kept cattle but went broke, not quite sure yet.'

'It must be in the genes!' I cried. 'It can't be a coincidence that I keep animals - just like my real granddaddy.'

Already I'd discarded my old one in favour of this new more interesting role model.

'Remember, it was probably the animals that made him go broke,' he said, swiping the elation from my credit card of hope.

'Anyway, what proof have you that this broke bloke was your dad?' I muttered sourly, not so keen to have him as a forefather after all.

'I'm working on it. But it's not my father I'm so interested in.' I'd never seen such a look of intrigue or rapture on his face.

'It's my real mother. You'd be amazed if I told you who she probably is.'

'Well who probably is she,' I said, amazed enough already, without knowing.

'I'll not say, until I have more proof. So that's why I wanted to ask you - now you're not using the attic studio for painting, can I use it as my private office and plug my laptop into your phone socket. I've got a modem.'

I stared at him even more amazed. It was only a few months ago that he'd bought a PC. Now he was talking laptops and Internets and modems. A fleeting ache shot through my heart as I remembered the paintings I'd planned to do up in the attic, set up ready with easel, paints and all the other art paraphernalia. One day maybe. But for now it was my father's space.

'Use it whenever you want,' I said. 'And let me know soon who you think your mother is ... even if you can't prove it. I'm dying to know.'

'I have to be sure before I divulge it to anyone,' he said secretively, eyes darting.

'Why?'

'Because if it gets out and it isn't correct, it could be construed as treason.'

'Treason!'

His eyes bore into mine. 'It could be good news for you,' he murmured. 'Although they're cutting the civil list down.'

I stared at him. Was he having me on? But the intense look in his eyes told me he was serious.

'And don't mention a word to your mother,' he said. 'She's hard enough to live with as plain Mrs Salmon. If she knew she were married to ...' His mouth clammed shut as he realised he'd said too much. 'I mean it Freda. Tell no-one. She knows about the Salmons not being my real relations. But the fact that my mother might be someone important is just between you and me.'

I tottered out to Hermione, my mind in a whirl.

'My lovely lovely girl,' I whispered to my recumbent pig. 'It seems as if we should have named *you* Princess, not your bright pink offspring.'

The rumbling piggy purr that had revved up when I began scratching behind her ear abruptly ceased and I looked behind me guiltily in case father had followed me out and heard me spill the sprouts to my girl, and Kermit the eavesdropper. Suddenly Hermione reared up, sitting on her haunches, peering regally down her upturned snout. Then she leapt up, cavorting around, snorting and squealing as if cheering. Kermit, caught the atmosphere of a royal birth and skipped around with her, bleating at full blast.

Over the cacophony I heard the thumping sound of someone pounding up the ramp and, twirling round, saw mother charging in, pitchfork clasped in her hands.

She stopped short. 'Good god,' she shouted over the din, 'I thought the animal thief had come, and I was out to get him.'

Carefully, I took the pitchfork from her. 'It's very brave of you,' I said. 'And I know someone in the government is advising citizens to have a go, but I agree with the police who say it's too dangerous.'

She turned on her heel. 'That's what you get trying to help,' she called sulkily over her shoulder. 'A bloody lecture from your only daughter.'

I was dying to ask her to come back to discuss the hot news imparted by father, but knew it was bad enough that I'd blabbed it out to the pig and the kid.

Now all I had to do was wait and hope he found out for sure who his mother was before ... before ... before he went home for more treatment.

Eighteen

At last I've discovered what Carl the carpenter and Robert Bambridge have been so secretive about. Robert, on his latest inspection visit, came over to the pig unit where I was in the shower room hosing Jesus down.

He pulled back the purple pig patterned shower curtain, saying, 'When you've finished with his ablutions, I've got something to show you in the stable block.'

Hurriedly, I dabbed Jesus dry with an old towel while Robert hopped from foot to foot like an impatient schoolboy.

I'd been hoping to clean up Hamlet but left him mucky to go off with Robert, puffing to keep up with him as he charged eagerly across the lawn.

Outside the door to the end room of the repaired stable block, Carl the carpenter waited, eyes as twinkling as Robert's.

'Come in and see,' he said.

Then he and Robert dived in before me, standing closely side by side.

'Your reception committee,' Robert explained, taking my hand, pulling me past them.

Forcing away the sensation of choking and the stench of smoke, forcing away the sound of crashing timbers, forcing away the feeling of intolerable heat, trying to forget I nearly died here, I let myself be dragged in, resisting the strong instinct to turn round and make a bolt for it.

'The concrete base had to have cracks filled in,' Robert was explaining. 'And we thought it safer to rebuild the back wall in breezeblocks instead of wooden planks.'

'Not only safer,' cut in Carl, 'but completely weatherproof.'

I wiped my hand across my forehead, shivered, wondering what all the fuss was about.

'See the new roof,' said Robert, pointing.

I looked up seeing new A-shaped timbers and cross beams and a new corrugated iron roof. For the first time I thought of the doves who'd lived there and wondered if they'd escaped. My neck began to hurt so I looked down at the breezeblock wall, suddenly realising there was a window there where there hadn't been one before. Was this what they were so keen to show me? A good idea. Welcome light inside what was once a dim area. But surely not enough for all the secrecy and excitement.

'Why don't you turn round,' suggested Robert.

And when I did I saw it.

To one side of the doorway I'd just walked through. A free-standing very large doll's house, the point of its gable roof as high as me. They'd been deliberately screening it standing shoulder to shoulder as I'd walked past. I gasped, dived at it, peered through its clear perspex front seeing a miniature bedroom, fully furnished, its walls painted pink. And peeping out from under the double bed were the shiny eyes of a chipmunk. Instantly it darted out and scurried down a flight of stairs. I bent lower, seeing the little creature arrive in a square hallway then scurry off into an adjoining dining room. A bushy tail was poking out from under a table and, as I watched dumbfounded, its owner sprang out and jumped at the one that had just come downstairs. Another one darted out from behind a sideboard and the three rolled around on the straw-covered floor, playing like rat sized, stripy, bushy tailed bear cubs.

I turned to Carl and Robert, tried to speak, but deep emotions clogged up my throat.

'Look at the other side,' said Robert, grabbing my elbow and shunting me round.

Upstairs, chipmunks were playing in a second bedroom and spacious bathroom. Downstairs two chased each other round and round a sofa in the sitting room and, in the kitchen, one popped in and out of open cupboards having fun. It was clearly a chipmunk's paradise. It was clearly also a creative wonder, a work of art, a joinery feat as amazing as the rebuilding of the Globe. And, quite unexpectedly, a tear slid out and slipped down my cheek.

'I thought you'd like it?' said Carl, scratching his head and casting Robert a bewildered look.

'I do like it. I *love* it,' I sniffled, wishing I had a tissue. 'Whose idea was it?'

'My idea,' said Robert, his face breaking into a relieved grin. 'My plan. But Carl here's the one who made it happen. It's all down to his expertise.'

'How ever can I thank you,' I said, at last finding a disintegrating tissue in my pocket and blowing my emotion-blocked nose. 'It will *make* our Animal Park.'

'You can repay me, when the pressure's off, by painting Poppy's portrait.'

'But, but, that's not enough,' I stammered.

'It's more than enough. Do it the same size as the one you did of me last year, and in the same style, and we can hang the two together.'

I thought of the portrait I did of Sidney Slocumb last year when he was the mayor, of what a thick gungy mess it was until Hermione knocked it off the easel and sat on it, accidentally creating a contact print on her broad backside and a work of subtle magic on the canvas. And the resultant commission by Poppy to paint Robert's portrait, and of the mess it was until an outrageous plan born of desperation had formed in my frazzled mind and I skidded my own bare bum over the thickly painted oils, once more creating a humiliating contact print on a fleshy bum and a work of subtle magic on the canvas.

'You don't have to do it until you have time.' He stared at me anxiously. 'You don't have to do it at all if you don't want to.'

'Oh, yes, yes, if that's what you'd like, I *will* do it,' I said vehemently, whimsically wondering if I could bear it, in either spelling of the word.

'Poppy and I would love it,' he said. 'But only when you have time, no worry, no pressure.'

Carl had stood by, fidgeting impatiently.

'You still haven't seen it all,' he announced. 'Come on, come and see round the back.'

And, round the back of the magnificent chipmunk house, he showed me that the whole of the wall was hinged down one side so it would open out and be relatively easy for cleaning. Then he pushed down a switch and all the lights in the house came on. It was truly a marvellous sight.

'Now come and see *this*,' said Robert, eagerly.

And, in a daze, I followed him over the other side of the room where the cupboard containing the candles had been. But there was no cupboard there now. Instead, against the rebuilt partition wall, was an array of hutches, four across, three high.

'In case you want to keep rabbits,' Carl explained.

'No! Not rabbits.'

Again Carl scratched his head and cast Robert a puzzled look.

'Thought you'd be pleased,' he said petulantly again.

'Oh I am, I am. We can keep guinea pigs.' I gulped. 'Hamsters ...'

Robert, who knew about the rabbit eating the guinea pig, patted my arm. 'Not all rabbits are like Nesbit's Dick,' he said kindly.

And once again Carl scratched at his head, this time casting his eyes up to the roof as if seeking help from on high.

Back in the kitchen I gabbled out the news to mother and father. Bernard, having been told, was already racing over to see for himself.

'The twelve-hatch array is wonderful,' I said, 'but I'm not sure what to put in the cages ... we can't really afford to feed any more animals ... besides, they'd all need cleaning out.'

'Fill them with twigs and leaves,' said mother. 'Pretend there are creatures inside. Give them interesting sounding labels.'

'Like what?' I asked, not catching on.

'Like ... Lesser Spotted Spiny Toad. Or, Deadly Tartan Snake. Make 'em up!'

'That's not cricket,' interjected father.

'Okay,' said mother brightly, 'go out and find one of those. I'm sure I heard one chirruping in the grass.'

'Silly bitch,' growled father, turning his attention to his food.

As we ate our evening meal, mother expounded on her zany idea. 'I went to a zoo once and spent ages trying to see creatures that never appeared because they were sleeping behind rocks or camouflaged against foliage,' she said.

'How did you know they were behind rocks or camouflaged if you didn't see them?' grunted father.

'Precisely,' whooped mother. 'My exact point. I just assumed that was where they were, they could have been non-existent.'

Perhaps it wasn't such a daft concept I mused.

'It would save a lot of worry on the excess droppings front,' I said. 'We've got more than we can handle.'

Bernard puffed back into the kitchen. 'The chipmunk house is brilliant,' he enthused, helping himself to his dinner, served up and in the Aga.

'Don't know why you don't just shovel all the animal manure up and flush it down your loo,' mother continued, shovelling up a turkey sausage and angling it into her mouth.

'Do you mind,' said father, pushing his plate away in a futile gesture because he'd already scraped it clean.

'And it's ridiculous to think that you could shovel tons of manure down a domestic lavatory,' said Bernard, taking my mother seriously.

'Why, would it put your sewage rates up?' she quipped, still milking what I presumed was a joke and, at the same time, livening up the table talk which she'd complained was getting too dull.

She sat through the ensuing howls of ridicule from father and earnest discourse from Bernard with a look of triumphant contentment raked across her face. Our eyes met in the midst of it and she winked.

Next day, however, a phone call out of the blue miraculously took the mounting dung problem off our hands.

'Reggie Thatcher here,' a man introduced himself, 'vegetable farmer from Orlford - 'spect you've heard of me?'

'No, I haven't,' I replied, cautiously.

'Have you not,' he exclaimed, rushing on, 'Alfred at the PDQ Piggery told me you've got a problem with too much muck.'

'Well, yes. For years our pig's dung has been tipped into a ditch and now we have the piglets and ...'

'And it's not a bottomless pit,' he interrupted.

'Quite.'

'Bottomless pit is very nearly bottomless piG. Get it. If you had a bottomless piG, you wouldn't have a problem.'

I held the phone away from my head to protect my ear drum as he cracked up at his own wit. Not another Bernard! I thought, dismayed.

'Anyway,' he said at last, 'you're lucky. I need fertiliser and well rotted pig manure is the best, especially natural stuff like yours. No chemicals. They call me Green Veggie Reggie and ...'

My pulse began to race.

'... you can't beat the taste of tatties grown in pig dung. Swedes thrive on it too. Parsnips. Carrots, the lot.'

'So, what are you suggesting?' I asked, hoping I knew what.

'What I am suggesting is that me and one of my men come along and dig out all your old rotted down pig manure from the ditch - that'll be the creme de la creme.'

'Will it,' I exclaimed, amazed.

'Then we'll leave a trailer with you to fill with new outpourings and will collect it when you ring to tell us it's full, leaving another empty one in its place.'

'Sounds exactly what we want,' I said wondering what the catch was.

'But first we must agree on a price.'

And then I knew what the catch was. He was going to charge us.

I sighed. 'How much will it be?'

'How about if we say twenty pounds a trailer load - you'll see the size of it when we come round.'

'Twenty pounds a load!' I gasped, knowing we couldn't afford any extra expense whatsoever.

'Twenty-five then, but that's top whack. It doesn't pay us to give any more.'

'You pay *us*?' I whispered, astounded, the realisation that we had a continuous on-line flow of filthy lucre quickly taking hold. Hurriedly, I repeated the words firmly with no question mark lurking in my voice. 'You pay us ... twenty-five pounds a load.'

'Yes, paid on the dot.'

'What size is the trailer?' I asked, trying to sound business-like. Attempting to hide that we'd settle on a trailer the size of a double decker bus, to get shot of it.

'I said, you'll see. I'll come round tomorrow morning and show you.'

I replaced the phone and ran out to find Bernard, seeing him down by the pig unit.

I cupped my hands round my mouth. 'You know the brown stuff we're up to our eyes in,' I yelled down. 'Well we're not any more. Reggie Thatcher's taking it all away.'

'Maggie Thatcher. Why does she want it?' he shouted back.

'To bomb Edward Heath or John Major,' I shrieked, on a high.

'More likely Brussels,' he called back, snorting.

I came down early next day to find mother already up, pummelling the contents of a saucepan with a potato masher.

'What are you doing?'

'Damn it, I wanted it to be a surprise,' she grumbled, whipping the masher away and bashing the lid on.

'It's all right, I won't look,' I said, laughing, as she rushed out with my biggest saucepan clutched in both hands. I wondered what kind of new recipe she was working on as I heard her plod up the stairs. It must be top secret to hide it in her bedroom.

Closely positioned against the jutting bridge of his nose, Larry's deep set eyes stared straight ahead as he clasped a mug of tea at our kitchen table. I pondered at such a design fault, for that great wall-like proboscis must surely block a full view from each side.

'Nice set up you've got here with your garden and the adjoining field, Mrs Field,' he said, nasally. 'When are you opening it up to the public?'

'On Saturday,' I said, a shiver of fearful anticipation shimmering through me.

'Weather forecast ain't good fer the weekend,' he said, loudly slurping his tea then staring into space again.

As I loaded the dishwasher I puzzled about him. He'd been such a wonderful help each morning and evening since he'd been with us, but from the very first day he seemed to know the exact lie of the land and out-buildings without us telling him.

'I like working with your animals,' he suddenly said, coming out of his reverie. 'Mr Bambridge is a good man to work for, but I prefer being here to the factory.'

And, as he spoke, he lifted one booted foot onto his knee.

I stared. Another person with small feet! Vernon Veal. Sidney Slocumb. Harry from school. And now Larry to add to the list of suspects.

'Which animal do you like best?' I asked, all innocent-like.

'I like them all, but my favourite is my namesake, or, at least, nearly my namesake.'

'Oh, you mean Lairy our lamb,' I said, smiling, my aroused suspicions assuaged by his choice of a creature who had not been borrowed. Unless, of course, the lamb was next on the list.

He scraped his chair back and stood up. 'Must get back to the factory now. Ta for the tea.'

After he'd gone I sat thinking. He couldn't be the animal borrower. Why would he want them? What would he do with them? All I did know was that he was worth his weight in pig nuts to Bernard and me. To have the burden of feeding and mucking out off our shoulders was such a relief, even if just for a while.

'Morning,' said mother, bouncing into the kitchen, happily smiling. 'What's for breakfast?'

'Eggs, if you like, fresh from the hens.'

'I might be a townie from Tooting but I know they aren't fresh from the pigs,' she teased with no trace of sarcasm, just light-hearted fun.

A surge of well-being flooded through me. In the short time they'd been with us the worried lines on her face had floated away like gossamer cobwebs on a breeze. The outdoor life, and sharing of the worry of father with us, had done wonders for her and that made me feel good.

'It was a brilliant idea of yours, suggesting we ask for Robert's advice,' I said, taking an egg from the bowl, picking off fluffy feathers. 'He's been such a help.'

'Any time you want brilliant ideas I'm your woman,' she said, blue eyes twinkling, wide mouth grinning. 'And I've got another brilliant idea tucked up my sleeve - but don't ask me yet, 'cos I'm not telling.'

I cracked the egg into the pan, and took up another.

'Your father's told me that he's informed you your grandparents weren't your real ones,' she said, eyeing me.

I nodded, turning away from her gaze. How much did she know? Had father given her a clue? I was dying to ask her.

'He's spent hours and hours trying to find out who they really were,' she said. 'At home, every minute he wasn't being zapped at the hospital, or wasn't recovering from being zapped, he spent on the Internet or poring over genealogy books. He's gone straight up to the attic now, without breakfast, to plug himself in.' She paused. 'I think he's on the trail but he won't tell me - did he say anything to you?'

Briskly I forked the eggs into a scramble wondering what on earth to say, but the sudden clatter of Hermione barging through the pig flap saved me. And before we could get back to the question, the pathetic crying bleats of Kermit outside the door took mother's attention away. She jumped up and opened the door to the little kid who hadn't yet plucked up courage to butt her head at the flap, even though it was protected by her two small buffers. For the first time I wondered if Hermione's frequent entries gave her headaches. I watched mother's engrossed expression as she stroke the little kid. At least for the time being she was distracted.

Reggie Thatcher, in a battered Range Rover disporting the logo GREEN VEGGIE REGGIE, was waiting in the car park field. We opened the double doors of the barn and he inched the vehicle forward.

He wound down his window. 'Did you say this is going to be the entrance to the Animal Park?'

'Yes,' said Bernard, looking dubious.

And my heart sank as I saw the problem too. Even if the wide trailer he was towing scraped through, it wouldn't manage the narrower doorway opposite, leading into the grounds. And, even if he brought a narrower trailer, there was a step to bump down. How stupid that we hadn't made some other means of access, I reflected, if only in case there was ever another fire.

Bernard stroked his chin.

'We'll have to incorporate a pair of gates in the fence that divides the car park from the animal park.'

'They'd have to be two metres tall, like the fence, so that when Kermit is fully grown she can't spring out,' I warned.

'Yup, that'd be okay,' said Green Veggie Reggie, who, far from being green was a sallow shade of yellow, with a distinctly oriental slant to his eyes. 'What d'you think?' he asked a sinewy tanned man in a black singlet sitting beside him.

'I was hoping to get stuck in today,' he answered, a whine of disappointment in his surprisingly high voice.

'Have to wait,' said Reggie consolingly. He turned to Bernard. 'When can the gates be made?'

Nesbit, who unbeknownst to any of us had been listening in at the end of the barn, suddenly spoke out.

'Not to worry, I say not to worry, Nesbit Batty's yer man.' He loomed out of the shadows towards us wielding a brace and bit. 'If Bernard here will come wi' me to the timber yard, I can knock up a pair of strong gates and get 'em hung by day after tomorrow, I say day after tomorrow.'

I saw Bernard's anxious face and knew he was worried. We'd already forked out to replace the three close boarded panels knocked down by the firemen in that uninsured fence.

'Can't you make gates from the panels you'll have to remove,' I suggested.

Nesbit came up close to me and I was heartened not to smell the slightest trace of alcohol on his breath, just peppermint toothpaste.

'Aye, good idea Freda. Then we'll just need hinges and handles and stuff.'

'Oh, that'd be *jolly* good,' said Bernard, looking relieved. 'I can pay for those few things on my credit card.'

And as the Range Rover and trailer bumped away back across the field, we three wandered along the fence to decide the best place to locate them.

'Gates could be incorporated anywhere in the fence between the barn and where it connects with Esmerelda's holly hedge,' stated Nesbit.

'Why not between the other side of the barn and our boundary hedge,' Bernard queried.

'Aye, that's a possibility. I say that's a possibility,' boomed Nesbit.

'Wherever you put them, make it so children can't undo them,' I cautioned. 'Otherwise the animals could get out.'

'If animals 'ave a mind to escape from this Garden of Eden, I say this Garden of Eden, they'd hop out through the barn,' observed Nesbit.

'Strangely, they don't. They're wary of going into unfamiliar enclosed spaces,' Bernard explained.

'And even if one did get bold enough to explore, it would be seen,' I added, 'because there'll always be at least one person in there when the front and back doors are open.'

'If thee says so, I say if thee says so,' said Nesbit, looking unconvinced. 'What about setting gates in fence right here, nearer to the barn than Esmerelda's. It wouldn't then interfere with the display arena.'

'Good idea,' I agreed, 'the trailer would be towed in to the left of the arena and be far enough away from Esmerelda's not to be a nuisance to her.'

'We should have thought of gates in the first place,' Bernard said ruefully. 'Supposing the fire brigade had to smash the fence down again to rescue you from another fire.'

'Oh, just supposing,' I said tartly, hurt by the innuendo that equated the value of my life with that of the fence.

But then he put his arm round my shoulders and whispered, 'Supposing you hadn't managed to get out by yourself and they couldn't have reached you.' He gulped. 'It wouldn't have only been you and Daisy who died, it would have been me too. I couldn't live without you.'

And my heart seemed to melt in his love's fiery heat. I stared at the wooden fence, inwardly gloating.

If, miraculously, any visitors did turn up on Saturday, they'd need to know what they were looking at so, rather belatedly, after Bernard had come back from the DIY store having bought the accessories for the gates, we made time to sort out the animal information labels stacked up in the garage by Mr Menabilly.

Bernard lugged one of the free standing A type notices up on to its stumpy legs, and we stood back and read the bold print:-

LARDARSE - A MALE LLAMA BEWARE THIS ANIMAL MAY SPIT. *South American ruminant allied to camel but smaller, humpless and woolly haired. A beast of burden.*

He turned it round. On the other side it read:-

A ruminant: any of various hoofed animals having a divided stomach and chewing a cud (food regurgitated from the first stomach and chewed again).

'That's a good sign,' I remarked to Bernard, 'easy to read and informative, but do you think some children's parents might object to him being called Lardarse?'

Mother came into the garage pushing the empty wheelbarrow which she'd lined with one of the newly laundered old towels we use to dry off the piglets.

Bernard, hands on hips, surveyed the sign.

'I think they'd think it was funny,' he replied at last.

'Thought I could help out by taking the signs down to their appropriate places,' mother said, adding, 'If you're worried about parents not liking the name Lardarse, what do you think some of them will think about a piglet being called Jesus?'

I stared at her. Could she be right? It had been the natural name for our first born who'd slithered from Hermione and lain immobile in the straw as if dead, then risen up fully alive again.

'The thought had occurred to me too,' Bernard confessed. 'Some people might think it sacrilegious.'

'But what can we call him,' I wailed. 'He's always been Jesus.'

'Why not call him Jim,' suggested mother.

'You can't call Jesus Jim,' I cried.

'Course you can,' she said, 'It's not as if you've got to do it by deed poll or anything. Only you two know what you called him. He didn't come labelled.'

'But Jim *isn't* Jesus,' I said crossly.

Bernard ran his fingers through his newly clipped crew cut.

'I think it makes sense,' he said. 'It's not as if you're changing the real Jesus's name. Not like you're getting the congregation to sing, Gentle Jim sweet and mild, or, What a friend we have in Jim.' He sniggered.

'I like that better,' asserted mother. 'They're always updating the Bible and hymns. Jim. It's more with-it. And you can shriek it out without it being blasphemous. Perhaps you should put it to the Archbishop of Canterbury - or whoever the boss man is.'

'What, and get a fatwah put on us,' chortled Bernard, now ridiculously in cahoots with my ma.

'But what about Mary, the next born,' I interrupted, trying to engender serious thought. 'Jesus went with Mary like Mohammed goes with Ali. Jim and Mary doesn't sound right.'

'Oh god,' exploded mother. 'A piglet called Mary won't offend anyone because no-one will know the connection with Jesus because Jesus will no longer be Jesus he'll be Jim.'

'And, if you need the two names to go together,' sniggered Bernard, still ganging up against me, 'instead of calling Jesus Jim you could re-name him Poppins.'

'But *why*!' I exploded, only just resisting stamping my foot.

'Mary ... Poppins,' he said, eyes twinkling, hand held up to his mouth like a stupid school girl containing the giggles.

'Why not bloody well call them Eliza and Doolittle,' I yelled, exasperated with the pair of them.

'Good idea,' he whooped.

'Or Pomp and Circumstance,' I snarled.

'Good idea,' he aggravatingly agreed again.

'Or Pompeii and Up Yours,' cackled mother, always quick to go off into the realms of vulgarity, a built-in genetic tendency I worry I may have inherited.

And Bernard cracked up too, so that the two of them were tottering around the garage screeching like undisciplined children whilst I stood watching like a po-faced school marm who'd lost control.

Gradually they calmed down. Bernard red in the face, spluttered, 'If you really don't like Jim, how about calling him Georgie, then we could change Hamlet to Porgie, and we already have Pudding and Pie. See. Georgie, Porgie, Pudding and Pie. Children would love that.'

My mind became tangled as I tried to adjust to the renaming of two of my babes. Was this confusion and sadness how father had felt when he was told he wasn't really a Salmon?

'Okay,' I finally snapped. 'Jesus will be re-named Georgie. Hamlet will be re-named Porgie.'

As I spoke my heart ached for the loss of the Prince of Peace and the Prince of Denmark.

'How sweet the name of Georgie sounds,' sang out mother.

'Porgie, Prince of Denmark,' added Bernard, still aiding and abetting her.

'So that's settled,' I snapped. 'Let's get on.'

Mother raised her eyebrows at Bernard then, giggling, trundled the LARDARSE LLAMA sign away whilst Bernard hauled up another board.

BIG BELLY BELLA FEMALE VIETNAMESE POT BELLIED PIG.

'I suppose we're going through all the rigmarole again,' I grumbled. 'I suppose you and mother will join forces and say we have to change Big Belly to something politically correct like A Bit on the Plump Side Tummy.'

Bernard stared at me with a sorrowful look.

'I mean, let's be uncontroversial here,' I said nastily.

Without comment, he turned the sign around:

Vietnamese Pot Bellied Pigs can live for 15-20 years. The breed is usually good tempered, but some individuals can be grumpy. A bad-tempered owner will often produce a bad-tempered pet.

'You'd better not go near her today,' Bernard said, smirking, then obviously thinking better about a full-blown guffaw, hauling out another sign.

By midday, the signs were all in place and I was in better humour. We went indoors and I called upstairs for father to come down to join us for lunch. I heard him dashing down and worried that he would fall but, almost immediately, he burst into the kitchen, face and eyes glowing. He hurried to where I stood at the open fridge.

'I've just discovered she was born in nineteen hundred!' he whisper-whooped in my ear.

'What's that?' asked mother, washing her hands at the sink.

'Nothing,' said father.

'Did you know that Jesus is now Georgie,' I informed him, changing the subject to distract her.

Mother looked suspiciously at father. Father looked dumbfoundedly at me. Bernard, opening up a tin of baked beans, said, 'But Mary is still Mary.'

'Although Hamlet is Porgie,' added mother, drawn in.

'And Green Veggie Reggie and his man have been today and are coming again when the gates are made to take a trailer-load of dung,' Bernard burst out jubilantly.

'And you lot are taking the piss,' father grumbled. 'The sooner I get back on line to communicate with sane people, the better.'

He stood up, looking perplexed.

And the sooner Saturday comes so we can see if visitors appear the better, I thought, excitement and fear flooding over me in equal torrents.

But by bed time the excitement had evaporated leaving only the fear. Just two more days before we knew our fate and my intestines were finding the wait intolerable.

Nineteen

I dialled Green Veggie Reggie's number. 'The gates are hung and ready to open,' I told him.

'Great! I'll come straight round with Butch and dig out some of that matured fertiliser in the ditch, I'm desperate for it.'

Twenty minutes later his Range Rover and trailer bumped over the grass and I ran over to the new gates, pointing at them.

'Look,' I said excitedly as Reggie jumped out, 'they're here.'

'So I observed,' he said, dryly.

The strong-looking one I'd seen before stuck his head out.

'Close them after I've driven through,' he instructed Reggie in his girlish voice, 'or all the little creatures will scamper away.'

'Quite right Butch,' said Reggie, stretching up to fold back the metal hasp that secured the top, then turning the handle to open them.

I watched Butch drive through, ripples of elation rolling over me like waves of sewage on a polluted beach. Soon it would be making the return journey full of manure and our ditch would be partly emptied - and our pockets partly filled. I smiled to myself as Reggie secured the gates shut.

'Don't forget to do it every time,' I reminded him.

'Course not,' he replied.

An hour later I had twenty-five pounds in my hand and joy in my heart.

'Keep it coming,' I yelled at Hermione as she sauntered past, exuding a little plop.

At last it was Saturday. Opening day. The excitement inside my chest was like a huge bird trapped in a small cage, flapping around in panic, suffocating me.

Nine forty-five. Just fifteen minutes 'til the doors were officially due to open, though mother had already unbolted them and was sitting at the desk just inside the barn ready to sell entry tickets .

'Are you *sure* you'll be all right?' I asked, worried about leaving her alone.

'What do you think I'll do, fall off the chair,' she said, back to her unnecessary sarcasm.

'Course not. But are you sure you'll be all right to sort out the money, say, if a crowd of people comes in all at once.'

'Freda, I'm a seventy year old sane woman. I can bid and get seven no trumps at the Bridge Club. I can do most of the cryptic crossword in The Times. I can cope with a daughter who dotes on her pig like an over-protective mother and her piglets as a fuss-pot grandmother. So don't go doubting my capability at coping with crowds.'

I started to leave, but turned back again. She and the large second-hand desk we bought last week were silhouetted against the brilliant June sunlight spilling in from the empty car park. The metal cash box glinted, in full view.

'Don't you think that should be hidden in the deep drawer,' I ventured. 'It contains twenty pounds worth of change.'

She snatched up the pad of numbered tickets beside the box and waggled it at me. 'And what about these, should I hide these away too! And then hide myself under the desk, or fold myself up in a drawer, in case a visitor intent on raping and pillaging comes in.'

'Just don't want twenty pounds stolen and you mugged,' I mumbled, knowing I was justifiably getting up her nose.

'Go off and see to the animals,' she snapped. 'You're keeping me from my book.'

As she spoke she withdrew a paperback from a drawer, its ghastly snot green cover displaying the title: *Bedding down with the farmer's wife*. She must have caught my look for she said.

'Don't worry, I *will* hide that when customers appear.'

'Good. I'll be off then. You're sure you can manage?'

She slammed her knuckles down on the desk and started to rear up, but the thinly disguised pain of the rash action made her plummet back down, hands clamped under her arm pits.

'I can take fivers off adults,' she said between obviously gritted teeth. 'And two pounds off children, and if people of mature age come too I'll charge them their concessionary price of four pounds and warn them to keep clear of you because you'll aggravate them into their graves.'

'Sorry, sorry, sorry,' I twittered, pecking her on the cheek, then really leaving.

'Georgie Christ!' I heard her mutter to herself, 'I thought she'd never go.'

As I entered the field through the doorway in the opposite long wall, I tried to imagine what it was like to be a visitor coming for the first time. The initial thing they would see was the sign Nesbit Batty had hurriedly made yesterday and stencilled in this morning. A red arrow pointed towards the newly mown show arena to the right and underneath were the bold black words:

PIGLET CHOW IN THE ARENA AT MIDDAY. DO NOT MISS IT.

Oh god. He'd been in such a rush he'd picked up a C instead of an S! I looked wildly about to see if miraculously Bernard was around with a marker pen in his hand but, of course, he wasn't. The only person I could see was Esmerelda leading Daisy out of her stable.

'Do you have a marker pen on you - preferably black?' I called, running down to her.

Esmerelda, a sardonic grin raked across her face, made play of searching for one about her person, then hauled a carrot out of a pocket asking if that would do instead.

'Hardly.'

'Didn't think so!'

She laughed then abruptly stopped, her dark eyes piercing into mine. 'You look wore out, en't things going right?'

I looked around the sunlit scene. Lardarse was gazing at me over the fence of his spacious compound, jaw swivelling as he contentedly chewed the cud. In the distance, Lairy was grazing, his plump little body gleaming white in the sunlight. Likewise, the now tethered Goolie and Goofy were also happily absorbed in nibbling grass, slowly circumnavigating their twirly whirly poles. Ducks quacked, geese honked and hens clucked. The glorious smell of new mown grass wafted in the air.

'Everything's fine,' I said, 'perfect, idyllic - just a letter on a sign needs changing.'

I focused on Daisy, almost under my nose. Her mane had been cut short like mine because of the singeing, but it seemed to be growing, and vestiges of fresh new fur were sprouting from the bald sore patches on her back. The angry red of her nose and hairless ears was gradually fading. As I gazed at her she suddenly leaned forward, muzzle close to my face, almost as if wanting to kiss me.

'You two got a special bond between you now,' Esmerelda observed without rancour. 'I don't know why you ever risked your life for my ... our ... your Daisy,' As she spoke her eyes were scouring my face. 'But you got good healing skin for one so freckled, your burns're fading fast.'

Tentatively, I fingered my face. With all the activity, my mind had been taken from the sore patches of red. And also, I suddenly realised, from the wax blobs the police found after the fire.

'There were some candles in a cupboard ...' I began.

But, a familiar voice called out my name and I turned to see Cynthia waving a ticket at me emerging from the barn. 'I'm your first customer,' she called triumphantly.

I patted Daisy, said goodbye, then ran up to my friend.

'Couldn't miss this spe...'

'Have you got a marker pen?' I cut in.

She gave me a funny look then delved into her shoulder bag. 'Nope. Funny that,' she replied. Then she grabbed my arm and towed me away in the direction of the gap.

'I've got a proposition to make,' she said.

'What kind of proposition?'

'Let me set up a tea room in one end of the barn - I'll fork out for everything, and run it, and you can take a percentage of any profit - it'll be like a kind of franchise.'

We stopped walking.

'Do you mean it!'

'Of course. I love baking biscuits and cakes, it's my hobby. And visitors would enjoy real home-made cooking. And maybe I'll do light lunches too. It'll help me as well as you. I've always wanted to run my own small catering business.'

'Are you sure?' I asked, staring in wonder at this short legged, wingless angel.

'Course I'm sure - especially now Sidney's finished being the mayor and has quit the Council. He clogs up the house. It'll give me a break away from him.'

'Yes, then. Yes please.' I kissed her on both rosy cheeks. 'When can you start?'

'As soon as I've bought tables, chairs, tablecloths, crockery, cutlery and everything that's needed, then set ...' She trailed off.

'What's up?'

'I'd forgotten. What about water and electricity in the barn?'

'You're okay,' I smiled, 'There was already electricity, but from years ago, so Robert Bambridge's men rewired it, and there was a mains tap outside which they plumbed inside. It was planned to be a tea room one day - we just didn't know how soon.'

'Cooee.'

Another familiar voice made me turn.

'Couldn't miss your opening,' called Poppy Bambridge. Then Robert appeared, his blond hair swirling as he hurried out from the barn.

He waved, handsome face alight.

'Just checking to see what the men had done,' he called. 'And wanting to be present on this auspicious day.'

Before I had time to greet them another familiar figure appeared, and another and another. And soon it seemed as if every child and parent from the village school and every Wood Hill villager was waving an entry ticket at me as they fanned out over the field.

'I must go and help mother, she'll be inundated.'

'No, you stay, I'll go and help her,' said Cynthia, catching hold of my arm. 'When the rush stops I can send your mother out for a break and sit there studying the barn - picturing my tea room.'

She hurried off and I stood in the sunshine greeting and chatting with neighbours and friends, the only cloud shadowing my happiness being the worry that there'd be nobody left to visit tomorrow - and for ever after.

As if the virtual reality of my earlier rose-tinted dream had magically changed to absolute reality, I watched eager children dragging parents around, heard the ones from the class I'd brought here on trial telling parents how brilliant the piglet display was to be.

Goofy and Goolie, both bright-eyed and bleating, strained eagerly towards Mrs Trugshawe as she approached them. I watched anxiously, saw with relief that as she passed their expressions were of rapture, like cigarette addicts inhaling someone else's smoke, and not of unrestrained lust. I wondered if we should put up a warning notice advising of the hazards of wearing Chanel Number Nineteen.

Pushing nightmare visions of headlines screaming *Goats rape visitor to new Animal Park* out of my mind, I wandered down to the stables and went inside, seeing excited children crowding round the chipmunk house laughing at their antics.

I left the happy scene and ambled towards the pig unit, now labelled PORKER PALACE. More nightmare visions of headlines screaming *Chanel sue new Animal Park for banning their Number Nineteen* broke into my head then ebbed away.

Bernard was in the yard holding up one piglet at a time, letting the children stroke them and answering questions. The rest of the piglets and Pot Belly Bella milled around his legs looking up at the faces peering over the wall at them, and I wondered who was most intrigued with what they saw, the humans or the swine.

I felt a tug at my arm and looked round to see Harry, he with the suspicious feet.

'Pigs can't sweat and they can get sunburnt so they should be under cover,' he admonished loudly.

And I marvelled at the knowledge of this petless boy. For he was right. Normally they'd go into the shade of their individual apartments of their own accord when the sun was too hot, but now they were too interested in all the people.

'Quite right,' said Bernard, who had overheard. 'And they need to rest before their show, so the piglets are going inside for an early siesta.'

'Apartments' he called loudly and, reluctantly, each piglet headed off to its room.

The impressed crowd dispersed and Bernard beckoned me over.

'I'd already worried about them getting burnt because there's no shade in the display arena, so I've bought tubes of special hypo-allergenic sunblock factor fifty to rub on them just before the show.'

'I'm very pleased to hear it,' said Harry, like an RSPCA spy lurking behind me.

I watched the people exploring the grounds and wished the tea room was already in existence. Not only must most of the crowd be in need of a sit-down and a drink, but a percentage of Cynthia's profits would be ours!

Mr Mole, father of Toby, one of the children at the village school, came over and pumped my hand enthusiastically. 'Well *done*,' he said, 'it's a great place, but there's one thing missing.'

'Oh. What?' I asked, annoyed. There were dozens of things missing, but today wasn't the day I wanted to hear about them. Shouldn't he know that.

'A play area for the kiddies when it's bad weather.'

So tell me about it, I thought, miffed.

'So some of the other dads and I have just been talking about it and we reckon between us we've got the skills and the time to design and make one - you just pay for the materials, we'll sort out the rest.'

'Do you mean it?' I asked, in an action replay of my response to Cynthia's tea room suggestion.

'Sure do,' he said grinning. 'We Wood Hill villagers always like to help a neighbour out, especially you.'

'Thank you, thank you,' I said, kissing both his rosy cheeks, in another deja vu experience. 'Show us the plans and we'll buy in the materials.'

As I said the last bit, a picture of my credit card, a heavy weight in place of the hologram, plummeted from a plane and bit the dust of our ground. But even as the film rolled, frolicking children played in the play area as their parents emptied their pockets to Cynthia.

I wandered around in a blissful daze. Possibly our Animal Park would put Wood Hill on the map, making it easier for helpful Mr Mole, our local Estate Agent, to sell houses. Maybe it could even push property prices up. And, being on the outskirts, the extra traffic wouldn't bother anyone. And all our animals would thrive. It was all turning out so well. Brilliant in fact.

I watched a young brother and sister laughing and jumping back and forth over winding rivulets running down from the spring. I followed a tributary down to the pond, saw children I knew throwing bread to the ducks. If we could divert a rivulet away, before it reached the pond, we could make a shallow miry pool where the pigs could wallow and coat their skins with protective mud. Cheaper, and more natural, than sunblock.

I glanced at my watch - just half an hour before the Piglet Show. I strolled across the garden towards the field, savouring sights, sounds and smells. Animated children were pointing out chickens with trousers, speckled hens, white crested bantams, poultry with fluffy hats. The fowl, both ornamental and otherwise, dutifully clucked and quacked, almost to order. Even Cussbert, somewhere unseen, let forth a rousing crow. If only he'd wait 'til this time every morning I thought, he being the only fly in the Animal Park ointment, as far as I was concerned.

Slowly I made my way towards the arena and a boy from the top class of the village school came running over.

'Mum says you can have Alma and Mike Baldwin, we don't want them any more,' he panted.

'Alma and Mike Baldwin!'

His mother hurried over, laughing.

'Alma's a beautiful soft doe with huge brown eyes,' she said, 'the most friendly gentle rabbit I've ever known.'

'How many's that?' I asked suspiciously. 'How many have you ever known?'

And she gave a wry smile, saying, 'Well, just the two actually, Alma and Mike Baldwin, I was speaking figuratively.'

'Why do you want to give them away?' I asked, desperately trying to think up a polite excuse not to take them.

'We go away each weekend and every school holiday and there's no-one to look after them.'

My mind went vacant. She stared at me quizzically, waiting for an answer, but the only thing that filtered into my head was the image of Nesbit's vile Dick gorging on our guinea pig.

'I had a bad experience with a neighbour's Dick,' I said, being careful not to name Nesbit.

'Haven't we all,' she said, rolling her eyes, and tipping her head towards her son in case I'd forgotten he was there.

'A rabbit called Dick,' I hastened to explain.

'So you're used to rabbits,' she burst out triumphantly. Then, wheedling, 'Please take Alma and Mike Baldwin, it would be such a load off my mind.'

The image of the assassin rabbit faded and my brain came out of its torpor. We had the empty hutch, still in the spare room of the mobile home. We also had the array of empty hutches that Carl had made. But still, once bitten by a finger mauling, guinea pig eating, rabbit, twice shy.

'It's kind of you,' I said, 'but no we don't want rabbits here.'

She groaned. 'I did think they'd be happy with you.'

It was nearly time for the piglet display and I wanted to get away from this persistent woman and get to the arena.

'Alma sounds okay,' I said briskly, 'bring her round some time.'

'But our Mike Baldwin would be devastated to have Alma taken away from him, he's not like Coronation Street's cocksure little spiv.'

It was nearly twelve o'clock!

'All right,' I snapped, 'we'll have them on a one week trial.'

As she bombarded me with effusive thanks I thought how lucky it was that we hadn't replaced the guinea pig so there was no new little creature for Alma and Mike Baldwin to gnaw on.

At last I arrived at the arena where nearly every bench seat was already full. I squeezed up on the end of one, next to Mrs Trugshawe.

'Oh hello Freda,' she said. 'Your goats are very friendly aren't they.'

I breathed in, smelling the distinctive perfume wafting from her. I opened my mouth then closed it again. She probably wouldn't re-visit, so there was no point.

By two minutes to twelve every visitor was sitting or sprawled out on the grass. I looked around. There wasn't a single stranger among them. But, if the piglet show was as brilliant as before, the word would surely spread.

I looked at my watch. It was time. Now it was up to Bernard. And our porkers.

'Mrs Field,' said Harry as he squeezed past me, 'Is a Piglet Chow a dog or a pig?'

'A spelling mistake,' I replied, knowing full well that he, an atrocious speller, just wanted me to admit it.

As the sound of the Sousa March started up, my skin burst out into goosepimples. And as Bernard, holding the tape recorder, followed by his amazing pink army hove into view, I shivered out of control. This was it. Our fate was held in the trotters of our grandpiglets.

Necks craned and a murmur of delighted disbelief blew through the crowd. I hugged my shaking body as our audience cheered.

They marched into the ring.

'STAY,' bellowed Bernard as if commanding a team of deaf dogs.

And laughter erupted as my babies bumped and squealed to a halt by the ramp in the centre. Now was the big test. How would the piglets react to an audience, and a large one at that? I continued to tremble with fear.

'SQU - AD, LE - FT TURN!' hollered Bernard as if addressing a section of the British army.

And with grunts of concentration and a shuffling of trotters they turned, some left, some right, till they were in a line all facing my way except Pudding and Lady who faced the crowd at the opposite side.

More laughter and applause greeted this and I saw the piglets' ears prick, watched their short-sighted eyes sharpen, saw their short necks crane, heard Duchess let out a frightened squeal, saw Princess go even pinker.

I saw Bernard's expression change to worry.

'TAKE YOUR BOWS,' he commanded.

And, thankfully, each one slowly spiralled in a complete circle as he had trained them, then knelt down, heads lowered.

And the applause was deafening.

My shivering subsided as the show progressed. They were superb. And when the climax came to Ravel's Bolero, the audience, as one, stood, calling *Bravo* and *Encore*, and I half expected red roses to be showered down.

And when my bright eyed Georgie-Jesus came speeding down the ramp, I half expected my swelling heart to literally burst with grandmotherly pride.

At five o'clock, after we'd shut the barn doors on the last of the visitors, I hared over to Porker Palace.

'You were all *brilliant*,' I extolled them as I opened the gate and they streamed out for their last meal of the day and their freedom time in the garden.

Draping myself over the top bar of the open yard gate, I lazily gazed up at them as they ate, seeing Mary and Pie finish first then race down to the spot where the broadest rivulets spilled out across the grass. I watched them as they splashed around, squealing and rolling in the icy water. And for a brief instant the son and daughter I never conceived were squealing and rolling there, and the old pain reared up like an ulcer you thought had gone. Georgie-Jesus, nose muddied through energetic rooting, trotted over to me. He looked up, smiling, and nuzzled my leg as if sensing my sorrow.

'You're my first-born grandchild,' I whispered down at him, 'and, as porkers go, I couldn't ask for better.'

I saw Hermione eyeing her released family from up by the cottage. Saw her eyes swivel to Kermit then her head jerk towards the mobile home. Saw the two of them slink off into the old yard, up the ramp, disappearing inside. I knew I'd have been a far more loving mum than she was if only I'd been given the chance.

Georgie-Jesus rubbed his head against my leg again. And I realised I had been given a chance, and this loving plump boy was part of it.

Bernard popped the cork and quickly filled a glass with the fizzing outpour of champagne. Then he filled the other three and handed them round.

'To our success,' he cried.

And we lifted our glasses, repeating, 'To our success.'

'Now I can tell you my secret,' said mother, taking a hefty swig.

I looked at father. *Mother's* secret. I thought the secret was his.

'You haven't got a secret Maeve, it's me ...' He trailed off casting me an uneasy look.

Mother stood up, went to a cupboard, took out a small bottle, came over to me, unscrewed the top and held it up under my nose.

'Smell *that*,' she said with pride.

I sniffed. 'What is it?'

'Isn't it fragrant,' she enthused.

'What?'

'This perfume.'

I sniffed again. Maybe there was the scent of something, but it was very faint and I didn't know what.

'I knew you wouldn't recognise it. No-one would. It's my own invention. Something to sell in the barn. The first item for your gift shop.'

'What the hell are you talking about,' roared father, all his old aggression resurfacing now he was feeling better.

'What I was doing when you came in and caught me at it,' mother said to me.

'Hope it was nothing disgusting,' said father, turning to Bernard. 'Come on, you don't want to listen to her nonsense, let's drink.' With that he glugged more champagne down and, despite the re-emergence of his domineering spirit, I was thrilled to see the progress he'd made since coming to stay. His colour was good. And his temper was bad. He was definitely almost back to his old self.

'Have you finished,' mother snapped at him, once again shoving the bottle back under my nose, then going over and doing the same to Bernard.

'What do you think of that?' she said, answering the question herself: 'Great isn't it.'

Bernard's strong nose wrinkled. 'That reminds me of something,' he said. 'There's the faint smell of hay.'

'That's it!' she whooped. 'See Freda, he's a better snitch on him than you. It's my newly invented perfume - remember when you caught me in the kitchen with the masher and the saucepan?'

I nodded, still not understanding.

'It was full of fresh hay boiled up in water and I was mashing the fragrance out of it.'

She placed the bottle on the table exposing its label. And there in carefully written gold lettering were the words *New Hay Perfume exclusive to the Fields.*

'See,' she said, 'even a double entendre - it'll sell like hot cakes.'

'More like cold pee,' guffawed father.

I stared at the yellow tinged water that did look remarkably like a urine specimen.

'Well done, ma-in-law,' said kindly Bernard. 'You've shown a lot of initiative there. It's a great idea. And maybe you could try out another batch made with lavender.'

Apparently fully satisfied, she sat down, cheeks flushed, smiling. He was right. She'd been trying. Trying to help us make a go of it.

I raised my glass. 'Here's to my inventive mother,' I said.

And after we'd all drunk that toast, I raised my glass again.

'And here's to my gutsy dad.'

Next morning I was so tired that even Cussbert's early morning call failed to catapult me out of bed and I drifted back to sleep.

'Come on Freda,' Bernard said shaking me. 'It's nearly nine - I've fed all the animals and mucked them out. We open up in an hour.'

And duly we opened up. And not one person came. Not for the morning. Not for the afternoon. Not for the whole day.

'Must have been because it was raining,' said Bernard.

And though I nodded, I didn't believe him. Everyone who ever intended to visit had come on the opening day. And that was it. Like a damsel fly, we'd had our one day of glorious life, and now we were dead.

That evening, walking around the grounds watching the piglets and Bella enjoying their freedom, I hardly had the strength to lift one foot after the other. It may have been the boggy ground that weighed them down. Or it may have been because all of the stuffing had been knocked out of my body into my boots.

I wondered how long the feed and straw would last before we were forced to shut down.

Twenty

Monday, I rang Green Veggie Reggie to tell him the trailer he'd left was full and, within half an hour, he was back with Butch in the Land Rover towing an empty replacement. Later, Bernard walked into the kitchen where I was making coffee. In his hand were five five pound notes which he waggled at me with glee.

'At least the money we're shovelling in at one end is coming out worth something at the other,' he said, 'so it's not all bad.'

'About five pee in the pound return I reckon,' father growled, taking his decaff from me.

'Not pee,' mother whooped, quick to see an opening. 'Shit!'

And we were all so relieved to have the fertiliser problem removed that we all laughed like sewers. But the jolliness didn't last long and glumness slowly drifted down on us like a dank sea mist extracting heat from a sunny beach.

Green Veggie Reggie and Butch turned out to be our only visitors. The sun shone on our garden of Eden, but the apple withered on the tree and my only temptation was to wring Cussbert's neck for wont of something more rewarding to do.

Tuesday, and it was almost as bad. The kindly sun came out enticingly at ten o'clock, but just three adults and five children were seduced enough to come out as well to visit us. Three times five pounds, and five times two. Twenty-five pounds all told - as much as a truck-load of dung. And that at the height of the season. Twenty-five pounds total income and dozens of mouths to feed, including my mother's which appears to take in the most.

And, even after bed-time, the misery continued. As soon as I'd finally drifted off into blissful sleep, Cussbert shot off a quick crow, waking me straight up again. But, as I tossed and turned in a vain attempt to regain unconsciousness, a plan slowly formed.

Next night about eleven, while Bernie was cleaning his teeth, I tiptoed out to the airing cupboard on the landing and removed our largest bath towel, then crept downstairs and out the back door, running quickly to the end of the garden.

As I drew near Cussbert's ark and en suite run I reasoned, as I had when I devised the plan, that it *had* to be the faint glimmer of early morning light that awoke him, compelling him to screech out the news to the world, so if I could block out all light, he wouldn't do it.

Stealthily I approached, knowing that Bernard had already done his nightly duty of shutting his darling safely inside. The air of the late June night was still, the sky glowing with faint warm light from the west and faint cold light from the rising moon.

Cussbert's head appeared, craning round from the archway of his ark, his startled eyes hardened as they settled on me. Uneasy cluckings quickly revved up to the high and low warbles of a teenager whose voice was on the turn. Adroitly, I flung the dark brown king size bath towel over the mesh of his run, engulfing his space in the total darkness of a full eclipse. Cussbert's loud squawking abruptly stopped. No winding down of sound. No gradual petering out like an engine deprived of petrol. Complete. Absolute. Immediate. Glorious silence. I'd found the solution! Unless the cussed bird had an alarm clock tucked away, the morning would break without the loud mouth knowing.

'You've been a long time,' said Bernard as I slipped under the duvet.

'Just went outside for a few minutes. It's a lovely moonlit night.'

At least I hadn't lied.

'That sounds romantic,' he said, taking my hand and gently placing it on his squidgy expanding bit.

Not *another* one to deal with, I thought, lying still, eyelids already heavily drooped in readiness for sleep. But he shook my shoulder complaining that we'd not had sex since mother and father had come.

'How d'you know when that was, been listening at their bedroom door,' I sleepily replied, attempting one of his sorts of joke.

'Come *here*,' he bellowed. And when I dutifully nudged up a little closer he said, 'I didn't mean you. I meant we've not had sex since your mother and father had come *here*.'

'There's so much to think about with the animals,' I murmured.

'*Precisely*,' he snapped. 'Whenever I try anything you just lie there half dead.'

'Well I'm tired,' I yawned.

'That's what I mean,' he said curtly, sighing heavily and humping over so his back was towards me like a spoilt school kid.

Fed up with his attitude and desperate for sleep, I nevertheless stupidly taunted him.

'Well why don't you *take* me like a man,' I recklessly said.

And with that he shot up, grabbed hold of my nightdress at the neck and with a grunt and an enormous tug he ripped it straight down.

'Is that man enough for you,' he snarled.

Astounded, I squealed out and thumped him on the chest, but he pushed me back and forced his hand over my newly exposed right breast.

'Is that you Bernard?' I asked the unknown dominant male in the darkness.

'No,' his voice answered. 'This is the *man* that you want.'

And suddenly, although my best nightie was ruined, the humour of it hit me and, as his expert hand began its seductive caress, mirth built up inside me and suddenly burst out in an uncontrolled roar.

'Go on. Go on then,' he reproached bitterly. 'Go on and ruin it. There's no pleasing you. Go on, spoil it all by cackling at my expense.'

And I did. I couldn't help it. Couldn't stop. That was my best nightie made of fine white lawn, a replacement for the one ruined in the fire, and the normally gentlemanly Bernie had just ripped it in half and somehow it seemed such a scream.

'Don't know what's so funny,' Bernard said sullenly.

And somehow that set me off even more and torrents of screeching giggles gushed from me in a series of bubbling cascades.

Imperceptibly, reluctant sniggers started up from Bernard, slowly transforming to noisy snorts then exploding into full-blown hysterics.

'Am I man enough for you now?' he gasped, taking me in his arms and once again taking advantage of his bodice ripping act.

And, gradually I found I was no longer as tired as I had thought. And, besides, when the love making was all over, at least I could go to sleep assured of a lie-in with Cussbert safely shut away in the totality of darkness under the towel.

The raucous reveille bit into my dormant brain like acid etching into metal. I stretched my arms and smiled to myself knowing that, although I still felt dead beat, it would have to be late. I turned to look past sleeping Bernard to the glowing red digits of the clock. Four forty-five! Four fucking forty-five!!! Bloody bumptious big-mouth bird. F words and B combined in an onslaught of inner cursing.

I tottered out of bed, torn fabric flapping. Then, knowing I'd never get to sleep again, stomped downstairs and spent 'til breakfast time trying to mend the nightdress, all the time wondering how I'd ever found such wanton vandalism funny.

The banging, sawing and general clatter of people at work came from the barn. I poked my head in and, through my fatigue haze, saw Nesbit, amazingly being aided by Sidney, constructing a counter for the tea room, and several men I recognised as fathers from the school erecting colourful apparatus in the children's rough and tumble area. A ramp and raised walkway that led, through a rope spider's web, to a short slide, had already been put in place.

'That looks *fantastic*,' I gasped.

'Just you wait,' said Mr Mole, beaming. 'You ain't seen nothing yet.'

'Is that old dresser okay for you?' asked Mr Trugshawe, pointing.

And there, behind the desk by the barn doors, stood a huge old pine dresser with shelves and cupboards.

'Thought you could display gifts on it,' he said. 'What do you think?'

'I think it's brilliant,' I said, rubbing my eyes, wondering if I were still asleep.

But, even as I spoke, I worried that all this time and effort and credit spent was a waste because no visitors or coach parties had booked to come, despite our advertisements.

Vernon Veal rang to say he couldn't make his usual monthly call on the twenty-eight of June because he was going off on holiday for a fortnight. Going off to have time to work out how to make poor innocent animals say *Oh that was gorgeous Vernon* or to set up a spare parts factory using modified pigs, I thought sniffily.

When I asked where he was going he said Africa, to watch big game. He sounded over the top excited and I wondered if the game wardens would miss a zebra or giraffe or other such wild animal in all that space, especially if just removed for one day. But, at least with our prime suspect out of the country, we had no need for night-time animal borrower watch duties this month I thought happily as I replaced the phone.

A plump zebra is wired up to Vernon's laptop and Vernon keeps jabbing a cruel spike into its tender side. Sharp angular peaks and troughs show up on the small LCD screen and Vernon smiles. A lion in the long dry grass prowls towards him. Slowly. Silently. Skulking low. Suddenly it pounces, its claws ripping into Vernon's back. He screams and I think what a pity he isn't wired to the laptop. The lion draws his talons down and down the vile vet's body, over and over, shredding him to bloody bits and, taking his chance, the zebra gallops away, laptop still attached.

It runs and runs, through long grass, through scrubland, into a jungle of trees where it collapses onto the ground, panting.

A familiar dark figure totters into the scene, staggers to the stripy creature which lies, tongue lolling, half dead. He spies the poor animal and gazes at it with dark shining eyes, then he bends down and strokes the laptop. He looks up to heaven. He says: It's a miracle Lord, I, Desmond Tutu was lost, but thanks to you I am found. Tenderly, he detaches the computer from the zebra, connects it to his mobile and sends out an e- mail for help.

'You're making noises in your sleep.' Bernard's far off voice cut into my consciousness. I felt his warm hand clasp my shoulder and gently shake it. 'What's up?' he asked.

'Laptop ... zebra.'

There was silence, then: 'Is that like Lardarse llama?'

'Stupid,' I sniggered, not opening my eyes.

'What's a laptop zebra then?'

'Vernon Veal was prodding a zebra in Africa,' I slurred.

'What disgusting dreams you have!' he said, edging up to me so I could feel his prodder at the ready.

Mother and father were at the table eating breakfast when Bernard came rushing into the kitchen. 'Lairy's missing,' he panted, 'can't find him anywhere.'

Plunging down the cafetiere knob, I stared at him aghast.

'He can't be. It's only one week since Vernon Veal rang - he's still abroad.'

'No. No. I mean Yes Yes. Yes he is. I've searched everywhere. Lairy has gone. Someone must have taken him last night.'

'Don't worry,' said mother soothingly, 'if the animal borrower has taken the lamb he'll soon bounce back, they always do.'

'Just a pity it's one of the animals that eats free grass and not one you have to *buy* food for,' growled father, cutting off a large section of his toast piled high with baked beans, mushrooms and scrambled eggs and shoving it into his mouth.

'I agree,' mumbled mother, cheeks bulging like a hamster filled to the eye sockets with grub.

'The lamb *can't* have gone,' I stated firmly, pouring coffee into mugs. 'You've missed him somewhere.'

'Okay, you go out and double check,' said Bernard wearily. 'If that's got caffeine in I'll have some.'

He flopped down, put his elbows on the table and shut his eyes.

I went outside to look and half an hour later Bernie joined me.

'You're right,' I groaned, 'I've searched every outbuilding, every nook and corner, every blade of grass. I've asked Esmerelda and Nesbit and the rest of the workers in the barn but they've not seen him. And they swear they've kept the back doors shut. Lairy has well and truly vanished and it can't be Vernon Veal.'

'Could be a copycat or, should I say, copylamb abduction,' said Bernard flippantly, his catnap apparently having revived the joke cells in his brain.

'Could be Vernon has an accomplice, such as a wife,' I put in, for the first time wondering whether such a weird person as our vet could have such a thing as a wife.

'Or a male partner,' said Bernard, meaningfully.

Mother wandered over. 'One good thing,' she said, 'none of the paying visitors will notice Lairy's missing because we haven't got any. Not one person in three days. Still, I'll have to go over and open up at ten, just in case.'

She didn't need to remind me.

I gazed at our glorious Animal Park. It was Tuesday June the twenty-ninth and the sun flamed as it was meant to. Animals grazed. Water fowl, exotic fowl and every other kind of fowl busied themselves, preening, pecking, swimming or sleeping. An occasional squeal or snort came from Porker Palace where the piglets rested in their apartments until their performance. Wild birds twittered and sang.

I wandered into the barn, to the end where the rough and tumble play area was now ready, hundreds of small plastic balls having just been tipped into the large padded open-topped box at the end of the slide. It all looked wonderful. Everything in brilliant primary colours. Everything new. The only thing needed being children.

New red and white checked tablecloths covered new square tables, with new chairs neatly tucked under them. Everything looked perfect. Too perfect. Perfectly dead.

The door of the Ladies opened, and Cynthia came out.

'What do you think then?' she said proudly, entering her domain, shifting a minutely crooked chair a fraction as she passed on her way to the counter.

'I think it's all ... it's all ... too much. And I'm sorry you've wasted your money.'

'No, no. I haven't wasted my money. It's been worth more than this lot cost to get away from Sidney. And, besides, the people *will* come.'

'Lairy's gone missing,' I burst out, 'and I wish the person who's stolen him would gradually take all our creatures away one by one and not return any of them because we can't afford to keep them.'

And when I'd finished that dreadful sentence I found that I was crying and mother, who'd just come in to open up, was thrusting a tissue at me. And in the midst of emotional noseblowing I heard Bernard, who I hadn't known had entered, exude a deep deep sigh, a moaning sound of utter defeat that gave my heart a headache and set me off sobbing again.

'Come on,' said Bernard eventually, 'come with me outside.'

We mooched away but hadn't got far before mother was calling after us to wait.

'I've opened the doors and asked Cynthia to keep an eye on them,' she puffed, catching up. 'Pointless in two of us wasting our time waiting for non-existent visitors.'

She didn't mean those words to upset me, but they did, and the tears started flowing again.

'Excuse me,' a man's voice called out, 'ze voman inside told me to come into die animal garten to find somevun to take zie money.'

'Quick, wipe your nose and pull yourself together you're a big girl now,' ordered mother. 'I'll run back and sell him a ticket.'

'We have lift-off,' whispered Bernard, squeezing my arm.

I peered at the owner of the voice, hoping my red-rimmed eyes wouldn't scare him back to Germany or wherever he came from. But he turned and headed back to the barn with mother, so all I could see was the back of his balding pate.

As I stared after them wondering if he'd try to pay in Deutschmarks, a movement by the stables caught the corner of my eye. I turned and what I saw made me catch my breath, for the top of a familiar tiny head was emerging at ground level from behind the end wall. And, slowly, the whole sweet rotund body on four fragile legs came into view. And it was Lairy, head down, wholly absorbed in grazing.

Lairy my lamb! Returned from being borrowed, ahead of time.

I didn't mean it about hoping all the animals would gradually be taken away I silently told any spirit who might be tuned in to my inner wavelength as I ran towards the sweet little sheep. But I knew that this mollifying thought couldn't rectify the damage done by my carelessly spoken words, because those words were lodged inside *my* head to be dredged up ad nauseum whenever I was on a guilt binge.

The man came back out with mother and another woman. From a distance the woman looked how our Queen Mother would have looked if she'd had red hair. The finely pleated skirt of her pale pink and powder blue dress billowed in the light breeze and my stomach tightened at the knowledge that my father was close to proving a connection to the grey haired one. I hastened to them.

'Otto Schwartzkopf,' he said, shaking my hand vigorously, 'comen to see your schvine kinder display - I haf been told it is gut.'

'You've been told right,' extolled mother, 'just you wait till midday and you'll see.'

'And my wife Helga,' he introduced.

I shook her ring-laden hand and winced at its unexpected crushing force. She didn't feel like our gentle royal maybe-relation and, close to, she looked nothing like her, maybe just the fluffy shape of her ginger hair. Her eyebrows resembled arched strips of orange peel which clashed harshly with the bright cyclamen lips.

'Ver iss everybody?' she asked, fingering a long necklace of massive pearls which hung navel length, its flashy clasp askew against her plump neck.

'Good question,' I replied.

The muffled trill of a phone came from the white bag that hung on her shoulder. Deftly she hoiked out the mobile, holding it to her ear drawing attention to a thick wrist bedecked with bracelets and an oblong watch with two sets of hands and dials.

'Ya,' she said, 'Ve are now here in ze Animal Park. Ya, the last time I talk to you ve vere in ze car. Ya, really, no wires. It vas moving.' She rolled her eyes at us and mouthed *sorry*. 'I do not know how the radio waves keep up with my voice. Ya, maybe it iss the other way around. Now excuse me please I vant to see vhat iss here.' There was a pause then, very aggravated. 'Ya, maybe it iss done mit microwaves. Nein, my ear iss not cooking. Nor iss my brain. Goodbye.'

'What kind of idiot was that,' asked mother tactlessly.

'An English one,' she replied with a smile that smacked too much of gloating satisfaction for my liking.

I looked down at her short fat feet encased in white peep-toe sandals and felt like stamping on them. Instead I made my excuse to leave saying I had to run the piglets through the shower.

Otto's bushy eyebrows shot up in surprise.

'She has to get them spruced up for the piglet show,' mother explained.

Now Helga's orange peel eyebrows shot up. 'Spruce ist ein tree iss it not?'

But I didn't waver in my escape, leaving mother to clear up the confusion.

In the shower room, I hosed down each piglet in turn with the icy spring water that they loved, zapping them with vigorous energy, roughly drying off each one as it left. So, we only had two people in the audience, but we had to keep up standards.

At twelve o'clock I was sitting on one of the bench seats with the Schwartzkopfs. From the first rousing strains of the Sousa march when the piglets and Bernard arrived to the final act when Jesus skateboarded down the ramp, they were clearly entranced.

'Mein Gott,' Otto kept saying, interspersed with Helga's gasps of 'Vunderbar' and 'Bravo.'

As the piglets took their final twirling bows Helga turned to me, face alight. She lifted her long loop of pearls and flung it round her neck with joyful abandon. Her eyebrows met in a fleeting MacDonald sign. She clutched her hands together then sunk them deep into the cleft of her bosom.

'It vass *awesome*,' she whispered.

And then, after hand pumping goodbyes, they left. And we were alone again with our eating machines.

'At this rate,' said Bernard dolefully at supper time, 'we'll have to close down in thirty days.'

'Better contact the Menabillys to learn how to find suckers who'll take on a job lot,' said mother brightly. 'They were brilliant at offloading theirs.'

Twenty-one

Mother puffed into the kitchen.

'Just walked into the village for some fresh bread,' she said, handing over a crusty bloomer from a carrier bag. 'Here, take a sniff at that.'

She wafted it under my nose.

'Mmm. Delicious,' I drooled, my inner being trying to ward off the aromatic temptation that I knew had the miraculous power to put on more weight than it weighed itself.

'A woman in the shop was saying there's gypsies camping in the woods - and not for the first time apparently.'

My mind, fully occupied with the battle to resist tearing off a hunk of bread and gobbling it down, only slowly filtered meaning into the words.

'Don't you see,' said mother. 'They could be the ones swiping your animals, not Vernon Veal.'

At last I gave in and ripped off a wad and, like a hooked fish, crammed the enticing bait into my mouth.

'Do they come to the woods once a month?' I mumbled.

'She didn't say once a month, she just said they come and go.'

As I inwardly lamented my capitulation to the fat-making lure, at the same time wilfully contemplating tearing off another bit, I tried to picture a gypsy creeping into our grounds down our sideway, or maybe through the gate in the boundary hedge linking Esmerelda's garden and the lower field. I tried to imagine him deciding which animal to borrow. The picture of a gypsy formed in my head. A swarthy face, black hair, dark mystical eyes. A face that, I suddenly realised, could be Esmerelda's. Maybe they were her relations? Maybe they were the sisters she once spoke of - her circle of friends?

I decided to go to the woods to spy on them, hopefully unseen, and not to tell anyone where I was going. A bad decision as it transpired.

'Just going to drive round to see Cynthia,' I lied to Bernard. 'Want to talk to her about the tea room.'

He and mother were relaxing for once, reading papers in the sitting room. Father was, as usual, up in the attic on the trail of his mother. It was seven p.m.

As I drove down Bramble Lane and turned into Primrose Hill, I wondered what on earth I was expecting to discover. Wondered even if I'd find out where the gypsies were camping. The woods were vast but I'd worked out the clearing I would choose if I were a traveller with a caravan, but if they weren't there I had no other idea.

After about a mile I spotted the *Mad Bess Glade Car Park* sign and turned into the rough patch of ground, seeing just one other vehicle - a red shooting brake - at the far end. I locked the car then set off briskly down the broad bridle path, observing imprints of horses' hooves and the faint pattern of tyre treads in patches of soft ground. I remembered years ago Bernard and I had lugged a picnic basket along this broadly curving path to the clearing known as Mad Bess Glade which flanked the near bank of a gently-flowing stream. There we'd stretched out on the short grass and kissed and cuddled like teenagers, though we'd been married for a good ten years. Hidden from view by the trees and bushes behind us and the barrier of dense bushes and silver birches across on the far bank, we'd been in our own private world, the only sounds the gurgling of water where it broadened to a ford, and the twitterings of birds. And my sudden squeal as a mosquito bit my bare bottom, I remembered, smiling.

Now, the sudden grating shout of a man came from the direction of the hidden glade, followed by a woman's scream.

I halted, shivering, wishing I hadn't come, wishing I'd told Bernard the truth of where I was going. A distant argument flared up, ugly, indistinct. At least the woman was still alive! I hugged myself, wondering if they were the gypsies or the people from the red shooting brake. Or other people. Dog walkers? Murderers! Fear gripped me by the scruff of the neck and shook the breath from me.

I turned back, hurried away, stopped, breathed in deeply, dithered. Didn't I want to know if the gypsies were the ones borrowing our animals. Wasn't I brave enough? Hadn't I rescued Daisy from an inferno? Was I really scared of a walk in the woods with some far-off shouting?

I turned back again, noticed a beaten track leading off to the left and, on sudden impulse, turned down it. This way would be safer. I would reach the clearing from behind, look into it from the cover of the woods without revealing myself. Brambles tore at my jeans and tall fronds of fern hit my face as I plunged deeper into the thick undergrowth, all signs of a track disappearing. Half remembered tales of the ghost of Mad Bess who had haunted these woods since she'd been murdered a hundred years ago set me shivering again.

The piercing chatter of a bird adjacent to my ear made me scream out and turn to run, but a trailing bramble grabbed hold of my sweater holding me captive. Moaning, I twisted round, carefully trying to disengage its thorns, but quickly abandoning caution and ripping myself free.

The agitated chattering continued alerting my dangerous presence to other birds. To other humans too? I wondered, trying to retrace my steps. I pushed back the twigs of a bush but abruptly the bird's harsh chatter ceased. I dithered again. What was there really to be frightened of? Modern gypsies weren't murderers, besides, I hadn't even established they were there. I'd come this far. I could go a bit further.

Sweating in the cool shade of the tall trees, I pushed through ferns, brambles and nettles, at last hearing the gurgle of the stream, at last coming to another trampled pathway, at last able to make unimpeded headway.

Ahead, shafts of sunlight cut through the gloom. Knowing I was nearly there, I eagerly strode out causing twigs to crack sharply underfoot. Immediately the deep ferocious barking of what could only be a large dog erupted. Then other yelping barks joined in.

I dived behind a holly bush, stood there half-crouching, yearning to be in the safety back home. I took a deep breath to calm myself, smelling, as I did so, the faint smell of smoke in the air. Terrible sounds and pictures blazed into my head. *Don't be a coward*, I rebuked myself, *the stable fire is in the past, forget it, let it die. And, if the gypsies are ahead, they won't hurt you. Their dogs are bound to be chained.*

I straightened, forced myself to take a step forward towards the sunlight shafting through from the clearing. I heard a man and a woman laughing together and the clink of metal. And at last I was at the wooded boundary peering around a tree into the clearing.

Across the other side, a long metal motor caravan gleamed silver in the low sun's rays, the swanky modern type you see at fairgrounds. A large mongrel, chained to one of its wheels, lifted its head turning gleaming eyes in my direction, pricking its ears. I stayed motionless and it settled down again.

An old-fashioned wooden caravan, in complete contrast to the other, was parked further along. It was painted dark green with red and cream flowers decorating every panel. Open shutters coloured in lively swirls flanked arched windows. An old bicycle leant against one of its wooden shafts, a twiggy besom against a wheel.

Two piebald horses were tethered nearby, at a distance from each other. The nearest to me turned its head and whinnied, pawing the ground. A rough looking man opened the door of the silver van, jumping down the steps. I held my breath, but he merely walked over to the dying camp fire, lifting a stick and poking at it, sending sparks flying, shooting images of other flying embers painfully into my mind. I closed my eyes until the pictures had gone. When I opened them I saw the man was bounding back up the steps. Without a backward glance, he disappeared inside.

I shifted, leaning forward to look round to the left, spying a tethered nanny goat grazing in the shadow of a tree. Further into the shadows, a chicken could be seen, its milk white feathers flecked with black.

A fat old woman appeared at the open doorway of the old fashioned caravan. She seemed to look in my direction and I ducked quickly back.

'Here chicky chicky,' she called, throwing down some corn, and the chicken I'd spotted, and two others, came running to it.

A twig cracked behind me and, too late, I realised someone was stealing up behind. I spun round, heard the stealthy movement transform to open running, saw the bulky dark figure of a man and a large alsatian hove out of the bushes, charging towards me, the dog barking ferociously at the sight of me.

Fear hammered pain into my temples and I ran for it, out into the open space of the clearing.

'Get her boy!' the man's rough voice yelled, and I heard the pounding of paws, heard the panting excited breath, looked back to see the powerful dog about to leap at me.

'Keep it off me,' I screamed, stumbling, falling to the ground.

'STAY,' called the man.

And the dog halted, close, menacing, quivering, snarling, wild eyed.

'Keep it off,' I screamed again, crawling back, awkwardly rising.

'He won't touch you if you don't run.'

But I didn't believe him. The dog crouched, growling, lips curled back from stained teeth, eyes fixed on my neck.

I put my hands up to my throat and screamed louder.

'Here boy,' the man said, patting the front of his thigh.

And the dog stood, panting, tongue lolling, disappointment in its mean eyes. Reluctantly, it dragged its gaze from me then padded back to him.

'Stay,' the man ordered, holding a flat hand up to the dog, then striding to me, roughly grabbing my arm in a strong painful grip.

'What's your game! You spyin' on us?'

'No. No, just interested,' I protested, trying to pull away.

'You come with me, see what someone else got to say about this.'

'No, I must get home,' I cried struggling.

'Not 'til you've answered a few questions,' he snarled, dragging me across the clearing. 'Heel boy,' he called back, releasing the dog from its obedient standstill.

I struggled harder but was no match against his strength and when the dog bounded to us I gave up trying, allowing myself to be dragged past the growling mongrel tugging at its chain.

'Look what I've found,' the man called as he hauled me up the steps of the picturesque caravan, dragging me in, slamming the door shut behind us, leaving the alsatian outside.

The fat old woman I'd seen before dried her large hands on her apron as she came towards me, beady eyes boring into mine. She scratched her large hooked nose then hitched up her ample bosom.

'What the bloody hell d'you think you're up to son,' she groaned. 'Let her go, you'll get us all put in clink.'

'She hasn't been for ne'er on five months, but I knew she'd come back,' he said, releasing his grip.

'What do you mean?' I cried, rubbing my arm. 'I haven't been to Mad Bess Glade for years.'

'You was acting suspicious, don't deny it.' He turned to the woman. 'Ma, she were skulking behind a tree, spying on the goat.'

'Sit down,' the old woman said to me, indicating a padded bench seat built into the wall. 'He was worried you was going to borrow our nanny for a while.'

Then she turned to her son, blaring, 'Do she look the sort to return things - look at her.'

What does she mean? I thought.

'What do you mean?' the man echoed.

'All that untidy curly red hair and green eyes and ripped blue jeans. Gorgios like that never return things.'

'Red hair and green eyes don't mean nothing,' he grunted.

'Maybe not, but women wearing torn trousers and torn sweaters don't bother 'bout nothing like returning things. I can tell yo ...'

'Have you had animals borrowed too?' I cut in.

The man's dark eyes lit up with surprise. 'What d'you mean, too?'

'My animals keep disappearing, but they always come back. When I heard you gypsies were in the woods, and not for the first time, I suspected you might be taking them. I put two and two together ...'

'Making five,' he grumbled.

'Same as you apparently,' chided his mother, flashing a one-toothed grin at me. 'D'you want a cup of something m'dear, no offence about your apparel, it's up to you, and you can't help your hair, we got Earl Grey.'

'Ordinary tea would be lovely,' I said, slightly mollified and slightly miffed.

'With sugar, by the looks of the paleness of your face - hot sweet tea for a shock, you're as white as our albino rat - he got borrowed, and that were no joke.'

The man must have seen my puzzlement.

'She thinks the white rat brings us good luck,' he explained. 'Most of our clan think it's white heather, she's gotta be different.'

She glared at him. 'Well he does bring us luck. It was proved. In the twenty-four hours he were away from us bad luck showered down on us, especially on me 'cos I cut me finger off.' She held up a truncated digit finger and waggled the stump at me.'

'Coincidence,' he scoffed, 'shouldn't have been doing yer whittling with such a sharp knife.'

'And it were a coincidence that yer dad died that very night and as soon as the rat were returned he came alive again.'

'Ma, you know he were drunk.'

'Drunk people don't stop breathing and lie on their backs with their eyes open.'

'Well me Da did. And why can't you get out there and sell lucky white heather like the others, make us some dough,' he grumbled.

'It's lucky white rats for me,' she said sullenly.

I imagined a white rat tucked into a button hole and, despite the fear still floundering around inside me, must have smiled.

'See, the gorgio thinks it's funny,' said the man. Then, 'Come on Carrot Head, I'll see you back to yer car.'

'Where on earth have you been?' cried Bernard. 'I was worried about you.' Tenderly, he took me in his arms and suddenly I began to cry. 'What's happened? It's dark. I rang Cynthia but she said you'd never got there.'

The warmth of his embrace, his tender concern, made me howl louder.

'I didn't ever mean to go to Cynthia's,' I confessed. 'I'm sorry. Can't explain why I lied.'

Footfalls sounded on the stairs then mother appeared. 'Told you,' she said triumphantly. 'She was like this as a kid. Always saying she was going to her friend's house then skiving off down the rec.'

Bernard led me into the sitting room, guiding me to the sofa, gently lowering me down then sitting beside me.

'Hermione never lounges here any more, not now she's got Kermit to think about,' I sniffed, sidetracked by the sofa's pigless state.

'Never mind Hermione, what about you, what's happened. Your sweater's torn. Have you been attacked?'

His worried eyes stared into mine, like clouded sapphires. God I did love him.

'I'm sorry Bernie, but I've found out the gypsies aren't the ones who borrow our animals.'

Bernard ran his fingers through his dark silver flecked hair. He turned to mother.

'Maeve, *you* mentioned the gypsies ...'

'Don't blame me for Freda's peculiarities,' she snapped. 'I just reported back what I heard down the shops - that the gypsies were in town. End of story.'

'I went to find them, to Mad Bess Glade where we had the picnic once, remember? To see if they might be the animal borrowers,' I snuffled.

And dear Bernard, instead of being angry, took my hand and squeezed it, creating considerable pain, not to my burns which had stopped hurting, but to my arthritic metacarpals which recently had been giving me gyp.

'And?' demanded mother impatiently.

'And they thought *I* was the animal thief, and one of them, a strong rough man, captured me.'

Bernard gasped.

'But he was only rough for a little while, until his mother came into it, and he held his alsatian off so it didn't bite me.'

'We'll get the police on them,' said Bernard angrily, jumping to his feet.

'No, no. They were nice people really. They gave me tea and we talked about white rats for luck, then he escorted me back to the car park. The red shooting brake had gone.'

'Red shooting brake!' said father, entering the room.

'Don't ask,' said mother, 'I'm losing the plot.'

'Father, I'd almost forgotten you were staying here, you spend so much time in the attic.'

'Yes and I'm almost there,' he said, tapping the side of his nose and winking.

'Almost not there - doolally more like it,' said mother whose kindliness towards him was disappearing in direct proportion to the rate of disappearance of the side effects of his chemo.

'The gypsies,' prompted Bernard gently. 'What did you find out?'

'That their animals had been pinched, then returned, every month when they camped in Bad Bess Glade. Up until March that is, when whoever the animal borrower is, switched from their animals to ours.'

'But why did he capture you?' asked Bernard.

'Because he was on the lookout for someone behaving suspiciously.'

'And that'd be you all right,' confirmed mother.

'Oh yes, that'd be Freda,' added father with relish.

'So long as you're safe,' said Bernie softly, crunching my metacarpals again.

'I suppose the gypsies were upset when their animals were borrowed because it delayed their meals,' said mother.

'You do talk rot Maeve, what in god's name do you mean?' roared father.

Guiltily, I realised I preferred him weak and drowsy and trying to be nice so we'd have happy memories of him than almost fully recuperated like this.

'We all know gypsies eat hedgehogs,' explained mother, rolling her eyes with the exasperation of explaining the obvious. 'So if their cherished hedgehog was taken they'd have to improvise with another meal until it was returned.'

'Lucky they don't have an *eat-by date* stamped onto them,' guffawed father.

'What don't?' I asked, losing the drift as I often did with my parents.

'*Hedgehogs*, obviously hedgehogs,' said mother rolling her eyes again, this time at my personal stupidity. 'She was always slow on the uptake,' she informed Bernard, smiling conspiratorially at father.

He did not smile back. 'Not only hedgehogs you silly bitch. Rabbits too.'

'Rabbit stoo!' shrieked mother. 'Get it. Rabbit stew.'

I'd had enough. I stood, glared from mother to father, then back again.

'I was really scared out there in the woods, and it's taken it out of me. I'm going up to bed.'

'Me too,' said Bernard, hastily following me out of the room.

'Sex mad,' I heard mother pronounce to father as we reached the stairs.

'Always was,' father replied.

'Doesn't take after you ...'

In bed, Bernard put his arm over me. 'Don't do that again,' he whispered. 'Not knowing where you were - I was terrified.'

'Not as much as I was,' I said, stroking his arm. 'And, despite all that trauma, we still don't know who the animal borrower is.'

'You've narrowed the field, though. It's definitely not the gypsies,' he sniggered.

I snuggled in to him. 'Should have known,' I said drowsily

'Known what?'

'Known it wasn't that burly gypsy, his feet were too big, though there must have been other smaller-footed ones around.'

Vaguely I drifted to sleep.

I know it is Tom Tom the Piper's son. I can see him. Running. Running away from me, a piglet tucked under one arm. I give chase and a hedgehog bounds up to me, all joyful like. Mother appears and runs alongside, pouring sludgy clay over it, wiping the smile off its pretty pointed face. 'One for the pot' she says, grabbing up the mud ball with protruding legs and dashing to a cauldron that dangles over a blazing fire. And I don't know which one to save. Poor piglet or poor hedgehog. But you can't cuddle a hedgehog so I set off after Tom Tom the Piper's son who has stolen my pig and away has run.

'You small-footed fucking pervert' I shout after him. 'I'm gonna get you.'

Twenty-two

Feeling like a naughty schoolgirl, I crept down the garden to Cussbert's night-time secure haven. Bernard was safely ensconced in a steaming bath and I was on a mission of revenge. As I lifted the hinged mesh side of the rooster's run, his arrogant eyes stared unblinking at me. Carefully, I positioned a two-belled alarm clock on the patchy grass by his feet. With a cluck of consternation he backed away into the ark where he stood in the opening, eyes darting between me and the clock, baleful dislike and apprehensive perplexity alternating with each sharp look.

'Sweet dreams old cock,' I whispered, 'but they won't last long - see how *you* like it.'

I think I laughed.

Silently he backed away out of sight into the darkness of his bedroom.

'What are you doing down there at this time of the evening?' mother called out, running towards me.

I froze. That was the last thing I wanted, my mother witnessing this! But quickly she reached me.

'Just putting the alarm clock in with Cussbert,' I admitted, avoiding her eyes.

'Are you all right in the head?' she asked, reaching her hand up to my forehead as if checking for fever.

'Perfectly,' I replied, shaking her off, bending to clip the mesh flap shut again, seeing Cussbert eyeing the clock with uncertainly from the safety of his ark.

'You did say putting an *alarm clock* in?' mother said.

I nodded.

'Do you have to give him a reminder call then?' she asked, looking astounded.

'No. He wakes me up too early every morning ... so I'm giving him a taste of his own medicine ...' I petered out, knowing I sounded pathetic.

'Didn't think you'd ever become a cock teaser,' mother said, killing herself, 'not at your age at any rate.'

'Very funny mother. The idea is that the alarm will wake him at three and he'll be too tired to crow then, and the disturbed night will make him get up late.'

She stared at me with the same look of pity that she used to give me when I practised my violin.

'And if *he* gets up late then I stand a chance of lying in till, maybe even, seven,' I explained, flaring, 'It's all right for you - you're in the front bedroom.'

Still she mutely stared at me. And I realised what a brilliant word dumbfounded was, for that was what she was, dumbfounded, and it took a lot of doing to dumbfound my ma.

'*And* I get my revenge on the bloody bird,' I yelled into the still dumbfounded silence, and marching away, cheered by the knowledge that at least she could no longer haul me back and send me to bed early.

'Wait till I tell you father,' mother threatened.

And I almost turned round and stuck my tongue out at her!

'Cock - a - doodle - doo,' the cock screamed, throat strained to its absolute screeching limit.

I turned over to look at the glowing digits. Seven-o-five. It worked!

I leapt out of bed, skipped out to the bathroom punching each fist in the air. If I could set the alarm clock every night I could get two more hours sleep each morning.

At breakfast, I confessed my jubilant news about Cussbert's delayed awakening.

'You woke Cu*th*bert up with an alarm clock at *what* time!' exploded Bernard, pronouncing the *th* over-strongly, like a kid with a lisp.

'But it worked,' I cried.

'Either that or the sleeping pill I slipped him,' said mother dryly.

Bernard reared up to his feet, eyes flashing like laser strobes. 'I will *not* tolerate my cock being woken with an alarm clock or being artificially sedated,' he roared.

And I thought: That is the trouble with owning a cockerel, it leads to such vulgar ambiguity. An ambiguity confirmed by mother's sniggers and mutterings about Viagra and my father.

And father, getting the gist, reared up to his feet too, so forcefully his half moon glasses shot half way down his nose.

'I'm off,' snarled Bernard, 'to muck out the pigs.' Then he twirled round like a prima donna and flounced out.

'And I'm off too, up to the attic,' growled father, shoving his glasses back up, 'to log on to the net.' He stomped off muttering, 'In cyberspace there's people with more common sense than you.'

'Nice pair we married,' commented mother raising one nostril in a cockeyed sniff as she gathered up dirty dishes, taking them to the sink and rinsing them off. 'Did you know the drain's blocked?' she asked, as she began to stack the dishwasher.

'Got the very thing,' I said, delving in the back of the cupboard under the sink for the plunger.

'Suppose we did rile our boys, said mother, quite thoughtfully for her.

'Yes,' I agreed, 'so let's suggest we all get together for a game of bridge tonight, they both enjoy that.'

I located the thick wooden handle at the back amongst J cloths, pan scourers and the rest of the clutter, and pulled it out. 'I wonder how the drain got clogged,' I mused aloud as I positioned its thick rubber hemisphere over the plug hole.

'Could have been when I accidentally dropped Alma Baldwin in the mud,' offered mother, obscurely.

'What do you mean?'

'When I carried her out of her cage for a little hop around on the grass she wriggled out of my arms and fell into the muddy bit where the pigs wallow.'

'But how did that block up our kitchen sink?' I asked, bemused.

She gave a sigh of exasperation. 'I brought her back here didn't I, to wash her in the sink, and how was I to know great clumps of her hair would come out.'

'Mother, you do *not* bathe animals inside the cottage,' I said, vigorously pumping the plunger up and down, hearing the mucky water leaving with slapping gurgles.

Thankfully, mother ignored the rebuke and, when the last dregs had gone, took the plunger from me, obviously going out of her way to be helpful.

'Good aren't they,' she said, twirling it in her palms. 'And not only for blocked sinks. I heard of a man who had a heart attack and his wife re-started it by pumping one of these up and down on his chest.'

She bent and opened the sink cupboard door but, instead of replacing the plunger at the back where it belonged, she laid it sideways across the front of the shelf. Knowing it probably wouldn't be needed for months, if not years, I decided to shift it to the back when she wasn't around. I'd got away with one potential flash point, not worth risking another.

'Time for me to go outside,' I sighed. 'I'm on a feeding treadmill. Twice a day, never ending. Duck pellets, pig feed, pony nuts, grain, vitamin supplements, carrots, stale bread. In one end out the other. Never ending. And all for only two visitors in one week.'

'And both of those German,' said mother enigmatically.

As I went outside I reflected on how the push and pull suction of a plunger could miraculously force a dead heart into action and decided it was probably more forceful and controlled than pressing down with the flat of ones hands.

Lairy lamb skipped over as I walked down the slope. Chickens came clucking around my ankles. Goofy and Goolie slowly circumnavigated their poles, peacefully grazing. It was a perfect day. And yet a python of despair squeezed all contentment from me. The silent tea room and rough and tumble play area stood ready and waiting, like ghost sites. Bottles of *New Hay Perfume exclusive to the Fields* lined the dresser shelf. But, no-one came.

'Sod off,' I snarled at Lairy, shoving his sweet little body away, adding another painful memory to the burgeoning banks of guilt memory cells in my brain.

As I kicked my way back, I wondered if there'd be enough storage space available to last me for the rest of my shortening life. The way I was filling them up with remorse, I rather doubted it. Perhaps that's when you died, I mused, when you'd saved as much guilt and regret as you could store and then the next bit you entered crashed the whole system. Then it hit me that that was what was so good about being a Catholic. When they confessed their guilt on their special service line to god, their cells were automatically wiped clean. For a second I considered converting, until I remembered I was an atheist.

'Sure I feel well enough for a game of bridge,' said father affably, shuffling his chair up close to the kitchen table, 'and it's nice playing in the kitchen by the Aga - I feel the cold more since the chemo, or maybe it's just my age.'

But it was chilly for mid-July and, after the depressive worries of the day, I too was looking forward to relaxing in the warm kitchen for a fun game of cards.

Mother, in fluorescent pink leggings and long baggy black sweater, hurried in holding a bottle of red wine. 'Bought this,' she said, handing it to Bernard to open.

I studied her. She looked terrific. Hard to believe she was seventy. She took her seat then turned to stare at me. The eyes never wavered and I knew that look.

'What's up?' I asked, not holding her gaze.

'You look exhausted - your forehead is setting into tram lines,' she observed.

Bernard caught my eye and smiled sympathetically, handing me a glass of the wine.

'It's good to see that your burns hardly show now,' he said in the kindly way a father might try to hearten an acne-ridden teenager.

I knew he meant well, but mother was right. I *was* exhausted. And no doubt my forehead could be scanned into a computer and printed up if we ever needed lined paper.

'Let's play bridge,' I snapped.

'Like that is it,' muttered mother, making a face at Bernard, adding, 'She was always quick to get huffy when she lived at home.'

Bernard handed me the pack to shuffle.

Grim faced, I pounded the cards up and down, sending half the pack flying.

Grimmer faced, I retrieved them from the table top and floor.

'Look at her,' said mother in an undertone. 'She used to get like that with her homework.'

'Why didn't you ruff,' shrieked father to mother.

'Because I didn't want to,' shrieked mother back.

We'd been playing for over an hour and, though I'd simmered down, the temperature was rising, and not just from the Aga.

Bernard dealt out the next hand.

Father, next to him, bid 'One spade.'

I said, 'No bid.'

Mother and Bernard no bid too.

'So that's it then,' said father, droopy eyelids even droopier with disappointment. 'One piddling spade.'

I led out a diamond. Mother, the dummy, put her hand down, exposing a perfect responding hand for father's opening one spade.

'I don't believe it,' said father sounding like Victor Meldrew. 'You've got ten points and four spades yet you no bi...'

Sudden gurgling sounds took over from the words. He clutched his chest. His blazing emerald eyes abruptly vanished under completely drooped shut lids.

'He's having a heart attack,' I shrieked, throwing my cards down as his body slumped forward.

Bernard jumped up.

'We must give him mouth to mouth,' he said briskly, gathering my father's long ungainly body up in his arms and flopping it down on the long table.

Mother dived under Bernard's arm. 'If anyone gives him mouth to mouth it's me,' she said forcefully, placing her bright red lips over father's pale ones.

'No! No! You're doing it all wrong,' shrieked Bernard, who'd done a first aid course in ninety eighty-nine and resuscitated four of the newborn piglets last year.

He hauled mother away and turned father's head sideways and backwards, poking his finger inside his mouth. 'Must clear obstructions,' he asserted, 'false teeth, tongue.'

'He doesn't wear false teeth you stupid bugger,' shouted mother, turning to me wildly yelling, 'What sort of a son-in-law *is* he?!'

She wriggled herself in front of Bernard again, her lipstick plastered lips hovering menacingly over father's.

'Hold it!' I said, grabbing her arm. 'Remember what you said about the plunger?'

Clearly not wishing to give up her good position she stood bent over, long wisps of hair falling onto father's face, lips at the ready.

'Yes, go and get it,' she said out of the side of her mouth, like a ventriloquist.

'But, but,' said Bernard as I barged past him to get to the under-sink cupboard where, mercifully, the plunger still lay in its erroneous place at the front.

In one lightning movement I grabbed it up and bounded back barging my way past Bernard again.

'But, but,' he stuttered again.

Mother straightened, grabbed father's shirt in both hands and ripped it open, sending buttons flying, exposing his chest. Then, reluctantly, she relinquished her prime place, standing back for me. In another lightning movement I lunged the rubber hemisphere down in a perfect encirclement of his left nipple, then slowly and forcefully pushed the handle down.

'That's his *right* side,' screamed mother, 'his heart's not in there.'

Sobbing, beads of sweat dropping from my forehead onto his chest, I pulled gently then tugged harder until, with a squelching pop, it released its sucking grip. Shaking, I took aim again and lammed it down over his other one.

'Are you sure that's right!' cried Bernard.

'Yes, yes,' I replied, pumping the plunger forcefully, yet slowly, up and down.

'No, no, it's his *left*, you idiot,' blared mother.

With a howl of pain, father shot up into sitting position.

I let go.

'Good god! What are you doing!' he yelled, staring down goggle eyed at the plunger jutting straight forward from his chest.

'Thank goodness, you're alive,' I cried, grabbing hold of the handle again.

'Course I'm alive!'

I tugged.

'Get off me!' he screamed.

I let go again.

Tentatively he took hold of it and pulled, but the vacuum was too strong.

'Here, give it to me,' commanded mother, at last getting in on the act. And with one mighty yank, accompanied by father's deafening roar, she tore it off him.

'What in god's name were you doing,' he screeched, getting off the table.

'We thought you'd had a heart attack,' I whispered.

'I almost did when I came round and found you attacking me with *that*,' he moaned. 'And look what you've done. I look stupid.'

Raised red weals on his white flesh encircled both nipples.

'*And* look at my shirt,' he moaned, indicating the sprouts of truncated thread where buttons used to be.

'Calm down Hector,' Bernard soothed. 'You may have had a cardiac arrest, you ought to see a doctor. At least sit down.'

Father plonked down on the proffered chair.

'I *didn't*,' he said firmly. 'I fainted. Anybody would if their partner was Maeve.' He glared at her. 'You should have said two or three spades with that hand and then we'd have been in game.' Then he turned to glare at me, adding, '*And* the kitchen was too hot.'

Fucking marvellous I thought, now I had part of the blame.

The lucky pigs were up the top of the slope eating their breakfast whilst I, their daily woman, tidied their apartments and scattered fresh straw.

Sometimes I wished I could swap places with them. It was all getting too much again.

'Thought I'd leave them to it and come down to see you,' Bernard said, entering the yard gate. 'You looked so unhappy.'

Then it all came out: The strain of the cost of the animals and no income. The worry that my cantankerous father, who refused to see a doctor, had some sort of heart trouble as well as his cancer and was about to go unconscious on us again. The living in a creative vacuum - no visits to the art club, no painting pictures, no artistic stimulation. With difficulty, I withheld the strain of keeping the secret of my potential blue blood from him.

He hugged me to him. 'We can manage without you now and then.' He took hold of my hand and led me out. 'Go up to the attic and get your painting stuff out. It's a lovely day. Go off somewhere in the country and paint the scenery. It'll do you good.'

I held back, making excuses, but he pulled me up the slope towards the cottage where the piglets were shunting their bowls around, snuffling up the last scraps.

'I'll go and finish in their apartments,' he stated. 'You go on off somewhere, get absorbed in painting a scene. It'll help get things in perspective - clear your mind.'

And I knew he was right. But, if I had time for painting I should start on Poppy Bambridge's portrait, the commitment that hung over me like the horrible sack of sick green gunge seen on horrible TV children's shows. But Robert had said there was no hurry, so I let the doomed portrait wait and half an hour later was in the car in my old jeans and tee shirt, painting stuff packed in the boot, and me filled with a glorious excitement, little suspecting I was about to come eye to eye with a frightening man. Though, not exactly eye to eye, as it transpired.

Twenty-three

I'd parked at the end of the main street in Orlford and lugged all my gear past the watercress beds, taking a narrow side track to, what turned out to be, the perfect spot. The clear trout stream which rushed gurgling over orange brown stones was in front of me, a copse of oak and beech trees lay behind.

I looked at my watch. Three hours since I'd made the decision to settle here. Three hours tussling with composition, colour mixes, what to leave out, what to put in, thinking of nothing but colour and beauty. On my easel was a stretched canvas laden with joyous strokes of bright oil paint released at long last from dull tubes. Ultramarine sky blended to cobalt blue, with distant bushes and trees misting into it. Blue-green reeds edged the crystal stream and wild buttercups and daisies bedecked the foreground. Already it was nearly finished and better than I'd hoped for.

A sound behind me brought me out of the picture, abruptly alert. I didn't move, arm held out straight, hand holding the hog hair brush laden with sap green almost touching the canvas. The sound came again, furtive, slow, the crackle of dry leaves and twigs compressed under creeping feet. I stayed immobile, hardly breathing, remembering the murder of a woman a few years ago just beyond this spot. A woman strangled in cold blood by the side of the watercress beds where people often walked. Here, I was even more vulnerable, off the beaten track where no-one came. It had been a calculated risk.

Another rustling sound, closer this time, drenched me with terrible fear. I had to get away, pack up quickly, leave. I rapped the brush down, lifted an open tube of paint with shaking hand, tried to screw its lid on, but the tiny top refused to engage with the thread.

A whistle piped up behind me: a soft two-tone signal for my attention. The lid jammed crookedly on the neck of the tube and I picked up another, repeating the process, desperate to pack up and escape. The whistle, high then low, almost friendly, sought my attention again.

Heart pounding, I slowly turned my head, squinting from bright sunshine into the darkness under the trees, eyes scouring the undergrowth, seeing nothing, but gradually acclimatising to the gloom and spying the give-away movement of a dark figure lurking in the shadows straight ahead. I turned away, panting in terror. Should I make a run for it, abandon my equipment? Or would such open panic galvanise him to attack? My legs began to wobble as I grabbed up a handful of dirty brushes and plunged them in turps.

The whistle piped out again, more insistent, more urgent. And, lured by the compelling call, I turned again. The dark figure was now crouching, trousers down, hand yanking vigorously up and down. I stared in repulsive fascination at the rough manhandling of the poor penis, brightly glowing in a narrow shaft of sunlight.

'Leave it alone,' I yelled, emboldened by the knowledge that a man with his trousers down couldn't run fast. 'You nasty pervert. Go on shoo,' I shouted. And I found I was waving my hands in flicking movements as I did getting rid of flies.

The hand pumped quicker and quicker, frantically jerking up and down as if intent on pulverising its defenceless victim. Abruptly, the bright sunlight went. Coincidentally abruptly, the shadowy figure came. Thankfully, I couldn't see the wanking climax.

Please make someone come along, I prayed, terrified he would now loom out of the darkness and attack me. My eyes roved the far bank of the stream. *A jogger. An OAP. Maybe someone walking their dog. I'm not fussy,* I persevered, on the off-chance there might be a god.

The sudden rustle and crackle of footfalls slowly treading bombarded my ears. God, his trousers were already back in place and he was walking! I couldn't look. I couldn't move. The stealthy sound continued. Grew fainter. Stopped. Was he standing close behind, about to pounce? Panic swept over me in icy waves.

Eyes half closed, arms raised to ward off attack, I slowly turned. But he wasn't there. Holding my kung fu position, I peered around, but couldn't see him. I waited, arms aching, then slowly relaxed my stance. I waited some more, breath gradually returning to normal, heartbeat coming off the boil. After ten minutes I decided the danger was over.

I surveyed the canvas. Just a little longer would do it. I took up the tube of burnt umber and unscrewed the crooked lid.

'It's fantastic,' raved Bernard.

'Yes, you haven't lost your touch,' agreed mother.

Then I told them about the man.

Bernard clenched his fists.

'How *dare* he,' he said. 'You must inform the police immediately.'

'But I can't,' I wailed, for I had thought of that myself, then rejected it.

'Why not?' asked mother eagerly, obviously sensing something smutty.

'Because they'll ask me what he looked like, and I didn't see his face!'

'You could describe what you *did* see couldn't you,' she cackled.

Bernard, grim faced, marched out.

That night, in bed, he burst out, 'I *hate* to think of that exhibitionist getting off on the excitement of you watching him.'

'If it's any consolation, he was much smaller than you,' I lied.

'It's no consolation,' he lied back, after a few minutes sighing contentedly then falling asleep.

Bernard left the table to answer the door and came back in with Sidney.

'Aye oop, sorry to interrupt, but couldn't wait to show you this,' he said, delving into a large plastic bag and hauling out a model Mallard duck.

'Very nice,' I said politely, noticing the green paint on its head was chipped.

'Aye, it is that. *And* it's remote controlled,' he said, beaming.

'Is this your new plaything?' Bernard asked, 'now that you've left the council - something for you to do?'

'Is it heck as like,' he said, still beaming. 'Nay, nay, I'm giving it to you. To attract visitors to your duck pond.'

'How do you mean?' asked Bernard.

'Can't you *see*. You could give visitors goes.'

'Goes at what?' I asked, obviously equally as clottish as Bernie.

He delved in the bag again. 'Give 'em this controller and let 'em steer the model duck through the real ones.'

'Won't it frighten the real ones?' asked mother, rather sensibly.

'Aye, it might, but think of the fun the visitors could have, guiding this model duck through.'

Bernard was looking thoughtful. 'Maybe it would attract customers,' he said. 'Maybe we could make a separate pond and get several remote controlled ducks and they could play games with them.'

'Have duck wars,' said mother brightly.

'Aye, you've got it. I've been wanting to help your enterprise and, at same time, draw customers in for poor Cyn who has nowt to do in her tea room but twiddle her fingers.'

Now I guessed at his alternative motive: he wanted to get some of the money back on his wife's investment. I sighed. But that's what we all wanted, wasn't it. It was worth giving anything a go.

'Let's go down to the pond and give it a gentle try out,' I suggested.

'Nothing too drastic,' Bernard warned. 'Presumably the speed can be controlled with this.'

He picked up the remote controller with its long metal rod and went to the kitchen door.

'Aye, the signal's picked up by that aerial on its tail,' said Sidney, puffing his chest out and waddling after him. Not unlike a mechanical duck himself I humorously observed.

Mother, Sidney, Bernard and I all trouped down to the pond where our water fowl were gathered, either on the water itself or at its edge. I wondered if they were as contented as they looked or if, under the surface of their unruffled feathers, they smouldered with resentment at their one clipped wing apiece.

A pochard sat asleep in the grass, its chestnut-red head twisted round, tucked into its pale wings. A red-breasted merganser stood on one leg, its delicate crest wafting atop its dark green head. Several tufted ducks and mallards cruised lazily across the dammed up spring water pond. I was proud of my new-found knowledge on water fowl, read up in a Bird Spotter's Book.

A white-fronted goose waddled away, honking. A gang of wigeon and shovelers hung around at the far side where the outlet cascaded over a series of steps, disappearing into a pipe going under our boundary. In the dense woods the other side, the water could be heard gurgling as it re-surfaced to rush down to the stream at the bottom of the hidden valley.

Carefully, Bernard placed the model mallard in the shallow water at the edge.

'Here, take this,' said Sidney handing over the controller to me. 'You have the first go - aim it at the duck, hold down the centre pad, the right one makes it go in reverse.'

Feeling as if I was about to switch on the TV, I pointed it at the false bird and pressed hard on the middle pad. Immediately, the duck with the chipped head shot forward emitting raucous quacking sounds. Immediately, all the other birds in the vicinity set up a commotion, quacking, honking, flapping their wings, going berserk.

'They're panicking,' shouted Bernard, snatching the controller from me, clicking wildly at the left pad, which hadn't been identified by

Sidney, sending the sham duck zooming round in circles, quacking louder.

I watched in horror as our entire fowl stock half-ran, half-flew away from the pond down towards the bottom of the garden. Bernard doggedly aimed the remote at the mock bird, knees bent, arms and back straight, like a yankie cop keeping villains at bay with his gun.

Mother, calling inanely for them to come back, sped off after them and Sidney followed suit, chasing after our fleeing flock, creating even greater mass hysteria. As if I'd taken root in the grass, I stood immobile, listening to the gathering crescendo, watching the demented birds ungainly attempts to launch themselves up into flight.

It was like seeing a horror movie projected in slow motion: webbed feet pounding at the air, untampered wings strongly flapping, clipped ones weakly wafting, like oarsmen rowing in circles with unmatched arms. But gradually, galvanised by the insane mass panic, one by one each heavy body lifted off the ground in low ungainly flight to land, unbalanced, wavering, on top of the boundary hedge.

Bernard remained crouching, still pumping wildly at the controls.

'Give it here,' I screamed, grabbing it from him, aiming at the circling duck and pushing two pads down together.

Abruptly, the chipped mallard let out a volley of earsplitting quacks. Immediately, all the teetering birds toppled off the hedge, disappearing over the other side. Straight away Bernard set off after them, long legs flying, veering past Mother and Sidney who were puffing their way back. The only duck left in our garden was the phoney mallard floating serenely around the vacated water, a stupid aerial stuck up its arse.

'Fucking marvellous,' I cried, all affectation at being a lady vanished with our birds. 'Fucking marvellous.' I repeated, rounding on Sidney.

'That weren't meant to happen,' he wailed. 'It were meant to be fun.'

He handed me the controller that I'd flung down on the ground.

'You'll need that to bring him in.'

'Come in number one your time is up,' mother called out through cupped hands.

'Very funny,' I snarled.

'Just trying to see the humorous side,' she replied, smirking at Sidney.

'But there isn't one,' I raged. 'We're back to having an empty duck pond.'

'Not entirely empty,' said mother pointing at the water. 'Look, there's Jaws.' I followed her finger and spied the glint of our little goldfish.

The one I'd forgotten existed. The one whose name I had meant to change in case it was a bad omen, but hadn't. But obviously should have.

'Think on,' said Sidney placatingly. 'I'll get you some more fish then you can sell little bags of fish food for people to feed them with. I've seen it done. And I know where you can buy the fish food cheap. Aye, you could coin it in. Money for old rope or, in this case, old fish food.'

Bernard trudged back. 'Not one to be seen,' he said mournfully. 'I climbed up and looked over but they're no doubt following our outlet stream and will soon get to the river at the bottom of the valley. We'll never see them again.'

And my soul bled for him. He loved those colourful birds almost as much as he loved his handsome Cussbert.

That night a contagious gloom descended heavily upon the cottage. Father said he felt tired and needed an early night. Mother said she might as well join him, and presently it would be time to go back to Tooting because his appointment with the specialist was due soon. And I noticed she sounded as if she didn't mind.

Bernard and I sat gazing at Hermione who'd seemed to sense our despondency and had for once left Kermit bleating outside to come in and join us.

'What are we to do?' I cried pitifully. 'The whole venture's a disaster.'

Bernard's hands went up over his face so I couldn't see his expression. 'Don't know,' he mumbled.

Hermione ambled up to me emitting little comforting throat rumbles and placing her snout on my lap. I stroked my dear girl.

'I could see if there's a teaching job going, not here in Wood Hill - I know Elizabeth's got a permanent replacement for my old job - but perhaps in Orlford.'

'But I want you here,' Bernard groaned, lifting his head, his wonderful black fringed eyes staring with an intensity that still had the power to make my legs, and other parts, go funny. 'And I want you to be able to do more painting,' he added. 'You're talented.'

And I wanted those things too, but knew I couldn't have them.

'I'll look in the local paper tomorrow,' I said, 'see if anything's going.'

But when I did look, there was nothing.

I knew then that it was only a matter of time before we'd have to close down. But how much time, I wondered miserably. And which of our precious animals would have to go first?

Twenty-four

'Why don't you go out in the sunshine with your easel and paint some of the animals,' mother suggested. 'I'll take over your jobs.'

I knew if I were to take time off for painting it should be Poppy's portrait to repay Robert, not one of our animals. But even thinking of it set my innards off.

'Yes, go on,' Bernard urged, ignoring the rumbles. 'Do some quick sketches. It'll relax you.'

Well yes, I could do quick sketches without too much guilt. Robert's commission would take many hours and, besides, I hadn't yet bought the canvas.

I gathered up my art stuff and lugged it outside. Two hours later three small pastels of piglets were completed and I was finishing off a water colour of Lardarse when a grey-haired couple appeared.

'The barn door was open and the woman behind the food counter said we should just came in,' explained the woman apologetically.

'Who do we have to pay?' asked the man.

I glanced around for mother but couldn't see her.

'Pay me, I'll get your tickets later. It's four pounds each if you're retired.'

'I like the tactful *if*,' said the man, grinning. 'I also like your pictures, how much do you sell them for?'

A quiver of excitement skittered through me. How much should I say? They hadn't taken long but I knew they were successful.

'Twenty-five pounds each the pastels and, when the llama's finished, he'll be fifty,' I ventured, not wanting to put them off with larger amounts. Besides, they were all unmounted and unframed.

The woman smiled as she scrutinised the piglet pictures taped to drawing boards leaning against the wire mesh of Lardarse's compound. She turned her head this way and that as she surveyed them.

'I like them all,' she said eventually, 'so don't know which one to choose.'

'We'll take the three,' stated the man. 'It's her birthday and she's mad on art, *and* pigs.'

'Here's to your success,' beamed Bernard, raising a glass of sparkling wine.

And the four of us clinked glasses across the table.

'Paint portraits of all the animals then reproduce them as cards,' suggested mother. 'Sell them in the gift shop.'

'Yes, *and* the originals,' added father. 'Get them framed.'

'And if it goes well,' said Bernard softly, 'we could employ someone to do your jobs, and you could do what you want to do, that is paint every day.'

'Someone like Enid Batty,' suggested mother. 'She ought to get away from Nesbit and build up some confidence.'

The bubbles filled my brain with fizzy exaltation. The decision I'd made at the beginning, to put keeping the piglets before my painting career, had been the right one then, but now I could do both.

'All we want are more of those kind of visitors with more money than sense,' said father, happily unaware that he'd just spiked most of the joyous bubbles fizzing inside me.

'All we want are more visitors, period,' added mother, finishing them off and directing my thoughts back down the grim path of selecting which animal was first for the chop. Or chops in the pigs' case.

The visitor we did get wasn't a paying visitor it was a visitor who needed paying, i.e. Vernon Veal the vet back from his holiday in Africa.

'How was it?' I asked him, for the first time thinking how like Woody Allen he looked.

His hands waved around in a theatrical indication of perfect bliss.

I bet those bony fingers have had practice at probing borrowed game, I thought, picturing unsavoury scenes.

'Freda, I can't tell you,' he proceeded to tell me. 'Being on safari's out of this world. The animals!' He latched one hand onto his narrow hip and flapped down his other in an action so camp I thought he must be putting it on.

'Did you know Lairy the lamb went missing while you were away - but he came back,' I interjected.

'Oh really? And you should have seen the zebras, they were divine.'

I wondered about asking him if he'd seen a lap-top too, but decided against it.

I followed him round as he checked out the animals, all the time talking ten to the dozen about lions and tigers and how *gorgeous* they all were.

Back in the cottage, he advised me to rub baby oil into the piglets' ears because they were all becoming dry and flaky. 'Poor little darlings,' he crooned.

And, despite myself, my heart warmed towards him. He truly seemed to love our babes almost as much as we did. Besides, he couldn't be the animal borrower. Last time he'd been too far away. At that moment I forgot the accomplice theory, especially when he generously said there was only five pounds to pay.

'Five pounds now,' he said, 'but if you are desirous of me fitting Hermione with a micro chip so that only she can gain access through the pig flap, you will have to commence saving. I've been making enquiries and, as well as the chip which I should insert beneath her skin, you will need a new door flap hinged down one side instead of across the top as at present.'

I'd forgotten mother's brilliant suggestion, passed on to him months ago.

'If ever we make money from this Animal Park, we'll get you to do it,' I said, knowing that that really meant never, so we'd always have to remember to bolt the entrance against incontinent intruders.

As I walked with him out to his car, I thought I'd risk testing him.

'Lairy wasn't the first of our animals to go away and come back,' I said, trying to sound casual, studying his face. 'They disappear regularly, once a month.'

'Strange,' he commented, with no look of guilt.

'And I forgot to tell you,' he said. 'I saw a hippo in a watering hole and thought of you.'

'Oh thanks!'

'No, no, dear lady. Thought of you inasmuch as the hippos reminded me of your sow, Hermione.'

Slightly mollified, I turned back, no nearer solving the mystery of who the pignapper was. He showed no signs of guilt. But, was he a good actor? I asked myself.

With me back in painting mode, I knew I *had* to tackle my obligation to paint Poppy's picture. Robert deserved it. Everything I was painting lately was turning out well. Why not this one? With feet of lead, I plodded to the phone.

'Hello Robert, Freda here. It's time,' I nervously blurted.

'What's time? Are you ill?'

'No. *I* have time. You said when I have time. Well I have time now.'

'Excellent,' he commented after a pause. 'I'm pleased. You deserve it. Time to do what?'

'Time to paint Poppy's portrait - to repay you for your kindness.'

'Oh no need. Really. But wonderful,' he said.

There had I been going through life for weeks menaced by a bag of sick green guilt hanging over me, and he'd obviously forgotten!

Briskly I said, 'I'll buy the canvas this afternoon. When will Poppy be free to sit?'

After a muffled conversation he replied, 'She says come here tomorrow afternoon.'

And I swear my heart stopped.

'How about here in the conservatory?' Poppy suggested.

I nodded. 'Good idea. There's no carpet to worry about.'

'Are you all right?' she asked. 'You seem a bit tense.'

'No, not a bit tense,' I said airily, unfolding the back leg of my French easel, and pulling it out to the length I guessed to be right. 'You position yourself in the cane chair, make yourself comfortable, while I set this up.'

Hand shaking, I screwed the extended leg tight.

Too late, I realised I should have dealt with the front two legs first.

I raised one knee under the heavy easel which incorporated a long drawer crammed with oil paints, and a deeper metal casing holding brushes, knives, linseed oil and turps. Wobbling on one leg, I stretched down to snap out the left leg but lost my balance and, as the easel crashed down, careered headlong towards Poppy.

'Ouch!' she gasped as I crash landed onto her.

'I omitted to tell you about Freda's peculiar working habits,' Robert laughed from the doorway, striding over and helping me up to my feet.

The portrait was blocked in and already her calm character was emerging. The garden had been hinted at in soft greens which perfectly complemented her pale blonde hair, violet eyes, and the pastel yellows, mauves and pinks of her sundress. It had taken just two hours.

'All for today,' I said, not wanting to chance my luck any further.

She didn't demur. Just stood up and stretched like a languorous cat.

'How long before it's finished?' she asked.

I remembered this stage with Sidney Slocumb's mayoral portrait, and with Robert's too. The blocking in of colour and shapes had been easy. It had been the next step that caused the trouble.

'Depends,' I answered cautiously.

She raised a questioning eyebrow.

'Depends on ... depends on how the final sitting goes,' I said, knowing she wouldn't spot the ambiguity.

I'd just come up from tidying the piglets' quarters when the phone rang.

'Hello,' I said moodily, still fed up to the molars by the lack of paying visitors.

'Ist that Frau Field?' said a voice I instantly recognised.

'Yes.'

'Otto Schwartzkopf here. Our organisation would like to bring parties of German families to your Animal Park on a regular basis once a week to see your schvine kinder display,' he said. 'In vun veek today ve vould like to bring ze first group.'

Suddenly my legs went weak and I crashed down on the chair. 'How many in each party?'

'About ten families, I sink between serty and forty indiwiduals,' he replied.

After I put the phone down I ran out to Bernard.

'I sink our troubles are over,' I cried.

I've left Poppy's portrait on hold and, in the last six days, have painted twenty small pictures of the animals in water colour, pastel and oil.

Nesbit, rather sweet now that he's an alcohol free person, has framed some of the pictures and hung them in the barn. He's also worked like a Trojan erecting a new pig holding compound and two stake and wire fences for Bernard's new piglet feeding brainwave which incorporates pig racing.

Instead of feeding them before eight and then again about four, their first meal is now to be at ten thirty. Yippee, say I!

Today everything was ready to try out the new regime.

At ten twenty I ushered the piglets plus Pot Belly Bella into the holding compound which backs onto the brick wall of Porker Palace, and fronts onto the slope up to the cottage. At the top, ten clearly-named troughs are spread out along a finishing line. The whole wide 'race track' has fencing on either side.

Ten pairs of piggy eyes watched Bernard fill each trough with sow nuts. Ten piglet throats squealed in ravenous excitement. Ten quads of trotters churned up the soft ground as they milled around my legs waiting for me to slide the new gate open for their breakfast charge.

I looked at my watch. Ten thirty. I waved to Bernard who stuck up his thumb.

'Are you ready?' I yelled over the squealing din. 'One, two, three, *go.*'

I shot the gate sideways and the stream of grunting piglets galloped out, gradually spreading across the whole track.

I chased after them seeing Georgie-Jesus reach the finishing line first. Immediately he stuck his head in the trough marked COUNTESS and greedily ate. (Serves her right I thought, stupidly pleased.) As each pig arrived it began scoffing from the nearest vacant trough.

'Look, look, Duchess has gone to her own named one,' I whooped.

Bernard ran over, his face aglow. 'We probably wouldn't be allowed to have proper betting,' he said excitedly, 'but we could get children to guess which one will home in on its own trough.'

'And we could give small prizes to any that got it right.'

'Yes. Like free entry another time, or a badge.'

We held hands and gazed at our babes as they hogged down their late breakfast.

'There's an unused blackboard and easel at the school. I'll ask Elizabeth Blessing if we can buy it, then I could write the children's selections down.'

'Good idea. Your mother could write the pigs' names in her beautiful italic handwriting across the top in white acrylic, and you could list the kiddies underneath in chalk.'

'Each pig's name with a number too, because we'd have to paint a number on each of their backs.'

Bernard looked askance. 'Hang on. I'm not at all sure about that.'

'Well otherwise how will the children know which pig is which? They wouldn't be able to tell them apart.'

Bernard nodded, looking sad. 'Makes fools of them in a way.'

'Better than making pork pies of them if we lose all our money.'

'Yes, you're right,' he sighed.

I flung my arms around him.

'But we won't lose our money,' I whispered. 'Our Animal Park is going to be a fantasmagorical success.'

'Don't tempt fate,' he replied.

But, unfortunately, I already had.

Twenty-five

Bernard crashed into the kitchen, face pale, hair dishevelled.

'Jesus!' he wailed.

'What's happened?' I cried, leaping up, grabbing his hand. 'Has someone attacked you?'

'Jesus has ...'

'Jesus is meant to *save* you not attack you,' cut in father.

'Jesus has *gone*!' Bernard moaned, shaking my well-meaning hand away.

'Georgie,' corrected mother pedantically.

'Jesus. Georgie. It's the same bloody pig,' he shrieked, rounding on her, aggression radiating from him like pulsating death rays.

'Oh. Pardon me for existing,' muttered mother. 'Good job we're going soon.'

'Sorry. Sorry, Maeve,' apologised Bernard. 'It's just that Jee ... Georgie has gone and not only is he our first born ...'

His voice screeched up higher and higher.

'... but he's the only pig that can skateboard.'

'Have you *tried* the other pigs,' asked father, scooping up a large spoonful of muesli. 'Maybe all pigs can skateboard given half a chance.'

'Yes, of *course* I've tried them ...' Bernard squealed, now full blown soprano.

'No need to start on him,' grumbled mother, unusually defensive on my father's account.

'Of *course* I've tried them,' he repeated in a slightly modified screech. 'But Jee ... Georgie is the only one who doesn't fall off. Of *course* I've tried them,' he reiterated, all attempts to soften his high volume screech now gone.

'Try blue tack on their trotters,' suggested father, surprisingly unoffended by the aggressiveness of his son-in-law, maybe because mother had taken on that role on his behalf.

'Or super glue,' added mother glibly.

'I can't stand this,' Bernard screamed, this time not only with no attempt at modification, but with renewed gusto.

He strode to the kitchen door and flounced out, slamming it behind him.

'And I can't stand it,' I cried. 'The Germans are due this morning.'

'At least they're not coming to bomb you,' snapped mother. 'You young ones don't know you're born.'

'Can't sit around chatting all day,' said father. 'I'm going up to the attic.'

'Chatting! He calls this chatting!' I cried.

'And I'm going out to the barn where I belong,' said mother, rising. I refrained from saying the obvious as she slammed out.

I marched to the hall phone. I'd had enough of our animals being systematically borrowed. I would have it out with Vernon Veal.

Viciously, I stabbed out his number.

'Have you taken Jesus?' I asked outright, not bothering with the niceties of weather and health.

'Do you mean have I been converted or something?' he replied in the kind of puzzled voice that could easily have been put on.

'No. Have you taken him? Physically. Picked him up and whisked him away?'

'Do you mean the piglet?'

'Of course the piglet.'

'Ah, no wonder I'm confused, I thought his name had been changed to Georgie.'

'Don't *you* start. It's bad enough with mother.'

'Am I being dim-witted here?' he asked plaintively.

'Let me put it bluntly Vernon,' I said, throwing caution to the wind. 'Have you or have you not taken our Jee-Georgie?'

'Certainly not. Why would I?'

'To experiment on of course.'

'No. No. No. All that talk about experimentation on animals was academic, I'm a respected vetinary surgeon. I'd never take a client's animal without permission.'

But, as I put the phone down I wasn't sure. He wasn't exactly going to admit to taking our animals and connecting them up to computers and voice synthesisers was he?

Cynthia hummed happily as she removed home-made fairy cakes from a large plastic box. I stood nervously waiting beside mother who was seated at the desk by the open back doors of the barn. Neither of us spoke as we stared up the car parking field to the entrance from Nuthatch Lane.

'*There* it is,' we exclaimed together.

The roof of a coach glided along above the top of the hedge then, with slow caution, turned into the field. As the coach approached us my stomach seemed to flip over, not with the adept control of a coin being tossed, but with the unbridled ferocity of a formula racing car somersaulting out of control. I clutched mother's arm as the long vehicle, gleaming with picture windows, drew near, then stopped.

'Operation Overlord has begun,' hissed mother in a confused state of excitement.

Hordes of children and adults spilled out onto the grass.

'It's going to be a disaster without sweet Jesus,' I moaned.

'*Georgie*,' mother irritably reminded me, though I hadn't forgotten - he was always sweet Jesus to me.

'No, no, it won't be a disaster, it'll be fine,' soothed Cynthia, standing behind her laden counter, eyes shining like lustrous conkers, buck teeth on permanent view.

'All right for you,' I groaned, 'it doesn't make any difference to you that our star turn has vanished. You can serve tea ...' I stopped aghast, seeing my friend's teeth quickly vanishing behind taut lips. 'Sorry, sorry,' I said, 'I'm a little distraught.'

'A *little*!' snorted mother scathingly. Then, out of the side of her mouth, 'Look out, the invasion's begun.'

A tall man with silvery grey hair and matching bow tie and moustache led the throng down to us.

'Tony Brownling,' he said, raising his voice above the foreign babble. 'I'm the English rep who will accompany the German families on each visit.'

He held out his hand to shake first with mother, then with me, and his grip was not too painfully firm nor too floppity soft and his expression was of the type some might call avuncular. At any rate I hoped he'd manage to sustain that pleasant look after he'd seen the piglet show without the spectacular grand finale.

'Otto asked me to give this to you,' he said handing over a cheque.

Mother immediately leapt up, beckoning the noisy mob who jostled behind him.

'Okay you vill now all come in,' she shouted.

As the colourful crowd streamed past us, she added, 'You vill go to see ze pig racing first in ze garden across ze field.'

'Sounds like the round-faced Gestapo man from 'Allo 'Allo,' whispered Tony Brownling, grinning broadly.

'Sorry about her,' I whispered back, 'she's my mother.'

'They're always a bit of a worry,' he said, winking.

'Come and see the pig race,' I suggested.

'Ze pig racing in ze garden,' he said in a perfect imitation of mother, sending Cynthia and me into fits.

'Send any other visitors out to us, and get the water boiling,' I said to Cynthia as we passed, 'there'll be plenty of time between the race and the show for serving drinks.'

And I was relieved to see her teeth were locked back into smiling position.

I glanced at her board on which she wrote what was on offer each day and saw she had chalked *29th July Ich nicht spreche Deutsch* at the top.

Outside, Esmerelda yahoo'd up from the stables and gave the thumbs up sign.

I thought it unusual she'd draw attention to herself, for usually she was reticent, but guessed she just wanted to demonstrate support.

As we walked through the gap, Bernard waved vigorously at us from Porker Palace yard then bent down out of sight behind the wall. He straightened, lifting a large wriggling piglet clasped awkwardly in his hands.

'That pig looks heavy,' commented Tony Brownling. 'How old is it?'

'Seven months, and they're getting too heavy for me to lift,' I said, hurrying forward, eyes latched on to the squealing piglet.

Grinning, Bernard waggled the piglet at me aiming its long back in my direction. There, clearly written in bright blue, was one straight line. Our number one child!

'What's the sudden hurry?' laughed Tony Brownling, puffing to keep up with me as I changed to a trot.

'Jesus has returned,' Bernard called out joyously, beating me to it, placing the protesting porker down.

'Is that man the local religious nut?' panted Tony.

'Something like that,' I replied. 'He's my husband.'

'Another family worry,' he observed as we reached the yard wall.

'Not really,' I laughed, introducing them and explaining the Jesus remark. Then Bernard ushered the ravenous porkers out to their new holding pen where they cavorted, squealing, vying with each other for best places by the starting gate.

I saw mother loitering by the duckless duck pond pointing out Jaws to the German families. *Come on. Come on, it's nearly ten thirty,* I inwardly railed. And luckily the growing porcine din made her look over. Wildly, I beckoned her to hurry then watched her shift her pointing finger up to us. I was relieved to see she allowed them to make their own way with no attempt to marshall them into line and frog march them over.

As they arrived, I invited each child to guess the name of the piglet that might connect up with its own trough. By the time I'd chalked up the last name, the piglets were squealing hysterically in ravenous anticipation of their food, making the children screech with laughter and their smiling parents stick their fingers into their ears.

Bernard had already filled their troughs with sow nuts and this time he was inside the compound at the starting gate with the cavorting squealing mob.

'One, two, three, go,' bellowed Bernard, sliding the gate open.

And, with a sudden crescendo of noise, they were off, trotters pounding, bums bouncing, as they raced up the slope. And watching those receding smooth bottoms with their sweet curly tails, I was filled with deep emotion. Without our love, without our hard labour, without our Animal Park, our adorable family would be dead meat by now instead of these joyous racing pigs.

'Do you serve pork pies in the canteen?' asked Tony Brownling. 'The German families love them.'

'No we do not,' I snapped.

'It's been a brilliant day,' enthused Cynthia as she wiped the counter clean. 'All my homemade cakes have gone, and the sandwiches, and I've lost count of how many cups of tea and coffee I sold.'

'And I've sold ten bottles of hay perfume and six of Freda's pictures,' beamed mother, rattling the cash box at me.

'Never mind about all that. What about the piglets' performance!' protested Bernard, pathetically desirous of praise.

'I'm off home now,' stated Cynthia, who hadn't seen the incredible show because she'd been busy preparing snacks for afterwards. She kissed me enthusiastically on each cheek then lifted her bulging bag and walked out all bent over sideways with the weight of her booty.

Bernard bolted the barn door behind her, the graffiti of disappointment scrawled all over his face.

I squeezed his arm. 'I was so proud of you and our ...' But I couldn't continue, the stream of words inside me entangled in a sticky sweet web of candyfloss love.

'Silly bitch,' said father, who'd just come in. 'She was always like this ... wasn't she Maeve.' Suddenly he was breathless. 'Remember,' he continued doggedly, 'when I won the ... father's egg ... and spoon race.' He paused, then inhaled deeply. 'And Freda couldn't talk because she was ... so choked with happiness.' Abruptly he sat down.

'I *wasn't* choked with happiness,' I burst out, suddenly articulate again. 'I was humiliated because everybody knew you'd stuck the egg on.'

He looked astounded that I knew and I was immediately struck with terrible remorse at having revealed the secret knowledge locked inside me for forty-three years. By the sound of my poor father, I wouldn't have had to hang on for much longer.

Next morning Tony Brownling rang. He's bringing a coachload of Germans next Tuesday as arranged but he thought the whole experience so outstanding, he's changing the itinerary of a group of Japanese families to include a visit to us the Thursday after.

'Nips and Krauts over-running the place. Never think we won the war,' grumbled mother as she pummelled more hay.

'Anyway ... we won't ... be here,' said father.

'No,' confirmed mother dolefully, 'It's time for his appointment with the oncologist.'

Her eyes locked with mine and unspoken sadness passed between us.

Their bags were packed and loaded in the car and we were having a final cup of tea together.

'I have ... something to divulge,' said father.

'What, that you've got flat feet,' quipped mother, bravely trying to hide the dejection of their leaving.

'As you know,' he continued, casting a glare at her. 'I have been ... trying to find who my real ... mother and father were.'

I scrutinised his face, seeing excitement lurking under the heavy-lidded tiredness.

'My father ... was a farmer ... no good at it though.' His eyes swivelled to Bernard. 'Good job ... it's only ... in Freda's genes, not yours.'

'My true mother ...'

He rubbed his fists into his eyes.

'... is the Queen Mother,' he blurted. 'I am her first born.'

An uncanny silence plunged down on the room.

Then mother's hoots of laughter rent the air, kick-starting normal sound vibrations back to life again.

'But, Hector,' said Bernard, frowning mother into silence, 'if that were the case, you would be king.'

'Precisely,' said father. 'You've got it. I've been diddled ... and now it's too late.'

Silence plummeted again, like instant deafness.

'It's not too late, you tell 'em' said mother mockingly. 'You become king and then the queen mother will be the king mother ... what a laugh.'

Father sighed deeply. 'My young ... half-sister... is doing a good ... job at being ... the queen, so I'll not upset ... the Windsor apple ... cart.'

'What a load of rubbish you do talk,' mother burst out.

'Knew you'd ... think that. But thought ... you all should ... know.'

He turned sad eyes on me. 'Sorry princess,' he said gently, pushing up off the easy chair, awkwardly rising to go.

And I burst out howling and hauled myself off the sofa, blindly dashing across the room and up the stairs, though whether it was because of the unfamiliar tender way he'd spoken to me or whether it was because he was going, maybe not ever to return, I didn't know.

Twenty-six

Nervously, I followed Poppy into their conservatory where she busied herself selecting a CD from a tall stack, no doubt deliberately keeping well away from the cane chair until my easel was safely up on its three legs.

Strains of the mesmeric Pachelbel Canon started up and she took up her position, elegantly sitting with ankles neatly crossed as before. Tentatively, I unscrewed tubes and squeezed thick juicy oils onto the palette. The gentle haunting music strangely did nothing to calm my jangled nerves and I picked up a brush with sweating hand, pummelling its stubby bristles into yellow ochre, terrified of putting one more stroke on the promising canvas.

I clasped the long fat varnished shaft at its tapered end, stepped back, surveyed Poppy who gazed back at me, an enigmatic smile twitching at her lips. I had to do it. I had to start. I had to make the first mark. With a flourish I flicked my wrist. With horror I felt the ochre laden missile slide through my grasp. With dread I watched the ochre laden missile zoom towards Poppy. With terror I saw it strike.

'Told you to beware,' said Robert, striding in from the doorway.

'But all I did was sit down,' wailed Poppy. 'Just look at my dress.'

And I *had* been looking at it, seeing its delicate pastel pattern smothered in yellow splats.

Whimpering, I grabbed up a wad of tissues, sloshed white spirit on, and tottered to her, dithering by her side like a nervous footballer wanting to tackle but scared to.

'That'll soon come off, it's nothing,' said Robert kindly, handing me the deadly paintbrush and taking the smelly wodge from my hands and starting to dab.

I hovered, hearing the final glorious chords of the Canon and wishing I were dead.

'Okay, all clear now,' said Robert eventually.

'Thanks,' said Poppy, nervously taking up her pose again.

'Thanks,' I quavered, dreading starting again.

Robert went over to the CD stack, pulled one out and inserted it in the player. 'I'll leave you to it,' he said, grinning impishly as he sloped off.

Loudly, the slow stately sombre sound of *The Death March* boomed out. *Dum dum di-dum dum di-dum dum dum dum dum.*

Poppy giggled.

Very funny, I thought, carefully jabbing at the yellow ochre again.

Slowly the resounding music continued. Slowly my brush strokes grew strong. Gradually I became absorbed, my eyes picking up the subtleties of my model, my ears picking up sounds of my father's death.

After almost two hours, Poppy yawned and stretched.

'That's all the time I can spare Freda,' she announced.

'Fine. Fine. You've been marvellous, a professional, hardly moved.'

She came up to the easel to look.

And it wasn't just her strong stench of turpentine that made me hold my breath.

There was silence.

At last she cleared her throat and the captive air burst out from my lungs.

'It's *fantastic*,' she exclaimed.

'You think so. You really think so,' I twittered.

'Yes I do. I wondered ... you know, with your nervousness ... but you've captured my look. But what about my hand.'

'It's not quite finished,' I explained. 'But I can add the finishing touches back in my studio ... now my father's gone.'

'Oh dear, has he, I didn't know.'

'No, no. He's gone back to his home.'

I wondered miserably how long it would be before the misinterpretation would be a true translation.

Bernard carried the compact heavy French easel up to the attic and I followed, gingerly carrying the canvas. I'd have to leave it a week to dry off a bit, then just ten minutes or so touching up should do it. And my debt to Robert would be paid. Yahoo.

Since my parents have left, Enid has taken mother's place in the barn selling entry tickets and we've had an increasing stream of visitors every day, word of our wondrous piglet display spreading, plus new flyers we've had printed and distributed to New Forest hotels and schools.

When I had told Enid we couldn't yet afford to pay her much, she'd requested that we paid her in pig manure!

I remembered her rapturous acceptance of the first sackful, with her sniffing the air above it and almost drooling, as if it were a delicious Cordon Bleu meal.

''Tis grand working here,' Enid declared as we were tidying up before shutting up shop today. 'And the fertiliser's doing wonders for t' garden.' She turned to Cynthia who was gathering up soiled table cloths to take away with her.

'Doesn't thee think 'tis grand working here too?'

'*Wonderfully* grand,' enthused Cynthia, stuffing the red and white gingham squares into a bin liner.

Enid handed over the heavy cash box to me, saying, 'Happen thee and Bernard like a game of bridge?'

'Yes,' I affirmed, surprised. 'Just fun social bridge, not the serious stuff that my mother plays at the Tooting Bec Club.'

I opened up the box and began sorting coins.

'Aye, Nesbit told me. So we were wondering if thee and Bernard would like to come to our bridge party next weekend.'

She turned to Cynthia who was flacking a clean tablecloth out over a table. 'Aye, and thee and Sidney too - it'll be a belated house warming party. All us old friends from up north will be coming down.'

'I had no idea that you or Nesbit could play bridge,' I said, carefully lifting a pillar of one pound coins and dropping it into a plastic bag.

'Not quite as daft as us looks,' she replied, giving a knowing sideways look, making me go red with embarrassment because I suppose that's really what I had meant.

'We'd *love* to,' I enthused, not really wanting to at all but anxious to cover up and make amends.

I lifted a pile of fifty pees and dropped them into another bag.

'And so would we,' said Cynthia, adding, 'Did you know we've been having lessons?'

Suddenly I thought I'd better read our *How to play Acol* bridge book again. At last the money was bagged up and the barn was ready to open up tomorrow. Cynthia and Enid departed, chatting together, and I hurriedly bolted the barn doors behind them then dashed back to the cottage anxious to ring mother.

'How did he get on?' I asked as soon as she answered.

'Considering he's the rightful king of England, not very well, he had to go by tube,' she said, a joke of sorts in her words, but not in her voice.

'What did the oncologist say?'

'He has to have more chemo.'

As I battled to stop tears spilling, I was thankful that ordinary people didn't have video telephones to give their emotions away.

'Give him our love and best wishes, and you keep your pecker up,' I quavered.

There was silence, then: 'I miss being with you,' she blurted.

And I lost the battle with the tears, now streaming down my cheeks.

'Maybe, maybe ... Great Piddlehurst General Hospital could treat him,' I snuffled. 'It's only twenty miles from here. If his doctor could arrange it you could come back here and stay.'

'*I love you,*' she replied.

'Ditto,' I returned, lips contorting.

And, as I put the phone down, I yearned to be able to rewind the tape and actually utter the three precious words that my mother had said for the first time but which I had ducked.

'Why are you crying piglet?' said Bernard, suddenly appearing.

'Dit ... dit ... ditto,' I howled.

'But I'm not crying,' he answered, perplexed.

'I ... I ... said ditto to mother.'

He scratched his head.

'Instead of ... I love you.'

'And I love you,' he said, getting the wrong end of the stalk, taking me in his arms and dotting a salvo of kisses on my wet cheek, making me wish even more that I had returned that simple three word reply. Then gently he whispered, 'Is it the monthly PMT?'

'You've been reading my woman's magazines again,' I cried angrily, wrenching myself from him, not understanding why fury had built up in me like molten lava in a previously dormant volcano.

'Thought as much. It *is*,' he stated, looking unbearably smug. 'Pre Menstrual Touch-the-short-fuse-and-retire,' he added, doing just that, skiving off outside.

'But I need you here,' I sobbed to the closed back door, working out that, indeed, my monthly curse was due any minute, the clever sod.

Nesbit came round to borrow our bridge table.

'I am delighted thee can come to our house warming do tonight, I say, delighted you can come,' he said. 'Some of me old friends are making the long trip down south to see us in our new abode. They love their game of bridge, I say they love their game of bridge.'

'And we love our game of bridge too, don't we Bernard?' I crooned, my usual happy equilibrium restored by the release of my monthly lava flow.

'Do you play Acol?' Bernard asked.

'Aye, that kind of thing,' he replied, looking devious as he lifted the folded table.

We went to the doorway to wave him off, watching him load the table into his car parked in the lane.

'I forgot to tell thee,' he called out, twisting round as he manhandled it in. 'When thee comes tomorrow evening, make sure you wear plen ...'

But the strong wind snatched his last words away.

'Make sure we wear plen?' Bernard pondered as went back inside.

'Maybe he said *make sure we have a plan*,' I suggested. 'A plan of conventions that we should write down.'

'Yes, probably that's it,' agreed Bernard.

I found I had a couple of hours to spare, plenty of time to finish off Poppy's portrait, so I bounded up to the attic to complete the masterpiece. Eagerly, I got out my paints and faced the canvas already in place on the easel. The languid violet eyes of Poppy gazed back at me and I grinned at her.

'I've captured you,' I whispered, 'your refinement, your charm, your beauty. Everything. Just a few finishing touches to get the sheen on your hair, your fingers defined and maybe add a darker outline to the low curve of your lips.'

One hour later I heard Bernard mounting the stairs. I stopped painting and he entered, handing over a cup of tea. I stepped to one side and gratefully sipped it while he stood surveying my work.

'It was jolly good before you started,' he ventured.

'*Before* I started, what about now?' I hissed, the cup rattling angrily in the saucer.

'You've plonked too much paint on,' he observed, reminiscent of his self-same words a year ago when I'd painted Sidney's portrait - before Hermione had sat on it.

'Impasto. That's called impasto,' I yelled, as I had done before.

'Impasto. In pasta. It's too much paint,' he replied, in a one year apart action replay.

I stared at the portrait, seeing he was right. I'd gone too far. I always went too far. Why hadn't he come up sooner with a cup of tea and told me to stop. It was his fault. All artists needed companions to tell them when to halt.

It had been the same with Robert's portrait. Too much gungy paint. Blotted off in a final reckless act on my own backside. *God! Not again, I couldn't bare it!* my whimsical inner soul cried.

Bernard sloped off and, with a wildness born of desperation, I attacked the wet paint. With the cushion of my thumb I mulched streaky bits together. With a turps-sodden rag I wiped thick bits off. With a palette knife I slashed colours together. How much time passed as I frenziedly set about it I have no idea, but I halted at the sound of Bernard's heavy footfalls plodding up the stairs again. Exhausted, I watched him appear, his hand clasping the stem of a glass full to the brim with red wine. Without smiling he handed it over.

He went to the canvas and stood staring, head tilting from side to side. There was silence, broken only by my long slurping intake of wine. *Say something, say something, you critical bugger* I inwardly entreated, scarcely able to stand the suspense.

'Stop now Freda,' he obligingly said. 'It's brilliant.'

Brilliant!

I threw my arms around him and kissed the gorgeous lips through which that fabulous word had just slipped.

'You're not just saying that because you're scared?' I asked him.

'Scared of what?'

'Me and my bad temper.'

'Oh, you've guessed,' he laughed.

But, when I looked at the canvas with new eyes I could see that it was pretty brilliant. I'd cracked it - and I wasn't talking bare bum cleavage here!

Next morning, I drove the wet canvas to the Bambridges, too worried that I'd start fiddling with it again to wait for it to dry.

'It's surpassed all my expectations,' raved Robert, eyes shining.

'I think you've really captured me, thank you so much,' gushed Poppy, hands clasped rapturously to her neat breasts.

'Be careful, it's very wet,' I warned, as I left.

And Robert said he would take it up to one of the unused bedrooms where nobody ever went in his vast Manor House.

'But I'll take my friends up to see it,' he stated. 'Won't be able to resist that.'

And, as I drove home, I dreamt of all the commissions to come.

Twenty-seven

Enid opened the door and I stared in wonderment at her. A daisy chain wriggled its way through her grey curly hair, scarlet lipstick enhanced what I now saw were beautifully shaped lips, and layers of floaty garments, in mainly yellows, reds and blues, bedecked her slight body.

'Thee always look so colourful,' she said, obviously correctly interpreting the look of astonishment on my face, 'so I thought I'd follow suit.' Her kohl lined hazel eyes surveyed me. 'Though thy outfit is toned down a bit tonight, aye, quite a bit. And didn't Nesbit tell thee to wear plenty of layers?'

So that's what he'd said. Now I wished I hadn't worn my little black dress and instead had chosen my navy mini skirt topped by the long jade silk blouse which could have taken tee shirts underneath and a jacket over the top. Although I couldn't see why it was necessary to wear layers for a game of bridge.

'I should've told thee myself, not left it to him,' she muttered as she showed us in.

A door burst open releasing a surge of noisy chatter along with Nesbit.

'Come in, come in,' he urged Bernard, pumping his hand. 'Enid, thee show Freda yer creations before we get down to some fun.'

'He wants me to show thee what I've been making,' said Enid shyly, leading me down a short corridor to the end room, 'but it's nowt.'

Not having a clue what was about to be revealed, I followed her in.

'There they are,' she said diffidently.

And scattered on the dusty top of a battered old table were about a dozen small sculptures of piglets in various attitudes, some stretched out lying down, some curled round, some sitting, some standing, heads down and up, tails twisted and straight.

I picked up one and stroked its rotund body.

'My Pudding,' I murmured. 'You've captured his looks *and* his character. The way his head is tilted, his one floppety ear. His tubby tum ...' And suddenly I was too overcome with emotion to talk.

'Well, thee's seen 'em now so come and meet us friends,' she said, obviously misinterpreting my silence.

At last I found my voice. 'I had no ... no idea you could do this,' I stuttered.

'It's nowt much. I studied ceramics and sculpture when I were young,' she explained, 'and I love doing thy animals.'

I picked up another piglet, a bowl clamped skew-whiff in its mouth, sly eyes peeking sideways.

'Our crafty Countess.'

'Aye, it's the mean one - I weren't sure of its name,' she confirmed looking pleased. 'And what does thee think of this?' She stretched up and took the model of a kid off the shelf.

'Why that's Kermit!'

'And there's this,' she added, lifting down a replica of Lairy our lamb.

And suddenly an idea spliced through my brain like a streak of lightning. Vernon Veal had been telling the truth. This woman under my nose was the animal borrower, not him. She'd only need to keep each one for a few hours to get the modelling right. Or maybe Nesbit removed them for her and sneaked them back the next day. He was always on the premises and knew where each animal would be. My mind was racing. His feet were too big to have made the imprint in the dung the first time, but maybe she had taken Pudding then, when he was small and easily portable. I tried to get a look at her feet, but the table obscured them.

'What's under there?' I asked, pointing to a tallish mound at the back of the table, covered in a plastic bag.

''T'is my latest effort,' she said, carefully removing the bag and some damp muslin, revealing a perfect llama in clay.

'He's based on your one,' she needlessly added, for it was Lardarse to a tee.

But that befuddled me. Lardarse had never gone missing, we'd have noticed. Besides he was too big to get in their estate car. But maybe she'd found a picture of one and modelled him from that.

'Have you decided which animal you're going to do next, after the llama?' I asked with feigned innocence.

'Aye, I'm going to have a go at one of your two adult goats. I were studying them t'other day. They jump at their own shadows, but they're champion, aye, especially the billy with the dangly beard and things.'

'I didn't know you came into our Animal Park.'

'Used to take Nesbit's sandwiches along when he rang on his mobile,' she said. 'Then I'd take a look at one or two of thy pets. Only ever saw thee once, busy inside the pig unit. Bernard's waved over a few times.'

I wondered why he'd never said anything, but guessed it wasn't worth mentioning.

'Where do you fire them?' I asked, edging round the table, even more keen to get a look at her feet.

'A kiln in t'garage,' she replied, traversing the corner, away from me. 'Most of them you've seen are stoneware, baked very hot.'

'Would you let us sell them in the barn gift shop? I asked, the matter of her feet abruptly swept away by another lightning strike of brilliance.

'Aye, I hoped that's what thee'd say,' she said, spiking my ego by obviously having had the lightning strike sear through her brain first.

But my mind continued on its creative sprint.

'They could be displayed in the barn and we'd take a percentage on any that were sold.'

'Aye, that's what I were thinking too,' she annoyingly said.

I followed her out, at last able to see her full length. Neat ankles led to sandaled feet which were larger than medium and certainly not as small as my recollection of the indent in the dung. But the memory was getting hazy and I'd never even been absolutely sure it had been a footprint anyway.

'How do you get such brilliant likenesses?' I asked, hoping to catch her off guard or give her the chance to confess.

'I look at them, me, and keep the image in my head,' she said, rather off pat.

She opened the sitting room door and ushered me into the din.

Nesbit bore down and grabbed my elbow.

Come and meet the gang,' he bellowed, guiding me round one of three bridge tables set up in a line down the room. 'Jack, Jack, I'd like thee to meet this long legged gorgeous redhead, Freda Field.'

A small man with a flat round face, snub nose and watery blue eyes smirked up at me. 'Enchanted, I'm sure.'

'She's me boss,' Nesbit said, guffawing.

'Thee! Thee with a boss. Nesbit Batty of Batty Building Works!'

'Aye, wouldn't thee like to work for her,' he said, digging his mate in the ribs, making me wonder if he'd succumbed to the bottle again.

'And she's not wearing much,' whispered Jack, rolling his eyes, causing a teardrop to fly out from the wettest one.

Why were they all on about wearing lots? I wondered anxiously, looking around for Bernard but my eyes arrested instead by the view through the French windows.

'What a transformation,' I gasped, remembering the run-down garden of the late Gertrude Smith when she lived here.

'Aye, that's all down to Enid and thy pig manure,' said Nesbit. 'Enid,' he bellowed, 'Enid, show Freda yer rhubarb, thee's got five minutes before the off, I say before the OFF.'

And all of their friends within hearing distance fell about making me feel even more ill at ease. We had come for a game of bridge but it seemed like it might be strip poker!

'That rhubarb were wilting 'til Enid brought home Freda's pigs' droppings,' bellowed Nesbit. 'Now look at it, couldn't be more erect. I say couldn't be more erect.'

'Thee'd better tack it instead of thy Viagra,' whooped Jack, setting off the howls of laughter again.

'Go out and look at it with Enid,' instructed Nesbit, pouring white wine into a large glass and handing it to me, then, I noticed, picking up a can marked alcohol free beer and putting it to his lips. So, he'd resisted the temptation even at a party, I realised with admiration, knowing I would find that hard.

'Aye, come with me Freda,' said Enid, opening the French windows and manoeuvring me out to the bed of flourishing rhubarb.

Last time I'd seen this large garden was when poor old ailing Mrs Smith had owned it and the rose beds that dotted the unkempt lawn had been straggly and overgrown, full of weeds. This was a transformation beyond belief. We walked over the newly mown lawn, passing neat rose beds, the weedless soil enriched with our fertiliser. We reached the end part which was now ploughed up and planted with rows of potatoes, carrots, beetroots, peas, runner beans, broad beans, radishes, lettuces and tomatoes.

'It's fantastic,' I exclaimed, almost as astounded as when seeing her sculptures.

'It's all down to me being paid in bags of thy manure.'

'Would you let us sell any produce you can't use yourself?' I asked, my mind now storming a path to a farm shop.

'Aye, that'd be grand, just what I'd hoped,' she replied, stealing my thunder again.

I was seated at a table with Jack as my partner, and a husband and wife team against us called Derek and Mavis.

Nervously, I twiddled with a short strand of hair, pulling it down straight.

'My mother's name is Maeve,' I told Mavis, to break the silence.

'Don't talk when t'cards is dealt will thee, just concentrate,' barked Jack. 'It'll be best for thee and me.'

My hair recoiled back to a corkscrew. My smile recoiled back to severity. My body recoiled back to sitting stiffly upright.

'With her attire, or should I say lack of it, she'd better play good,' commented Derek, leering.

Before I could ask why, Nesbit got to his feet at the far table.

'Here are thy instructions. I say here are thy instructions,' he bellowed. 'Them that's played strip bridge afore knows the form. But for them others, we play four hands, then stop.'

Strip bridge! I pushed the chair back, ready to escape, but Jack scowled at me, dislodging a few more tears, and put a finger to his pursed lips.

'We'll wait for them that plays slow to finish their hands,' Nesbit continued. 'Then, as most of thee present know, comes the strip part of the bridge.'

Excited giggles rippled round his northern cronies.

'*Strip* bridge!' exclaimed Cynthia. 'We haven't learnt that one in class.'

'What's this strip bridge all about then?' complained Sidney obviously aggrieved to be the only northener who wasn't in on it. 'Is it the weak no trump or the strong?'

'Don't get annoyed,' admonished Cynthia. 'It'll be a bit of fun like a special booby prize.'

'Is it 'eck as like,' hooted Derek.

'Any road up, we're all waiting to see a few boobies,' exclaimed Jack loudly, causing all the northerners except Sidney to fall about.

Shocked into inactive muteness, I watched vibrant Enid almost falling off her chair. She'd always been just plain insipid Enid I reflected, not this fetchingly attractive confident woman in on this strip bridge lark. Then I remembered her in the jodhpurs at the *teaching Nesbit a lesson* evening and realised this wasn't the first time she'd cracked open her protective shell. There was more to her than I'd first thought, and not only brilliant sculptures, green fingers and biggish feet.

'Right ever-y-body,' called Nesbit. 'Thee all knows what to do. I say thee all knows what to do. So let's get dealing.'

The pack was passed to me to cut and, as they were dealt out, I twisted round to see Bernard, who I'd just realised had not uttered a word. But his back was towards me and I could just see Cynthia, his partner, staring glumly at her cards. I wondered how they would get on together as I organised mine into suits.

The bidding was unremarkable and Derek and Mavis, our opposition, won the contract, finishing in four spades, Mavis being the dummy. Jack, my partner, led a heart which I won with my only heart, the queen. I led back a club.

'Why didn't thee lead back my suit,' hissed Jack, 'that could cost me my shirt, that could. Mind you,' he said, brightening, 'it could also cost thee thy frock.'

I noticed a little smile bounce back and forth between Derek and Mavis. What was I doing here! Maybe I could feign illness. I tried to turn my head to seek out Bernard, hoping he too would turn round and we could exchange messages with our eyes, but the muscles in my neck had locked solid.

'Why didn't you ruff,' berated Cynthia loudly behind me. And I pictured my poor Bernard's mortified face.

At last the interminable round was over. Four games had been played and Jack and I were two hundred points down. We waited in the kind of silence that precedes a violent storm while Bernard's table finished their final hand.

'Now thee'll see what thee's let us in for,' Jack whispered excitedly, patently putting all the blame for our losing onto my slumped shoulders.

'No wonder we lost, we were in the wrong contract,' Cynthia's aggrieved voice whined out loud and clear, their game now obviously over.

Nesbit jumped up and walked across to a cassette radio.

'Right ever-y-body. First round has been completed. Those couples with minus scores stand yourselves up and walk into the middle, I say walk into the middle.'

With legs as wobbly as if they'd been filleted of all supporting bones, I tottered with Jack to the centre of the room and stood with the other two losing pairs.

'Oh good, Freda's lost!' Nesbit hollered.

And suddenly it occurred to me that this was his way of getting his own back on his pre-teetotal horse humiliation.

'Now, all of our gallant losers must take off one item of clothing for every hundred points they are down. Freda, how many points did thee lose?'

'Exactly two hundred,' Jack answered snappily for me.

Nesbit pushed a button on the radio cassette player and the raucous sound of *The Stripper* started up, suggestive and sexy.

'Okay Freda, two items,' Nesbit bellowed, 'and let's see 'em come off with panache.'

Horrified, I watched a man called Les start up wild thrusting actions with his skinny hips as he started to unknot his tie, bony elbows jerking ceilingward in time to the music. Astounded, for the third time in one evening, I watched Enid waggling her bottom and flamboyantly discarding one of her flimsy tops.

'Come on Freda, let's see thee wiggle,' roared Les as if I was yards away from him instead of within ear drum shattering distance.

I looked down at myself, seeing my black dress, knowing that underneath was just a pair of skimpy red satin briefs and a matching bra.

'Free - da, Free - da,' a chant set up and, panic stricken, I bent down and eased off one of my high-heeled sandals, then the other. Unwillingly, I clasped one in each hand by their back straps and half-heartedly twirled them around my head.

The Stripper continued playing and I continued begrudgingly twirling as the well-known music jerked along: dee dum THUMP, dee dum THUMP, da dee da daa dee da da da da. And strangely its seductive rhythm got through to me and, without at first realising I was doing it, my bum began to gyrate, my eyes began to half close, the wine I'd been constantly sipping began to kick in and, as the music reached its familiar climax, in an act of reckless abandonment, I let one sandal go, giddily watching its flight across the room 'til it smacked full force into the front window. As the shattered glass came crashing down and my sandal went flying through, a rousing cheer went soaring up. I stopped twirling my remaining sandal, stood swaying, unsure whether to make a run for it or take a bow.

'Well thee soon got into it,' grumbled Nesbit, picking up shards of glass and placing them in a waste paper bin hastily provided by Enid.

Jack, who had also opted to take his shoes off to account for our minus two hundred points, made great play of putting them back on again saying that with splinters of glass on the carpet footwear should remain on and that I, Freda, should put my sandals back on my feet and remove two other items from my body. But, crushed into instant sobriety, I refused to remove one other thing.

'I only have one sandal and I'm not feeling well,' I said, which was now true. 'And I want to go home,' I added, realising I sounded like a pitiful schoolgirl.

'I'll take you,' Bernard said firmly, handing me the missile sandal he'd just retrieved from outside.

'And I'm going too,' stated Cynthia.

'And me,' said Sidney, rounding on his cousin Nesbit, saying, 'You make me laugh, you. You come to Wood Hill to be me neighbour and you don't have decency to tell me about yer strip bridge in advance.'

'I knew it were a mistake inviting them,' grumbled Nesbit in an undertone to Enid as they removed packs of cards and glasses from the table they'd borrowed from us, then folded it down.

Their old friends, now redistributed around the remaining two tables were swigging back alcohol and chatting animatedly as they waited. Les, the one with the dancing elbows, was not only tieless but trouserless too. Jack had put his shoes back on and was loudly demanding that Enid hoovered the carpet, all the time flashing sharp glances of blame at me.

At the door Nesbit shoved our table at us. 'Thanks for the loan, he said stiffly.

'Sorry I broke your window,' I muttered.

'Next time don't let loose with clodhopping sandals,' he replied, quickly shutting the door on us.

'Next time!' I exclaimed when we were safely tucked away in the confines of our car.

'There'll never be a next time,' Bernard grimly confirmed 'But I was proud of you, never thought you'd go to such drastic lengths to get us out of there.'

'Well, it was no good waiting for you.'

'I was too busy fending off Cynthia. What a total waste of an evening.'

'Not a total waste. If it hadn't been for this evening I wouldn't have seen Enid's amazing sculptures or her garden produce, all of which we can sell in the barn.'

'It's exciting running our own business isn't it,' he commented as a few minutes later we pulled up outside the cottage.

'Yes, the future's looking *so* rosy,' I trilled, hopping out, careering forward and diving face down on the gravel.

'Sweet piglet,' Bernard cried, rushing round. 'What happened?'

'I lost my balance and by dose is broken,' I wailed thickly, 'and by dees too.'

'Your poor nose, your poor knees,' he translated as he helped me up.

Gingerly, I moved one foot forward, but abruptly stumbled sideways, just saved from another plummet by strong Bernard.

'Your heel's broken,' he observed. 'That's why you fell.'

Hand cupped over my pulsating nose, I limped to the door, heel flapping, Bernard supporting me.

'Poor darling,' he said tenderly. 'It must have cracked when you hurled it at the window.'

'But it was worth it to get out of there,' I croaked.

Though up in the bedroom I wasn't so sure. To add to the imperfection of my still faintly burn-scarred visage was a swollen grazed bright red nose which looked as if it was a false one stuck on by some cruel prankster.

'How am I going to face visitors with *thad* dose?' I wondered out loud.

'Why not hire a clown's outfit and put on some entertainment before the piglet display,' Bernard brightly replied, and then wondered why I groaned and rushed off in floods of tears.

In the seclusion of the bathroom I groaned even louder as teardrops hit my poor grazed nose like an onslaught of salty bee stings.

Two days since my crash landing and still my scabby knees hurt and my nose glows red.

'I look a sight,' I moaned. 'My dose is still like a clown's.'

'It's *not*,' said Bernard forcefully, evidently having learnt his lesson. 'You can't even see there's ever been the slightest damage to your lovely little snitch.'

'It didn't make me go blind,' I blared, hobbling out to the garden, Bernard carrying my painting gear, slavishly willing to help because he'd inveigled me into saying I'd paint a picture of his wonderful Cussbert.

'I'm not stupid you know, I can see what it's like in the mirror,' I chuntered on.

We reached the ark and run and Bernard went idiotically clucky like a father swooning over his first child.

'Who's a lovely boy then,' he crooned to the eager-looking cockerel who thought he was about to be let out into the foxless early morning freedom of the garden.

'Cut the lovey dovey cackle,' I snapped, snatching my easel from him. 'I want to be finished by ten when the gates open, I hate being watched - with or without a ripe tomato in place of a nose.'

'It isn't a tomato, it's pale and lovely,' he lied, almost tugging at his forelock as he spoke.

Then he bustled about, obsequiously anxious to please, setting up the easel, adjusting its legs so I could sit on my low stool stiff legged to save my fragile knee scabs from cracking. Carefully, he placed the canvas on the support, then deposited some old rags and a large bottle of turps on the grass.

He threw a handful of corn through the mesh at the far end of the run and, as Cussbert pecked, he briefly lifted the ark end, inserting a cross triangle of wood so the cockerel was forced to stay on view.

Awkwardly, Bernard helped lower me down to the stool, and then handed over my palette. I pulled the easel drawer out, picked out seven tubes of oil paint and some charcoal. And, at last, I was ready to start.

'Yahoo,' called Esmerelda jogging over to us from the gap.

'God, why is *she* here,' I muttered, not expecting an Almighty answer.

'En't it a nice day,' Esmerelda puffed, grinning at me, her eyes doing a double take on my face. 'What you done to your nose? It's bright red,' she observed.

I flung a glare of reproach at Bernard, then snapped, 'I'd like you both to go, I need to get on.'

'I dunno. I was only being sociable,' Esmerelda complained, mooching off.

At last alone, except for a few inquisitive chickens, I surveyed Cussbert. I had to admit that he was a beauty. The ruff of deep orange feathers around his neck shone in the sunlight, his erect comb and dangly discs that hung either side of his beak were a glorious rich crimson, his arched tail feathers gleamed green and black as they wafted in the breeze. His beady eyes stared at me glinting with even more malice than usual because the seed had all gone and he knew I was in some way responsible for his protracted imprisonment in the run.

I selected a fine stick of charcoal and began lightly sketching on the canvas, all the while Cussbert emitting warning rumbling growls. I wouldn't have been at all surprised if he'd suddenly opened his beak baring fangs.

The main shape roughed in, I began squeezing out colours then eagerly loaded my brush.

As I worked, Cussbert's growling changed to a benign purr, then stopped altogether. Gradually he slumped down, resigned, bored, eyelids drooping. But I wanted him standing proudly like a matador, cruel pride glinting from sharp eyes. I clapped my hands, and let out a shrieking imitation of himself crowing. With a squawk, he reared up, head high, immediately alert. Instantly, I smacked down more paint, wondering if I'd somehow managed to call out something meaningful in fowl language, whichever way it was spelt!

Slowly realising he'd been conned and there was no approaching danger, he settled down again, eyes gradually closing, beak pursed.

Again I clapped and crowed at him but, this time, he merely looked at me with a sneering expression which patently said: *Do you think I'm an utter fool who'd fall for that one twice.*

So I cupped my hands and clapped even louder, emitting an even more raucous succession of *crowing COCKADOODLEDOOS*.

And this time Cussbert rose up flapping his wings, eyes flicking, unsure.

Quickly I jabbed on the last few strokes to complete the picture.

'Freda, Freda,' called Bernard, haring down from the cottage. 'What's happened? Are you all right?'

'Freda, Freda,' called Nesbit, haring across from the gap. 'What's happened? Are you all right?'

They reached me simultaneously, both panting.

'Just painting this uncooperative bird,' I said, feeling foolish, 'but I've finished now. Thanks for flying to my rescue anyway, both of you.'

'It's *fantastic*,' Bernard exclaimed, at last sighting the painting.

'Aye, it is that,' agreed Nesbit. 'It'll complement Enid's sculptures in the gift shop. That's why I'm here - delivering boxes of them to the barn. They're on the floor so thee can display them how thee wants on the dresser.'

'That picture is *not* for sale,' Bernard stated. 'It's mine.'

'Aye, thee loves that rooster doesn't thee. It'll be grand to have his picture as a memento for after he's dead.'

From the appalled look on Bernard's face, I guessed he'd never ever considered his proud cock could ever die. But then probably no man did until it happened.

Back in the cottage I looked at my watch. Five past ten.

'Jolly good timing,' remarked Bernard. 'Enid should have opened the barn doors by now. I'll go out and get the piglets ready for their race.'

At twenty past ten I glanced out of our French windows and what I saw made me gasp.

Twenty-eight

Hordes of people were pouring through from the field. It seemed as if there were hundreds of them. I banged my mug down and ran out to the garden, seeing Bernard ushering the piglets out of Porker Palace to their holding pen round the side.

Attracted by the new notices we'd scattered around advising visitors of the twice daily pig races, the crowd was yomping across to the unit like an attacking army and, by the time I reached there, they were milling around, jostling each other to get a good look at the piglets.

As I tried to push my way through, a scruffy boy whined: 'We've just seen all them bleeding ponies in the New Forest, why d'we wanna see flippin' pigs.'

'So you can learn where bacon come from, case they arsk yer at school,' answered a man I took to be his father.

'Excuse me,' I snapped icily, my way blocked.

'We was here first, don't shove in,' complained a fat woman.

'Let the lady through,' bellowed Bernard, observing my predicament. 'She'll write your children's names ...'

But, even Bernard's strong voice became lost in the rising clamour.

'Forget the betting,' Bernard shrieked at me.

'Betting?' a stocky man repeated. 'Hang on. QUIET all of yer. There's betting.'

And, as if he'd cast a magic spell plucking all their tongues out, silence fell.

Fearing the spell might be short-lived, I dived in.

'Each child who wants to bet should chose the name of the piglet he or she guesses will go to its own named trough at the finishing line,' I pronounced.

Tongues rapidly came back into muttering action with: *It's only fer kids/ No bloody Tote/ Who cares anyway/How much does it cost*?

'I shall write the child's name on the blackboard under his selection,' I continued brightly. In fact far more brightly than I actually felt because dealing with this lot made me feel extremely tarnished. But, doggedly, I carried on: 'It costs nothing, but any who've guessed correctly will receive a prize.'

'No skill in that,' said a man sulkily. 'Don't know their form.'

'Wozza prize then, Rudolph?' asked a young lad, sniggering and pointing out my nose to his friend.

Still holding the brightness on my face, though now it wasn't only masking tarnish but also rising anger combined with worrisome fear at what they'd think of the prizes, I took a badge from my pocket and held it up.

'One of *these*,' I trilled, reading from it: 'I've *been to Freda's And Bernard's and it's FAB.*'

''Tain't fab so far, it's naff,' commented someone.

And the noise level quickly rose, competing very successfully with the squealing of the frenzied piglets desperate for their food.

But despite the baleful disparagement, about twenty children lined up to tell me their choice, so it wasn't until ten forty that we were ready.

'Okay to start,' I yellowed over to Bernard who quickly raised one arm, creating anticipatory piglet mayhem around his legs.

'One, two, three, GO,' he shouted, releasing the squealing mob to the fenced- off wide track.

'The black bastard's slow,' guffawed a man, 'not like our Linford.'

And I stood there watching our family race, overcome with deep sadness. I should have known that all sorts of visitors would come, including nasty ones.

'Cor, look at them go mum,' said a bright eyed girl. 'Never seen a pig before.'

And my spirits lifted a little. Maybe this would let city children see that farm animals weren't just dead meat in the supermarket or cooked meat on their plate.

Ten sets of trotters pounded the grass, ten little tails swished on ten bouncing bottoms. Giggling, squealing children ran up the side keeping pace with them, calling out encouragement, yelling their names. I followed after them.

'Come on number five, go fer yer Princess dish,' a girl called.

'Pie! Pie! Get yer finger out,' yelled a boy.

'Ten. Ten. It's there. It's there. Look. Big Belly, go get it,' called a pretty black girl, pointing to Bella's trough.

'Change course me old Dutch,' a father called, presumably supporting his daughter's choice of Duchess.

'Come on Georgie my son,' yelled another supportive father, galloping alongside, long black hair flying.

And suddenly I was glad we'd changed our first born's name. *Come on Jesus my son* coming from someone like him just wouldn't seem proper.

Piglets homed in to the zinc troughs along the finishing line, snouts immediately down, grunting in concentration as they urgently gobbled. I marvelled that two never went to the same troughs as I watched Pudding dash to a vacant one at one end, and Big Belly Bella dash to the only other vacant one at the other side.

Bernard had run up behind them and was whizzing along the line checking. He straightened, eyes roving the crowd until he saw me, then he pointed down at Porgie, our erstwhile Hamlet, giving the thumb's up sign.

He cupped his hands round his mouth and announced: 'The winner is NUMBER TWO, PORGIE.'

Groans of disappointment welled, but one excited voice called, 'It's mine. It's mine. I bet on Porgie.'

I located the voice and saw it was another jolly looking dark skinned girl.

I hurried over to her. 'What's your name?'

'Kylie,' she said softly, her long dark lashes sweeping down as, bashfully, she stared at the grass.

'Come back down the slope so I can check it on the board,' I said, and we ran down together, closely followed by an excited gang.

Seeing her lone name there under TWO PORGIE, I took out a badge and pinned it on her tee shirt.

She turned her velvet brown eyes to me. 'Ta very much miss,' she said. And, impulsively, I bent down and kissed her.

'Crap that is,' said a tall skinny kid who'd been peering at the prize. 'Who knows what Freda And Bernard's is? FAB what? It don't say.'

And, with a jolt, I realised he was right.

The crowd scattered and I made my way over to the barn to see how Enid was coping.

'Look,' she said, when I arrived there. 'Look, three of them, all from London.'

I looked out and saw three long coaches in the parking field and a smattering of cars.

'I've sold ninety adult tickets, that's four hundred and fifty pounds,' she said joyfully and sixty-three children's at two pounds, that's one hundred and twenty-six on top.'

'And now my dears you can add to that,' said a goatee-bearded man with a posh voice who appeared from behind the new screen displaying my art work, 'because I'd like to buy these pictures, all of them.'

I blushed, not realising anyone was in the barn as we talked so openly about the takings.

'Do you happen to know where the artist is?' asked the man, extracting a gold credit card from a leather wallet.

'I'm sorry, we can't take those,' Enid informed him.

'Oh can you not, what a pity,' he said. 'I never carry much cash on me.'

My heart sank. Were we about to lose this fantastic sale?

'I'm the painter,' I told him. 'Do you have a cheque book - I could take a cheque.'

'Ahh, my dear woman. Such talent. I am enchanted to meet you, ecstatic that you are here in person.'

He grabbed my hand and squeezed it, not letting go, staring hard, a look of rapture in his deep set slightly skew whiff eyes that both seemed to focus on my nose.

'My, my nose is red because I fell down,' I stammered, embarrassed by the close boss-eyed scrutiny.

'Your protuberance is of no concern to me,' he said. 'It is your gift.'

Was he taking the micky? I shuffled my feet and smiled unsurely at him.

'Your wonderful ability to apply paint is all that concerns me. The fact that your exquisite freckled face framed by your pre-Raphaelite titian hair is crying out to be captured in oils, without the redness of the proboscis of course, is of no matter now, it is your artistic genius that is my interest.'

I shuffled my feet again, embarrassed that Enid was present listening to this tripe. He must be some old weirdo intent on making a fool of me. I looked out to the sunlit scene outside and saw, for the first time, a gleaming silver Rolls Royce at the edge of the parking field.

'My card,' he said, handing me an expensive one with gold deckled edges.

In amazement, I read: *Basil Argue, Basil Argue Gallery, Old Bond Street, London W1.*

'I'll be back with my cheque book soon. And I'll take as many of your pictures as are available at that time. And, by the way, your prices are ludicrous. You can add *at least* five hundred to each.'

A streak of red nose flashed before my eyes as I spun my head round to Enid. 'You must see Enid here's sculptures,' I urged, indicating the boxes Nesbit had dumped down by the desk.

Enid giggled nervously. 'Nay, nay, they're nowt,' she protested, nevertheless leaping up and tearing at one of the lids.

He sighed. 'Ah well, before I go, I may as well just see.'

She opened up the flaps, delved into crumpled newspapers and pulled out the perfect replica of Pudding. I saw Basil Argue's offset pupil's sharpen.

'Let me see another example,' he ordered, the tip of one digit finger pushing through his thin beard to place on his hidden chin.

She scrabbled around then lifted out the model of Lairy our lamb.

'Mmmm. Both excellent renditions,' he murmured. 'But we couldn't possibly take them. Get them cast in bronze though and I'd consider showing them in our other Gallery in New Bond Street.'

He turned to me. 'Give me your card dear lady, and I shall ring you informing you when to expect me back.'

'I ... I don't have a card, but ... but I'll write it down for you,' I stammered, delving into my pocket for some paper, coming out with a crumpled piece on which I scrawled my name and number down.

As I handed it over I smelt a waft of something unsavoury and saw on the back: *Received - one load of pig dung, Reggie.*

He tucked it into his inside pocket, then shook my hand.

I felt sick. This rich man was going off with a stinking manure sales receipt secreted inside his light grey suit.

As he strode away to the sleek silver car by the hedge, my febrile imagination pictured him extracting the pungent scrap from his pocket at an exclusive Private View and everyone within nose shot fainting.

'I shouldn't smile if I were thee,' sniffed Enid. 'Happen that's the last we'll see of that one.'

'Yes, happen you're right. I bet it's a line he spins to look big and, even if it's not, he'll probably not come back to humble Wood Hill Village or our Animal Farm. I wonder why he came here in the first place? It's way off the beaten track.'

Twenty-nine

Mother and I, between us, have organised father's ongoing treatment to be at Great Piddlehurst General, starting next week, so Nesbit came in to help with the animals while I drove toTooting to collect them, mother not wanting to drive.

As I drew up I saw her peering anxiously out of the window.

She hurried out.

'He isn't so good,' she warned, after we'd kissed. 'He's still in bed.'

I ran up the stairs and along the passage. At their bedroom door I halted, pinpricks of dread prickling my skin. I pushed it open. And there he was gently smiling at me, the DEATH sign propped up beside him as before.

'She still thinks I'm on it,' he said sleepily.

'On what?' I asked, rushing to him, kissing his forehead.

'On my death bed of course, he flared. 'But I'm not. Just too ... lazy to get up, a sloppy ... old man. But now you're ... here I'll put my dressing gown on ... and we can get going ... to your place.'

He lay back on the pillow, recovering his breath.

'Not before you get dressed,' commanded mother, pulling the duvet off him. 'Freda's not going to drive all the way to Hampshire with you in a dressing gown and those awful maroon and blue pyjamas. You look like a cricketer rigged out for a one day match. He's got nicer ones,' she said, turning to me, 'but he won't wear them.'

'I have *not*,' he blared.

'Yes you have. The ones I bought you last year.'

'I'm not wearing ... horizontal ... blue and white ... stripes. That's QPR ... and they're rubbish.'

'That's just because I support them,' said mother out of the side of her mouth. 'He's cussed like that.'

She turned to him. 'Just put on your crown and ermine then, but get a move on, Freda hasn't got all day. The animal dung's piling up every second we dally here.'

At last two suitcases and a bulging grip were in the boot of the car and father, "properly" dressed, was in the back, mother in the front "so she could direct me". (As if I hadn't got there on my own!) Almost as soon as we set off she forcefully ordered me, despite my protests, to turn into a one way system to take a "shortcut" to the motorway. We then spent fifty minutes driving round Tooting in heavy traffic with father saying *Silly Bitch* to mother with the reliable timing of a metronome.

By the time we did reach the motorway mother was retaliating with her *Stupid Dog* ripostes, the rhythm of their squabble taking on that of the wheels of an old clickety clack train. *Silly Bitch Stupid Dog, Silly Bitch Stupid Dog*, and so on until, just as I was on the point of jamming the brakes on and ordering both of them out onto the hard shoulder, father dropped off to sleep.

'I knew I'd win,' said mother smugly, making me want to clock her one.

Three hours since we've been back in the cottage. Father has slept the whole time up in their bedroom. Mother has done nothing but complain about Enid "nicking my job".

'There are plenty more jobs now,' I told her. 'The business has picked up and we get dozens, sometimes hundreds, of people in each day. You could take groups of people round.'

'Round what?' she snapped, deliberately being awkward.

'Or you could direct them to the chipmunk house, show them how the lights go on. Visitors often miss it.'

'Bloody brilliant. A highly responsible job.'

'And while you're there in the stable block, you could make sure they see Alma and Mike Baldwin, they're often missed too.'

'Still only two rabbits - big deal,' she scoffed. 'Why don't you let them get together - you know how they'd breed.'

'And introduce them to Daisy ...'

'Still all mangy from the fire.'

'Not mangy. She's healed up as well as I have.'

'I can still see where your burns were on your face,' she snapped, her finely chiselled nose coming so close I thought she'd etch out some new scars.

'What's up mother?' I finally said, exasperated with her.

'Nothing,' she said shrugging and making a face. 'Just that Enid's got my job and your father's dying. Nothing for you to bother about.'

I took her in my arms and we both wept. If Bernie were dying I knew I'd get into funny moods.

The phone went.

'I'm Gary. You don't know me,' a man's unrefined voice said, 'but I've heard you take on unwanted pets.'

'Yes. Yes, I do sometimes, it depends.'

'On what?'

'On whether they're harmless ... I warn you, we're picky with rabbits.'

'I see. How about a parrot? Does he fit the bill.'

Then he burst into raucous laughter, saying, 'That's rich innit. Fit the bill. Get it?'

As I laughed politely with him, words of rejection were forming in my mind.

'He comes with an aviary delivered free of charge at the same time as I get shot,' he added, spiking my prepared reason.

'What's the parrot like?' I asked guardedly.

'He's real cool.'

'But what kind is he?'

'He's a Green Fronted Amazon. As soon as you clock him you'll fall fer him. He's a handsome bird.'

Visions of another Cussbert rose.

'His name's Cocky. Cocky by name, cocky by nature. Struts around as if he owns the place, real wicked.'

Visions of the other Cussbert enlarged and menaced.

'But he's kinda sweet, kisses your cheek, all that sort of thing. It'll be a wrench for me to leave him.'

'Is he noisy?'

'No. Quiet as a mouse. I gotta fly soon. Are you up for him or not?'

'I'd like to try him for a few days,' I said prudently.

'No time. I'm off to Heathrow pronto. If you don't want him, I'll be forced to let him go.'

'Let him go where?'

'Let him fly away, like I'm going to do, though I'll stand more chance of surviving than that poor bugger.'

My mind stumbled. I didn't want the poor parrot to be shredded to bits by a hawk, or frizzled to a charred corpse by overhead electric cables, or to die from starvation, unloved and nutless.

'I'd like to see him,' I said, weakening.

'No time. He comes unseen with a mobile perch as well as the aviary. And I'll start you off with two bags of nuts. Can't say fairer'n that. If I had time I'd sell him, but I'm giving you the lot.'

'Well, that is generous,' I admitted.

'Settled then - be with you in under three hours, then I'm off.'

There was no time to discuss it with Bernie but, by the way he worshipped that other colourful bird, he'd be bound to be keen on a new one.

'Okay, bring him round,' I said.

There was a deep sigh, then a gruff, 'You'll not regret it. What's yer address?'

'Wisteria Cottage, Nuthatch Lane, Wood Hill.'

'Right mate. See yer soon.'

After I'd put the phone down I wondered if I should have given our whereabouts to a stranger who was urgently off to Heathrow. Maybe he was a wanted man, a murderer, who would do us in and steal our car?

'Rubbish,' said mother when I confided my fears. Any man who owns a parrot must be all right. I *love* parrots,' she added, thankfully well and truly brightened up from her previous mood.

That was the first time I'd heard her even mention parrots let alone love them, but I didn't say anything.

'Who's a pretty boy then,' she said in that kind of special voice people use when talking to bird brains, obviously practising.

'Nesbit's lending a hand outside,' I told her, 'so I have the whole day free from my duties. How about if we make something special for dinner tonight, something father will really enjoy ...'

But I couldn't carry on and voice the reason for wanting him to enjoy a special meal because the powerful emotion inside me refused to organise itself into words that might make the reason come true.

'Yes, let's,' said mother, brightening even more. 'He loves steak and kidney pie, so how about if I make the pastry while you whizz down the shops for the meat.'

And two hours later delicious smells were wafting from the Aga.

'Hope he doesn't sleep too long,' mother said. 'He'll not sleep tonight and ...'

As if hearing his wife's hopes, father's limping footfalls sounded overhead, then thumped down the stairs.

'Smells good ... what's for dinner?' he panted, leaning against the kitchen doorway, sniffing the air.

'Parrot pie,' mother joked.

'Carrot pie. Hope we're ... not going all ... vegetarian,' he said, plonking himself down at the table, chest heaving.

'Carrot pie!' exclaimed Bernard, entering through the back door.

'Not *carrot* pie, *parrot* pie,' chortled mother.

I was just about to open the Aga to get out the pie when a volley of sharp raps sounded at the front door. I hurried to the hall, flinging the door open, knowing it would be the new member of our family.

And sure enough, there on the step a very big parrot, in a livery of blue and yellow plumage, stood tied by its ankle to a free-standing chromium plated perch at my eye level. Solemnly it stared at me. Slowly it winked.

'What is this parrot doing on our doorstep?' asked Bernard, coming up behind me, sounding remarkably like John Cleese.

'I haven't had time to tell you. He's come to join our family.'

'Sorry,' a man called from the garden gate. 'He's nutless.'

'I didn't know parrots had to be castrated,' Bernard whispered, putting the idea in my head that perhaps if Cussbert were done he'd lose his raucous maleness and be easier to live with.

Mother wriggled her way between us. 'Oh, he's *beautiful*,' she gushed, lifting her finger up to his hooked beak which immediately opened and latched on making her yelp.

'Cocky don't hurt, he's only playing,' the man said, now joining us. 'Gary,' he said, sticking his hand out. 'Gary Bitter's the name.'

I stared at this shaven-headed Gary in horror. I'd seen body pierced young people in Great Piddlehurst precinct, but not as gruesome as this. This man had so many bits of metal puncturing his puckered flesh it was like witnessing the victim of a deranged torturer who'd been let loose with a staple gun. It was only by holding my breath and pursing my lips that I didn't immediately throw up all over him. I let the breath out and looked away from the cobbled up eyebrows, the drilled lips, the perforated nostrils, the ring edged ears, turning my eyes to the parrot who had released mother's finger and was standing motionless, staring at her.

'It didn't hurt,' she pronounced. 'And I think he likes me. Have you got those rings through your nipples?' she asked, blue eyes twinkling like a naughty schoolgirl as she addressed the young man.

'And through me penis, it's wicked innit,' he replied, making as if to unzip his trousers, but not going through with it.

My stomach flipped over again, and I put my hand up to try to ensure any rising vomit would be held in check.

'You'll never get through an X-ray machine at the airport with that lot,' Bernard observed.

And I noticed that all the metal rings and staples and bits and pieces minutely stirred as tiny ripples of worry spread over his whole being.

'I thought you said the parrot was a Green Fronted Amazon,' I said, suddenly aware of the disparity in its colour description.

'It is.'

'But it's blue and yellow.'

'Look, take a decko here.' Gary brushed his finger down the gorgeous ultramarine blue chest of Cocky, stopping half way and lifting the feathers. 'See. Four green ones. Suppose they should have called it A Tiny Bit Green Fronted Amazon,' he conceded.

'It's wrong,' I said indignantly. 'A Green Fronted Amazon should have more than four green feathers on it.'

'Then it'd look like a giant budgerigar,' Gary argued. 'Anyway, that's what the label said when I picked him up.'

There was a silence while I, and no doubt Bernard, pondered on whether we were taking on stolen property here. And the doubt must have shown.

'Well, are you up for it or not?' he said, anxiously glancing back down the path as if expecting someone.

And, whilst I wondered if I was up for it or not, the bird suddenly burst out laughing, sounding just like a very jolly old woman.

'He's a hoot in'ee,' said Gary, hooting himself in long inhales and exhales of breath, encouraged by mother also falling about, hooting herself.

When they'd both recovered, mother said, 'Look, look, when he puts his foot up to scratch his head you can see underneath his claws and it looks like a tarantula with two missing legs ... aaaah, isn't he sweet.'

'Wicked,' Gary agreed.

I looked at the parrot's snakeskin covered feet, both firmly on the perch now, noticing their peculiar configuration of two toes forward and two back, but failing to spot the sweetness my mother observed.

'I'm starving,' father's rasping voice called from the kitchen. 'Come back ... and we'll start ... on the parrot pie.'

The man's eyes narrowed. He looked at his parrot. He looked at his watch.

'Me check in time's real soon but this parrot isn't gonna be turned into no pie, I'd sooner let him go.'

'He means *carrot* pie,' giggled mother, pointing at her ears and mouthing: *my husband's deaf*. 'Cocky will be quite safe with us, won't you diddums.'

And I was astounded. I'd never heard her call any creature diddums before. She truly did seem to love parrots, especially this one. And then the terrifying thought shot into my mind before I could stop it: *It'll be company for her when father's gone.* Oh why did unbidden notions like that spring into your head filling yet more guilt cells, I wondered miserably.

'Bye bye Cocky,' Gary said, running his tattooed fingers first over the small smooth feathers on the parrot's head, then through the short bluish stubble on his own. 'I wish you luck in your new life. You wish me luck in mine.'

All eyes were turned to the parrot, but he didn't say anything, just stood staring mutely and adoringly at mother.

Gary turned at the gate. 'The aviary's in bits out here.'

Bernard and I walked down the path in time to see Gary climbing into a battered van. The engine clattered into action sending dirty fumes belching out from the back. And, with a wave of his blue patterned hand, he was gone. Lying against the hedge was a pile of rusting mesh panels, wooden struts and bits and pieces.

'What have you done?' exclaimed Bernard.

'Got my mother a friend by the look of it.'

Nesbit suddenly appeared round the side of the cottage. He walked up the front path to us.

'I heard thy voices, I say I heard thy voices, so I thought I'd come and tell thee, I'm packing up fer the day. What's this thee's got here then?'

'A heap of junk,' said Bernard, kicking a panel, sending flurries of rust falling.

'Nay, nay, Bernard. Not a heap of junk. That looks like an aviary in bits if I'm not mistaken.'

I was impressed. 'How did you know that?' I asked.

'Easy. Look. We used to keep budgies. See bird crap all over it.'

'Could you do something with it?' Bernard asked.

'Aye. First get rid of the rust wi' a wire brush, give all t'metal a coat or two of red oxide, then spray paint it whatever colour thee wants. It'd be good as new. I say it'd be good as new. But why d'you want an aviary?'

'For that parrot over there,' I said, pointing to the front door where the bird and mother still stood bonding with each other.

Father tottered up behind her. 'Where's my dinner?' he demanded, words spilling out in one quick rush of hunger.

'Here,' mother answered, 'just got to pluck him.'

Two days since we acquired the parrot. Nesbit is erecting the aviary to abut the outside wall of the barn so visitors will immediately see him as they walk out onto the field.

Meanwhile, Cocky sits docilely in the sitting room, not attempting to unpick the knot in what looks like an old dressing gown cord that attaches him to his perch, not attempting to fly, not attempting to talk, not doing anything but eat fruit and nuts bought at great expense from the village shop; and to plop onto sheets of old newspaper lovingly placed on the carpet beneath him by mother - though *not* cleared up by her, of course.

'He hasn't got much personality,' Bernard commented at lunch time.

'He *has*,' said mother aggressively, but not continuing to explain what.

I could see father revving up his thoughts and lungs to disagree, then the phone rang.

'It *keeps* doing that,' father burst out angrily, immediately looking peeved that the gathered up breath had been squandered on the unplanned eruption.

'Well it *is* a phone,' howled mother. 'Bloody BT, better change to Cable and Wireless, maybe they've got a different system, maybe ...'

Thankfully, I escaped to the hall.

'Hello.'

'Basil Argue here.'

I held my breath and heard my heart beating as if it had only just switched itself on.

'I shall be visiting my old friends Robert and Poppy Bambridge again on Friday. May I come on to you then - say, four o'clockish?'

So that was why he was in our backwater. So that was how he knew of my paintings. He wasn't a line-shooter after all. Enid and I were going to make our fortunes!

'You may, you may,' I replied, failing to keep my voice from whooping with unsophisticated joy.

After we'd said goodbye I rushed back into the kitchen to tell the others.

'That parrot ... has as much character ... as a ... tin of sardines,' pronounced scowling father.

Oh god, they were still at it. I'd hoped to miss out on the row.

'Tin of sardines,' mother jeered, 'can't think of anything but a tin of sardines.'

She turned to me. 'Sardines have got lots of character haven't they. You tell him. You open the tin and you never know what's going to hit you - big ones, small ones.'

'Yeah, yeah,' I said wearily. 'Some in oil, some in tomato sauce.'

'See,' she said. 'Freda knows about sardines.'

And I realised that was one of the few times she'd ever actually credited me with knowing about anything.

'Who was on the phone?' asked Bernard, mercifully changing the subject.

But, before I could say, the phone started trilling again.

'I'll go this time,' he said, beating me to it.

I tried to hear who it was but couldn't hear a thing because of my bickering parents.

'Okay ... I agree,' said father. (An amazing statement which made me concentrate.) 'Dead sardines ... in a can have more ... character than that parrot ... I was wrong.'

The only other time I'd heard him say he was wrong was when he'd let mother choose their kitchen flooring and she'd chosen puke green and mauve vinyl tiles and he'd kept on for ever saying: *I let her have her choice and I was wrong*.

A squawk came from the sitting room and mother leapt up.

'He never makes a sound. Something's happened,' she said, rushing out in alarm.

Bernard came back in, everything about him gleaming - eyes, teeth, expression, the lot. It was as if the whole of his being had just been buffed up by an over-zealous dentist whose polisher had run amok.

'Guess what,' he said.

'What?'

That was Tony Brownling. Not only does he want to bring another Japanese group next month, and the usual coachload of German visitors on Thursday, but he was just checking it was okay for three other coaches of Danish tourists to come this Thursday too. Apparently they love pigs.'

'Course ... they do. Danish bacon ... excellent with eggs,' chipped in father.

'Tony asked for a special quantity discount and we settled on four pounds for adults instead of five, but the children remain at two, because that's cheap enough already.'

I flung my arms around his neck. 'Bernie, we've done it. We've succeeded!'

'You'd better get some new badges made quickly,' advised mother, 'or we'll run out of prizes.'

'Yes. I'll ring them right away, get them to print the new ones with *I've been to Freda And Bernard's Animal Park and it's FAB*.'

'That *is* fab,' Bernard agreed.

'That should be *and it's FAB AP*,' said mother, pedantically.

But we ignored her, staring at each other, bright eyed with excitement, neither of us suspecting the true new wording should be: *I've been to Freda and Bernard's and it's a Sodding Awful Disaster! FAB SAD.*

Thirty

That night after mother and father had gone up to bed, Bernard got out the whisky and two tumblers then sat beside me on the sofa and poured out two hefty measures.

'Let's drink a toast to us and many more coachloads of FAB visitors,' he said, smiling tenderly at me.

'Yes. To us and our FAB Animal Park,' I said, swigging a mouthful, feeling its fiery path course down my throat, feeling Bernard's hot hand sneak between my legs.

'And here's to the piglets, long may they perform,' I sang, taking another large gulp then holding out my glass for a top-up.

'And here's to their mother, the lovely Hermione,' he carolled, re-filling both tumblers.

I sniffed the Highland Park malt, catching its peaty aroma and hint of smokiness, before glugging more down. 'And maybe we can get her mated again to produce another litter of performers,' I said, even taking myself aback with the dazzling idea.

He stared at me, sapphire eyes glistening with emotion. 'Then we could have a backup troupe in case any of our babies ...'

But he couldn't go on. He took another mouthful then picked up the bottle and topped us both up again, quickly reinserting his hand between my warm flesh.

We sat in contented silence for a long while, steadily drinking.

'More pigletsh,' he finally whispered, his glistening orbs turning maudlin.

I took another long sip, feeling the powerful spirit blurring my brain like a smudgy rubber.

'Le'sh-go-upshtairs,' suggested Bernard.

'Yesh-le'sh.'

'Le'sh take thish up,' he said, waggling the bottle. 'There'sh a little more left inshide.'

'Yesh le'sh. I'll take theshe too,' I said, clasping a tumbler in each hand and slowly toppling off the sofa.

Ripples of high pitched girlish giggles cascaded from Bernard. 'Tha'sh very funny,' he hooted. 'Come back up and do it again!'

'I will not - tha'sh hurt my knees and they've only jusht healed from the lasht time.'

'Why did you fall off the shofa before,' he howled, joined suddenly and terrifyingly unexpectedly by a sudden roar of laughter from the corner.

I turned to see Cocky, shifting from one foot to the other, staring at us. He caught my eye and started chortling again, so realistic that if I couldn't see his open beak and short fat tongue, I'd think an old woman was hiding there.

'It wash Cocky,' shrieked Bernie, tottering up to his feet, hauling me up to mine, dragging me out to the hall. Peals of hearty laughter came from behind us. 'He'sh good fun,' observed Bernie, pausing to change direction, lining himself up with the staircase before launching us both upwards, stumbling and crashing, giggling and shushing, slowly ascending, eventually reaching the summit where we teetered, mustering our combined strength not to fall back down again.

Chuckles floated up from downstairs.

'Full shteam ahead, wooo wooo,' Bernard loudly whispered, rocking backwards before gaining forward momentum, tiptoeing with high-kneed exaggeration past my parents' bedroom, reaching our open bedroom doorway where we became tightly wedged together, screeching and SHUSHING until, finally, I burst through, leaving Bernie, kind of wafting in the open space.

Come on, come on, don't just vacillate there, I inwardly moaned, my body primed for passionate action. I slammed both tumblers down and embarked upon a wiggly strip-tease dance brazenly facing him instead of the usual full frontal facing the wall.

Waving the bottle still clutched in his hand, he lurched eagerly towards me, miraculously kicking the door shut behind him as he shot forward. He halted, swaying. He put his finger to his lips.

'We mushn't wake your parentsh up,' he shouted, crashing the bottle down on the bedhead shelf.

I slipped a bra strap over one shoulder and winked, smiling alluringly at him. Galvanised by such seductive charm, he began feverishly tugging at his belt. I slipped the other strap over, gyrating both shoulders in sexy circular movements, wishing he'd hurry.

'Bloody buckle ish locked,' he moaned, jerking at the leather strap.

'Fanshy you wearing a chashtity belt,' I giggled impishly, lifting one foot and wiggling my big toe in his crotch.

'Not funny Freda,' he cried. 'I can't get the hole off the shpike. I'm shtuck and my prick ish ready.'

My supporting knee suddenly gave way and I took a header past him onto the bed.

'It ish, it ish, it's ready and it hurtsh,' he cried, yanking and pulling wildly at the belt end.

I stumbled off the bed, stood, leaned forward, unhooked my bra then whipped it off, twirling it round my head in gay abandon, playing for time, wishing he'd buck up and disrobe himself. But, Bernard ceased all effort and stood, fragilely balanced, watching my sexy performance, head going round in circles in time with my bra.

For god's sake get a move on I silently implored, flinging the bra in the air.

Bernard's head ceased circling, though his eyes carried on for a while.

'Tha' could shet the housh on fire,' he said, frowning up at the 38B black satin cups dangling from the lamp shade above him.

'Tha' *could* shet the housh on fire,' I agreed, 'but not *definitely*. But one thing ish definitely on fire, and that ish my Beatrish. But you can't shee it becaush it'sh hidden between my legsh.'

'I'd put out your fire if I could get my jeansh off,' he bellowed, collapsing down on the bed.

'Jusht give it a pull,' I encouraged leaning over him. 'No not my boob,' I screeched as he grabbed me. 'Your shtrap.'

Desperate eyes, like those of a baby seal about to be coshed by a cruel culler, roved over my face. 'Pleashe releashe me ...' he started, like a poor interpretation of Frankie Vaughan, and I was tempted to join in because I like that song, but he fell back blubbering and the seal image came back so I desisted.

I lay down beside him and patted his fully clothed body as if consoling a small distressed child. Slowly his little sobs died away and his breathing became slow and even. I was playing the motherly part too well and the bugger was drifting asleep!

'Oh no you don't,' I said, jabbing him sharply in the ribs and grabbing hold of his fly zip. 'Get your trodger out this way.'

He shot up, abruptly awake. 'I can't do it. I've never been any good making love out of my flysh. You know that.'

I knew that all right. I remembered a couple of humiliating experiences before we were married, standing in shop doorways.

'I will help you get your troushersh off my shweet lover, ' I said, casting my knickers and then my sandals off, though it would have been easier the other way around. 'Jusht wait till I am fully undreshed.'

'But you *are* fully undreshed. I can shee your breashts. I can shee your ginger ...' He leant forward, eyes sharpening. '... your ginger and grey pubic hair. I can shee you are fully undressed.'

'No. *No*. I shtill have thish on,' I informed my unobservant man. And in one deft movement I pulled the eyelet hole in the thin leather strap back off its metal spike liberating my watch. 'Shee, I can release buckles, I'm a fucking exshpert!' I crowed.

'I could be a fucking expert if I could get my fucking pants down,' he snarled, mood turning nasty, grabbing the end of his belt again and tugging so hard he flipped himself right over onto his front.

'Shtay there,' I commanded, delving under his body for the belt end, dragging it upwards with all my frustrated might, hoisting him back again, at the same time hoisting the hole clean over the spike.

'Shtand up and get 'em off,' I commanded. 'You're free.'

'Shweetheart, you are *brilliant*,' he hollered, still lying there. 'Now undo my zip.'

A volley of angry bangs on the bedroom door abruptly machine-gunned my ears.

'Undo your bloody zip yourself,' mother's voice bellowed through the solid wood. 'Some of us want some sleep!'

Bernard lay unmoving as if dead, jaw dropped down, eyes glassily staring up at my dangling bra.

At last my lips regained the ability to move. 'I shtayed a virgin till our honeymoon becorsh of my mother'sh door rapping,' I said bitterly.

'Well, you're not shtaying a virgin in our own home,' Bernard squealed, awkwardly rising up off the bed where he stood wobbling like an inebriated yogi, one foot lifted to remove his trouser leg. Slowly at first, he began hopping, then longer hops born of the need to keep upright.

'She'll not shtop me,' he re-avowed as he gathered speed, careering past me. 'Not in my own houshe,' he panted careering back to crash-land back down onto the bed, one leg at last now mercifully bare. There he lay, grunting, fighting with his tight jeans, until finally winning the battle and, laughing in hysterical triumph, flinging them down on the floor. 'Now for the jolly old shocks,' he said, twisting his foot back up.

While his slow and, by now, *un*tantalising disrobement was going on, my eyes were darting from his writhing body to the solid door wondering if mother was lurking behind it ready to pounce. It was no good, I had to see.

'Where you going?' he cried shrilly. 'I'm almost there.'

'Cover yourself up,' I snapped, hand on the door knob.

'But it'sh taken me all thish time to uncover myshelf,' he moaned.

Quickly, I yanked the door open, but there was no headlong entry of mother. I peeked out, and the only thing that moved was a spider. Carefully I shut the door then bounded back to the bed, throwing myself down next to my naked man. Grateful that, at last, my lusting frustration would get seen to.

He flopped his arm over my waist but that was all. I waited. Nothing moved.

'What'sh up?' I asked, perturbed.

'Nothing'sh up, that'sh the trouble,' he mumbled. 'It'sh gone back down.'

'You don't love me,' I grumbled.

'Yesh, yesh I do. My head is full of love for you ... but it hasn't reached downshtairs.'

'Why, did you leave your penis in the shitting room?' I said, rather nastily.

'Shilly Freda. Downshtairs - my old friend in the pubic garden.'

'What'sh happened to your old friend in the public garden?' I asked, exasperated at this change of subject.

'Not the public garden ... the *pubic* garden.'

'I see. How can I help you?' I asked, realising suddenly that I sounded just like a shop assistant. *Can I help you sir, double glazing, conservatories. We're good on large erections.*

'Remember when I pleasured you with the tangerine - rolled it all over your body including your ... you know what?'

I flushed at the erotic memory.

'Well, will you shink of shomething kinky - to get me going?' he said in a small embarrassed voice that didn't sound like my Bernie.

'I will. I will,' I vowed, yearning to help my poor dear man. I sat up and looked down at his little old friend curled up asleep, no doubt pissed out of its tiny little mind, incapable of standing. I looked back up at my darling's face, eyes squeezed tightly shut. I looked up higher to the Highland Park wide mouthed bottle on the shelf above him. Maybe he'd find it erotic if I placed his little old friend inside, I thought, not thinking of the consequences.

'Keep your eyesh closhed,' I instructed.

'Be kind to me shweetheart,' he whispered, a smile of hopeful anticipation on his lovely lips.

'I'll be kind,' I said, mustering husky sexiness in my voice. 'We're short on tangerines, but ... keep your eyes shut ...' I stretched up and lifted the bottle down, '... but long on whisky.'

'Are you going to anoint me with it dearesht ?' he asked, quivering slightly.

'Better than that,' I purred, not knowing I was lying. 'Just relax because it's time to put your little ship in the bottle.'

Fastidiously, I picked up his floppety old friend between forefinger and thumb, feeling a minuscule wiggle of interest before heading it into the wide clear neck of the bottle.

I watched excitement grow on his face. 'Ooo, there's shomething hard and cold, what are you ... Ow ow, it's hurting,' he shrieked, eyes flashing open.

We both looked down. His little old withered friend was now a pulsating puce giant jammed fast inside the solid confines of the glass.

'For god's sake get it out,' he screamed, veins on his forehead and penis bulging in unison.

'For god's sake I agree,' called mother's voice from their room.

'For god's sake I'm trying,' I cried, not knowing whether to try to tug the fleshy cork out of the bottle or to rush over and stand guard against the door.

'Do something,' screamed Bernard.

'Yes do something,' called mother.

So I let the bottle go, causing even louder howls of agony to vibrate the air as the falling weight pulled Bernie's rigid old friend sideways, nearly uprooting it. Fleet of foot, I bounded to my dressing table.

'What do you shink you're doing?' howled Bernard.

I picked up the only thing I could see to whack it with.

'I'm going to smash it with my hand mirror.'

'Smash what?' screeched Bernard, rearing up, grabbing the bottle, holding it upright in both hands.

'Yes smash what?' called mother, sounding intrigued.

'Smash the bottle of course,' I raged.

'Smash the bottle!' screamed Bernard. 'You will not.'

There was a pause whilst I looked at the door and listened for mother, but she kept silent.

'Oh, oh, oh, it's all right now,' sobbed Bernard.

And I dragged my eyes back to him, seeing the bottle now raised, parted from his battered old friend who had curled back down to recoup.

'Never do that again,' he screamed.

'No, I vow I never will.'

'Thank god,' cried mother, 'then we can all get some sleep.'

I heard mother's footfalls and turned my back on the kitchen doorway, busying myself with picking out the hard squashed-up little flies that passed for sultanas in my bowl of muesli.

'What a night,' mother moaned, entering.

Reluctantly I turned, seeing her straw hair drifting in clouds to her shoulders. Absently, she pushed a hank of it up, searching to secure it with non-existent combs.

'What a night,' she said again, letting the lock of hair go.

I turned back to the dead sultanas, face burning, head throbbing.

'I overslept due to you know what,' she said, coming up beside me, casting a meaningful sideways look.

Don't you dare mention it, I inwardly implored, taking a sip of water into my dehydrated mouth.

'How are we this morning then?' she asked.

Did I imagine the snigger in her voice, or was she just being cheery?

'As a matter of fact my arthritis is playing up,' I said, hobbling to the fridge for some milk. 'My hips and back are stiff,' I unwittingly added, feeding her the next line.

'Not the only thing that's been stiff recently,' she said, now definitely micky taking.

Father, breathily singing *Life is ... just a ... bowl of cherries* entered the kitchen. 'God ... what a night ... I've had,' he said.

And I cringed.

'Oh yes?' said mother, a stupid grin raked across her eager face.

'Yes ... I dreamt Hermione ... was dead,' he said, finishing off the happy tune in a breathy disconnected hum.

'He goes out like a light,' said mother, winking, taking my arm. 'He didn't hear anything.'

And suddenly I felt grateful to her and choc-o-bloc with filial love.

'Where's ... Bernard?' panted father, his rare musical rendition over.

'He got up early ...'

A snigger burst out from mother and I glared at her.

'He got up early,' I repeated, 'to make sure everything and everyone's in place - today's the big day when the Danes and the Germans come.

Larry is lending a hand as well as Nesbit and Enid - and she's bringing some of her garden produce to sell, so it's all got to be displayed.'

'And I'm helping too,' said mother hastily inserting bread into the toaster. 'As soon as it's ten o'clock I'm going over to help sell my hay perfume and your pictures and Enid's model animals, and her vegetables.'

Suddenly the back door crashed open and Bernard tottered in, eyes wild, hair dishevelled, hand held theatrically up to his brow.

'Hangovers don't suit you,' commented mother, scraping margarine onto toast, spraying brittle rasping shotgun pellets into my fragile brain.

'The piglets are ill,' Bernard whispered. 'Ring Vernon. QUICK!'

I knew when I heard that last word, shouted, and with no adverbial ending, that something was terribly wrong.

Thirty-one

Vernon knelt beside Georgie-Jesus who lay on his side blindly staring into space.

'He's still bravely smiling,' I quavered.

But Vernon ignored me and got on with what he was doing.

Porgie, suddenly staggered into view and I guessed he'd heard my voice. 'Porgie ... Hamlet ... here baby.'

His ears twitched then he ran full tilt at me, blundering into my legs.

'It's all right, I'm here,' I whispered, gripping his shoulders.

He looked up with unseeing eyes then opened his mouth and screamed. Appalled, I pulled him to me, but the sound set the others off and the air became rent with squeals and screams that blended into one relentless high-pitched screech that bit into my heart like a power drill.

'I can't bear it, do something,' I beseeched Vernon.

But he didn't reply.

Pudding blundered out of his apartment and into the yard. Keeping one hand on Porgie's quivering body to let him know I was still there, I craned to see what he was doing. In horror I watched him falter, vacillate, then run forward straight into the wall where he crashed down on the concrete crying pitifully.

'I can't bear it, do something,' I sobbed again.

Vernon stood up and peered over to the yard where Bernard was just lifting poor Pudding.

'As I thought,' Vernon muttered. 'Both troughs are empty.'

He turned to me. 'They all have salt poisoning,' he pronounced.

Bernard strode over, face ashen, Pudding lying limply in his arms.

'I heard that. My fault. I didn't notice. The gravity fed pipes from the spring must be blocked.'

Carefully he lay Pudding down in line with Georgie-Jesus then crouched between them, head bowed.

'I should have checked,' he groaned.

'Yes you should,' snapped Vernon.

'Quick, we must do something. Get them some water.' I cried.

'Wait a second while I check the females,' rapped Vernon, darting off.

Bernard stroked Georgie-Jesus's head.

'I should have given them more free time to wander, lap up water from the pond, but yesterday all I did was rehearse them, for today, their *big* day. Ironic isn't it.'

And the look on Bernard's kind face made my soul ache.

'And the unblocked outlet pipes would have taken every vestige of water straight away.'

'So, one minute there was water, the next minute none,' I whispered.

Vernon came running back.

'Okay, time for immediate action before they all die. But you must do it correctly.'

I thought of the gates about to be opened to the hordes of FAB visitors. They'd have to wait.

'My babes can't die,' I moaned. 'What must we do?'

'Pour water gently across the sides of their mouths. They might start to lap it up eventually.'

'Might?'

'Yes. Might. If we're quick. But really we need a team of helpers with so many sick pigs to deal with.'

I heard a sudden babble of voices, looked across to see Nesbit blithely bringing a large group over in our direction. Then Esmerelda appeared with another lot close behind.

I ran out towards them.

'We need help,' I screamed. 'The piglets are all dying. We need buckets of fresh water and people to drip it across the sides of their mouths.'

'There is a large schvine behind you. It look okay,' a blonde girl said.

I spun round to see Hermione, eyes wild, ears flat, galloping down the garden towards the pig unit, at last picking up the high-pitched vibrations from her dying brood.

'That one's the mother. She has her own separate water supply up in that mobile home,' I said, suddenly shivering violently in the hot July sun.

'All Danish boys and their mothers got to come with me,' said Esmerelda, taking command. 'We'll go to the stables over there and find buckets and containers, then we got to run to that pond and make a human chain to pass water up to them pigs there.'

I saw Bernard stagger out of the yard, one of the disconnected heavy zinc troughs clutched against his chest, heading for the pond.

A gust of Danish chatter blew through the group then quickly died.

'All Danish girls and their fathers got to go with Nesbit Batty here,' instructed Esmerelda, pointing to dithering Nesbit. 'You go up there to the mobile home and take anything from any room that will carry water - en't just buckets - even cups and plastic bags will do. Then you got to join the rest in the line. And it en't no good you being slow. By the sound of it you gotta act quickly.'

A tall blond man gabbled to the jostling mob in their strange Danish language. Then children and parents grouped and hurried away in a hubbub of excitement.

I ran back to Porker Palace, opening the yard gate for Bernard as, knees buckling, water slopping, he struggled in.

'Here,' Vernon instructed. 'Georgie is one of the worst. Freda, take this old beaker I found and trickle some water over the side of his mouth. Don't pour it directly in, it could get into his lungs and cause pneumonia.'

Grateful to have something positive to do, I knelt weeping beside my child and dripped water across the upward tilt of his smiling mouth.

Gradually a clamour of voices could be heard. Commands were being given in English and Danish and also what I recognised as German. So the Germans have arrived too I thought as I trickled water onto my first-born grandchild. *Rise up,* I inwardly begged him. *Please rise up from the dead like your namesake did, please.*

'God, this is awful,' said a familiar voice..

And I looked over to see Tony Brownling opening up the yard gate to let the top end of the human chain in.

'Take that bucket to Princess over there - the pinkest one - she's the worst of the girls,' said Vernon to a fair haired boy. 'Get your mother to hold her still on her side whilst you drip the water across the corner of her mouth. Not *in* it.' He looked at the mother. 'You understand. Not *in* it.'

'Ya. Ya,' she answered. 'Ve konnen.'

'You go to the fat black wrinkly pig,' Vernon told a strong looking man. 'She is panicking and crashing into things, hurting herself. You have to be strong and hold her, while your daughter drips the water.'

The girl shrank back looking scared.

'Remember, the pig is much more frightened than you,' said Vernon. 'And her life depends on your courage.'

The girl pulled back her shoulders and led her father to where Vernon pointed, but from where I sat low down, I couldn't see poor Big Belly Bella. I pictured her thrashing around in panic, imagined her ugly squashed-up face even more wrinkled in fear and her dangling pot belly dragging at the concrete as her legs gave way and it dawned on me that I'd grown to love our late arrival almost as much as our own.

'Every pig has two attendants and water,' I heard Tony Brownling say, 'so put any extra containers of water down here inside the yard wall, then leave quickly. We don't want the piglets worried by too many people. Your water will be used later.'

I craned my neck and saw eager children and their parents doing as they were bid.

'Thank you everybody,' shouted Tony. 'Obviously the pig racing and the midday show cannot now take place, but you are free to wander around these lovely grounds and see the other animals, or go to the barn and play in the rough and tumble area or get something to eat or drink. Or you can look over this wall to see the progress of these poor creatures, just so long as you don't make a sound.'

'What happened to them?' piped up a tiny boy perched high on his father's shoulders. 'Did an alien come down and zap them?'

Hoots of laughter from the older children were quickly quelled.

'Nein,' said one big boy. 'I sink zay was all poisoned.'

Vernon, sweating profusely, stood up. 'Their water supply was cut off,' he explained, 'and salt has built up in their bodies because it couldn't be flushed out by the natural process of drinking and urinating.'

Hot tears wetted my cheeks and moistened my lips with their salty shame. I lifted the beaker, aimed a few more drops of clear water across Jesus's mouth and, slowly, very slowly, the tip of his tongue slid out. Almost dizzy with hope, I dripped more of the crystal liquid, watching the thick muscular organ reshape itself, as if it were a separate animal, to gather up the drips. Then he closed his mouth and swallowed.

'Sweet Jesus is saved,' I cried joyfully.

'Georgie,' said mother dogmatically, her head suddenly appearing over the wall.

And I wished I had a wooden ball to shy at the coconut head.

'God I'm tired,' said Bernard, staggering into the sitting room, eyeing his favourite chair then crashing down on the sofa.

'What's ... the time?' puffed the favourite chair's occupant, already packaged up in his pyjamas and paisley dressing gown ready for bed.

'Half past ten,' said mother, drifting in, rubbing some sort of white cream round in circles on her face.

'What a day,' I groaned, going over and sitting next to Bernie.

'Don't know what you're so doleful about,' said mother, homing in on the silent Cocky by the French windows and air kissing his beak.

'Don't know why I'm so doleful,' I shrieked. 'All of our piglets at death's door all day and hordes of visitors turning up expecting them to perform. And you don't know why I'm so doleful!'

'They all said it was one of the best days of their stay - didn't they diddums,' she said to the bird.

'Silly bitch,' growled father from the depths of Bernie's chair.

'Well they did. I was with them. You weren't. Nor were you diddums,' she said to the blue and yellow thickoe she was besotted with.

'Never mind talking to dopey diddums,' I snapped angrily. 'Talk to Bernie and me. We were the only ones left dripping water across piglet mouths when all the visitors had left.'

'Quite. You were otherwise engaged. I was free to mingle with the people. All the ones I spoke to told me they'd enjoyed being part of the drama. The kids thought it was great. They're dying to get home to tell their friends how they helped.'

'Is that true?' asked Bernard, who'd been slumped back with his eyes closed but was now leaning forward with them open.

'Course it's true. Not only that, the kids made whoopee on the rough and tumble equipment and the parents filled in the time watching them by eating and drinking - Cynthia's hit the jackpot.'

I remembered Cynthia coming over after the visitors had gone. Remembered how I'd snapped at her that "couldn't she see I was busy resuscitating pigs". Remembered how she'd slunk off without saying anything. I am beginning to realise that if my theory about people dying when their guilt cells are all full is correct, then I've not got much longer to live.

'Not only that diddums,' said mother. 'They've cleared the gift shop out of hay perfume, bought all Enid's carrots and onions and three of her model pigs, and four of Freda's pictures, so your grandma had better get the brushes out again. And I'd better get boiling and pummelling.'

I stared at her, amazed. Amazed I had a new grand-relation and amazed that, providing all our babies survive, the dreadful day hadn't been a complete disaster.

'How were the piglets when you left?' I asked Bernard.

'All of them can stand and drink by themselves except Countess who laps if you pour water at her mouth but is still too weak to lift herself up off the straw.'

And an unbidden memory reared up from a guilt cell reminding me how often I'd wished that if one of our grandpiglets had to go it would be the Countess.

'She's so sweet the way she steals the others' possessions,' I burst out, causing Bernard to cast me a sharp look and then look perplexed.

'I'll put a ... notice on the inter ... net if you like,' panted father.

'What, telling the world that Countess can't stand up!' scoffed mother. 'Daddy's so silly sometimes isn't he diddums.'

'Telling ... that the piglet races and enter ... tainment is ... not on 'til ...' He looked at us. ''Til when?'

'Vernon says, all being well, they should be back to full strength by this time next week,' I said.

'Providing their supply of fresh water is kept up,' added Bernard, looking wretched.

'Lardarse is a pack animal,' said mother. 'Why not buy two large water containers to strap on his back and take him to the water outlet behind the pond to fill them. Then he could carry them up to the piglets. It'd be good entertainment for the visitors.'

'Mother, you take my breath away sometimes,' I gasped. 'That's *brilliant*.'

'At last she realises diddums,' mother aggravatingly said.

And I wished I were a vacuum cleaner to hoover the compliment back up inside me.

'Bed time,' yawned father.

'I pray to god that Countess will be saved,' I inexplicably said, rising.

'She can pray to god till the cows come home,' said mother, 'but he won't come up with the bacon unless he's a mind to, and he's not known to be strong on saving pigs - only ever saved two from an abattoir as far as I know.'

'God never saved ... two from ... an abattoir,' father rasped.

'Yes he did. Butch and Sundance. Remember? The Tamworth two?' mother argued, eyes flashing, not giving an inch to her ailing man.

'That wasn't ... god.'

He started panting.

Mother stared hard at him. I stared at him too. Seeing with a shock how thin he'd become. How pale he was looking.

'You're right,' conceded mother. 'Why would god save a couple of tasty porkers and let all the others have their throats cut for us to eat. It doesn't make sense.'

'Precisely,' said father, looking astounded at her capitulation. Then, in a quirky aside to the room he added, 'Being mortally ... ill has its advantages.'

Then his pallid face lit up with a grin which chipped a bit off my heart for ever, matching the chipped off front tooth he exposed.

'You've broken your tooth,' mother observed. 'We must get you to a dentist.'

Father, always terrified of dentists, gathered in his breath, then let it out in one long uninterrupted memorable sentence:

'I'd rather have a barium enema than go to the dentist,' he declared.

'Didn't know you had the choice,' said mother.

'The two things aren't connected,' said Bernard, still able to be puzzled by my zany parents even after all this time.

'Course they're connected,' said mother. 'Your teeth are in your mouth and a barium enema is shoved up your jacksy. They're connected by the elementary canal.'

'Alimentary,' I corrected.

'Oh yes, alimentary my dear Watson, I think not,' she scoffed, adding, 'Night night diddums,' and air kissing the clamped beak again. 'Come on Hector,' she ordered, clasping father's hand and trying to haul him up. 'Let's get to bed.'

'First ... I have an idea.'

We waited, all staring at him.

'I can't help ... out with the ... animals. Too much ... work. But I can ... organise signposts ... to guide ... people here.'

Mother's face turned to incredulity then contorted to jeering mode.

In the dangerous pause, I silently pleaded with her: *Please don't say anything, not now, look at him.*

I watched her staring at him. I watched her expression sadden, transform to tenderness.

'Yes, he's good at signposts,' mother at last confirmed.

Thirty-two

Ten days since the terrible day when our dehydrated porkers were nearly vaporised into pillars of salt. Mother quips that if they had died we could have made the most of it by getting Cynthia to sell bags of pork scratchings, then she curls up adding: *with stick-on labels saying already salted*. But I know she has come to love her great-grandpiglets really and it's just her peculiar way.

The piglets are all back to normal now, performing brilliantly, especially their new routine, dancing prettily with high heads and pointed trotters to The Dance of the Sugar Plum Fairy, which brings much laughter and applause. Countess was the last to recover but is now fully restored and back to her old stealing ways, bless her.

Father has been amazing. He's organised signwriters to make eight signposts and liaised with the Highways Department for Council workers to erect them on all routes leading to Wood Hill. He said he'd used his creative initiative and altered my wording, which frankly bothers me, but it's good for his morale and will no doubt be okay, so I've left him to it.

'Can't wait to see your signs,' I remarked at breakfast.

'Is ten ... minutes too long ... to wait?' he said, his sudden grin looking extra big in his shrunken face.

Ten minutes later came a knock at the door.

'Does Mr Salmon live here?' asked a man with an orange fluorescent top over his donkey jacket.

'Yes. I'm his daughter.'

'Good, he said you'd tell me where to put it. Come to the van and look. We've erected all the others but need to know whereabouts in Nuthatch Lane you want the last one.'

The signpost! Eagerly, I followed him down the path to his van where he hauled out the two legs of a sign.

'What do you think?' he said, holding it upright.

On a large rectangle of brilliant yellow, written in zinging blue, were the words: *FAB CAZ Private Park open to the Public.*

'What's FAB CAZ?' I asked.

'Don't ask me, I just do me job. Where do you want it put?'

But to tell him where I really wanted it put would have been too rude.

'Stick it ... stick it at the junction with Bramble Lane, along the road there.'

I hurried inside where Bernard had come back in and was stacking the dishwasher, and father was still sitting at the table.

'What do ... you think?' he asked, eager eyes roving my face.

'The, the colour scheme's terrific, the blue on the yellow really stands out.'

'To match ... the parrot' he explained.

Obviously kow-towing to mother, which proves how ill he is, I reflected miserably.

'Umm, the trouble is, I can't quite work out what FAB CAZ means,' I ventured.

I saw Bernard stop stacking and turn, pitching me a worried enquiring look.

'Wondered ... if you'd ... get it,' he said, smiling proudly.

'Well, FAB is obviously Freda And Bernard, but what's CAZ?'

'Children's ... Animal Zoo. I thought ... it was mem ... orable.'

'What about FAB CAF, Children's Animal Farm?' asked Bernard.

'Too much ... like an ad. for ... Cynthia's tea room,' he explained, looking pleased that we now knew he'd already thought of that.

'What about FAB CAP, Freda And Bernard's Children's Animal Park?' I asked.

'Thought it ... sounded as if ... it was extolling ... a brand of ... those Dutch things ... women use.'

He coloured, never having spoken about such things to me before.

An awkward silence fell, broken eventually by good-hearted Bernard.

'I *like* FAB CAZ,' he stated. 'It will be our new logo. We'll get ads and posters displayed, spelling out the acronym.'

Father leant back and smiled contentedly.

His tired eyes met mine, a look of loving care in their dark green depths.

I'd been about to query the contradiction: *Private park open to the public.* Instead, I said, 'Thank you so much for all the trouble you have taken.'

And was rewarded with another contented smile.

More and more people visit every day now, and we have so much money coming in we can afford to employ Larry early mornings and evenings when he's not working for Robert. And we can pay Enid in fivers instead of bags of manure, which, as she says, is a blessing, because her garden is full up to the gunnels, or, at least the flower bed edges, with rich fertiliser.

Nesbit, despite his saintly protests, has been reimbursed to some degree for his past work, and continues to help out whenever needed. From what Enid said the other day, to wit: *oh god, now he's turned to god*, it seems that Nesbit's need for spirit inside him has transferred to the Almighty's spirit, so now poor old god is having to listen to the woes and desires of yet another pious soul.

With all this help, I now have time to paint, usually doing quick sketches before the visitors come, then working them up in the attic studio during the day, popping down now and then to make sure FAB CAZ is running smoothly. Then adding the final touches after the last pig race, when the public have left and we're back to being a Private Park *not* open to the Public.

Basil Argue came the other day and bought most of my creations, upping the prices by hundreds on condition I paint pictures in a different style for our gift shop, signing them with a pseudonym. I have just finished a couple, painted in acrylic and signed Red Salmon. When I told father, thinking he, as Hector Salmon, would be delighted with the fun name, he said he thought that, as these were the cheapo pictures, they should be signed Pink Salmon, not Red. I suppose he has a point, but I'm not taking it. My hair's always been red, except for my faded frumpy years coming up to fifty.

A group of twelve are coming today at eleven o'clock. Mother took the booking and said they were going to pay in Euros. So I left my painting of Daisy and waited by Enid at the entrance to inform them we could only take sterling.

At one minute to eleven a white mini-bus entered the field and zoomed towards us so fast I was scared its brakes had failed and it would crash straight through the barn wall. But it screeched to a halt about a foot away and its side door slid open and I was astounded to see a variety of clergymen spill out. One of them, a bulbous eyed fellow with a halo of wiry sticking-out hair around his pink face, lifted his long black frock exposing hefty boots, and strode towards me.

'You are expecting us,' he said, fingering the weighty cross on his charm necklace as if superstitious that he'd pick up something sinful from me if he didn't keep contact with above. As he spoke the other men and a couple of dog-collared women formed a neat line behind him.

'Are there twelve of you?' I asked, to be sure it was the right group.

'Twelve, like the apostles. We haven't gone metric,' he said.

And I fell about at his quip until I saw his face was straight.

'Just had a funny thought ... about my pigs,' I said lamely, trying to justify my sudden burst of hilarity.

Then his face cracked and he chortled, 'You were right in the first place, it was a joke!'

'Freda Field,' I said stiffly, holding out my hand, feeling a twit.

'Father Badbreath,' he replied.

And I stared at him uncertainly. But his eyes remained grave as he stared back, shaking hands.

'Pleased to meet you Father Badbreath,' I mumbled.

And he burst out into sharp short attacks of ack ack laughter, setting off all the others who tottered in and out of line, hooting and howling like fools.

Father Badbreath, or whatever his real name was, at last simmered down and began delving in the deep folds of his cassock, finally pulling out a purse.

Remembering why I was there, and feeling more than a little miffed, I snapped, 'We don't take Euros.'

'Don't take EUROs! That's discrimination. That's what we're against.'

Out of my depth with this peculiar man, I tried to explain. 'FAB CAZ is a relatively small concern and we don't take foreign money - it costs too much to convert it.'

'What's foreign money got to do with it?' grumbled one of the flock.

'Euros. We haven't joined the single currency yet.'

'And I hope we never will,' offered an owlish looking man, who I think had been responsible for much of the hooting.

'Our group is called the EUROs - the Ecumenical Union of Religious Organisations,' explained Father Badbreath. 'We're here to assess whether FAB CAZ is a suitable venue for our EURO Sunday School summer outing.'

'Oh,' I said, feeling my face grow hot. 'In that case it'll be five pounds each and you'd better come in.'

'And, by the way, he said, grinning, as he stood aside for his disciples to lead in, 'my name is really Father Goodair, I like a joke.'

Now I've got three of them at it, I silently lamented. *Bernard, mother and now this f ... f ... funny fellow.*

'It's been top-hole,' said one of the twelve apostles. 'I've never seen anything like those piglets, the children will love them.'

They were standing in a bunch beside the aviary, newly erected by Nesbit and, for the first time, accommodating the parrot. One of the vicars was up close to the cage, throwing his head from side to side with such vigour he seemed in danger of having his neck sawn through by his dog collar. Cocky, one claw clasped firmly round his perch, the other clutching high up on the mesh, was twisting this way and that mimicking his movements with silent relish.

With mild interest, I watched the ever increasing antics of the decapitating head, shadowed with ever increasing gusto by the parrot.

Finally the vicar stopped, ruefully rubbing the sides of his neck.

'Does the dear creature talk?' he asked.

'Never,' I innocently replied.

'Pity,' he responded, drawing out a large handkerchief, flapping it out and gathering it back loosely together, raising it up to his ample nose, where he held it at the ready whilst drawing in a prolonged breath.

The parrot craned forward watching intently, beady eyes glinting.

The vicar, at last fully primed, let out the captured air plus whatever was dislodged from his nostrils, in one lengthy rasping raspberry.

'Stop that fucking farting,' squawked the parrot.

A tall thin Father sniggered in the stunned silence.

'I'm not sure this is a suitable venue for the Sunday School children after all,' said Father Goodair.

Mother of course found the whole story hysterically funny when I told them what had happened that evening.

'Who's a clever diddums then,' she sniggered to the monster who'd pretended to be dumb, now back tethered to his perch by the French windows.

'They've booked up for sixty children to come on August the twenty-seventh,' I said. 'Providing the parrot isn't within earshot.'

'Better kill ... the bugger,' said father, just to annoy mother, squandering the little breath he had in his lungs on laughing.

'Would you like me to run you to Great Piddlehurst General tomorrow?' I offered, knowing mother always took him, but thinking that maybe they needed some space from each other.

'I'll take him. I want to,' snapped mother, taking her eyes off the parrot to lob me a glare.

'I'll take him. I want to,' squawked the bird, mockingly.

And mother looked pathetically hurt. It was as if her best friend had suddenly turned against her for no reason. I looked at father's dull darkly shadowed eyes. I looked at Cocky's brightly shining yellow rimmed ones. And I knew she needed this friend.

'Who's a pretty Cocky boy,' I said, encouragingly.

And the parrot went off into gales of laughter, screaming raucously like a shamelessly drunken woman, setting us all off, sparking my father's eyes with a flash of emerald.

I came in at five to ten having blocked in the basic outline and colours of Alma, our heavily pregnant rabbit with the huge expressive eyes.

'Had a phone call while you were out,' said mother, eyes veritably dancing.

'Oh yes.'

'From the BBC.'

'Are you sure you've got the letters right?' I said, remembering the EURO fiasco.

'Perfectly. They're sending a crew along on August the twenty-seventh to film the piglet show.'

I gasped. 'Are you sure?'

'Sure I'm sure. It's to go out on Southern News.'

With trembling hands, I wrote the booking in our newly bought Appointments Diary, seeing it was the same day that the sixty EURO Sunday School children were coming, seeing it was the day after the full moon. An asp of unease slithered into my breast. Hadn't there always been a bright full moon when the animals went missing? Supposing a star performer was borrowed and not returned in time. There was too much at stake to ignore. If our animals were in danger of being nicked, the Police Force must become involved. Then hopefully they could enjoy a bit of nicking of their own. I dialled the station number.

'Hello, is that PC Compton?'

'Roight enough,' replied the familiar slow voice that represented our Hampshire Constabulary.

'Freda Field here, remember?'

'Roight enough,' he replied again. 'You lost your pig *and* your mother last year. Hysteria Cottage. Oi'm good at names.'

'*Wisteria* Cottage,' I corrected.

'If you say so, but my name seems more appropriate.'

'The BBC and the EURO children are to visit FAB CAZ next Friday and as it is the day after the full moon I am worried that one of the animals will go missing the night before, in other words the night OF the full moon, and won't be returned in time for Bernard to put on a good show unless, of course, as sometimes happens, the animal in question turns out not to be a piglet.'

There was a head-scratching length of silence, then:

'Can oi get this straight. Is this a problem with your pig and your mother going AWOL again?'

'No, no, no. Hermione is too big to be pignapped and my mother doesn't come in to it. It's the others. Pudding was the first, then Kermit, then Hamlet, then ...' I had to think hard. 'Then Lairy, yes he was the next. And last has been Jesus.'

'Jesus went missing?'

'Well I still think of him as Jesus but really he's Georgie.'

'Can Oi get this straight Mrs Field ... Freda. Are you reporting missing persons? Because if you are and they've all come back they are not missing and you are wasting moi toime.' He paused. 'Although, granted, after Jesus came back he disappeared again.'

'They are all animals. They have all been stolen. They have all been returned. As far as I remember - because I did not keep a diary at first - they disappeared once a month, at the time of the full moon. Don't you see. The animal borrower strikes when he has light to see by.'

'Ah. Oi see.'

Another head-scratching silence percolated through the ear piece, then:

'Do you think he doesn't have a torch then?'

'I don't know. Maybe he thinks torch light would be seen from our bedroom window, whereas in the light of a full moon he can hide in the shadows before pouncing. God knows what he does to them,' I cried, my imagination in full creative flight producing a horror show in the dark private auditorium of my mind.

Vernon Veal in the guise of a fox lopes across the stage, electrodes in hand, small-footed, pet-hungry. As he disappears the other side, Harry comes on dangling our sweet little kid by her back legs then flings her full force at the head of a man I somehow know to be his father. Silently they vanish and a fat old gypsy woman bounds on holding up a lucky white rat by its tail. She walks straight towards me and waggles it enticingly, before falling off the front of the stage. Enid Batty and Lairy lamb struggle together as they cross my vista. Then Larry, our wedge-nosed, small-footed helper stealthily enters from the wings, but I don't see what he's up to because I crash down the safety curtain.

'So what are you asking me to do?' queried PC Compton's plaintive voice.

'All I'm asking,' I said forcefully, 'is for you, and/or some of your men, to come to our Children's Animal Zoo on the day of the night of the full moon.'

'The day of the noight ... of the full moon,' he repeated, clearly trying to come to grips with the concept.

'Yes, and the morning after.'

'Yes and ... the morning after,' he repeated, grappling with the simple phrase as if it were a complex Shakespearean speech.

Hold the aggravation in, I willed myself, *it's never good to blow your top, especially when you're asking big favours of a policeman.*

'You'd be doing us and the whole of our neighbourhood a big favour,' I said, changing my voice to wheedling, though I'd never been much good at that, at least not with Bernard.

'Well oi'd loik to do our neighbourhood a favour,' he said, responding at last but still re-hashing my words. 'But how would that be?'

'How that would be,' I said, suddenly realising I too was getting into repetitive word re-hashing mode. 'How that would be is when the BBC come and film our piglet display, and if it is the usual brilliant show because all the porkers are present, Wood Hill would be on the map.'

'But supposing it weren't a piglet that were taken?' he asked, for once using words of his own.

'Good question. If Lardarse or any one of the other creatures went missing, think how disappointed the EURO Sunday School children would be,' I patiently explained, because I'd already thought of that.

To which there was another long silence, of the length where not only could he have scratched his head, he could also have gone out and had a pee. At last he said:

'All roight Mrs Field ... Freda. Oi don't know who Lardarse is but if the children will be disappointed by his disappearance oi'll arrange police surveillance. Me and one of moi colleagues will come to you on the day ... of the noight ...'

An image of the cogs in his head slowly turning, seeped into my mind.

'... of the full moon,' he finished triumphantly. 'And also, if necessary, the day after ... the noight ... of the full moon,' he whooped.

And, as I replaced the phone, a shiver of fearful anticipation ran through me. Soon we should know who'd been tampering with our animals - and hopefully why.

And then I remembered something Esmerelda said months ago. When FAB CAZ was just the glimmer of an idea:

You can have Daisy, you en't obliged to buy her, just so long as my son, if he ever comes home, can have access to her.

Esmerelda's son! The man who was in prison for murdering his father. But, perhaps he wasn't. Perhaps he'd escaped. Perhaps he was holed up secretly with Esmerelda. On the only time I'd ever been in her house, when Nesbit's Dick was served up to eat, I'm sure I'd heard a creak from upstairs. Perhaps he had a fetish about animals, not just the donkey. Perhaps he was like Welsh farmers who apparently didn't just shear their sheep but shagged them as well. I quivered, picturing horrible, yet tantalisingly erotic scenes.

'How'd ya like to come to bed with your little ewe?' I whispered to a startled Bernard.

'Don't you mean with your little *me*?'

'Ewe, me, whatever,' I bleated, knowing it was impossible for him to be shocked by picking up on the spelling.

'You, me, whatever what?'

'Whatever creature you want. How about if I'm your little pussy?' I said coquettishly purring.

'Don't know what you're on about, but it sounds good,' he said, dragging me upstairs.

And, as we made love, lewd pictures of Queen Pasiphae of Crete, bent over inside the wooden cow structure contrived by Daedalus, her bare bum bulging out the back, reared up in my mind. And, as Bernard fiddled with the top of the tube of KY Jelly, the rampant bull rammed its enormous manhood home. Only now I was in that wooden cow. I was that Queen. And I screamed loudly, one quarter in disgust and agony, three quarters in wicked delight.

'But I've not done the lubrication yet,' said Bernard, perplexed.

I look up in my agony seeing the Great Piddlehurst Labour Ward sign. 'Bear down with the next contraction,' says the nurse and my body hardens in the grip of torturous steel. 'Push again, harder,' she commands and I scream out loud as I split apart. 'It's a bouncing boy,' she says and I look down between my bloody legs to see the Minotaur, half-bull, half-man. It pulls itself up to its legs and lows weakly. 'That'll teach you to fool around with cattle, you silly moo,' sniggers the nurse, wrapping my baby up in a swaddling bath towel. 'But I just wanted to know what it'd be like to couple with a bull,' I howl. 'I don't want a minotaur son, I want Hermione my daughter.' 'Well you should have coupled with a swine,' she says scathingly, somehow knowing my precious daughter is a pig.

Thirty-three

It is late afternoon of the day of the night of the full moon. PC Compton, in plain clothes, plods around the grounds, hands laced together behind his back, eyes flicking.

'En't that our local bobbie over there,' Esmerelda called, running over to me.

'Yes I think it could be doesn't Daisy look sweet now her fur and mane have grown back.'

She gave me a sharp glance.

'Why is he patrolling the grounds like that? I been watching him from the stables. He turned up 'bout half an hour ago and that's his third time round.'

A tall thin man strode over to us.

'Hello hello hello,' he said. 'Nice day, though rather cloudy.'

I looked up at grey clouds amassing, already blocking out the sun. Full moon or not tonight, the animal borrower would need a torch unless that lot blew over.

'You're a copper too,' said Esmerelda, accusingly. 'What you doing here on my land?'

The man I'd secretly met and knew to be Detective Sergeant Perpendicular, on loan from Great Piddlehurst Station, turned on me.

'Am I to understand this is not your land.'

'We use it,' I explained. 'With Mrs Oven here's permission,' I added sheepishly.

'I ask again,' said Esmerelda, drawing herself up to his top button height, 'What you doing here on my land?'

'We have reason to believe, from Mrs Field here,' he said, 'that an animal of unspecified type is at risk of being abducted from these grounds sometime late in this day of the night of the full moon,' he said, obviously well-rehearsed by PC Compton. 'Or actually during the night of the full moon,' he added.

'Oh yes,' said Esmerelda, darting spikes of reproach at me through dark lashes.

'Or on the day after the night of the full moon,' he P.S'd.

'Suppose no-one were going to tell me,' grumbled Esmerelda, darting more angry spikes in my direction. 'Me, a partner and friendly neighbour who has let you use my land free of charge to get you going. A partner and friendly neighbour who you were going to keep in the dark on this day of the night of the full moon.'

'*And* the actual night of the full moon,' chipped in Perpendicular. '*And* maybe the morning after the night of the full moon too.'

'The fewer people who knew the better,' I mumbled. 'But you're right, I should have I told you.'

'Too right,' she said. 'En't no doubt about it. We'll discuss next month's rent tomorrow - the day after the night of the full moon. You can afford it now your zoo's doin' well.'

Miserably I went away. Esmerelda was right. I should have told her. There was no way her son could have escaped without the whole of our neighbourhood and the police force knowing. He couldn't be the animal molesting borrower. She deserved to have been kept informed.

But my mind was quickly taken off Esmerelda by a burly man running over from the barn.

'You Mrs Field?'

'Yes.'

'Savvy Scaffolding - the woman in there said you'd open the gates for us.'

'What for?' I asked the back of the man who was already hurrying off.

He turned. 'To get me truck in of course - can't traipse through the barn with bundles of scaffolding, there's only two of us, besides it's heavy.'

He turned again and hurried back towards the barn, turning his head as he went to make sure I was following.

'Come *on*, love,' he called. 'We're on a tight schedule.'

'But who sent you?' I asked, jogging after him.

'The BBC - they need a tower block built for tomorrow.'

'Oi would loik you to make an animal inventory now that you have shut the doors to the public,' PC Compton said. 'As far as Detective Sergeant Perpendicular and Oi can tell, nothing untoward has happened so far. Pigs are still snorting, goats are still bleating, et cetera. Nobody has been seen secreting an animal out of the grounds. But there was a lot for just two pairs of oiyes to keep watch on - especially while those scaffolders were on the scene. Oi hadn't been informed about them. There is therefore a small chance we just moight have missed something, so a full catalogue of creatures for us to check against is required.'

It took ages going round checking and listing the animals but at last it was done and I tore the A4 sheet off the pad and handed it to PC Plod.

'Oi needed it in duplicate,' he complained. 'Thought you'd have realised that.'

Detective Sergeant Perpendicular looked over his shoulder. 'Are you sure this register is accurate,' he asked, slightly menacingly I thought, glad that I'd never done anything wrong because he suddenly seemed the type to give a covert whack on the kneecap during interrogation.

'I'm not quite sure about the chipmunks,' I admitted. 'They've been breeding and I don't know exactly how many there are. I counted fourteen, but there may have been one or two small ones hiding.'

'Hoiding, where?' said PC Compton, taking out a notebook from his blazer pocket.

'Under sofas, or chest of drawers, or behind curtains,' I said. 'They could be out of sight anywhere.'

'You let them in your cottage?' exploded PC Perpendicular. 'We weren't told there were animals at risk of being borrowed for nefarious purposes in there.'

'No, the chipmunks live in their own house - didn't you notice a large dolls' house in the stable block?'

'Yes, it was infested with stripy rats.'

'Nefarious purposes?' queried PC Compton, picking up rather late. 'Do we know the animals are borrowed with such intent?'

'No, no,' I said. 'We've no idea why they go missing.'

'Mark my words,' said Perpendicular darkly, 'it'll be nefarious. Those animals will be vily used before being returned. Such depravity relies on the poor creatures being unable to make a statement or identify their attacker on account of being dumb.'

Images of Vernon plugging a "poor creature" into a voice synthesiser arose.

'So, there are *no* animals insoide your cottage?' demanded PC Compton.

'Well, only Cocky the parrot - he's been grounded for swearing till the EURO Sunday School children have left.'

PC Compton scratched his head. 'How do you ground a parrot?'

'Remove him from his aviary and tie him to a perch indoors. It's just a term, being grounded, his mobile perch is in actual fact quite a way off the ground.'

'Really?' said Perpendicular bestowing me with another dark look and I wished I'd said attached to his perch, not tied, for the thought bubble sprouting from his head read: *Should the RSPCA know about tying?*

Bernie, heavily scented with Chanel Number Five and looking dishevelled, having enticed Goolie first, then Goofy, into the vacant stall next to Daisy, hurried over. 'I'm getting as many animals as possible behind bolted doors. Freda and I will join you out here after dark.'

'And we'll stay till one a.m.' I rushed, in case they should think we were to do the whole night watch with them.

'In the meantime, I'm going to shower and get some food,' said Bernie.

PC Compton was stationed in the barn, looking out the window towards the field. If the full moon had been on display he would have been able to keep an eye on the compound containing Lardarse and Lairy the lamb, and the stable block containing Daisy, the two goats, the chipmunks, Alma and Mike Baldwin and their four fluffy babies. As it was, he looked into profound darkness.

Detective Sergeant Perpendicular was positioned by the hedge right down the end of our garden. If the moon had been out he would have been able to see the ark and run containing Cussbert, and Porker Palace containing the nine star performers and the non-performing black one. As it was, he also looked into profound darkness, alleviated only by light spilling from the French windows of the cottage way up at the top, Cocky's silhouette and magnified shadow swaying like an eagle about to swoop.

Bernie and I sat side by side in the mobile home, peering out into the darkness, listening to snoring grunts from Hermione and sighing bleats from Kermit.

Suddenly, a blaze of moonlight flared out from a rent in the clouds, lighting up a dark figure who headed towards Porker Palace. I stiffened, hearing Bernard's quick gasp.

'Don't move yet,' he said. 'Just watch. We'll catch him at it.'

A dark sweep of shadow sped across the grass, plunging the garden back to blackness.

'I can't see him, let's get out there,' I cried. 'Pick up the torch, we'll confront him.'

A sudden flash of moonlight burst through again and in that strobe of light I saw the man had reached the wall of Porker Palace, just a couple of paces from the yard gate.

'He's going for the pigs again,' muttered Bernard, rising, snatching up the torch.

I concentrated on the darkness where I'd last spotted him.

Abruptly, the moon became fully exposed, revealing PC Perpendicular, also fully exposed, peeing against the wall.

'Why did you walk all the way over to the piggery to pee, when you had all those bushes behind you?' whispered Bernard later when we crept down to him to tell him we were off.

'Because I'm from Southampton,' he replied, as if that were sufficient explanation.

'Leave it,' I whispered, sure that Perpendicular would be embarrassed if the subject of his peeing was enlarged upon.

'And people from towns don't pee in bushes, they pee against walls,' he added, completely unabashed.

And with that new piece of city folk law confounding my head, we left him.

'Can't wait to get some kip,' yawned Bernard, leading up the stairs.

'Nor me.'

But in bed I lay wide awake, brain racing, wondering who the animal borrower could be, knowing that if our gallant policemen were successful, by dawn break we'd all know.

Thirty-four

'At the time of our handing over to the police officers from Orlford Station, all of your animals were present and correct,' stated Perpendicular, wiping marmalade off his chin. 'So, the animal borrower has not yet struck.'

'As far as we are aware,' added PC Compton cautiously. 'Don't forget the chipmunk stock could not be verified.'

'It doesn't matter about them so much,' I said, provoking another sharp look from Perpendicular which had clear RSPCA informant underglares.

Bernard burst in through the back door.

'They're here,' he whooped. 'The television crew has arrived.'

Through bleary eyes I saw it was seven thirty. I'd been up since five. I took another gulp of strong coffee.

'I heard them coming into the parking field,' Bernard babbled, 'so I opened up both gates and the convoy drove in. Three lorries, one huge, all emblazoned with BBC RESOURCES ...'

I watched him as he spoke and could see him as a schoolboy, blue eyes sparkling, hopping from foot to foot, cap screwed into a scroll in fidgety hands, only now it wasn't a school cap it was part of an old towel used to dry off the pigs.

'... They're setting up their equipment. Fifteen or twenty people. All to film our pigs!'

Our eyes locked, and in the silent void when my heart stopped beating, a vision came to me of my piglets being driven around Wood Hill in an open float, villagers throwing flowers at their famous and most loved neighbours.

'Time to go,' said Perpendicular, making me squeal out because I'd forgotten he was there.

He rose from the table and jerked his head doorwards, eyes on PC Compton, who I'd also forgotten was there.

'Yes, oi'll just go out first to make sure the men from Orlford Station have been briefed correctly on their length of stay here.'

He looked at me for confirmation of what was to come.

'They stay here today ... the day *after* the noight of the full moon ... oiyes peeled, until the piglet show starts. Then, providing all noine piglets are present and correct, they can go off duty.'

'Quite right,' I said, trying to imagine a correct pig. 'Or they can watch the show if they're interested. Thank you so much for keeping our animals safe. It's the first month that one hasn't gone missing.'

'So far,' Perpendicular warned. 'Maybe the animal snatcher somehow got wind of our presence. Maybe the depraved perv will be skulking, watching, waiting, ready to strike.'

PC Compton yawned in a noisy, long-lasting, open-mouthed gape that eventually had me fearing he'd been struck by lock jaw. Then, in splendid synchronisation, his mouth slowly closed and his arms slowly stretched.

'Oi can't abide noight duties,' he said, rising. 'Sometimes a policeman's lot is not a happy one.'

And I thought they were going into full Gilbert and Sullivan as Perpendicular's low voice repeated, 'Happy one.'

'Police! Police!' Cocky's squawky voice suddenly shrieked out from the next room, provoking Perpendicular to bound out to the hall, one hand hovering over his jean's belt where a firearm would have been if he had one.

'Police! Police!' the parrot squawked again.

Following, I saw Perpendicular's demeanour transform from gung-ho bravado to prudent stealth. Silently, he flattened himself against the wall beside the open sitting room door, his lean body facing outwards, chin drawn into his long thin neck, arms straight down by his sides, palms pressing into our pale pink emulsion, looking amazingly and aptly perpendicular. I watched from the kitchen door, unsure how to tactfully reveal to the vertical copper that the voice was that of a parrot. I opened my mouth to speak but Perpendicular shook his head, his eyes sparking warning. Gingerly, he peered round into the room.

'Police! Police!' observed the parrot, going off into peals of realistic laughter.

'The parrot. Remember?' I said, apologetically.

And, whereas being spotlit peeing against a wall hadn't fazed him, playing cops and robbers with a parrot obviously did.

'*Should* he be shackled to that perch all day?' he blustered in his RSPCA menacing tone, face going scarlet.

'He's usually in his aviary,' I explained, 'but the Sunday School children are due here today.'

'So?' he said, raising half his top lip and the whole of one eyebrow in a face- distorting sneer.

'And the parrot swears.'

Perpendicular looked unconvinced.

PC Compton, back from briefing the two replacements, came and joined us.

'Hello, hello. What's going on here?' he said sleepily, extracting a hanky from his pocket and loudly blowing into it.

'Stop that fucking farting,' shrieked the parrot, eloquently backing me up.

'I see,' said Perpendicular, emphasising the *see*. 'Not at all suitable for children. But if you want to get rid of him we'll keep him down at the station. He could be useful.'

'How?' I asked, puzzled.

'Unfortunately, farting is rife in the Great Piddlehurst Station.'

PC Compton, looking relieved, no doubt because he was stationed at the sweet smelling Wood Hill outpost, said, 'Oi'd loike to get home to moi bed.'

'Don't forget. We'll take on your parrot if you want to get rid of him,' Perpendicular reaffirmed as they left.

Alone at last, Bernie and I stood face to face, holding hands.

'This TV programme could be the the turning point,' he said, an emotional tremor wobbling his voice.

'Yes. The publicity to bring crowds flocking day after day so we'd be able to afford to look after the piglets and all the other animals for ever,' I said, feeling tears pricking and wishing he'd let go my hands so I could wipe my eyes.

'And soon we might be able to employ people to do all the donkey work.'

'Esmerelda does that,' I hooted, doubling up - at least as far as I could with my hands held tightly.

'And go off on holiday - a Caribbean cruise.'

'Or an African safari.'

'Too many animals to be a real holiday,' I giggled.

Abruptly Bernard let go my hands and his eyes transformed from merry sparkle to horror-struck consternation.

'Oh my god,' he exclaimed, turning. 'I didn't shut the gates.'

'I expect the TV people did,' I shouted at the open kitchen door.

'All nine piglets, and Big Belly Bella, are here,' he announced as I entered the yard.

'So the show will go on.'

'For sure.'

'Were the gates open?' I asked.

He nodded. 'I've secured them shut and told the television people to let me know when they want to leave.'

'So, it's all okay then?'

'I hope so. I saw Lardarse, Daisy, Goolie and Goofy as I ran back here. But I haven't seen Lairy or Hermione or Kermit.'

Sudden fear prickled my skin. Hermione. My girl. The pig I love and adore as a mother loves and adores a daughter. The pig who presented us with our grand-piglets. My big fat child who, I just realised, has been shunted into the sidelines by her babies.

'Why don't you go up and check in the mobile home,' suggested Bernie. 'Hermione and Kermit are probably there waiting for their food, they often are if I'm late like today. You know where the pig nuts are kept don't you. And I usually give Kermit a handful of hay though she doesn't really need it with all this grass.'

'Look, there's Lairy over there,' I said, my worries about Hermione stupidly allayed by the appearance of the grass cropping lamb.

I jogged up the slope and puffed into the old yard.

'Hermione,' I called, as I ran up the ramp.

But she wasn't in her bedroom opposite and nor was her little goat shadow.

Quickly, I searched the other rooms, but they weren't there. Sharp jabs of fear pulsated through me. I remembered last time, just prior to the Christmas before last when she vanished. I remembered that dreadful day sitting waiting for the phone to ring while hundreds of local people searched. I remembered it wasn't only my pig that had gone missing then, it was also my mother. My mother who, it turned out, had taken Hermione away. But this time the blame wasn't my mother's, it was the carelessly unshut gates.

I ran back to the cottage.

'Mother, father, are you there?' I yelled up the stairs.

Father appeared at the top.

'Your mother ... went out early. Said she wanted ... to make sure the barn ... was ship-shape.'

His anxious eyes looked down at me.

'Don't you worry,' I said. 'Get some rest, you look weary.'

I rushed out to the barn.

'Mother.'

But the only human sounds were the talking and laughter of the TV people as they prepared nearby.

'Mother,' I called again, looking around, seeing the place had been newly tidied. I stood still, trying to hold down the panic, trying to think what to do. I looked at my watch: a quarter to nine. One hour 'til Enid Batty was due. One hour fifteen minutes 'til the doors opened. One hour forty-five minutes 'til the piglets' race. Two and three quarter hours 'til *the* show.

I dithered. What should I do? Hermione and Kermit could be in danger. Lost. Getting further away with each passing minute. Could, at this very instant, be being knocked down by a car, or even a bus, or a lorry if they'd got as far as a main road.

Then the thought struck me. Maybe the open gates were a red herring. Maybe the animal borrower had struck again, despite the Orlford coppers on duty. I looked out and saw the two of them skulking together down the bottom of the field, both in jeans and chequered shirts, both looking like coppers in mufti. Both lighting up crafty fags. With them on patrol, the animal borrower could easily have struck.

Maybe when the evil borrower had snatched the little kid my brave girl had refused to leave her side. Maybe he'd been lumbered with the Large White sow. Or maybe the animal pervert was enlarging his vile repertoire by dealing in twos. Or maybe he liked an audience, albeit a pig or a kid.

Images of disgusting unions permeated my mind and I wondered how such kinky pictures could be conjured up by my innocent brain. At any rate I was glad no-one else had access to my sleazy inner skull.

I looked at my watch: ten to nine. I had to do something. Tell someone. But who? Father was ill. Mother had vanished. Bernard was busy. Esmerelda was tucked up in her farm house due to sally forth and let Daisy out at some unspecified time.

It was up to me. I had to go out of the grounds and search. I raced back through the gap and up the slope, hoping in vain to see Bernard en route. I charged round the side of the cottage and out the front gate to Nuthatch Lane where I stopped, faltering, not knowing which way to turn.

Leaves sighed in the strengthening breeze as if commiserating with me. A bird twittered. A squeal sounded way off in the distance. I cocked my head, straining my ears for that sound again, but it wasn't repeated.

I ran across to the five-bar gate at the other side of the lane, surprised to see it was ajar. I took a step in, eyes raking Tinkers Field, wishing I could see the far corner that dropped down out of view. I listened harder. Heard the chug-chug of a far off tractor at work in a field, but no more squeals. Maybe it had been the sound of the tractor's wheel scraping against a stone? Maybe its engine was faulty? I dithered. To run to that far corner would waste precious time if they weren't there, and surely there'd be some sign of two animals and maybe a mother.

I turned back.

Last time Hermione and mother were missing they'd been at the school. That was where I should look. And, if I didn't drive, I could look into gardens and fields as I jogged along, keeping an eye out for dollops of pig dung or sprinklings of kid droppings - or strands of long blonde hair. Dread filled my throat with a solid lump of fear and I couldn't swallow.

Move woman move!

But supposing they weren't at the school?

Act on instinct. Imagine you're a pig. Do something.

I took off, trainer-clad trotters pounding past the entrance to our parking field, streaking past the exit, coming to the holly hedge behind which Esmerelda's farmhouse hid. I slowed down. Stopped. Should I call in and ask for her help? But she might be outside at the back, on the loo, in the bath. She might not even open the door. And valuable time was passing. I looked at my watch: nine-o-two. Oh god!

I took to my trotters again and, grunting with the effort, at last reached the junction with Bramble Lane. I flagged, gasped for breath, glanced across at our sign:

FAB - Freda and Bernard's Private Parts open to the Public

Oh no!

Some ignorant clot had spray-painted out the *k* and written *ts* in its place.

Vile thoughts of chopping off the hands of all graffiti goons surfaced as I crossed the road and turned right into Bramble Lane, heading towards the school. Then the recollection of mother's apparent mis-hearing when I'd originally told her of our Animal Park overrode the images of gore. Could she have changed the sign? Was she leaving a trail? Was she in trouble? Or, had she done it on purpose, just for a laugh?

Oh mother, where are you? And are you with my kid and my babe?

I hurried along, too puffed out to run.

At last the tall oak tree in The Bungalow garden came into view. Enid and Nesbit! They were always willing. They would help. My spirits rose. Galvanised, I ran. Reached their gate. Hurried down their path. Knocked on their door. Waited, like an overstretched balloon.

Come *on*. Come *on*. Open the door.

And at last, reluctantly the door did open and Nesbit's face slowly eased round it, body unrevealed.

I gabbled out my dire news.

'Nay, Freda, there's nowt to worry about, I say there's nowt to worry about. The pig won't have got far.'

He made as if to shut the door on me.

'But you don't understand. It's an emergency, you must help me,' I screamed, in an outrush of high pressure air.

'What's happened?' called Enid, pushing Nesbit briefly and accidentally into view as she manoeuvred in front of him.

But, in that fleeting moment, I saw his towelling robe fall apart, revealing an erect member clad in a strawberry pink condom.

'Sorry. Oh, sorry, sorry,' I gasped, backing away from the unusually flush-faced Enid.

'Not time to open up yet is it?' she burbled, clutching her satin wrap round her slim body.

And Nesbit's voice from the depths of The Bungalow uttered mumbled words that couldn't quite fathom, but got the lewd drift of.

'See you later, back at the ranch,' I trilled with forced gaiety that vainly attempted to fool her I'd witnessed nothing.

I heard the door slam shut behind me before I was two strides down the path.

As I tore along the lane, I pondered on his strawberry pink encasement. Condoms, fruity or otherwise, had played no part in our lives due to my inability to conceive, but Nesbit and Enid were of retirement age, so they had no worries on that score either. So, why did he use them? And did other male OAPs make love with colourful packaging on their trodgers I wondered in awe. Were we missing an erotic thrill, or could it be something to do with staving off arthritis?

But all thought of old men's penises gradually vanished as I hurried along, peering over hedges and walls until at last, ahead, I spied the long brick wall of the school. But, as the entrance came into view, I cried out loud. Groaned at my own stupidity. The wrought iron gates were padlocked shut. It was August. The school was closed!

Dispirited and exhausted, I turned round and headed back home.

As I half ran, half walked, past the offensive signpost into Nuthatch Lane, I looked at my watch: twenty to ten. Urghh!

Two cars were driving from the opposite direction into the parking field ahead. I pictured Enid rushing around to be on time to unbolt the doors. Wondered if Nesbit had been deflated after I'd gone. Wondered if my interruption had delayed proceedings, making her late for work. And today of all days.

Three cars passed me and turned into the field. What should I do? Keep looking? Take time out to tell Bernard? He'd need to know. He'd need me there for the pig race betting whatever happened. Maybe the missing trio were back in place. Maybe they'd never been absent. Maybe I'd missed seeing them.

I reached the cottage, staggered round the side, seeing Bernard walking through the gap leading Lardarse with head collar and rope.

'Where've you been?' he called up. 'I couldn't let Lardarse out with all the TV people here, he might have turned nasty, but he needs exercise.'

'Bernard! Bernard! They've gone,' I gibbered, tottering to him.

'I was hoping *you'd* do this,' he fumed, trying to hand the rope over to me as I joined him.

'I can't find Hermione, or Kermit,' I panted. 'And mother's vanished too.'

He stopped walking and I felt Lardarse's warm breath on my neck as the tall creature came up close behind me. I glanced round to see the llama's jaw gyrating ominously. I drew back. His long lashed eyes gazed into mine, then, slowly he leaned forward, lips puckered. I stood motionless, at the ready to duck the stream of gob. But, tenderly he kissed me.

As I rubbed my damp neck I heard a hubbub and looked across to see visitors spilling out onto the field. Oh god, Enid *had* come (supposition I realise!) and she'd let them in early. And, soon, the EURO Sunday School children would arrive.

'I need your help here, in these grounds,' said Bernard, wild eyed.

'Just let me ring for help first.'

'P.C. Compton, I'm sorry to disturb you.'

I heard the sound of a yawn. Then his reproachful voice: 'Oi've been up all noight.'

'I know. I know. I'm sorry. This is Freda Field. I rang the station and a recorded message gave your number. I didn't know it was you until I heard your voice. But even if I did ...'

'There's only the two of us stationed at Wood Hill ...' he said, stopping to yawn loudly again, '... and the other constable is off sick. And so will oi be if moi sleep is interrupted. It makes people go round the twist.'

'Hermione's gone missing,' I blurted.

'Oo Arr,' he said with immediate alertness, 'the animal borrower finally struck.'

'No, the gates were left open.'

Another long yawn crept out of the phone into my ear.

'Is that the Large Whoite that went missing sometoime ago?'

'Yes. Yes.'

'The one that went AWOL with your mother?'

'Yes. Yes. And they're both missing again. *And* Kermit.'

A long groan now penetrated my head.

'You wake me up to tell me your mother's gone off on a jolly with the pig again, plus a flippin' *frog*!'

'Not a frog. A kid. A baby goat. They jump like frogs. She's like a shadow to Hermione - you must have seen her when you were on patrol here.'

'Who, your mother?'

'No,' I screamed, panicking at the actionless time passing. 'The little female goat.'

'Oi don't wish to be rude, but you sort it out. If they're still missing in twenty-four hours contact the Station. Oi'm going back to moi sleep.'

And suddenly the purring snore of the telephone was all that oozed from the phone.

I looked at my watch: ten twelve. Oh god. The Sunday School children were due at ten fifteen, and I should be over in the barn to greet them. I dashed out but, as I reached the gap, saw children in pairs being marched out of the barn like a file of dejected prisoners.

I stopped, seeing Father Goodair and some of the previous apostles marching beside them, plus a stern-looking nun in full regalia.

'Halt, two, three,' balled the vicar who I recognised as the one who'd done the head dance with Cocky.

Abruptly they halted and the vicar strode back to the aviary where he once again performed vigorous head tiltings, but this time evidently searching for the disgraced bird.

'The parrot is not here,' he confirmed in a bellow. 'Pro - *ceed.*'

And the POWs set off again, now led by Father Goodair, cassock flacking in the wind like an ill-set sail.

'Halt,' he bellowed when they were near the gap, then, 'Dis - MISS.'

And the silent disciplined children exploded into a shrieking raggety mob which charged forward, crowding and jostling to escape through the gap, knocking out the little breath I still had in me as they stormed past. Father Goodair, who hadn't spotted me, turned back to the barn where I guessed he'd put his feet up with a cup of tea and one of Cynthia's homemade buns.

I chased after the escapees to attend to my blackboard duty, yearning to get it over and done with and go out searching again.

I forced my way through.

'Form a QUIET line to register your selection of which piglet will connect up with its named trough,' I shouted.

But, far from forming a quiet line, they swarmed hither and thither, noisily shrieking.

I yelled out the order again, seeing other children with mums and dads pelting over to join us. I surveyed the chaos aghast. About a hundred frenzied children were pushing and shoving, screaming out piglets' names and numbers read from the board.

I saw Bernard's horror-struck eyes under black hairy eyebrows that had knitted together like copulating caterpillars.

Suddenly, shrill silencing blasts from a gestapo whistle stabbed through the din and I spun round to see the nun, cheeks swelling in rhythmic billows as she pumped air out. Abruptly the hubbub died.

'ALL EURO SUNDAY SCHOOL CHILDREN LINE UP BEHIND ME, SILENTLY AND QUICKLY,' she roared, her face seeming to inflate in the tight confines of her wimple.

With a scuffle and muttered whispers, a queue formed behind her.

'ALL OTHER CHILDREN LINE UP BY THE RED HAIRED WOMAN,' the red faced nun rapped.

And, mutely, other children, with whispered instructions from mothers and fathers, formed a queue beside me. Never had I thought I'd be so grateful to a prison warder sister of mercy. I almost felt like running to the top of the slope singing *You go to my head, like the sound of music,* but the Julie Andrews image didn't remotely fit and, besides, the pain of my missing trio suddenly flooded back and I wanted to run to the top of the slope to escape outside and search for them.

Rapidly, I began scrawling racing selections on the board and, in ten minutes, all names had been registered.

As Bernard held up one arm and the pigs squealed, I was reminded of the sound in the lane. Had it been the tractor, or Hermione in trouble? But a sudden gust of wind sent the blackboard crashing off the easel and the thought from my head.

'Oy! That's dangerous,' complained a father, dragging his son away from where he had just nearly been hit. 'We could sue yer if that 'it 'im.'

I thought of the BBC cameraman, soon to be perched high on the scaffold tower beside the show ring and the fear of being sued was quickly overridden by the fear of a cameraman being blown off his perch and plummeting onto one of my piglets.

At last the interminable pig race and badge giving was over. Already it was gone eleven. Something dreadful had happened, I knew that. Or someone would have reported seeing a pig and kid on the loose, and maybe a mother. They were off the beaten track and I now knew where I had to look. It had been obvious all along. I hared across to Tinkers Field and stood just inside the gate, eyes darting. A distant squeal, as chilling as a finger nail scraping down a blackboard, made me wince. That was definitely my pig, and she was in trouble.

Half demented with fear I charged across the rutted ground towards the hidden corner but, half-way, my foot plunged into a grass-hidden hole, twisting my ankle, throwing me down. I groaned, pushed myself up, stood awkwardly facing my invisible goal. I had to get to the low corner of the field, the force was pulling me.

Wind buffeted me from behind, sending my tangled curls streaming forward, flashing dangerous red in and out of my vision. I pushed a hank back behind one ear and, as if exposing my ear hole made the difference, picked up faint sounds of a cry for help. Mother! It was my mother.

'I'm coming,' I cried, dashing forward with all the speed I could limp.

The ground began to drop away and the low corner gradually became visible. First the tops of bushes. Then quick flashes of Kermit's bouncing head. Then the tops of my mother's head and Hermione's. Then the boggy mire in which my baby floundered. Then the rough ground on which my mother lay.

'Hold on there,' I screamed, cantering down the slope with the uneven gait of a chimpanzee.

Good foot solidly down, bad foot lightly down and quickly up. Good foot solidly down, bad foot lightly down and quickly up. Rhythmically I galloped towards them, seeing with horror that, far from floundering, Hermione was stuck immobile in the centre of the bog and mother, splattered all over with mud with the even splodged pattern of a leopard, lay on her back on puddled coarse grass, a long thin branch clutched in one hand. Kermit, bleating with the intensity of a pneumatic drill, jumped up and down, wild eyes swivelling between Hermione and me.

'What kept you?' mother moaned as I stumbled towards her.

I knelt in a puddle, took her poor muddied hand in my clean one.

'Mother, mother,' I cried. 'What's happened? Why are you here? Why are you flat on your back?'

'Saving your pig, that's why I'm here. And I'm flat on my back because I've ricked my ankle and I got tired of sitting up.'

'It's the rutted ground,' I said understandingly. 'I've just done the same. I feel as if mine is broken.'

'Trust you,' she snapped, hauling herself up into sitting position. 'Always got to go one better.'

If she could make snotty remarks like that she wasn't too bad I thought, hurt. I turned to survey Hermione. My poor lamb stood up to her armpits in gungy mud. I dreaded it was slow-sucking quickmire and that imperceptibly she was disappearing. Our eyes met and she let forth a series of short and long honks which, I knew from past experience, was her piggy morse code SOS.

Kermit trotted over on mud clogged hooves, nudging her damp little nose up under my hand in a sweet gesture, then she turned her strange horizontal bar pupils towards Hermione and bleated pitifully, begging me to save her friend.

Mother leaned forward, clutching her fat red ankle in both muddy hands.

'I was tidying the barn,' she said. 'I went out, saw the television people, saw the gates had been left open, looked up the parking field to see Hermione and the kid running out of the entrance into Nuthatch Lane. You weren't around, nor was Bernard, so I ran after them and found they were already halfway across this field. By the time I'd caught up with them, the pig was in the mire. And so was I when I fell down and couldn't get up.'

'Oh mother, thank you,' I cried fervently.

'Don't thank me,' she snapped. 'If I'd known what was going to happen I wouldn't have bothered. I'd have happily left them to get on with it. Hours I've spent in this hell-hole, in agony and bored stiff. And look at my new flares, ruined! Cost a fortune these trousers, *and* they're the height of fashion.'

She repositioned her hands and groaned.

'Oh mother, thank you,' I cried again.

'Oh shut up keep repeating yourself,' she ungratefully said. 'Just see how you get on extracting your pig from that bog. I've tried. My god I've tried. I've tried with sticks and stones and shouting. But it's impossible. She's stuck fast. We'll have to get a tractor or the fire brigade.'

I turned to my darling porker. Our eyes locked. I held out both hands. 'Come to mummy baby' I crooned.

And with the sucking sound of jelly releasing from a mould, and a peppering of rapid squeals, she pushed one front leg forward against the pressure of the bog, then a hind one, then the other front and the other hind. And slowly, leg by leg, trotter by trotter, squelch by squelch, honk by honk, my big fat girl came forth from the thick mire, like Aphrodite coming forth from the sea foam.

'Fucking hell,' exploded my mother.

And I was astounded. That was the first time I'd ever heard her use that word.

The kid, in a series of robust leaps, sprang to her beloved's side, resuming her normal close position, like a Siamese twin connected by invisible two inch threads.

I stroked Hermione's big mud-splattered head, gently cooing to calm her. 'Never mind the fucking pig,' yelled mother, getting into the swing of it. 'What about me!'

I hobbled away from Hermione back to her. 'There, there,' I soothed. 'Let me try and help you up.'

I bent down, inserting my hands under her armpits, then forcing them through to lift her light body on rigid arms like a mechanical forklift.

'Shall I roll up your trouser leg to stop it flapping when you walk?'

'I *can't* walk,' she exploded. 'I can't even put my foot down.'

She hung on to me, balancing on one foot. I looked round for inspiration and my eyes were arrested by Hermione's broad back.

'Maybe you could ride Hermione, you're very light,' I said, at a loss for something more constructive to suggest.

'You think I'm a fucking cowgirl,' she cried, now in full effing spate.

'Or maybe *I* could give you a piggy-back ride,' I rashly offered, forgetting for a moment my damaged ankle, then realising with surprise that the pain had subsided to a mere faint ache.

'Not with your broken, or was it fractured, ankle,' she sniped. 'You're not being a martyr on my behalf. If anyone's giving me a piggy-back ride it'll be the real macoy.' She jerked her head at my pig.

'You mean you'll really give it a go?' I asked, astounded, because it hadn't actually been a serious suggestion.

'I'm hungry, thirsty and in agony, so fucking yes.'

She shivered and I eyed her anxiously.

'Well, do something,' she snapped.

Hermione was sauntering off ahead with Kermit as if nothing had happened. 'Here baby,' I called.

But she carried on up the steep slope, oblivious.

'HALT PIG,' yelled mother.

And my big strong girl obeyed, sending Kermit into an immediate frenzy of leaps and bleats as she tried to undermine mother's command. Slowly, with mother hopping and moaning, we made our way to the porcine chariot and, fending Kermit off, manoeuvred mother, bad leg by the pig's side.

'Try and throw your damaged leg over,' I urged.

'Can't you wipe her down a bit. Just look at her.'

I looked down at the gently rounded pink back that abruptly changed to gungy brown below a plimsoll line running under her tail and round her body to the lower part of her neck.

'Just throw your leg over, your trousers will wash.'

'Suppose I've no option,' she grumbled, lifting her leg back and tilting forward, like a clumsy ballerina. Gingerly, I hung onto her waist as she slid her back leg over Hermione's tail.

'Oh, oh, it hurts where my ankle touches,' she cried.

'Be brave,' I encouraged, heaving her up.

'Don't let go,' she begged, at last astride my porker, one hand clutching at my shoulder, the other down on the pig's neck.

'You look all twisted,' I said, pulling her back a bit, making her yelp.

'Don't *do* that!' she reproached. 'The bristles spike right through to my flesh.'

Hermione's eyes swivelled round to me, their whites gleaming like a mad creature's. She let out a stream of grunts which I knew meant: *if you care a sausage for me you'll get your mother off my back*. I thought of times in the past when Bernard had expressed the same sentiment, though not nowadays I hastily amended, not wanting more unkind thoughts to be filed away in my already jam packed guilt store.

'Come on my girl, giddy-up' I commanded, keeping a firm grip around mother's waist with one hand and patting the pig with the other.

'Watch out,' squealed mother, 'you'll have me off.'

Hermione began lifting each hind trotter in turn without making any progress, as if the front two legs didn't work, and I began to worry that it was the prelude to her kicking both back legs up in the air to buck mother off. But it wasn't, it was the equivalent of revving up an engine for a hill start and, when the hind legs had achieved optimum momentum, the fore legs began to move, and suddenly my pig was walking.

Mother, legs splayed, torso twisted, squeaked out in fright.

'I don't feel safe,' she cried.

'There, there,' I said inadequately again.

'You're getting so fucking repetitious,' she hollered. (And I carefully held back from telling her she wasn't doing so badly on that front herself.) 'Can't you get this pantechnicon of yours to walk without rolling like a fucking ship.' (Manfully, I still bit my tongue.)

'Just be glad she's walking at all, it's steep here,' I said, hanging on to mother and kicking out at Kermit who leapt around bleating loudly in overt jealousy.

Slowly we processed, me hobbling, the kid bouncing, Hermione getting into her stride once we were on the flat, making almost stately progress.

'Georgie-Jesus, this is uncomfortable,' groaned mother. 'I'm doing the splits sideways for the first time since I was ten. And I'm twisted so much my back is killing me.'

'Not for much longer,' I soothed.

And silently, except for groans, snorts and bleats, our strange caravan traversed the wide field until at long last we were out through the open five-bar gate and crossing Nuthatch Lane.

As we reached the other side, clapping and cheering broke out from behind the fence in the parking field and my heart ached. The show that would put us on the map had started, and I wasn't even there.

'Where's Hector?' mother suddenly asked.

'Still in the cottage, in bed I think, he didn't look too good earlier.'

'Well I don't want to go in and worry him, just look at me.'

I stared at her mud-splattered clothes and her mud-splattered hair, untidy hanks falling over her anxious white face. I looked down at her swollen ankle sticking out from the cream and red flares. The sight of his wife in this plight would undoubtedly worry him. And he patently had enough of that of his own.

'Maybe I could clean you up a bit in the barn,' I said doubtfully.

'Yes, yes, that'd be it,' she agreed. 'There's always hot water and towels in the Ladies and Cynthia keeps a hairbrush and a mirror round the side. Your father mustn't see me like this, it'd do him no good.'

And I was touched. Sometimes in the past I'd wondered if she really loved him. This unexpected thoughtfulness proved she really did.

'And all the visitors will be at the show,' I said, warming to the idea, 'so no-one will see us.'

'Yes, yes. It'll be a longer walk but we've come so far.'

'Right,' I said guiding the plodding Hermione towards the entrance to the parking field, seeing, as we entered, a cameraman high up on the scaffold tower, his back to us.

Strains of The Sugar Plum Fairy and a sudden burst of laughter, followed by cheers came from over the fence.

Concentrating on keeping Kermit off my back, metaphorically speaking, and off Hermione's back, literally speaking and, at the same time, holding mother in place, it wasn't 'til we reached the barn that I saw the doors were shut fast. We halted in front of them, Kermit lightly bouncing, Hermione emitting sighing grunts and peering up at me with pleading piggy eyes.

'Enid must have closed the doors while the show was on so she could go and look,' I moaned.

'We can't go back,' mother whispered weakly. 'I'm all in.'

'Then we'll have to open one of the gates in the fence and go in that way.'

Mother nodded.

'Everyone's eyes will be on the piglet display to the right. We'll sneak round to the barn on the left.'

'Okay,' groaned mother.

'Not far baby,' I whispered to Hermione, tapping her backside to get her going again.

'Not far for you,' blared mother, thinking I was talking to her. 'You're not doing the fucking splits on a fucking pig.'

I pondered on whether she'd keep this up when the pressure was off and father was within earshot.

We reached the gates and, manoeuvring Hermione to one side, I pulled mother up from leaning on the porky neck to leaning precariously against the fence, her fingers gripped round a post.

'Don't let the pig move,' she cried fearfully.

Terrified Hermione would do just that, I rushed to the gate, stretched up and pulled the hasp over then grabbed the handle and turned, pushing the left gate open.

I dived back to mother. 'Okay. Now hang on to me.'

And we set off again, slowly turning into the grounds, weary Kermit still lowly leaping and wearier Hermione pathetically grunting.

'Hang onto her neck a minute,' I said, mindful that this whole sorry expedition was because someone had not closed the gate.

As I secured it shut, gales of laughter erupted from the show ring again.

I turned back to mother who was clinging onto Hermione's neck and sliding sideways, her bad foot almost down on the ground.

'Not long now,' I comforted, half lifting her back into position, mindful of the spikes.

As we set off again for the last few steps to the barn, I looked back, looked up, and found I was staring straight into the lens of a camera aimed by the fiend who was twisted round on his spying platform on top of the tower.

Wickedly, I prayed a gust of strong wind would spring up and blow him and his equipment down, smashing the camera into smithereens onto the ground - but clear of my pigs of course.

I looked back again as we turned into the safety of the barn, but the cursed lens was still aimed upon us.

So much for prayer.

Thirty-five

'What a day,' sighed Bernard. 'The television crew said the show was brilliant, even though the piglets' frisbees kept coming back at them because of the strong wind.'

The strong wind that hadn't gusted strong enough to detach that spyman off his perch, I reflected miserably.

'They said it made it funnier,' Bernard added, handing me a tumbler of whisky.

Mother hobbled in leaning heavily on a walking stick, her ankle encased in the removable support supplied by the doctor. She wore a knee-length white towelling dressing gown, and a blue towel was wound round her wet hair.

'Do you feel better after your bath?' I asked.

She sank down into a chair. 'Much,' she said, closing her eyes and resting her head back.

I studied her. Without the bright twinkle in her blue eyes, without her wide smile, without her straw-coloured hair swathed up on top with its fetching loose tendrils, she looked frail and more vulnerable than I'd ever seen her. I wanted to take her into my arms and hug her close to me.

'I can feel you're looking at me Freda,' she snapped, 'and I don't like being scrutinised without my makeup on. Thank *you* very much.'

'I'm not,' I lied, quickly turning to look at the television that was flickering in the corner with the sound off.

Bernard picked up the remote control. 'It's the main news now and the regional news straight after. I'll put the sound up then,' he said. 'That's when we'll be on.'

I saw his hand was shaking.

He couldn't see my inside was shaking.

But maybe we'd been too far away to be in focus. Maybe they'd only show a snippet at the end. In any event, they'd be bound to broadcast the full wonders of the display and our Animal Park would be made.

Mother opened her eyes and I noticed how weary they looked.

'Have a whisky,' I offered.

'Oh sorry, ma-in-law,' Bernard said leaping up. 'My mind is on the show. Is Hector coming down?' he asked as he poured from the new bottle of Highland Park.

A vision of his pulsating appendage stuck fast in the neck billowed into my head.

'What're you smirking at?' said mother, none too kindly. 'Thought you were meant to have a broken ankle.'

'Well I haven't,' I said. 'It's okay now. It's only when it swells up that it hurts.'

I grinned meaningfully at Bernard, but the subtle innuendo was lost on him.

'It brought the house down when Jesus came down the ramp on the skate-board for the grand finale,' he said, his whole being radiating rapture.

'Georgie!' said mother irritable. 'And they say it's old people that forget.'

'But his trotters only just fit on that board now, he's getting so big and fat. I'll have to try and make a larger board, or think up a new finale.'

Father suddenly appeared in the doorway.

'I understand ... the piglet show ... is on soon,' he puffed.

'Yes, yes, soon,' confirmed Bernard, ushering father into his chair.

'Nice and ... warm,' said father smiling appreciatively.

'Look,' I squeaked, 'put the sound up, the main news is ending.'

I glanced at my watch: nearly twenty past nine. Southern News finished at nine thirty so we had ten minutes. Enough time to make us famous.

A thrill shivered through me, like the moment before my first sex. I blanked my mind to the disappointment.

'And here is news in the South,' said a newsreader who I'd never seen before but looked as if he'd just left school. 'Read by William Just.'

'And Elizabeth Violet,' added a woman with a tall hairstyle and a low neckline.

Pictures of horses in a glade surrounded by trees came onto the screen.

'It has been reported that New Forest ponies are being sold to the French to eat,' said the woman.

The scene changed to a man.

'I 'ave to say zat we French people prefer to eat British 'orses to British cows,' he said.

'Never mind the horses, what about our pigs,' roared Bernard.

'Not only do zay taste better,' the man continued, 'but zay do not make you go mad. At least, as far as we know.'

The picture faded and the boy newscaster reappeared.

'So much for ponies and frogs,' he said, sniggering. 'And now on to our other main news story.'

Bernard leaned forward.

'This is it,' he muttered.

But a picture of Great Piddlehurst General Hospital appeared.

Now father leaned forward.

'That's where ... I go,' he said, beaming.

And for the next few minutes it was all about dirty wards and hard working nurses, though it might have been about dirty nurses and hard working wards for all I took in. Three minutes to go and no sign of a piglet. I looked at Bernard who had slumped back and shrivelled as if all of his innards had been vacuumed out of him.

Great Piddlehurst General finally disappeared and the school kid announcer came back.

'And to end with, a peculiar sight in Wood Hill Village at a dippy place called FAB CAZ.'

And the overhead shot of the back view of mother riding the pig, muddy and bedraggled, legs splayed, twisted round hanging on to me, appeared. The camera zoomed in to a close-up as we slowly processed away.

I stared in horror at the picture. My god, my bum looked big!

Then I turned, looked up, hair flying around looking awful. My horrified eyes grew bigger as the dastardly cameraman zoomed in, eventually filling the screen with my mouth which was twisted in ugly consternation. Abruptly, a close-up of mother's swollen ankle appeared.

'Looks as if there's been an outbreak of foot and mouth disease at FAB CAZ,' said William Just, exploding into peals of school boy laughter.

Relentlessly the nightmare rolled on, finally and horrendously ending with a shot of my trainer-clad foot kicking out at the kid.

'Ooops,' said William Just. 'Whoever she is, she doesn't like goats.'

I groaned. Bernard groaned. Mother groaned.

'What was ... all that?' asked father, astounded.

'That's what I'd like to know,' said Bernard grimly, clicking it off. Breakfast was eaten in virtual silence. None of us had been able to sleep and even father had come down to join us.

'I tossed and turned ... all night,' he said.

'All I was pleased about,' said mother, 'was that none of my Tooting Bec Bridge Club friends would have seen it - it *was* only on in the south wasn't it?'

'Yes,' I confirmed, in my first utterance of the already long morning. I peered at my watch: one minute to seven.

The rattle of the post-box heralded the arrival of the post.

Bernard, always naively optimistic that something other than junk mail and bills would be delivered, leapt up and fetched it.

'Look,' he said, coming back. 'A postcard to Cocky from Rio de Janeiro. Dear Cocky,' he read, 'plenty of beautiful Brazilian birds here so feel at home, though am missing you. Went to a parrot show where macaws rode bicycles and tight-rope walked, but none of them could skateboard as well as you. Hope you're being looked after okay, Gary. P.S. To the new owners - forgot to say, don't pass wind or blow your nose in company!'

'Diddums can skateboard, isn't he clever,' whooped mother, eyes back to sparkling.

Bernard looked thoughtful. 'Could be the answer to my prayers,' he said.

How come yours get answered, I thought, miffed. Then realising it was probably because he had more faith and also his request only involved a substitute skateboarder, whereas mine involved the mortal plummeting of a BBC cameraman. But skateboarding parrots. Really. I ask you god!

'I've no need to try to make a giant skateboard now,' exclaimed Bernard, obviously so pleased he'd forgotten the disappointment of the TV show. At least for a while.

'Just going to look at the news in the other room,' he said, leaving the table, clutching the card, but failing to conceal the front which, I saw for the first time, had bare-breasted beautiful Brazillian women parading on a beach.

Mother beamed proudly at me and father as if, somehow, the parrot's balancing skills and Bernard's relief and pleasure were all down to her.

The familiar strains introducing the breakfast news wafted in.

'Pity my true ... identity isn't ... realised,' said father. 'If I were ... king, I could ... have had some ... influence on that TV show.'

'Not on the BBC, you couldn't,' said mother hotly. 'They're not into influence.'

Father's eyes blazed and I knew that if he had been in full charge of his lungs a row would have followed.

'COME IN HERE,' bellowed Bernard from the sitting room. 'Come on, come quickly. WE'RE ON!'

Mother grabbed hold of her walking stick and I rushed over to father to help him up. We stumbled out to the sitting room. And there on the screen were our piglets.

And for five full minutes on the BBC main news, our porkers hogged the screen.

'Well wasn't that marvellous,' pronounced the mature-looking announcer, as it faded, adding, 'That amazing Piglet Display can be seen every day at midday at FAB Children's Animal Zoo, Wood Hill. And, at ten and four thirty, those very same piglets race for their food and it's free for children to bet on which one, if any, will home in on its own named dish. Remember, it's FAB and you can't afford to miss it!'

We all sat grinning like Hampshire cats.

I should have known, I thought. *Should have had confidence. After the first shock of the honeymoon, it all came good.*

Thirty-six

Nearly a month since our FAB CAZ was given the wonderful exposure on TV. Not only the breakfast show, but all news programmes that day. Then came the ITV cameras. And newspapers, local and national. Visitors have poured in and we've been able to buy two good quality poultry units to keep the poultry safe, each with six nest boxes with outside access so we can easily collect their eggs. Ten remote controlled ducks have been ordered for war games on the pond. And we're in the process of buying a pony to give children's rides, and another parrot to keep Cocky company. Six villagers work here part-time and a retired farmer has taken over management of the animals. And so our empire grows. And the best bit of all is that Cocky is fantastic on the skateboard which, unfortunately, gets right up Jesus's snout, but pleases the rest of us, including the audiences. Luckily, with the smile the piglet inherited from his affable father fixed permanently on his lips, I am probably the only one who realises just how upset he is. Of course I make it up to him with extra titbits and cuddles, knowing full well what it's like to resent a showy squawking bird which is worshipped by Bernard.

I paint all day to my heart's content, knowing Basil Argue will buy all of the pictures signed Freda Field for huge amounts, and that the ones designated for the gift shop, signed Red Salmon and lower priced, will eventually sell.

The only shadow on our perfect world is the animal borrower for, although we thought he hadn't struck last month, Bernard is becoming more convinced that one of the young chipmunks had gone missing on the night of the full moon, though why he thinks that is a mystery, "explained" by him as a "strong feeling". But, the good thing is, that's prodded him into fitting security locks to all the doors in the stable block, and buying padlocks for the aviary, the poultry units and the gate to the pig unit yard. Though any person intent on pinching a porker could easily bunk over the wall. When I asked him about protection for Lairy the lamb and Lardarse, he said we'd continue to put Lairy in the llama compound each night, relying on Lardarse's spitting power to ward off any abductor.

Chief suspect as far as I'm concerned is still Vernon Veal, who comes every two weeks now to worm, inject, pare and generally keep the animals in good nick. And, now that we're doing so well, we insist on giving him a proper fee. Recently he told me that his dream of fitting animals up with voice synthesisers so they could give vent to their feeling had taken a giant step forward because he'd perfected the software. *All I need now is permission to try it out on an animal*, he had said, making my flesh creep.

Mother reckons Vernon wouldn't be so open if he were the one and that Sidney Slocumb always looks shifty to her. But, as I said, he's always looked shifty to everyone, even before animals were being appropriated for god knows what.

Thinking of shifty brought Nesbit to mind, but before his conversion, for to see him these days you'd think he'd had a blood transfusion replacing all of his shared Sidney genes with those of Tony Blair, or some other such current saint. Godly goodness shines from his alcohol-free body with the irritating aggravation of high volume pop music at the hairdresser's. Then the thought struck that maybe it *used* to be him, borrowing animals for Enid to sculpt, but now he'd seen the light which illuminated how much grief he caused me, he had stopped.

Tonight, the night of the September full moon, we should see. But, for *we* should see, substitute *I* should see, because Bernard, radiating happiness like a three bar electric fire, said: *not to worry, whoever it is always returns them, so who cares*.

But *I* care. I don't like to think of our creatures being used for nefarious deeds, despite Bernard saying that if they were they must like it because they always came back looking pleased.

Which took me back a bit because I'd never imagined an abused creature actually enjoying it.

'Tonight is the night of the full moon,' I reminded him.

'So?' he airily replied, stepping into his pyjamas.

'So, I thought we could hide in the back room of the mobile home to see if the borrower returns. If he goes to the field first he'll find the animals all locked away except for Lardarse and Lairy in the compound, but he's already borrowed the lamb and hasn't ever taken the same one twice. Besides, Lardarse would protect him.'

Bernard yawned.

'So he'll be forced to try his luck with the piglets in our garden,' I continued. 'And then we'd see him.'

'Well, you keep watch,' he said, hopping into bed. 'I've a busy day ahead and I'm off to sleep.'

It was hard to keep awake as I sat staring out into the darkness. A solid hour of boredom for what? Nothing. Perhaps it really had been Nesbit and he'd reformed and no-one would come.

I yawned, stretched, closed my eyes, opened them. And then I saw it. A movement in the gloom. I narrowed my eyes, focused, discerned a furtive figure creeping. All of my senses jangled, vibrating with tingling anticipation. I craned forward. Was it Vernon Veal? Was it? But it was too dim to tell.

Suddenly the monochrome garden flared into moonlit colour and now I could clearly see the trespasser on our silver green lawn and shock waves of terror surged through me, for he wore a long black cloak with copious hood, just like the Grim Reaper. Minus his scythe.

I held my breath, half wishing he'd turn so I could see his face yet terrified, if he did, he would see me. Fear bit into me like sharp teeth into a peach. I wanted to turn away, run out, escape. But I held back, fearing he'd fly over and grab me instead of an animal, and take me away to god knows where for god knows what purpose, before returning me, used.

Clouds slid over the moonface, dimming its light. I strained my eyes, just making out the terrifying black figure dithering in the middle of the lawn. Then, suddenly, he started moving, heading straight down towards Cussbert's ark and run. But, I knew Bernard's lovingly made sanctuary from the fox would offer no protection against this wicked being who was gathering speed, cloak billowing, as he bore down on the unsuspecting bird.

Quickly he reached his goal. *Stay inside*, I silently implored my Bernard's precious cock, as I never ever thought I would. The clouds thinned to translucence and, in the faint light, I saw the cloaked figure lift the end of the run with one hand and hold the other out, craftily cupped. And, slowly, Cussbert ventured forward, head jerking, each claw precisely placed, heading for the bait. Gradually, the tempter moved the enticement back. Timidly, the cockerel continued forward.

Get back, get back, I silently yelled again. But my Bernard's cock, always wilful, reached the lure and began trustingly pecking. Slowly, the wicked being set the end of the run down, then continued moving backwards and round. Soon he would be facing me. Soon I should see who it was. But suddenly, the scene was plunged into darkness again by a dense wodge of cloud.

I peered into the gloom and could just see the dark figure gathering Cussbert up off the ground. Too terrified to run out and stop him, I watched him hurry back across the grass, stopping by the gap in the hedge. And, in a sudden dazzle of moonlight, I saw him drag a lidded basket out from under the laurel and place Cussbert inside. But the garden was now plunged into total blackness, turning me blind. I kept staring at the spot but, in the next bright moon-flare, saw he had gone.

I *had* to find out who it was. I *had* to follow. But, god, I was so frightened.

I forced myself to stand on shaky legs, blundering out into the passage, past slumbering Hermione and Kermit, through the swing door, down the ramp, across the old yard and out into the garden. I glanced at the cottage where Bernard slept. Should I go in and join him? Should I flee to his safety? Should I give up? I'd never ever been so scared in my life before. But I had to know. And, if it were Vernon, as I still suspected, what harm could he do me?

I hurried as best I could in the darkness, halting at the gap before venturing through. This is where he'd disappeared. Supposing it wasn't Vernon. Supposing it was someone truly evil? Supposing he was psychic and somehow knew I was on his track and was waiting, hidden, ready to pounce. Panting as silently as possible, I dared peer round the hedge. In the racing cloud patterns of shadow and light I could see the figure at the far side of the field, the billowing of his cloak skew-whiff, impeded by the heavy basket hooked on his arm. He reached the gate leading to Esmerelda's garden and opened it, swirled through, turned left towards the valley, and vanished from sight.

Giving way to full volume panting, I sped after him, reached the gate, tentatively opened it, crept through, afraid he would be waiting, afraid he would hear me. But, the moon was fully displayed now and, in its harsh light, I spotted him a long way off on the path that led from Esmerelda's garden down to the wooded valley, his unladen arm stuck out sideways, counterbalancing the weight.

Hugging the hedgerow to my left, I flitted from shadow to shadow, tailing him, dreading every moment he'd turn and see me. But soon he'd disappeared into the blackness of trees. Now I dared move out from the safety of shadows into the stark moonlight, rushing down across the open tract to the gloominess of the woods.

Secreting myself behind a wide trunk, I squinted round. Through gaps I could see him in a largish clearing, lit by pencils of moonbeams, his back still towards me. I darted to the next tree and then the next and the next, till I dared get no nearer. Sweating, I stood still, waiting, watching. Fearing.

At long last the figure slowly turned. I stared. I rubbed my eyes. Stared again, gasped with the shock. For there, facing me, clearly illuminated by a ray of shimmering light, was Esmerelda, horribly naked beneath her long cloak. She bent over, hideously dangling, and flipped back the lids of the wicker basket. Then, she looked down tenderly at my Bernard's cock and blatantly stroked it.

How dare she! How could she be the wicked animal borrower? She was our partner, our confidante, our neighbour, our friend, that woman from Rugged Farm whom we'd only gradually, and misplacedly as it was now transpiring, learned to trust.

I was about to dash out and confront her but a rustling in the undergrowth made me stop. Could she have an accomplice? I faltered. Saw another woman emerging from the trees, then another, and another, until there were a dozen or more, all droopily naked under hooded cloaks.

One weirdo I could tackle, but not a whole asylum! I pressed myself against the trunk and prayed they'd not see me. This was no ordinary meeting of women, I realised. This was her circle of friends. Her coven. And not good white witches either. These were all bad black ones. A clique of crazy females who did something each month to my animals. And I had to find out what.

I stayed watching, scarcely breathing, petrified.

Not one of them spoke. It was eerie. Twigs snapped, dry leaves crackled, a distant owl hooted. Swift black slashes of silent bats swept overhead. As each woman arrived, she sauntered around on no apparent set path in the confines of the clearing 'til eventually about a score of them filled the glade, sinister and mute.

Suddenly, Esmerelda clapped her hands sharply, making me jump.

With no word of direction, no holding of hands, they formed two concentric circles. I stared, mystified at the perfection of them. And then I spied a ring of unlit candles positioned on the ground. Their guide. Their guide which, if lit and left, would leave a ring of wax blobs. Like the one found in the stables after the fire that cost Daisy and me our manes - and nearly our lives.

Anger raged through me and I made to step out, to reveal myself, lambaste them. But, Esmerelda clapped again and I pulled back. Abruptly, they half turned and began walking, following each other round, each circle moving the opposite way. As each circle member came face to face with the other they halted, stared into each others eyes, then jabbed two fingers vigorously into the air. When each had been thus greeted, the circling ceased and they all smartly turned to face inwards.

The sound of feet crashing through the undergrowth, accompanied by puffing grunts of exertion came from the valley side. I stared into the shadowy depths and spied two new cloaked figures emerging, each clutching the end of a long rectangular heavy-looking object. Fearful curiosity replaced my angry boldness and I stayed hidden, watching and listening.

At last, the groaning newcomers stumbled into the glade and lugged their heavy burden through the two circles of silent witches into the centre. There they carefully placed it down in a wide shaft of moonlight. Then, slowly, they pivoted on the spot, jabbing their lewd vee sign greetings at each of the others. This ritual over, they bent down and pulled legs out from the rectangle, turning it upright. And now I could see it was a trestle table of the wallpaper pasting kind. I wondered if they'd next produce some paste and flock paper, and decorate a tree. Nothing seemed impossible with these lunies. My thoughts then did a double take. *These lunies!* So, it wasn't a coincidence our animals disappeared once a month *on the night of the full moon*.

A pure white cloth was produced from somewhere and the two draped it over the table then moved away to join the others. I trembled, terrified of what this secret sect would do to me if they discovered me spying on their weird ceremonial rite.

Esmerelda stepped forward. She placed the wicker basket containing my Bernard's cock on the gleaming cloth. Hands held together in supplication, she bowed to it three times.

'Gather round sisters of the coven, you got to come closer, step through the ring of fire,' she sang in a strange high-pitched voice. Then, in a lower-pitched sing-song aside, she added, 'though since the stable conflagration the candles got to stay unlit.'

The women moved forward stepping between the candles with care, holding their long cloaks against themselves for protection against non-existent flames. Shoulder to shoulder they encircled the trestle table in one thick evil loop.

Esmerelda started up again, voice even higher: 'We meet as per usual at the time of the full moon ...' her delivery was now even more sing-song like a demented Welsh woman, or even an Indian: '... with our living sacrifice, as the spirits say we got to.'

My ribs seemed to be being crushed by unseen forces, making it hard to breathe.

Esmerelda opened the basket and gently, very gently, took the cockerel out, nursing it tenderly in her arms, protecting its wings.

In her weird new voice she sang out again, 'Witches of the Great Piddlehurst and District sacred coven, we are gathered once more to make our living sacrifice.'

She then placed Cussbert back into the basket.

There was silence at first then a weird chattering started up - random words and sounds as the witches began prancing and leaping around, breasts springing and falling back in a fascinating variation of bounces. Then gradually the strange chattering settled into a rhythmic incantation as they chanted in unison:

'We offer this cock to thee lord. We offer this cock to thee lord.' Over and over until it became hypnotic.

Esmerelda stood stiffly to attention in the centre as the chanting droned on. But, suddenly, her hand moved up to her mouth and stayed there. I watched in awe, wondering what was to come. Then, to my amazement, she released her hand, blowing a kiss at the basket.

Abruptly, the dirge changed to, 'We kiss this cock for thee lord. We kiss this cock for thee lord.' And as each woman passed the front of Cussbert's prison she too blew a kiss into the air.

Esmerelda raised her hand. Silence fell. She opened the basket once more, delved her arms in and carefully drew out our heavy rooster. He looked at her with glinting moonbeam eyes, his comb proudly erect. He didn't struggle or even cluck as she settled him on the table, then tilted him over quite slowly onto his back, spread-eagling his wide wings across the spotless white cloth. My mind was reeling. Why wasn't he screeching and crowing, squawking and struggling as he would if I'd tipped him over backwards? What power did wicked Esmerelda hold over my Bernard's magnificent cock?

Again, with no word of command, the smallest woman - so small she might have been a dwarf - came forward from the circle and held Cussbert's scaly legs down, pressing his elegant claws against the virgin whiteness. Mutely, two others stepped forward and held down each beautiful wing.

I gazed at those long flight feathers and was filled with anguish at their beauty and with the guilty memory of how many times I'd threatened to kill him.

An evil high-pitched whispered chanting started up, turning my blood to icy slush:

'Sacrifice. Sacrifice. Sacrifice.' Their grotesque faces lit up and darkened as they moved forward and back between shadows and harsh lunar light.

Esmerelda again held up her hand and again the silence was instant and absolute. To my horror I witnessed an axe being passed to her raised hand, its lethal silver blade glinting horrendously in the cold moonlight. Carefully, she positioned it above Cussbert's scrawny neck. In horror, I watched her lift it higher, ready to strike. And I couldn't bear it.

Screaming, I dashed out from behind the tree into full view and Esmerelda, with a sharp gasp of surprise, dropped the axe, its blade slicing clean through Cussbert's defenceless neck. The dwarf woman and the other two who held him jumped back, howling. Blood gushed from the open cross section of neck onto the pristine table cloth, soaking it scarlet. Cussbert's vacant eyes stared at me from the detached head, a claw gave a final twitch.

I heard a low voice grumble 'I'll never get that stain out, it's damask.'

'You *idiot*,' shrieked Esmerelda, turning on me. 'Look what you made me go and do - we never kill the creatures we borrow. You should know that - we always return them in the same condition as we found them.' Absently, she fitted Cussbert's head back onto his neck.

'You've beheaded him,' I sobbed.

'No, *you* did it,' she screamed.

'You lay off my animals in future,' I fumed.

'Too right I will. It's put me right off sacrificing,' she replied, repositioning Cussbert's head which had lolled over sideways.

Muttered protests came from the circle of women.

'If we can't get the FAB CAZ creatures, and we've already done all the gypsy ones, what're we to use in future?' grumbled the fattest witch.

There was silence. Then:

'How about insects?' some weird bright spark called out.

Esmerelda's face lit up. She gave up on Cussbert's head and drew her cloak around her, turning to face the mob. 'Witches of the Great Piddlehurst and District Coven, it has been suggested from the forest floor that from the time of this full moon onwards we shall sacrifice insects to the spirit gods, how say you?'

And, from the energetic vee signs jabbed into the air, I guessed the answer was yes.

She glared at me. 'At least those innocents will be safe on our sacrificial table without you startling me into murdering them.'

She was right, I thought miserably, but then I remembered the fire.

'It was *you* who burnt the stables down,' I counter-attacked. 'It was *you*. You who nearly killed me. *And* your donkey. So don't you go talking to me about murdering innocents.'

A flash flood of guilt surged across Esmerelda's face.

'Well we set it all up in there 'cos it looked like it were gonna rain and then it didn't so we took your piglet out and set it all up again here in the woods.'

'Forgetting to snuff out the ring of candles!' I exploded, maddened by her unrepentant stance.

She nodded her head. 'I got to admit I felt bad 'bout it ever since.' But then she flared up with a remembered thought. 'But it were your piglet's fault, setting up all that honking an' wriggling. Took our minds off things. It did, didn't it sisters. You were there. It were that pig made us leave them candles aflame.'

And the sisters earnestly jabbed their two fingered agreement into the air.

'You cannot blame my poor terrified pig for your negligence,' I screamed, incensed, my eyes roving the circle as a sudden gust of wind blew all their cloaks back. I stared at the strange naked assortment and suddenly, and unexpectedly, I was dying to laugh.

'So, if you ever touch one of my animals again' I snorted, 'I ... I shall set the police on you.'

'Ooo nice!' a voice muttered as I swept off, retracing my steps on the route that led back to Bernard: the man who worshipped the ground Cussbert's claws used to walk upon. The man who was never going to believe the crowing cock's demise wasn't planned. The tender loving husband who would undoubtedly give me hell.

'The only compensation,' said Bernard, having spent a whole week moping, sulking, weeping and wailing, and being horrible to me, 'is that I have the oil painting you did of Cuthbert to remind of his beauty.'

He slid under the duvet next to me.

'I'm sorry Bernie,' I said for the hundredth time, 'but it was an accident.'

'I know. I know. You were trying to help.'

'And it was very scary.'

He snuggled up and kissed me for the first time in seven days.

'It must have been very very scary,' he agreed, 'seeing Esmerelda with nothing on but a cloak.'

And we both went off into prolonged high volume hysterics.

'Cut the cackling you two,' shouted mother from across the landing. 'It's midnight and the king and I want some sleep.'